LOVE IN
THIS TIME
OF SILICON

for Jan Hughes —

good friend, dear friend

Best wishes

Biddum Pginla

January 14, 2004

Minneapolis, MN USA

2954-IGIN

LOVE IN THIS TIME OF SILICON

Biodun Iginla

2954-IGIN

To order additional copies of this book, contact:
Xlibris Corporation
1-888-7-XLIBRIS
www.Xlibris.com
Orders@Xlibris.com

CONTENTS

For Maya, Nelson, and Julie

1

Missoula: Tuesday, June 22, 1999

Katya to me:

—If you go to Paris with Francette, don't come back to me.

—Well, I'm definitely going to the conference in Paris. Francette and I are traveling together, and I'm staying at her apartment. And I told you many times. We're just friends.

—I don't believe you're just friends. If you remember, I read the e-mail she sent you when I was sitting next to you on the couch the Wednesday night before I left for Moscow.

—I won't deny she has fantasies about whatever she might want to develop with me. But it's mostly in her head.

—And you want me to believe you haven't done anything to encourage her? I know how you operate. That's one of the reasons you go to Bernice's. You like to flirt with the women there.

—Well, I haven't been flirting with Francette.

—Can you honestly tell me you haven't sent her erotic or even suggestive electronic mail?

—I haven't. Look: I'm definitely going to Paris. Francette and I will be on the same flight from New York to Paris. I'm staying at her place because it'll save me a lot of money. Paris can be expensive. I know this from having lived there. And I'm broke these days, as you know.

—Of course. Why didn't you tell me about this trip or this
  conference until Saturday when I got back? You picked an
  interesting way to welcome me back. Is this another variant of
  the payback?

—No. I never told you because the trip was finalized when you
  were
  in Moscow. All this time we were waiting for her father to
  send me a ticket.

—Her father? Her father got you the ticket to Paris?

—He's head of the Archive. I told you this, remember?

—How cozy and cute. All in the family. I can't believe what I'm
  hearing. And you had to tell me this the last minute?

—You never called or even e-mailed me from Moscow, remember?

—How can you say that? I called you twice! You weren't home, so
  I left voice messages.

—You didn't call me again.

—I told you: I was busy all the time I was there with the Pushkin
  thing and seeing old friends and relatives. And it's very difficult
  calling the US from Russia.

—Well . . . you didn't leave a number for me to call you back, so I
  had no way of getting hold of you until you got back.

—How very convenient all this is for you. If you go don't come
  back.

—I guess that settles it. I'm definitely going. I'll quit Missoula on
  Thursday.

—Why wait that long? How about leaving tomorrow?

—I need the time to make arrangements for UPS to ship my stuff
  back to New York.

That's how Katya Brodsky and I broke up two days ago. I
began writing this narrative this morning on my Powerbook 5300
because—especially now that I'm approaching forty—I have to
make sense of the way I have conducted my diasporic life in the
90s. In a way my whole 90s life that drifted had to get to this
point. It seems inevitable to me now that Katya and I had to meet

last August; gradually fall in love in the fall and then acknowledge this to each other in January; try to make the relationship work; try to live together since the beginning of May when I got back from Jerusalem; and finally: break up last Sunday, June 20, after *she* got back from Moscow Saturday afternoon, June 19.

A few events of my own life during the latter half of the 90s have been somewhat significantly imbricated with Missoula, so it seems to me that I need to track and unpack my own relationship to this dusty sprawling Western town (and also what inexplicably bound me to Katya) if I want to make sense of my life during the decade that is now closing out the twentieth century and the Second Millennium. Specifically, as Dorit Levin said about me in the mid-90s, "Your life was full of experience, although it was unfortunate that there had to be so much of it, so much so that you had to unload a shit-cargo of it through therapy." In a sense, what my mother told me when I was in high school in New York seems appropriate here, even "if"—pun intended—it was derived, as I found out later, from Rudyard Kipling: "If you can bear to hear the truth you've spoken, twisted by knaves to set a trap for fools . . . you'll be a man, my son."

*   *   *

2

Missoula: Tuesday, June 22, 1999

Katya and I moved in together, into a one-bedroom apartment in the Babs Building—one urban myth says it was quite busy as a brothel during the Wild West days—on South 4th Street West, when I got back to Missoula from Jerusalem last May 2. I had been in Jerusalem for two months freelancing for *The Jerusalem Post*, the English-language Israeli daily, a gig that Katya in fact had arranged for me through one of her close friends. Without knowing this at the time, my reentry to Missoula began the very last phase of my entire year there. To repeat: a few portions of my life in the mid to late 90s are entangled with Missoula. Given that I was born and raised in New York, how exactly did my connection with this economically depressive college town begin?

I first went to Missoula in the summer of 1992 to visit an old graduate-school friend who was now teaching at the University of Montana. First off, I was forcefully impressed by the monocultural Montana demographic: white, parsimonious, healthy, nature-loving, and friendly, set at the vortex of reality and myth, and surrounded by all those splendid mountains and stunning vistas where several weather systems were visible from a distance.

The friend I visited was born in France, and he had come to the US to study and then decided to stay and work. He got married to an American woman, and they had a son together before they split up. After graduate school at Columbia University, he became an itinerant professor in several midwestern universities before he finally landed at the University of Montana in 1988, where he eventually attained tenure in 1994. Never really the outdoor type in France when he was growing up—born in Paris and raised in Toulouse, he quickly came to appreciate the mountains, hiking trails, and camping sites in Montana. Missoula was changing and expanding quite rapidly in those years. Signs of this expansion were everywhere, especially in those outer neighborhoods, like Pattee Canyon and South Hills, that were littered with newly built bungalows with tacky architecture. Shortly before I got to Missoula, my friend (let's call him Jacques Berthelot from now on) had just bought one of these bungalows in South Hills (a house currently worth three times what he paid for it in 1992), and he was dying to introduce me to the thrills and pleasures of whitewater-rafting and backpack camping. And I most certainly was dying to get out of claustrophobic New York City. The many hikes we did up Blue Mountain and Lolo Peak that summer, the camping at Glacier National Park, the exquisite dining on buffalo burgers washed down with red wine, and the skinny-dipping in the hot springs and mud-baths of Hot Springs were definitely tonics (well, maybe spiked with a little bit of gin) for a psyche exposed to and blasted by the raunchy subways and the gritty sidewalks of New York. In any case, that was my first concrete encounter with the Other that Montana is to New York. I had had a previous virtual encounter with Missoula via Kim Williams's colorful and folksy dispatches in the mid-80s for Susan Stamberg's *All Things Considered* on National Public Radio.

*   *   *

3

Missoula: Wednesday, June 23, 1999

Now that UPS has picked up my eight moderate-sized boxes for a two-day ground shipment to New York, I can now relax and resume this narrative. I was taking a chance arranging this pickup on my last full day in Missoula. I fly back to New York tomorrow at 2 PM. But I needed Monday and Tuesday to pack all my stuff in Missoula into eight boxes, following a triage process getting rid of ballast luggage. I also needed the time to say goodbye to friends over drinks and dinner, or both in some cases.

The rest of Sunday after we broke up in the morning was a waste in some respects. I was surprised to discover that I was distraught about the breakup. After Katya left the apartment for her office at the university to "work on her book manuscript," I called a few friends around the US to break the news. Then I slept on the couch in the living room for two hours, since I had had very little sleep the night before: I was out until 4 AM. I got up around 1 PM., called my friend Mark, a painter with a day job at the US Forest Service, and told him the news. He and I had spent Saturday afternoon (shortly after Katya came back from Moscow, she and I had a brief argument and I left the apartment in a huff and met Mark) and evening together playing volleyball, picnicking, and then drinking and dancing with six international women students—from Hong Kong, Japan, and Ireland—at a disco on Brooks Avenue. Between dance sessions we had managed to discuss most of what I was going through with Katya. He said from what I told him the night before, he wasn't that surprised that we split up. He then invited me over to his place, which was within ten-minutes walking distance from Babs. After I got off the phone with him, I crossed the street to Holiday to get a liter of red wine and went to his place. We drank the whole bottle and talked some more about Katya and about women in general.

Sunday night, Katya and I had a nasty fight after she got back from her office.

—I want you to sleep in the bedroom tonight. I'll sleep in the living room.

—No, Katya: *I'll* sleep in the living room. *You* sleep in the bedroom. I can watch TV and get on the Internet out here.

—Yeah. That's all you've ever done at night since we moved in here, at least while I was here. Watching TV and surfing the Internet. I knew that would happen. That's why I never wanted cable.

—I don't *surf* the Internet. I *work* on the Internet. Remember, I'm collaborating with my friend Michael in Hong Kong on that screenplay, so I need to be online with him, especially at night because of the time-zone difference.

—Pardon me. Whatever. I'll need to use the treadmill in the morning, like around 7.

—Don't worry: I'll be up by then.

—*You'll be up by then?* Since when did you start getting up that early?

—Since you left for Moscow. You know, Napoleon said the world belongs to those who get up early.

—Napoleon? You're quoting Napoleon on me? What does he have to do with any of this?

—Well . . .

—Oh I get it. That little prick Frenchman dreamt—and tried hard—to rule the world. I guess *you* have your own fantasies about ruling the world. You're well on your way. After all, you're running off to Paris with your little Frenchwoman.

—How does that follow logically? That's quite a leap, no? And how do you know Francette is a little woman?

—Francette means "little France" doesn't it? I know a little French to know that.

—That's another leap, Katya. You're too smart to be making these illogical links. For the record, she's at least five-six. Hardly little. She's taller than you are.

—So? And I don't give a fuck what Napoleon said.

—Well . . . you don't have be hostile to Napoleon.

—I'm hostile because you cited him.

—Well . . .

—So you waited till I left before you changed your habits.

—What are you talking about?

—Getting up early.

—Well . . .

—You also waited until I left before you invited all your friends over for dinner. The new friends you made before and after I left. When I was here you watched TV at night and surfed the Internet. While I was away you invited all your old and new friends over to dinner.

—So I made new friends after you left. We moved into this apartment May 2, then you left for Moscow two weeks later. So what if I made new friends while you were away? I made the friends for us.

—Bullshit! You really don't want me to meet your friends. Mark was interested in hanging around last night to talk to me when he came to pick you up. But you were in a rush to get going. And you never introduced me to the blonde women you like to flirt with at Bernice's. I suppose you had a few of *them* over to dinner too.

—Well, yeah, I had Trish over.

—*You had Trish over?* Did you fuck her again too?

—No, I didn't fuck her again. You know I fucked her only once, in my only one-night stand in many many years, before you and I became an item. We've already been through this a million times.

—Yeah you fucked her then. And I also believe you fucked her here while I was away. You penetrated her. But you won't penetrate me. You won't fuck me. You've never fucked me in this apartment. But I'll bet you've fucked Trish here. And I suppose you're looking forward to fucking Francette in Paris.

—Oy vey, Katya. This shit is really getting old. Now that we've broken up I don't want to go through it again. I don't want even want to hear it. You know too well why I won't penetrate you. We've been through all that ad nauseam.

—You used sex to blackmail me. You never forgave me for not breaking up immediately with Glen when you and I became an item.

—I won't even respond to that.

—Since we're on the subject, I heard from the grapevine that you finally got to fuck Nina in Jerusalem . . . as a big-time payback for the Glen business.

—Nina?

—The only Nina . . . Nina Jacob, you fuck-face. I suspected you had a thing for her right after I introduced you two. This is how you pay me. I get you the gig at the *Jerusalem Post*. I introduce you to a friend so she could help you out. You show me your gratitude and anger by fucking her. I mean, God! How could you fuck her?

—I didn't! Whatever grapevine you're talking about got it all wrong. Sure Nina and I hung out together. She was part of the little group of friends I had when I was there. Otherwise we were with the whole gang every evening and every night. She and I were out alone only a couple of times.

—Yeah: my sources said you two fucked one of those times. Your last night in Jerusalem in fact. You guys went out to dinner at a little café on Ben Yehuda Way, near Zion Square. She cried on your shoulder regretting that you were leaving. Then she took you to her postmodern apartment on Derekh Ha'Shalom where you fucked her.

—I think I know who your source was. And he got it all wrong.

—How do you know my source was a he? How do you know Nina
   herself was not my source?

—Nina could never have been your source. And if she was . . . she
   lied.

—You're so fucking naive.

—I'm in fact positive your source is a guy. And I know who he is.
   That guy wouldn't know reality if he fell over it. He had no
   clue about anything.

—I don't believe you! You're a liar! But not even a good one. You're
   worse than a gigolo.

—Don't insult me!

—You fucking liar! I don't trust you! I should have never have
   trusted you! Did your first wife ever trust you? I wonder. After
   all, she left you, didn't she?

—You won't get anywhere there. How and why Sarah and I broke
   up is really none of your business. I already told you the reason
   FYI, that's all.

—I meanwhile was up front with you right away about Glen. I
   was involved with him for a year before you and I became an
   item. I simply asked you to give me time to break up with
   him.

—You took your sweet time breaking up with him. And I will ask
   you this again: Did he really *have to* come and visit you for a
   week from South Carolina while I was in Jerusalem? You want
   me to believe that you two never fucked that whole week?

—Why bring this all up again? I told you a million times: Glen's
   trip was planned in July, before I laid eyes on you for the first
   time, and way before you and I became an item. I did finally
   break up with him, didn't I? Are you going to Paris with
   Francette just to make me pay yet again for all this? And when
   will your payback eventually end? I finally broke up with Glen
   because of you, didn't I?

—Yeah, you *finally* broke up with him two days *after* I came back
   from Jerusalem and *after* we moved in together.

—Jesus. I told you I didn't want to upset him in March and April while he was studying for and taking his MBA exams. So you pay me back by not fucking me before I went to Moscow. How ironic: Before I broke up with Glen you were fucking me. After I broke up with Glen you stopped fucking me.

—Look, this is hopeless.

—If you say it's hopeless, then I too don't give a fuck anymore! I want you to sleep in the bedroom tonight!

—Listen, Katya. We broke up this morning. I'll be gone perhaps forever from your life Thursday. Let's not make all of this any more unpleasant than it already is.

—Yeah it's over! And I said I want you to sleep in the bedroom tonight!

—No. I'll sleep in the living room. You can't control me anymore. We're no longer an item. Mark did confirm to me that Russian women like to be in control. For instance, in the way you controlled the Glen situation from beginning to end.

—Mark knows about Russian women, does he? He has Russian-Jewish heritage, and he thinks he knows about Russian women?

—He went out with a Russian woman last year.

—Am I a Russian woman to you? Didn't I tell you I feel more Jewish than Russian, even if I was born in Moscow and grew up there?

—I'm positive you told me the exact opposite—that you felt more Russian than Jewish.

—Now you're insulting me! I can throw you out of this apartment tomorrow morning or even tonight! I have the legal right! My name is the only one on the lease!

—I see.

—If you don't behave yourself and treat me with respect . . . you'll see what I can and will do!

—What are you going to do?

—Wait and find out, you fuck-head!

Then she stormed out of the living room into the bedroom and slammed the door. About ten minutes later, I knocked on the bedroom door. She told me to come in. She was in her typical position in the bedroom as well as in the living room: Lying down on the bed or couch reading by the lamp.

—Katya, I'm sorry. You've been very good to me. Let's make the next few days pleasant before I leave.

—What did I ever do to you? I loved you and took care of you. In return, you've behaved like a teenager.

—I'm sorry. The Glen thing was poison. Our relationship never recovered from it. I warned you about this.

She did sleep in the bedroom Sunday night. Since then she's been staying at the house of one of her students. She didn't come home Monday night. Around 1 AM., I called Jacques, her departmental colleague at the university, to see whether he knew where she might be. Jacques and I had had coffee at Bernice's Monday late afternoon, when I told him about our breakup. Jacques told me then that Katya had melted the five-month ice between them early that afternoon—an ice that she had frozen on him, inexplicably to him and to me—when she blathered out *her* side of the story. This development was ironic enough, since Jacques and I went through our own five-month cold war because of Katya's ice, and since Katya and I met more or less through Jacques to begin with.

How did I meet Katya?

*   *   *

4

Missoula, Wednesday, June 23, 1999

Before I came back to Missoula to live intermittently for a year, from July 15, 1998 till tomorrow June 24, 1999, when I jet out at 2 PM., I had been back in the intervening years every summer, each time to visit Jacques. We had spent most of the time with his friends and colleagues at the university at private (sometimes dinner) parties, at drinking sessions at downtown bars, or at outdoor picnics at Caras Park and elsewhere. In July 1998, I was again living in New York, and again I was becoming claustrophobic and dying to get out into open spaces and big skies. And Sarah and I had broken up a about a year before after a very involved and intense four-year relationship, including marriage, in New York and Minneapolis. (In fact, in summer of 1996, Sarah and our then six-month-old daughter Shoshana were with me for my annual trip to Missoula.) Jacques invited me to join him and his group of seven on an extensive camping trip to the Olympic Peninsula and Glacier National Park. The three-week camping trip was soon transformed for me into an extended one-year sojourn in Missoula because I needed a break from New York to work on revising my novel according to the specifications of my publisher.

Let me tell you a little bit about myself: I am a freelance writer and cultural analyst, generating "content" for new media around the US and the world. Within mainstream broadcast media—currently MSNBC—I more or less function as a producer on contract. I also do basic research for cultural institutions., like museums and book publishers. The bulk of my everyday work consists of writing essays, reviews, and reading essays and books on politics and culture, digesting so-called journals of opinion in politics and the arts (mostly online), jargony academic journals, daily and weekly newspapers, and dogged research—through hyperlinks—that I do mostly online: This essentially means that I can do most of my work anywhere in the US and the world—as long as I have a computer with access to the Net. I send and receive projects as attachments on my web-based e-mail, My Yahoo, which can be accessed anywhere in the world from a computer with an Internet connection, sometimes from my laptop's "Global Village" modem. I download or upload material into my online workstation, a virtual PC (my assemblage of file managers, file transfer protocols, and e-mail at http://www.fusionone.com) and then work on them, so I really don't have to worry too much about crashed hard drives or misplaced or defective floppy disks. My clients most of the time even electronically direct-deposit my checks into my online bank account.

I communicate with friends and relatives mostly by e-mail, which is the only reliable way to contact me, as I might be anywhere in the world at anytime. (In fact, when I sometimes initiate a voice-connection with friends, usually the first question they ask is "Where are you?") My e-life, as it were, lived on speed, is an admixture of user IDs, passwords, e-airline tickets, e-boarding passes, airline name tags, airport outlets for my laptop, and multiple time-zones. In fact, the one period when I flew across time-zones so frequently, I ceased to believe in jetlag: I flew so often that I inhabited my own time-zone. (A few months ago, a friend, Elizabeth Arnold, the national political correspondent for National Public Radio, spent a week in the North Pole. She e-mailed me from up there. In response, I asked her what her time-zone was. She e-mailed back: "My time-zone is whatever I want it to be." Of course! I thought.) During that period, I woke up one morning in Tokyo, had lunch in the afternoon in Hong Kong, and slept the same night in New York, all adding up to a 36-hour day. And my New York brick-and-mortar apartment is on the fortieth floor, with a sweeping view of most of the West Side of Manhattan and New Jersey, so that some times at night when I'm dozing off in front of my TV by my living-room window, I have the illusion of being on an airplane over the city, descending and watching an in-flight movie. And in fact, one of those nights, as I was waking up, I reminded myself to fasten my seat-belt.

(In real-time, my day in the US is split into two day-time-zones, so to speak: In New York, for instance, my day-time-zone for Europe and the Far East begins at 3 AM Eastern, and overlaps with my day-time-zone for domestic US, which ends around 7 PM Eastern. The period between 7 PM and 3 AM is spliced into a four-hour chunk of sleep and some naps. But even this little routine gets disrupted from time to time, so to speak, as when I begin the Europe and Far-East time-zone at midnight—before one of my sleeping periods—that then bleeds into the routine one.)

So I could afford to live in Missoula and still do my work. Jacques was extremely generous letting me stay at his bungalow in South Hills for most of the year—intermittently, since my sojourn was punctuated by several weekend "cyber-saver" visits to Minneapolis to see my daughter Shoshana (I resisted Katya's efforts to accompany me on these visits: She wanted to meet Shoshana, but I didn't want that to happen just yet); a three-week working visit to Hong Kong and Tokyo from November 17, 1998 to December 8, 1999; and a two-month stint in Jerusalem from February 26, 1999 to May 2, 1999.

I met Katya for the first time at Jacques's when she came over to dinner one warm August night in 1998. She had arrived in Missoula the week before to fill an unexpected opening in the department of foreign languages at the University of Montana. Her predecessor had dropped dead of a heart attack early summer while drinking with his students at a bar in downtown Missoula. Katya had been living and freelance teaching in Washington DC for two years, and she was hired at University of Montana after a quick one-week search and an on-campus interview. In other words, like me, in early August she had no idea she would be living in Missoula.

I met Katya for the first time in 1998. She was the one crucial woman who made me recognize and realize—probably unintentionally—the vortex of my life in the 90s. So 1998: Since I'm a journalist who writes about politics and culture, please indulge me the following chronicle of highly significant events in the world and in the US that year.

*   *   *

1998.

In the subcontinent:

India and Pakistan inaugurated an incipient nuclear arms race when each detonated nuclear tests. Just two months after Hindu nationalist Atal Bihari Vajpayee became prime minister, India unexpectedly set off an underground nuclear explosion near the border with Pakistan. About two weeks later, Pakistan responded with several nuclear tests of it own, despite international pleas of restraint. Since China had enabled Pakistan to develop nuclear capability, this event underscored the emergence of China as both a superpower (albeit one that the US pretended not to acknowledge) and a regional power, further underlying that the situation in the subcontinent was triangular.

In Southeast Asia:

The whole region (except Singapore) caught an economic flu. The economic collapse in Thailand in late 1997 had set the foundation for the economic flu that spread throughout Southeast Asia. First, banks in Indonesia failed and the value of its currency plummeted. Malaysia soon followed suit, and Prime Minister Mahathir bin Mohammad denounced and jailed his heir apparent, Anwar Ibrahim, blaming him for Malaysia's economic downturn and for the subsequent protests all over the country. Hong Kong's turn came next, and there the situation was compounded by an epidemic that compelled the authorities to destroy the island's whole population of chickens. Finally, Japan's economy, the world's second-largest after the US, began to experience its worst recession since World War II, and everywhere experts speculated about an imminent deflation.

In Russia:

The whole economy collapsed and the ruble was devalued. In a futile effort to stem the downward spiral, Premier Boris Yeltsin dismissed his entire cabinet twice in 1998. Russian financial emergency soon spread through the Commonwealth of Independent States, particularly to Ukraine and Belarus, whose Soviet-style planned economies were highly dependent on Russia.

In the US:

The Clinton-Lewinsky sex scandal eclipsed all other news events in the US in 1998. Clinton's foreign-policy triumphs in Northern Ireland and the Middle East paled next to the media glare generated by his affair with Monica Lewinsky, a young White House intern. Various allegations (widely and confusedly reported by the media to be repeated here) enabled Independent Counsel Kenneth Starr to extend his 41-month investigation of the Whitewater real-estate deal involving the Clintons to the Clinton-Lewinsky sex scandal.

"The Starr Report," the product of his $45 million investigation, was released to the House of Representatives in September and subsequently posted to the web-sites of most broadcast, print, and online media. The voluminous tome read less like a legal document and more like a soft-porn NC-17 screenplay written by a sex-obsessed writer. As Dorit Levin put it to me later (see below), "Monica Lewinsky gave the most expensive blow-job in history." In December, after various media had inflicted the politico-sexual telenovella on the US and the world, Clinton became the second president in US history to be impeached by the House of Representatives. (He was later acquitted by the Senate at the beginning of 1999.)

*   *   *

Back to Missoula and Jacques and Katya. After the three-week camping trip, I had originally planned to stay at Jacques's for one week and then head back to New York. But then Jacques told me about the Five Rivers International Film Festival that was coming up in Missoula at the beginning of September. Since he specialized in film and theory at the university, he was in charge of the festival's academic component, which he conceived and organized around the triad of technology, capitalism, and narrative. And since my own work in recent years has focused on the Janus-like two-headed monstrous regime of capital and technology, he wanted me to give a presentation at the festival. I agreed, telling him that in fact I had a number of drafts on my virtual PC I could consult as a possibility. Jacques at that time then suggested that I could stay in Missoula until the festival, that there was indeed no point in going to New York only to come back in a week for my presentation. I stayed in Missoula until the festival, which began three weeks after I met Katya. She came to the presentation: I gave an account of how capital and technology had both set up visual regimes full of nomadic subjects, and then analyzed these regimes at work in Ridley Scott's *Blade Runner*. Katya told me later that she began to fall in love with me from that point on—in spite (and as it turned out independently) of her involvement with Glen, whom she had met that summer at Georgetown University in DC, where she had been an adjunct instructor of Russian the whole academic year before. Glen had been one of her students: He was taking Russian to prepare for a career in international finance in Russia.

After the festival, Jacques asked me about my plans. I said I was heading back to New York, to the three-year freelance contractual work that my union, the Writers Guild, had negotiated for me with the cultural desk at MSNBC, but more importantly, heading back to the revision of my first novel. My publisher had demanded that I substantially rewrite major portions of it, especially those that were more autobiographical than fictional.

The novel, which began its manuscript life as *Nomadic Lives* and was transformed by my editor into its hardcover one as *In the White City*, was, like most first novels, certainly semi-autobiographical. It told the story, in first-person narration, of several romantic triangles set in the worlds of media, art, and academia. In the main triangle, the narrator, a media researcher and cultural analyst, is caught between his love for his current partner, a professor of cultural theory, and his obsessive attraction to an artist. His dilemma reflects his ambivalent relationship with academic culture and his fascination for the art and media worlds. Set in the 70s, 80s, and 90s, the novel also illustrates myriad shifts and intersections of events and experiences that mark cosmopolitan life in contemporary American culture.

My publisher, afraid of a lawsuit, especially wanted me to rewrite the chapter that dealt with the sexual harassment of a male African-American book editor by his boss, a white "cultural-leftist" "putative-Marxist" woman. This event closely mirrored my own experiences in the early 90s when I was working for a major TV network in New York. The event was widely covered both in local and national print media because it happened way before the Clinton-Lewinsky farce, and precisely because it went against the grain of stereotypical male-predator sexual harassment cases. Since this chapter as I had written it formed the linchpin of the entire novel, revising it would have seismic ramifications for the narrative and structure.

From his discussions of the manuscript with me, Jacques knew the amount of work I needed to do, so he suggested that I stay in Missoula at his house in South Hills to focus on it. He said that I could sublet my apartment in New York and live at his place as a guest, free of the economic hassles of a mortgage and lodging, and that living in Missoula would reduce the pressure of freelance work and free me up to work almost exclusively on the novel. Jacques made me an offer I couldn't refuse.

I went back to New York at the end of August to renegotiate my contract with MSNBC and to sublet my apartment. My subletter,

Dorit Levin, was a New York-centric woman I had met for the first time in 1989 at HarperCollins, when I went to visit my friend Karyn Ross, a senior editor there at the time.

Since 1989 is quite significant in my life—when I met the one woman who has meant so much to me in my life so far, and since I'm a journalist whose areas are culture and politics, following is a chronicle of the significant events that happened that year.

*   *   *

1989: Several crucial events were happening all over the world. I remember thinking at the time that it was an incredible year to be alive. Mikhail Gorbachev captured it best when he said earlier that year: "We are leaving one epoch of international relations and entering another." (I was actually introduced to Gorbachev in 1988, in London at a book party that HarperCollins-UK had organized for the publication of the English-language edition of his *Perestroika*, but alas, I never had a honorable chance to talk to him.) Let's look at a few of these events, both global and domestic.

Communism collapsed in Europe, precipitating the end of the Cold War: Powered by Gorbachev's reforms (which were to disinstall the Soviet machine itself in 1990) and his renunciation of Moscow's imperial power in the so-called second world, movements for market economy and (so-called) emergent democracies toppled communist dictatorships throughout Eastern and Central Europe. The transformation began visibly in Hungary, which opened its border with Austria, after which thousands of Hungarians streamed across Austria on their way to (West) Germany or sought asylum in West German embassies in Prague and Warsaw. In Poland, the government finally legalized the Solidarity movement (nine years after Lech Walesa formed it) after months of unrest and negotiations. Then two million East Germans flooded into West Berlin while the guards along the Berlin Wall did nothing. The guards still did nothing while the East Germans began dismantling the Wall. In Rumania the government's security police killed some seven thousand citizens before insurgents finally executed a defiant-to-the-death Ceausescu and his wife. Czechoslovakia's "Velvet Revolution," historically grounded in the so-called Prague Spring of 1968, had begun with student demonstrations, and then culminated with the election (coronation was more like it) of dissident and affable playwright-activist Václav Havel as president.

In Panama, President Bush had an ax to grind with General Manuel Noriega, commander of Panama's armed forces and the nation's de facto ruler. The US government accused Noriega (a generously paid CIA informer since the 60s) of selling US intelligence to Cuba and of also allowing Colombia's Medallin cocaine cartel to ship drugs through Panama to North America. Finally, running "out of patience" (according to a US government communiqué that I managed at some point to get hold of), Bush sent 25,000 troops chasing after Noriega, arrested him in his "palace," flew him to the US, and put him in jail in Miami, where he sat for months and months while the US government tried to sort out the tangled mess of its history with him. As a sardonic friend of mine put it then: "A dog relentlessly and furiously chasing after a car finally catches it: What then will the dog do with it?"

In South Africa, Frederik W. De Klerk began the reforms that would eventually dismantle apartheid, free Nelson Mandela from prison after twenty-seven years (my father had corresponded with Mandela in the mid-60s shortly after he was jailed in Robben Island Prison, and I was thrilled to meet him in New York in 1990 during his first visit to the US), lead to democratic elections, and result in the election of Mandela as president.

In China, Mao's heir, Deng Xiaoping, sent troops and tanks into 100-acre Tiananmen Square to kill some of the thousands of students, workers, and intellectuals who had been staging three weeks of prodemocracy demonstrations. The incident met with worldwide condemnation. The leader of the protesters, Liu Gang, was granted asylum in the US in 1996. Once ranked third on the Chinese government's list of "most wanted" student protesters, he was arrested in June 1989 and sentenced to six years in prison and "two years deprivation of political rights" (whatever those might be). After Liu's release in June 1995, he was kept in isolation (with no telephone communication) in his remote hometown of Liaoyan. In 1996 he violated his "parole" (or exile) and went to Beijing, and from there he was smuggled to the US. In Boston, where he first stayed, Liu, with a masters degree in physics, said he expected to stay in the US and go to school: "I've just applied to go to school now, to some universities in Boston and other places." Then White House spokesman and windbag, Spin-Doctor Michael D. McCurry, said the Liu case should not further damage relations with China. "We are confident we can maintain the broad constructive engagement with China which reflects the status of our current bilateral relations," he said.

In the United Kingdom of Great Britain and Northern Ireland, ninety-five people were killed, and many more injured, at an English soccer tournament match between Liverpool and Nottingham Forest. Thousands of fans piling into the already overcrowded stands of Hillsborough Stadium in Sheffield crushed spectators against a metal "safety" fence encircling the field. The fence they were trapped against had been put there to begin with to prevent combative spectators ("hooligans," in British parlance) from storming the field, as they were wont to do. The lethal surge happened when police, fearing that locked-out late-arriving Liverpool supporters would wreak havoc in the streets (as they were also wont to do), opened exit gates to let them in.

In Iran, the Ayatollah Ruhullah Khomeni issued a *fatwa* (the Islamic death sentence) for Salman Rushdie, an Indian-born British novelist, for writing *The Satanic Verses,* his first novel to deal with London and which caused an uproar among Muslim fundamentalists for perceived blasphemy against Islam. The Ayatollah urged all "zealous Muslims" to execute him quickly. Rushdie immediately went into hiding. (In 1998, a more secular government of Iran assured the British government the *fatwa* would not be enforced, but Iranian officials also pointed out that this assurance was not binding on "freelance" zealots who might still carry out the order. At the time of this writing, Rushdie lives in New York with his third wife and appears at various events with limited security.) The *fatwa* gave a material (and chilling) twist to Jacques Derrida's theoretical linkage of writing with death. (Early in the year, before the *fatwa* and shortly after *Satanic Verses* was published in London by Penguin Books [Viking-Penguin was to bring it out in the US a month later], I met Rushdie and his then wife, Marianne Wiggins, an American novelist, in New York when they were both scouting for an apartment to buy in the city. They were living in London at the time and thinking about moving to the US. Karyn Ross (who was Wiggins's editor at HarperCollins) introduced me to them at her apartment in Manhattan. As all four of us sipped red wine in Karyn's living room, Rushdie wondered out loud whether he had exhaustively mined all the three crucial aspects of his cultural heritage for his novels up to that point: Pakistan in *Shame*; India in *Midnight's Children* ; and Islam in *Satanic Verses*. I remember him as quite arrogant, as he dismissed offhand all the protests in London and India that were then just beginning about *Satanic Verses*. He and Marianne Wiggins were to separate a year after the *fatwa*.)

In Iran, the Ayatollah Khomeni died "of natural causes."

In France, Irish-born self-exiled Nobel-Laureate writer, Samuel Beckett, died of respiratory problems in a hospital in the Massy section of Paris. Beckett's work, which I greatly admire, often explored, among many others, the themes of impotence and ignorance. One of my favorite Beckett lines is from a short play called *Company* : "The fable of one with you in the dark. The fable of one fabling with you in the dark. And how better in the end labor lost and silence. And you as you always were. Alone." (I have a personal anecdote about Beckett: In 1979 during my junior year abroad in Paris, I was on the 21 bus with a girlfriend, heading back to the Cité Universitaire from the Latin Quarter. On rue Gay-Lussac, at one of the stops, a man with the authentic likeness of Beckett got on the bus. "Hey, that's Samuel Beckett!" my friend yelled. "Shh," I said to my obviously embarrassed friend, certain that he had heard her. Surely enough, he promptly got off the bus the next stop.)

In the US:

Crippled by recession, the high price of oil, and labor strikes, two airlines went belly-up: Eastern and Pan Am, the major American airline that, with its imperial and latently racist Clipper service, pioneered America's link with the third world.

Two electrochemists at the University of Utah announced at a press conference that they had achieved nuclear fusion—the process that powers the sun—in a jar at room temperature. Dubbed "cold fusion," the phenomenon violated known physical laws and promised (still promises: These scientists claim they're still "working on it" at the time of this writing) cheap, clean, virtually unlimited energy.

Michael ("Mike") Milken—the prophet of the high-risk high-yield "junk" bonds that fueled the many mergers and acquisitions of the high-greed decade of the 80s, and that more or less concretized the arrival of the postnational stage of capital—was indicted on ninety-eight fraud and racketeering charges. Junk bonds empowered Wall Street raiders (mostly members of "Gen X") to seize control of multibillion corporations and prepare the terrain for the erasure, on one crucial register, of the nation-state.

The tanker *Exxon Valdez* hit a reef, pouring 11 million gallons of crude oil into the pristine waters of Prince William Sound, near the southern terminus of the Alaska Pipeline. The resulting slick fouled one thousand miles of shoreline in one of the world's most ecologically sensitive regions. The spill was the biggest in US history, doing tremendous damage to wildlife: An estimated 580,000 birds and 5,500 otters were killed. The disaster occurred because the Captain of the ship was drunk: Consequently, he then entrusted control of the ship to an unqualified third mate, and the Coast Guard in turn then failed to warn the ship that it was miles off course. Reports claim that right after the ship stuck the reef, and a startled fellow officer asked the drunken captain what the problem was, the captain thumped his own chest and responded: "You're looking at it."

And Spike Lee's *Do the Right Thing* was released in most theaters near everyone everywhere. Set in the Bed-Stuy section of Brooklyn on what its director called "the hottest day of the year," the film explored relations between the locals (including an Afrocentric militant, an angry and slightly incoherent rap fan, a carefully noncommittal pizza-delivery man, and three bitter street-corner "philosophers") and the non-African-Americans who work—but do not live—in the neighborhood (including an apparently decent Italian pizzeria owner, his two racist sons, a choleric Korean grocer, and brutal white cops). The film ended with contradictory quotations on self-defense from Martin Luther King Jr. and Malcolm X. Several film critics accused Lee (whom I was to meet later at a party at a friend's townhouse in Park Slope, and who, as I recall, was quite obnoxious to almost everyone that evening, including my friend himself) of endorsing violence as the only response to racism, and the critics predicted that the film would incite riots in major US cities (it didn't).

*   *   *

Now back to Dorit:

Dorit was Karyn's editorial assistant in 1989. Karyn was a former lover of mine who put me through the wringer by capturing me in a vicious and painful triangle with her husband, from whom she'd been separated for six years, and whom she was planning to divorce when we were together—until she changed her mind and heart. When I met Dorit in 1989, without my knowing it, I set off yet another intense psycho-sexual—maybe even lesbian—triangulation of Dorit-Karyn-me, and a chain of events that endured through the 90s, and that eventually led me to where I was to end up at the edge of millennium. But I'm getting ahead of myself.

I sublet my apartment to Dorit, successfully renegotiated my contract with MSNBC under the supervision of the Writers Guild, and flew Northwest Airlines back to Missoula, to Jacques and his community of friends, which now included Katya.

*   *   *

5

Missoula: Thursday, June 24, 1999

—Do you have the keys?

—Right here.

—I've arranged to have your line disconnected.

—Oh, OK . . . Jacques is driving me to the airport.

—I know. He told me. I just saw him in the department.

That was more or less the only verbal exchange Katya and I had this morning when she came into the apartment around 11 AM. As I said before: She has been staying with one of her students since Monday.

As I write this I'm waiting for Jacques to show up. He's supposed to pick me up at 1 PM. for the twenty-minute ride to the Missoula "International" Airport. My flight is at 2 PM. and typically, I have an e-ticket and nothing to check. I'll walk to the gate, get my boarding pass, and board the plane with the first-class, business, or specially handicapped, people because I've racked up so many miles with Northwest Airlines to make me a "preferred" World-Perks traveler. I have too many miles: I once told a friend that it's too bad I couldn't pay my mortgage or buy groceries with the miles I have banked up with Northwest. Right now, I feel compelled to narrate another exchange, a decidedly sexual one, between Katya and I yesterday afternoon and late evening.

Since Monday, Katya has been coming to the apartment during the day when I wasn't here for a change of clothes and perhaps for a shower. Yesterday evening when I came back here, I found her soiled underpants right smack in the middle of the bathroom floor.

This was definitely not typical behavior. The Katya I've come to know this past year is as clean a freak as I am. Some background: I was used to wearing her underpants, which she found quite amusing. This practice began one morning when I ran out of clean underpants and she suggested I wear her boxer shorts. More background: You already know somewhat implicitly that for the last two weeks of our active relationship I refused to penetrate her. She told me that one morning when I was out running, she picked up my underpants when she was about to do the laundry, and was quite disgusted and angry when she sniffed *my* semen in them. She surmised, correctly, that I had masturbated into my underpants the night before instead of penetrating her, thereby "wasting" the sperm that should have flowed into her.

So make of this what will, but this is what I did last night: I picked up Katya's soiled underpants and put them in the laundry basket. Then I picked up her clean underpants from her dresser and masturbated into them while thinking of a composite of Dorit Levin and Karyn Ross, then put them at exactly the same spot where she had put her soiled ones. She hasn't gone into the bathroom yet. I'm hoping that when she finds her underpants, she'll realize exactly what happened when she sniffs my semen.

*   *   *

6

New York: Saturday, June 26, 1999

First off: It's so great to be back in New York. But then I'm also looking forward to jetting off to Paris for the annual conference that L'Archive de la paix (Peace Archives), which Francette's father directs, is organizing this year around the topic of NATO and Kosovo, a conference that will be attended by writers and intellectuals around the world, and that will present Jesse Jackson with a peace award for springing the GIs from Milosevic. The Archive sent me a free ticket to cover the proceedings, and then I've made separate freelance arrangements to write up the conference for *Salon* and *Le Monde Diplomatique*.

I'm staying with friends in Park Slope in Brooklyn. Dorit is still subletting my apartment on West 57th Street. In a way it's a wash: She pays the mortgage and utilities. And I would rather sublet to a friend. She and I have managed to maintain a close friendship since we met at HarperCollins in 1989, and especially since our brief romantic interlude in the early 90s. Much more about Dorit later. Right now I have a number of options: I could kick Dorit out of my apartment and move back there. Or I could continue to stay with friends until I decide whether to move back to New York permanently or move to some other city. I'm not sure what I want to do. I'll think things over in Paris. Francette de Vallièress will fly in from Los Angeles on Tuesday. Wednesday we fly to Paris together. Katya might be right after all about one thing: Francette might have designs on me. We'll find out what she might have in mind soon enough.

When Jacques came to pick me up at Babs in Missoula Thursday at 1 PM for the ride to the airport, Katya and I exchanged goodbyes. No hugs or kisses. Just two words. That was all. Hardly a fitting end to a passionate six-month romantic and (excepting the last two weeks when we were physically together) intensely sexual relationship. And Katya and Jacques simply exchanged frosty hellos.

The situation that Thursday afternoon in the apartment at Babs, near the Clark-Fork River and Higgins Avenue, at the edge of downtown Missoula, was certainly odd: one that none of us—Jacques, Katya, nor I—could have predicted when Katya as well as ten others came to dinner at Jacques's house on the slopes of South Hills, five miles away west, toward Lolo, when we met for the first time, that warm August night. The day after that dinner, Jacques and I talked about Katya in French and English, but mostly the latter.

Jacques to me:

—You and Katya seem to have really hit it off. You two were yakking for most of the evening.

—Yeah. We talked mostly about Israel, about Jerusalem.

—She's quite a combination: Russian-Jewish-Israeli.

—Her mother lives in Jerusalem. Her father still lives in Moscow. They split up when Katya and her mom emigrated to Israel.

—She's extremely fluent in English, considering.

—Yeah, she speaks with a British accent and Russian intonation. Another odd combination.

—I wonder what her politics is like. I can't get a read on her.

—Well . . . she's anti-Zionist for one. That's why she emigrated here after staying in Israel for only four years.

—I still wonder about her politics. I wonder which faction she'll end up with in the department.

—I'll guess not with yours.

—We'll see . . . don't you have relatives in Jerusalem?

—My in-laws. Nigiste's immediate relatives. She's Ethiopian
Falasha. Remember I told you her family was airlifted from
Ethiopia to Israel in 1984.

—Yeah, you told me. She went to Hebrew University and now
works as an administrative officer in the Israeli Embassy in
Tokyo? And
that's how she met your brother, who is cultural attaché at the
American Embassy in Tokyo?

—Yeap. My brother, born in New York of Nigerian parents, works
at the American Embassy in Tokyo. He met his wife, an
Ethiopian Falasha who is now an Israeli working for her embassy
in Tokyo. They have a daughter, whom they're raising Jewish.
That's diaspora for you.

—Indeed. Your family is amazing. Nigiste. Nice name.

—It means queen in Amaric.

—Where's your other brother again? The scientist?

—In Baltimore—Johns Hopkins, remember?

—Yeah, the geneticist. Your brothers are so accomplished. So are
your parents. Is your mother still teaching?

—Yeah. She has more students than she can handle.

—And your dad?

—He's still at the UN but will be retiring soon.

—Now you . . . you're the bum. What happened?

—Recessive maybe regressive genes, now getting back to Katya. I
like her.

—You like all thin Jewish women.

—Katya isn't what you call thin.

—You're right there. But she has a nice curvy body.

—You like that kind. But what an interesting combination of a
face: Slavic and Jewish. The nose is Jewish, the cheekbones
Slavic.

—I still wonder about her politics.

—I can tell you one thing: She's not a Marxist. Otherwise she
would have stayed in Russia. Another interesting combination:
a non-Marxist anti-Zionist.

—You're probably right. She might even be reactionary.

—Are you attracted to her, Jacques?

—Hell no. My hands are full with Chris.

—Is that right? The sex is better now?

—We're still working on that.

—You have to *work* on it? It's either there or it isn't.

—That's easy for you to say, Mr. Stud.

—Your American expressions amuse me.

—Are *you* attracted to Katya?

—No, but I could be in another lifetime.

—Better grab her in this one, since Sarah has thrown you back into the market. You probably won't do better around here.

—I've seen some very attractive women in Missoula.

—Naive coeds, mountain women, retro hippies. They look okay, and some even gorgeous, until they open their mouths.

—You're such an elitist, Jacques.

—The pot calling the kettle black.

—I should be telling you that, given that you have a fetish about black women, and that you're what in New York we call a wigger.

—Wigger?

—A white nigger. Get it? The term's from hip-hop culture.

—I feel honored, especially coming from you. You have very high standards about race.

—Oh come on! You're really getting Americanized. How long have you been in this country again?

—Twenty-five years.

—1974. You came here in 1974? We met in 1978. Twenty-one years ago. Man! Time really flies.

—Deleuze said it.

—Someone said it way before your Deleuze. Time's arrow.

—Correction: our Deleuze. Who's the someone who said it?

—One of the Greeks. A pre-Socratic, I think.

—Probably Empedocles.

—Makes sense. Deleuze stole it from him. Empedocles was one of his favorites.

—You remember the joke that went around France and the US shortly after Deleuze jumped out the window?

—That he jumped out the window because he wanted to see time fly?

—I was in Paris at the time.

—Yeah, I know. You called me in New York to give me the very bad news.

—Back to Katya. Ask her out.

—She's really not my type. She's Jewish and all that. But she's not my type physically. She's yours though. Maybe *you* should go out with her.

—I got Chris.

—New Yorkese too. You picked that up in New York.

—Of course, but I should remind you that that particular usage is not restricted to New York or the Eastern Seaboard.

—Don't go smart on me. Jacques, why do we mostly speak in English?

—Because we're in the US.

—I guess we spoke mostly French when we spent some together at your parents in Toulouse.

—We had to. My mother neither speaks nor understands English.

—And your father pretends not to understand English.

—You saw through him there. Look: You can at least fuck Katya.

—Jacques, I'm not a fuck machine like you. I have to be invested emotionally.

—What about Trish? You fucked her the first night you laid eyes on her, you dirty old dog. Were you emotionally invested in her?

—I told you many times: That was a strange night. You know I never do that. It was your fault: You and Christine dropped me off at Rob's party one hour before the it supposed to begin. I started drinking way too early . . .   before the food was ready. Before I knew it I was stroking Trish's cheeks.

—Chris and I were surprised to see you two with your arms around each other. One thing led to another. And when you guys later tumbled into her bed at *her* house, she moaned and screamed for what seemed to be a very long night, you said.

—Trish moaned and screamed. She came several times.

—She came several times? My God. That woman is like a whore in bed.

(Disclosure: Jacques and Trish had had an on-again off-again two-year "affair" before he ended up—and during the time he was—with Christine.)

Jacques:

—Still, I think you should go out with Katya. She can teach you Russian.

To repeat: Katya and I didn't become an item until September 1998. After that warm August night, Katya was part of Jacques's local community of friends.

Jacques's somewhat closely knit community of friends consisted of all kinds, but I'll identify only the ones who will figure prominently in my narrative: me; Katya; Casey Jones, a college professor whom Jacques suspected of being asexual, his life uncluttered, as it were, by love or lust; Janice Lehman, a wannabe writer who lived in an old school bus parked in her friend's backyard; Rob Radin, a cyber-entrepeneur who owned his Internet company; Rob's wife Laura Jacobson, an aspirant painter who had a day-job teaching art in continuing education at the university; Christine Ford and Trish Van Cleve, two divorced blonde women, in a sense casualties of capital, trying to recover from failed marriages and careers and abusive husbands. (More about Trish and Christine below.) We had a regular schedule of sorts: On Sunday mornings we hiked on several mountains: Lolo, Blue Mountain, Sentinel, among others. After the hikes—which sometimes took several hours—Jacques and Christine made dinner for everyone. We ate, we drank, we talked about politics and culture. We went to movies. We went to perhaps too many drunken dinner parties and utterly wild blowouts—fueled by nicotine, alcohol, gossip, and casual sex—

around town, from the dilapidated houses on the Northside, to the "bougie" cottages in Rattlesnake, to the charming houses by the university, to the nondescript box-bungalows on the slopes of South Hills.

At one of these parties in late August, I met Bryn, a coltish gamine twenty-three-year-old talented artist who was also a forest-preservation activist. She had a day job doing retail work at Worden's Deli on the corner of North Higgins Avenue and Pine Street. High on the sauce herself, she—sometimes including her friends, who were in fact quite interesting in many respects—introduced me to seedy karaoke bars on and off Brooks Avenue, and to legendary (for the locals) bars on North Higgins and environs (The Old Post; Mulligan's; CharlieB's; Oxford; Am Vets; Missoula ["Mo"] Club, and others). Bryn told me that as a writer I had to experience first-hand local scenes and flavors before writing about them.

I integrated Bryn somewhat into Jacques's community. Everybody liked her, but Katya did not. Katya in fact was there when I met her for the first time at the party. She told me about two weeks later that Bryn was a retard.

—I like Bryn.

—What do you like about her? She's a retard.

—No she's not. She writes too, you know.

—She's a retard. What do you guys talk about?

—Lots of things. But mostly local politics. She wants to start a little magazine.

—About what?

—Local politics. Maybe the local art scene too. Have you seen her paintings at the art museum?

—Yeah, I was curious about her art. So I checked it out last Friday, during the so-called Gallery Night. She's a good painter, no doubt of that.

—She knows quite a bit about art.

—She's too young for you, isn't she?

—She's twenty-three, going on thirty-five. But you're assuming we're an item. We're just friends.

—That's what you think. I've seen the way she looks at you and
   hangs on to every word you say. She might have a father complex
   there.

—I'm not that old.

—Thirty-eight is getting up there.

—Thanks a lot!

—She wants to fuck you. Women know these things.
   She surprised me somewhat with the f-word.

*   *   *

7

New York: Sunday, June 27, 1999

Katya was quite wrong about Bryn in all respects. She was neither a retard nor all that naively young. And even if she might have been attracted to me physically, she never wanted to sleep with me, as Katya crudely asserted to the contrary with extreme prejudice. And we never slept together. However, Bryn's first few hours with me in Missoula at the wild drunken party where we met would appear to substantiate Katya's suspicion. Interestingly, Katya was at the same party but left after thirty minutes when she felt Jacques and I ignored her: She complained to me a few days later that we were instead seduced by the teenage "coeds"—as Jacques would put it—who flooded the party that night. Here's how Bryn and I met that late August night.

Missoula: Saturday, August 22, 1998

Trish Van Cleve had the wild party at her house that August night of the new moon. Katya and I had alluded to Trish in an earlier entry. Trish and I had had a one-night-stand casual sex at this same house before she had this party—and before I met Katya—after another drunken dinner party that Rob had at *his* house. And at this point Katya did not know this fact, although I was to tell her later. Trish was a theater "teaching specialist" (fancy title for exploited wage-slaves in contemporary American universities) at the university, and she had organized the party for her theater students from the year before, to welcome them back for the subsequent academic year. In fact, this "reason" for the party was simply a pretext to get a bunch of hedonic sybarites and nymphs together, on a warm night in Missoula, so that they can all get drunk while indulging in sexual foreplay—or in some cases the sexual act itself onsite. In Missoula people drum up the mildest excuses—or none at all—to have a drunken dinner party or blow-out.

Jacques, Christine, Katya, and I went to the party together. At this point in August, the four of us had formed a subgroup within the regular community. The raison d'être for this subgroup made sense: Christine was Jacques's mostly live-in main squeeze; Katya and Jacques were in the same university department; and I was Jacques's longterm friend living at his house. By the time we got to Trish's sprawling house on Arthur Avenue and University at 9 PM, half the partygoers were already drunk. Most of them were women in their late teens or early twenties, clad in costumes of all colors and personages (theater majors!). Two designated women photographers, one costume-cast as Diane Arbus and the other Annie Leibovitz, were darting about the rooms taking shots of various people in different poses and scenes. Two expansive rooms staged loud dancing music, with appointed DJs dressed in grunge.

As the four of us negotiated our precarious path though bodies, scenes, and rooms toward the kitchen for badly needed drinks, Jacques said to me in awkward French, purposefully using unnecessary subjunctives, loosely translated as follows:
—I want this party to be incredible. Look at this scene! I wish I
    hadn't brought her.

I chuckled but said nothing. Christine spoke and understood very little French, whence the subjunctives. Jacques was positive she wouldn't pick up the difficult constructions. She was a graduate student in sociology specializing in death studies. Although her program had no foreign-language requirement, she decided to take the first year of French in 1995, with Jacques as her instructor, which was how they met. She was his physical type: average height, mesomorph, blonde, neither striking nor unpleasant to look at. Yet he told me over the years that he was not that sexually attracted to her, even though she was a "nice" person, and that he was definitely not in love with her: one of his many contradictions that I had ceased attempting to comprehend years before. He had also told me over the past years that he was trying to break up with her. In fact, he did not invite her to the camping trip I mentioned earlier. So they had been fighting quite bitterly since we got back. But I'm digressing: Back to Trish's party.

We got our drinks and traced our path back toward the front of the house and ended up on the porch, sitting and chatting with three women, Jacques's acquaintances. One of the photographers— the Annie Liebovitz wannabe, of course!—found us a curiously stylish group worthy of a few shots: a Frenchman dressed up in a dark-blue jacket and khaki pants, loud yellow shirt, and colorful foulard; a plain-looking bleach-blonde woman with very tight blue stonewashed jeans (in 1998!) and bright-red shirt; a Russian-Jewish woman with a Jewish-Slavic face wearing a long loosely fitting beige formal dress and black high-heel shoes; and an African-American man all in black: beret, shirt, pants, ankle-length boots, with two large gold hoops on each ear. At some point Trish joined us and introduced us to a few drunken students. She suggested that we partake in the festivities instead of doing "discourse," that we mingle, that we go inside and dance with the others, and that we stop being elitist intellectuals.

We went inside one of the dancing rooms. Jacques plunged into the crowd and disappeared. Christine stood by herself trying to survey the scene until someone recognized her and asked her to dance. Katya seemed awkward and lost, as though on another planet. I simply stood there, sipping my wine, unable and unwilling to engage her in conversation, and it was too loud to sustain one in any case. At this point a woman grabbed me from behind and asked me to dance with her. Her drunken state did not conceal her attractive young body: dark hair, thin, somewhat tall, multiply pierced, packed like me in an all-black attire and high black boots, including a Hoqey beret like mine. The DJs had put on some zoukous music. I looked at Katya and shrugged, as the woman dragged me toward the dance area.

That's how I met Bryn.

After we danced through two pieces we came back to Katya exactly where we left her. I introduced them to each other. Katya was polite but a little frosty. After an awkward minute she said she was leaving because she was tired. Then she left without saying goodbye to the others. I offered to walk her home, since Jacques had driven us to the party, and she had left her car at home. She declined my offer, saying she didn't have to walk too far. Her impulsiveness and her response to my gesture should have been early red flags, which I chose to ignore or deny.

*   *   *

8

New York: Monday, June 28, 1999

I just got off the phone with Dorit. I told her that I was back in New York, that Katya and I broke up, and that I was headed to a conference in Paris with my friend Francette. She asked me about the conference but surprisingly not about Francette. Then she said she wasn't that surprised about my split up with Katya given what I had told her about Katya. Then she wanted to know whether I had time for dinner before leaving on Wednesday. I said maybe, that I'd call or e-mail her later tonight about that. What might Dorit be up to? I forgot to ask her if she's seeing anyone. We've had a curious relationship ever since Sarah and I broke up, and especially since she's been subletting my apartment. We voice-linked and e-mailed each other two three times a week when I was in Missoula. We tell each other everything—at least we try to. I'm not sure how to define our "relationship." I'd like to probe this further. But tonight, when it's also a full moon, I'd like instead to get back to that other night of the full moon in Missoula.

Missoula: Saturday, August 22, 1998

After Katya left abruptly, Bryn and I went back out to the porch for some air. I was sipping wine. Bryn was swigging beer from the bottle. She lit up a joint and offered it to me. I took a deep drag. I used to smoke cannabis in high school in New York. But into my sophomore year in college I stopped because I developed an allergy to it. These days I take a drag or two if offered, usually at a party.

Bryn:

—You're the dude Vanessa told me about.

—Dude? I like that. Vanessa? Trish's kid?

—Yeah.

—You know her?

—Yeah. She's a friend of mine. I came to the party with her.

Vanessa was Trish's twenty-two-year-old daughter, whom I met
the night I spent at Trish's, and who lived with her forty-two-year-
old mother.

—Is that right? Missoula is a small place indeed.

—That's right. You wanna hear how she described you to me?

—I'm curious.

—She said you're a cool mother-fucker.

I laughed out loud.

—Now that's very clever. Do I look like a mother-fucker to you?

—To her you *are* a mother-fucker! You fucked her mother, after
all. You know what else she told me?

—I'm all ears.

—She said you guys kept her awake all night. First, her mother
was moaning and screaming her head off. Then when you two
finally fell asleep you were snoring so loud the windows rattled.

—Oh no. I had no idea I snored that loudly.

—People who snore are not even aware of it.

—I've been told that. But do I seem like a real mother-fucker to
you, like in the hood?

—Not at all. But you look cool . . .

—Glad to hear it.

—I can't believe that we're dressed alike. We look good together.
We look like a totally cool couple.

—We do?

—Yes! That's not that hard to achieve in Missoula.

—Is that right? Our world as will and idea, as Schopenhauer said.

—Chopin who?

—Scho-pen-hau-er. German philosopher. He said we first will whatever life we want to live, then it takes root in our mind as a tenacious idea, then some of us eventually translate that idea into reality. In other words, we have complete control over our lives, if we work on it. In other words, if you want to look cool, you look cool.

—Awesome. Maybe I'll tune him in some day. How do you spell his name?

—S-c-h-o-p-e-n-h-a-u-e-r

—You dance very well. Are you a musician?

—No I'm not.

—You look like a musician.

—People often mistake me for one.

    I again:

—And I'm not really a good dancer. I dance only when I'm drunk.

—Well you dance very well, drunk or not.

—Thanks.

—Are you drunk? I am, totally.

—I know you are. I'm almost drunk.

—Almost drunk?

—A little buzz, as distinct from totally drunk, like you. I drank four glasses of wine really fast.

—I was surprised to see you here at this party. There aren't many blacks in Montana. A few here and there, in Great Falls and Missoula.

—Missoula I can understand. College town. But Great Falls?

—There's an army base there.

—Ah ah.

—What do you do then? What brings you to Missoula? I assume you're from somewhere else. I've never seen you before. And I get around.

—I'm a writer. And I'm here revising my novel.

—You're a novelist! Awesome! You must know that there's a group of writers here. Do you know any of them?

—I know a couple: Bryan Di Salvatore, a friend of a former lover of mine in New York, and Tom McGuane. But he lives north of here.

—Cool.

—Actually this former lover of mine is married to a former Missoula writer. He now lives in New York with her.

—Cool.

—Do you realize that Bryan is Bryn without the a?

—Ah, a wordsmith. Bryan reviews film for *The Missoulian*. New York. Is that where you're from?

—Yeah.

—Cool. I've never been there.

—You're missing a lot.

—I know. I plan to be there some day. Are you a rude New Yorker? People from New York are supposed to be rude and aggressive.

—You're right. New Yorkers are rude. You want to hear a joke about that?

—Sure. Totally.

—Well then. Here goes. Four guys are walking down a street in Manhattan: A Saudi Arabian, a Russian, a Korean, and a New Yorker. A reporter with a microphone intercepts them and asks: "Excuse me, what's your opinion about the meat shortage?" The Saudi guy says: "Shortage? What's a shortage?" The Russian says: "Meat? What is meat?" The Korean says: "Opinion? What's an opinion?" The New Yorker says: "Excuse me? What's excuse me?"

—Totally funny.

—Everyone in the US should live in New York sometime. It's a unique place on earth.

—How so?

—It's the most multicultural multi-ethnic city in the world. Every race, every culture, every ethnic group is represented there.

—Awesome! Really awesome! That's what's totally missing around here. That's why I was drawn to you immediately.

—Oh oh. Mandingo!

—Why oh oh? And what's mandingo?

—You don't get that reference? It's from slave narratives.

—No. What are slave narratives?

—I guess you're too young.

—Tell me the reference then.

—Never mind. Am I in your fantasy?

—No no. Not like that. I like things and people to be different. People look too much alike around here. Just like me. I totally blend in.

—Where's your friend Vanessa?

—Who knows? She's around here somewhere. She's a free spirit, like her mother.

—You seem quite young. Are you a student as well?

—I'm twenty-three. And I'm totally done with school.

—What do you do now?

—I'm a painter.

—Really? For real?

—Yeah, totally. For real. My paintings are in a few galleries around here. And the Art Museum has shown me a few times.

—How interesting. How did you get started?

—I've painted since I was four. How did you get started writing?

—Well, I've written since I was twelve.

—Are you totally a novelist?

—I write mostly nonfiction actually. Politics and culture. I'm learning how to write novels.

—Do you have an MFA in creative writing?

—No. I don't need an MFA to write.

—Are you a freelancer or on staff somewhere?

—Actually I'm a freelancer on contract with MSNBC right now.

—MSNBC? Does that have anything to do with NBC?

—It's cable. The ms stands for Microsoft. Jointly owned by Microsoft and NBC. CNN's main competition. Jacques gets it here through Montana Cable. I forget the channel.

—Awesome! Are you working for them from here? That's why you're wearing your press pass?

—I'm not working for them right this minute.

—You don't need your badge at this party.

—I know. I sometimes wear it to look cool.

—You totally look cool. You don't have to wear your press pass in Missoula.

—Oh sometimes I do . . . to get into gallery openings.

—All of them are totally free.

—Maybe you're right. Anyway, I'm more or less on sabbatical this year while reworking my novel.

—That must be totally cool making your living as a writer.

—Freelancing is great, but it has its downsides. I have to pay my own health insurance.

—I'm glad I don't have to do that. My day job pays for that, which is why I have it to begin with.

—What's your day job?

—Retail work at Worden's. I make the sandwiches. Do you know where that is? Downtown on the corner of Higgins and Pine.

—Yeah. That's a cool deli. Almost New York. Jacques likes to buy his wines there.

—Who's Jacques?

—You've never met Jacques? I thought you got around. Everybody knows Jacques.

—Well *I* don't.

—He's my friend . . . from way back. I'm staying at his house. We went to grad school together. He teaches French at the university. Katya is one of his colleagues.

—Katya. She's got an attitude. What does she teach?

—Russian.

—She's Russian?

—Yeah. Russian Jew.

—I like coming to Trish's parties. You meet some totally interesting people.

—You seem interesting yourself.

—Thank you.

>   She then leaned over and kissed me on the mouth—really

hard, rolling her tongue into mine. I thought oh-boy, here we go, as I tasted alcohol and caught a potent whiff of patchouli. Just then, Jacques showed up with an emaciated remotely attractive woman who looked thirty or forty, who had on very loose-fitting pants that were sliding down her waist, revealing part of her butt, and who seemed drunk out of her skull. She said nothing during the subsequent exchange.

Jacques:
—Hey. I can see that you're enjoying yourself.
—I am.
—Who is this charming young woman who is dressed like you?
  You both look like clones if you overlook the obvious.

I, laughing:
—And what might the obvious be?
Jacques, ignoring my question:
—Aren't you going to introduce me?
—Bryn, meet Jacques. We were just talking about you.
—Oh, no. What bad things have you been telling mon chère Bryn?
—Oh this and that.
Bryn, to Jacques:
—He's been telling me how you like to seduce and fuck women.
  Bryn was laughing. And I, somewhat taken aback:
—What? That's not true.
—Well I do like to seduce and fuck women. He's right.

Bryn:
—See?

I:
—Who is your companion? Jacques, you're being rude.
—Oh excuse me. I'm sorry. This is Janice.
—Where's Christine?
—I don't know. Where's Katya?

—She went home. She seemed a little pissed.

—Not surprised. Now that's one woman who seems to need a lot of attention.

Bryn to me:

—See? I was right. She has an attitude.

Then Bryn to Jacques and Janice, somewhat abruptly:

—Nice meeting you.

Bryn again, to me.

—Let's dance some more.

Without giving me a chance to respond, she then dragged me forcefully inside, toward one of the dancing rooms.

To sum up: By the end of the evening—around 3:30 AM— everybody was more or less drunk. Jacques and Christine left without me. Bryn told them she would drive me home. A few minutes after they left, Bryn invited me to her house for some more drinks, presumably before she drove me back to South Hills. (She lived in a house on Spruce Street in downtown Missoula, a few blocks from Wordens, where she made sandwiches for her day job.) I drank more wine. She drank more beer and smoked another joint. She first put on some rap music. Puff Daddy. Busta Rhymes. Beastie Boys. Then she switched to a Toumani Diabate CD that I actually have, something called "Nouvelles Cordes Anciennes." (New Ancient Strings) I was surprised. After about an hour and half, she said:

—Listen. I'm totally tired to drive you all the way up there tonight—or I guess this morning. The sun will be coming up in another hour. And I'm totally drunk. I don't trust myself to drive you in this state.

—Yeah, I totally don't trust you to drive me either. What do you propose?

—You can stay here. I have only one bed. We can both sleep in it. But let's get something straight: I don't want to fuck you, OK?

—Sure. I don't want to fuck you either.

—Great. I think we're going to be very good friends.

So that's how I met Bryn in Missoula. Totally.

*　　*　　*

9

New York: Tuesday, June 29, 1999

I have three hours before Francette shows up after flying in from Los Angeles. I e-mailed her directions about getting here from La Guardia.

As I said: I'm staying with friends in Park Slope. My friends are a couple: let's call them Alan and May. They have a sixteen-year-old son: let's call him Nelson. Al and May both work in the finance industry: he as a foreign-currency trader for Bankers Trust, and she as a new-tech analyst for Goldman Sachs. They all live in a three-story townhouse on Prospect Park West that they bought for a cool two million bucks.

When you walk in the front door you're in a vestibule that leads into a huge living room. Beyond the living room is an expansive kitchen totally outfitted with industrial metal cabinets and a restaurant-type range. Beyond the kitchen is a deck with chairs and plants. They sometimes have barbecues on this deck. Beyond the deck is a backyard with two trees and a garden full of herbs. This is just the first floor. You walk up the stairs to the second floor. There's a narrow hallway that feeds three rooms and a bathroom. One of these rooms is Nelson's. His door is locked most of the time, mainly to seal off the hip-hop and rap music he listens to constantly, even when he's on the Net. (At some point last year when I asked him how he felt as a Euro-Asian boy listening exclusively to rap and hip-hop, he responded: "I grew up in Brooklyn: Why wouldn't I listen to rap?") He has the TV on at all times, usually on mute. One room is the "family" room: This is the entertainment center for the whole family: A very spacious living room fitted with a huge audiovisual system. There's art on the walls—as is the case downstairs as well, lest I forget. The third room is the guest room—*my* guest room, as I like to remind them. For this house on Prospect Park West has become my home in New York since 1996 when I sublet my place to Dorit. You walk up to the third floor, into the penthouse. Al and May's own cozy living space: short hallway, bedroom with a skylight, bathroom with a skylight, and huge closets. There's a door leading out to a deck they've built on the roof, also with chairs and plants. They also sometimes have barbecues here in the summer and way into the fall as well. Guests have to through their bedroom to get to this deck, but Al and May don't really care, which should give you a clue to their generosity in the way they share their space and wealth with friends.

Al and May have many friends in domestic US and internationally. Even though friends stay with them all the time (one friend even stayed for as long as six months at some point!), I've managed to time my sojourns in New York so that I can stay in the guest room. I have backups places that I seldom use. I'll tell you a little bit more about Al and May later: They're a very interesting and extremely generous couple. He's a white American born and raised in Los Angeles. He speaks only English. She's Chinese-American born in Indonesia, raised in Hong Kong and Hawaii. She has an American and British passports. She speaks English with an American accent, and she's also fluent in French, Dutch, and Chinese. She told me at some point that her father once accused her of being a "banana" (yellow on the outside but white on the inside), but I knew for sure that was far from the truth.

Right now I want to tell you about Dorit. We went out for a drink last night. I was supposed to call her about a possible dinner before I jet off to Paris Wednesday. But I was working late until 11 PM. Then I called her, surprised she was home, and suggested we meet downtown for a drink. She thought it was a good idea. I wanted to see Dorit before Francette got here because any plans I might with her after that would have to involve Francette, something I wanted to avoid, somewhat inexplicably. So we agreed to meet at the Cornelia Street Café, our favorite place when we had the romantic interlude in the early 90s, before I got involved with Karyn Ross. Cornelia Street Café was packed. Alas, they had no room for us, so Dorit came up with an idea: Why not walk over to S.O.B.'s on Varick and West Houston and listen to the roots raggae band Israel Vibrations. Or better still, walk over to the Zinc Bar on West Houston Street between La Guardia Place and Thompson Street. It's only ten minutes away. There's a five-dollar cover charge, but it's worth it, Dorit said, because that night from 11:12 PM till 2 AM, Marianne Ebert was singing Brazilian music, alternating with Nkosi Konda and Peace of Mind's robust Afro-Caribbean percussion.

(Perhaps this is the appropriate point to declare that Dorit is most certainly a certified "wigger." She is one white woman about which I can assert without a doubt that she has thoroughly processed all the ramifications of racial difference and discrimination.)

Dorit, as we crossed Sixth Avenue to wind our way through Third and Sullivan Streets toward West Houston:

—If you're broke I'll treat you. In fact, the whole evening is on me.
—You're sure?
—I'm positive.
We got to Zinc Bar around 12:30 AM. We had no problem getting in. The guy at the entrance recognized Dorit and waved us in without the cover charge. That means two extra merlots, Dorit said as we settled at a table.
Dorit:
—Yo! You're looking well.
—So are you. It's been a while. When did we last see each other?
—Not that long ago, really. Spring of 1998, before you went off to Montana . . . into Katya's outstretched arms.
—Don't be too harsh. It still hurts . . . a little bit.
—Are you still in love with her, do you think?

—No I don't think so. But there is some residue. The breakup was as nasty and ugly as I told you.

—Sorry. I'll rephrase then: The last time I saw you was before you went to visit Jacques in Montana.

—OK, you're forgiven. The last time we saw each other we had lunch at the bistro in the Peninsula Hotel, on 55th and 5th. You didn't want to stray too far from either home or work.

—That's right. 55th seems well located between 57th and 8th, and Times Square.

—By the way, apropos the elegant Peninsula: I found out the other day that that was where Jon Voight, as the aspiring hustler in *Midnight Cowboy*, came to meet one of his rich but lonely female clients, and was promptly thrown out.

—I knew that. It was called The Barclay in the film.

—Indeed. Speaking of work: How's *The New Yorker* treating you?

—Can't complain. Things have calmed down somewhat after Tina. Remnick is doing a good job, keeping all the advertisers and Si happy. Not an easy task. And I'm good: They're letting me do exactly what I want to do.

—That's great, I couldn't believe all the media hoopla in the wake of Tina's departure.

—The media has, or have I guess, always been obsessed with my rag since it was launched, thanks to the drunks at the Algonquin Round Table.

—Rather more with Tina these days don't you think?

—I think more with the rag. Tina inherited a historical legacy. Of course her personality added more kindle to the whole combustion.

—Word has it that Renata Adler is writing a nasty kiss-and-tell book about all the major players there, from William Shawn through Lillian Ross and Robert Gottlieb to Adam Gopnik.

—Yeah, I heard that too. Somebody pried a manuscript loose from the publisher. There are some copies floating around. But I haven't seen one yet.

—Before I forget: Your piece on Afro-Paris in April was fabulous! I meant to e-mail you about that but forgot.

—Thank you. I guess you had your hands full in Jerusalem.

—I had my hands full in Montana too, even while I was in Jerusalem.

—Oh God. Katya. I told you that wouldn't last. A Russian Jew by way of Israel. And from everything you told me about her. For the life of me I couldn't figure out how and why you guys got together. She's not your type at all. You should have listened to me.

—You're right. It was a huge mistake. Must have been the Montana mountain air that got into me.

—Or all the beers and buffalo burgers and the militia out there.

—The buffalo burgers are great.

—Oh, come on. Maybe. I've actually never had buffalo.

—You have to try it sometime. It's distinctly different from cow meat.

—Not here in New York. I have to head West.

—Katya and I getting together seemed logical and perfect at the time. We were both at a strange moment in our lives. Our parallels somehow intersected, you know . . . timely, in a Deleuzean sense.

—Dear God. Don't go Deleuzean on me tonight. I left him behind when he jumped out the window. I had to get on with my own life.

—Sorry. I guess he would have wanted us all to get on with our lives.

—So you're off to Paris?

—Yes.

—With Francette.

—Yes.

Dorit, using the media code-word for nonmedia people:

—Tell me about Francette. That's a name that's never come up before. Is she a civilian?

—Most certainly yes. She's a professor.

—Really? You seem to like hanging out with academics these days: Jacques, Katya, Francette.

—I met her in the early 90s, shortly after my thing with you. She did some freelance translation work for me. She came recommended by a friend.

—Was her work any good?

—Yes, yes, in fact. I was quite surprised. She translated the stuff I did on France's resistance to global capital into French for Le Monde diplomatique.

—This was when you were still with CBS. Around the same time that Karyn the predator-bitch got her fangs into you and lured you into her lair on Horatio Street.

—You're being harsh again.

—Sorry again. It's just that I will never in the world forgive her for what she did. And how she did it.

—What did she do again? And how did she do it?

—You know exactly what she did. And exactly how she did it. Remember you were an accomplice as well. Some things are better not repeated.

—Yes, I know exactly. And you're right: Let sleeping dogs lie.

—Tell me a little more about Francette.

—Francette and I have become friends since she worked for me. She's an academic but fancies herself a writer.

—Where and what does she teach?

—UCLA. Cultural studies.

—Oh God . . .   cultural studies. If I hear that phrase again I'll scream.

—I know what you mean.

—What does she fancy herself writing? Academic books?

—Yeah.

—That doesn't make one a writer.

—I guess you're right there. She told me she's working on a memoir.

—Dear God. An academic writing a memoir. That would be a cure for insomnia. Have you seen drafts of this quote unquote creative writing effort?

—Yeah. She and I have exchanged writing projects. I sent her the manuscript of *In the White City*. And she wants my feedback on the memoir project.

—Oh God . . .

—You're being too harsh. She's a nice woman.

—Hey maybe her feedback will make your novel a bestseller.

—That'll be the day.

—So you're going to Paris together. Sounds like great fun! Where are you staying?

—Her place.

—Her place?

—Yes. She has an apartment in Paris.

She winked at me. I:

—It's not what you think. We're just friends. I'm staying at her apartment because I'm broke.

—Of course. Does she actually own the apartment or is she renting?

—She owns it.

—She must be loaded.

—Her parents are loaded. I think they're aristocrats. They bought her the apartment I think.

—So she teaches at UCLA but keeps an apartment in Paris.

—Yes. Some people live like that.

—Nice. What does she do with it when she's in LA?

—She's sublet it to a friend of hers—who lets her stay there when she's in Paris.

—That's nice. Is this friend male or female?

—Male.

—So they're an item?

—No: he's gay . . . a gay doctor.

—I see. It must be a big apartment to accommodate everyone.

—She said it's a four bedroom. One of the rooms is used as a study.

—So when you're staying there you'll have your own room.

—Of course.

—That's not obvious. Where's the apartment?

—In the 10th Arrondissement. Rue Fénelon, right next to St Vincent de Paul, she said.

—I know that area. Not too far to the north is Gare du Nord, and not too far to the south is Gare de l'Est.

—That's exactly what she said. You must know Paris well.

—*Hello?* I lived there for only three years.

—To repeat: I'm staying at her place with her only because I'm broke. She and I are just friends, the kind that dear Plato recommended.

—I believe you . . . So you're broke. Your wallet is always thin.

—I'm working on making some money.

—That'll be the day. What are you planning—winning the lotto? Or maybe the screenplay you're working on with your friend in Hong Kong will hit big and win something at Cannes or even the Oscars!

—As a matter of fact, I might play the lotto. That's an idea.

—Back to reality. Now that the bit with Katya is over, you can use Francette as a rebound.

—You know I don't believe in rebounds. I didn't do anything with anybody for a year and a half after Karyn, remember?

—Bull. You hooked up with Sarah eight months after that bitch Karyn broke up with you.

—I broke up with her.

—Bull: You dumped me for her, then she dumped you for her husband. Justice done.

—I repeat: She didn't dump me. I was the one who opted out of the triangle she was trying to set up with her husband.

—Right. Actually, who broke up with whom in a relationship is always academic.

—I guess.

—A rebound always fails. But then maybe one has to go with it, knowing it'll fail. As long as the other person knows this as well, everything's cool. Your thing with Katya failed, after all.

—Katya was not a rebound.

—That's what you say. Katya might even be a rebound from Sarah.

—After two whole years? Are you kidding? And you're forgetting that I was not involved with anyone during that time?

—No I'm not. I know you weren't with anyone during all that time. I made sure you weren't with anyone. I kept you company, my friend. I consoled you.

—For which I am very grateful, and for which I've thanked you dearly.

—And for which you're always welcome.

—You know, they say some marriages never terminate with divorce, especially when kids are involved.

—I think I know that. But does that mean that you're still in love with Sarah?

—Of course not, at least not consciously.

—What will you do after Paris? You'll be there for two weeks?

—Yeah. And then I'll have to come back here to think.

—You'll come back to New York to live? You have to stop this nomadic life sometime.

—Who is not nomadic these days, except for dinosaurs?

—I'm a dinosaur. Listen: At some point you've got to stop roaming around the world among mostly strangers.

—Ah. Elias Canetti once said that the most peaceful place on earth is among strangers. Listen: I feel completely at home at airports, that anthology of generic spaces.

—What do you mean, generic spaces?

—The contemporary airport is a collection of shopping malls, food courts, bars, and lounges. These are the generic spaces.

—You feel completely at home in an anthology of these generic spaces?

—Yeah. Can I tell you something funny?

—Sure.

—Al and I were drinking together quite late the other night.

—I suppose he was staying up late playing the market at Tokyo-Nikkei.

—You have that right. His assistant Jeremy, who usually handles that market so that Al can get some sleep, was in Bali on vacation.

—Bali. How nice.

—Anyway at some point Al asked me: Do you know what really gets me? I responded, what? He said: The weatherman says it's 75 Fahrenheit at the airport, and I thought, who gives a fuck? No one lives at the airport. Then yours truly told him: Well, I do!

—Funny. And clever. Did you make that up?

—No.

—Oh boy. This is bad. But trust you to come up with a literary reference for things personal. Was Canetti really talking about you? Your life is not that generic.

—Well . . . I have to be myself. Right now I consider myself one of the new nomads.

—Tell me about this new nomad. I'm all ears. I really want to know more about where your head is at these days.

—Dorit: You've seen this new nomad on countless occasions in our big cities, and mostly at our airports. You do travel, right?

—First the generics, then we'll get specific about you. Deal?

—Deal. The new nomad began to exist with the production of new technologies, when capital and technology began working for each other.

—I see. Like Janus with the two heads.

—Precisely. It doesn't matter where the new nomad's body is anymore. He's plugged into teletopia wherever he is. The new nomad's motto seems to "Be everywhere, and also here."

—What does the new nomad's body live on? He must live on something.

—He lives on speed. The speed of time-light.

—Time-light? Ah ah. You mean the time it takes to transmit data: the speed of light.

—Exactly. You're reading my mind.

—But didn't I just read somewhere that scientists have recently revealed that they had succeeded in breaking the speed of light?

—That's news to me. How did they do that?

—By sending a pulse through a chamber so fast that it exited before it entered.

—Dear God. Really? Can you try to remember where you read that?

—Probably *The New York Times*.

—When?

—Withing the last month or so.

—I'll do an archival search on their web-site.

—If I remember I'll e-mail you the reference. Now tell me more about this new nomad and super-light-speed.

—The new nomad lives on speed—or perhaps soon, super-light-speed—in the time that capital and technology have produced. This time is like a prison.

—Capital has locked time up?

—Right. By working together to erase the distinction between work-space and home-space, capital and technology have captured all of time and turned us all into their inmate-slaves, into their civil servants.

—Not all of us. Not all of us are plugged into their machines.

—Of course. You're right. But listen: The people who are plugged in are those whose profession involves producing, analyzing, and circulating money, words, codes, data, audio, video, and images—the dot.com crowd, editors, musicians, artists, video and movie producers, media content-providers, writers, designers, investment bankers, currency traders, and even salespeople, thanks to e-Bay and others.

—Very well put. In fact, geekspeak already has two terms for the human body.

—I know wetware is one of them. What's the other?

—Meatbot.

—That's good!

—Let's get back to this idea of our being civil servants of time. If you're working in these industries you just listed, you're this civil servant . . .   or this slave that's a piece of the machine, whether you're the employer or employee.

—Right. Right. They're both enslaved. You remember what Ben Franklin said about time and money.

—Time is money and money is time.

—Money is time saved as a valued commodity. One is rich because one has saved more time and has more saved time, that is, money, and one is poor because one has saved less time and has less saved time, that is, money again.

—So then according to this theory the poor or the homeless or the unskilled or the unemployed have no quote unquote valued time, no stored time, but only quote unquote naked or real or actual time.

—Right. And no employer is interested in or wants to buy this real and actual time, even at a discount. In other words, the homeless or the unemployed or the unskilled have only their own naked time to waste.

—You know, I read in *The New York Times* the other day that the richest fifth of humankind earns 86 percent of the world's income, while the poorest fifth earns 1 percent.

—That's really scary, Dorit.

—And unfair. Let's unpack this: If this new nomad is working on the computer he's living in the time of capital.

—Right.

—The time of capital is present to him on the screen of his monitor.

—Right.

—Again: this quote unquote present time is different from real time.

—Right again Dorit: When you see this nomad at cafés working on his laptop and also talking on his cell phone while drinking lattes, he's working in an environment that has no relationship whatever to real time as such.

—I guess we can use your friend Al in Park Slope to graphically illustrate your point.

—Yeah?

—He has a Quotron in his home study, so he can check trading in London, Paris, and Frankfurt at 3 AM New York Time. And at around 7 PM in New York, the market in Tokyo is open, since the time-zone there is about fourteen hours ahead of New York's.

—Right.

—From time to time, so to speak, he intervenes in these markets to trade and transfer currency in millions of US dollars. Time in Tokyo and London and Frankfurt is present to him on the screen of his monitor, where he lives, in his real time in Brooklyn.

—I couldn't have put it better myself. I ran into one of these new nomads the other day.

—Yeah? Where?

—At La Guardia. She was a definitely a thirtysomething like you. And she had only three midsized pieces of luggage, which included her laptop. I can recognize a laptop case when I see one.

—So did you talk to her? I know you: There's no way you would pass up the opportunity to talk to someone like that.

—Of course I talked to her. She had just jetted in from Istanbul by way of Boston. She'd been in Istanbul for ten days.

—On business no doubt.

—No doubt. She couldn't have gone to Turkey on vacation. Otherwise she wouldn't be a new nomad.

—What industry is she in?

—Are you ready for this one?

—Try me.

—She designs genetic drugs.

—That took her to Istanbul?

—I asked her the same question. Industry conference, she said. Something organized by the UN.

—So what else did you guys talk about?

—We chatted as we waited for cabs. She told me that she could afford to travel that light—even overseas—for long periods of time because she packed travelers clothing: you know, the kind that you wash in your hotel room and that dries in just five minutes. I don't believe in jetlag anymore, she told me at some point, somewhat jauntily, heartily, and triumphantly.

—Did she tell you about her traveler's underwear as well? You know, the kind that dries in two minutes?

—Give me a break, Dorit. Her face did remind me of Monica Lewinsky.

—Oh God . . .

—Speaking of which, what do you think of the whole Clinton-Lewinsky business?

—Oh God . . . the most expensive blow-job in history.

—Yeah, forty-five million dollars worth of taxpayers money.

—Maybe more, thanks to that closet queen Starr.

—The whole thing's unfortunate. Clinton deserves credit for the shape of the economy.

—Right: the US is the only country in the world in great economic shape.

—Somebody needed to cut off his dick.

—That's one person whose inalienable right was the happiness of pursuit.

—He's been so good for big business. You know he was the first Dem since Roosevelt in 36 to be elected to two terms.

—Yet, here's a guy who's despised thoroughly by Republicans, impeached by the House, and tried and acquitted by the Senate.

—Yeah. You know who actually was behind us in line at La Guardia?

—Who?

—Norman Mailer. I talked to him also. He said he was just coming back from Paris.

—He was alone?

—Yeah.

—That sexist pig!

—Oh come on, Dorit. You haven't forgiven him for the fight he had with the feminists a long time ago—specifically, with Kate Millett?

—Not even that. It's what he said about the novel that I'll never forgive him for.

—What did he say about the novel? He's said a lot of things about a lot of things over the years. I can't keep track.

—He said the novel is a great bitch, and we've all had a bit of her.

—That's bad. But he's written some good books.

—I like *The Executioner's Song.*

—On Gary Gilmore. But he borrowed Truman Capote's style from *In True Blood.*

—But I don't want to talk about Norman Mailer. Let's talk about you. How do you fit into this paradigm of the new nomad in the time of capital that you set up? You jet around the world all right. But you're also broke most of the time. You have little saved time, but it seems you also do not have any naked time.

—Right: Saved or naked time: I have neither. I lose out on both. How is that possible?

—You're Uberman.

—You flatter me. I'm just complicated.

—You mean you're fucked up.

—Put that way . . .

—What are you going to do?

—I'm not sure what I'm going to do. I could go back full-time with MSNBC.

—Yeah, you could do that instead of fantasizing about the lotto. Then you'll make money and pay me back the three-thousand dollars you owe me.

—You know I'll pay you back.

—Yeah, right. I won't hold my breath. Don't worry about it. I was just kidding. I told you already: Consider it as a gift.

—Thanks. But I'll pay you back. I promise you.

—Do you want your apartment back? Just give me the three-months notice, as we arranged.

—Hell no. I've given up the notion of living full-time here. I've done it all here: born here, grade school, high school, college, grad school, yuppie-life before marriage. What else can I do here?

—How about married life?

—I've done that with Sarah for four years. Are you forgetting that?

—I meant married life in New York, not in Minneapolis.

—Ha ha ... I stand corrected. But I was here with Sarah, married for one year.

—Indeed. Do you remember our first date as a romantic couple?

—You mean at the Time Café?

—No. That was *before* we became a romantic couple, remember? We slept together for the first time at your place *after* we ate at the Time Café. We also saw *Hiroshima Mon Amour* that night for post-prandials.

—I remember that well.

—OK, I'm waiting. Tell me about our first outing as a romantic couple in 1990.

—We went out to dinner at Acquario, at Bleecker and the Bowery.

—Right. What did we have?

—I had cornish game hen.

—Your favorite. What else?

—Couscous.

—Of course. What did I have?

—Portuguese fish stew. For an appetizer you had Acquario's fresh grilled sardines. For appetizer I had something called *harira* : lentil soup made with lamb stock and filled with lamb, onions, and chick peas. And we both downed two bottles of fine Côtes du Rhone between us, as usual.

—Very good! I'm impressed. Can you describe the atmosphere at Acquario that night?

—Sure. Brickwalls and lit candles. Small space. Cozy and warm.

—Very good.

—Why are you asking me all this? I know you like good food. But why?

—Just testing you. You know I love to do that.

—Are you seeing anyone, Dorit?

—No. I haven't had a main squeeze—as you would put it—since Rick.

—Yes, Rick what's-his-face, who's gone on to fame.

—I didn't want to go there with him. Been there, done him.

—I've never understood why you dropped him. And I don't understand why you're not with anyone right now. You've never lacked suitors.

—Suitors do not necessarily husbands make.

—Are you looking for a husband?

—I'm thirty. If you put one of your ears to my chest, you'll hear my biological clock ticking. I want kids.

—You're still young. You have plenty of time. You'll find someone.

—In New York? Fuhgeddaboudtit!

—How's your mother?

—She's OK. As batty and as fun as ever.

—You guys are really close, as I recall.

—We have only each other.

—Is she still at Mount Sinai?

—Is she still ever? She was promoted to chief surg eon of her department three months ago. So we don't see each other as often.

—That's a great job! The chief surgeon of the surgery department in one of the most prestigious medical centers in the world.

—Yeah, I'm so proud of her.

—So you should. Say hello to her for me.

—I sure will. You know she was very fond of you.

—I remember.

—She was hoping that we would get married. She told me then that she was glad we combined our DNAs.

—Is that right?

—She always asks me how you are. What you're up to.

—You do tell her, don't you?

—Of course. I tell her as much as you tell me.

—How's your brother?

—He's still in Holland. But he moved from The Hague to Amsterdam.

—Is that right?

—Amsterdam is more hip than the Hague. Who would want to live in The Hague? I once visited him there. I almost died that time.

—Is that right?

—That's right.

—So what does he do then—commute to The Hague from Amsterdam?

—Two three times a week. He's doing most of his international legal research online these days. From home. Like you.

—Like me indeed . . .

—For the past month or so he's been exchanging erotic electronic messages with a woman in New York who claims to be twenty-five.

—Or with a man who claims to be a woman.

—Right. I told him to tell this woman that I wanted to meet her here in New York, but he refused.

—So you and your mother really have just each other for sure. Is your dad still out of the picture?

—He's been out of the picture voluntarily since I was five.

—You told me years ago that he's remarried with kids.

—Living in Chappaqua with his new family.

—Are you ever in contact with him?

—Once or twice a year. Rosh Hoshana. Yum Kippur. He's Orthodox, remember?

—Yeah, I remember.

—Well . . . how is *your* mother?

—She's fine. She's still teaching Arabic to her students in Harlem.

—She's quite amazing, as I recall.

—Yeah. She really liked you.

—I know. She and I really hit it off. I remember thinking, how ironic, a Jew and an Arab hitting it off. Only in New York.

—You know, she's not quite an Arab.

—I know, you told me, she's Fulani, Arab-like, but not Arab.

—Yeah, big difference.

—Not that big, as I recall again. After I met her I did some research on the Fulanis. They're a Semitic people who somehow crossed the Sahara into West Africa.

—You have that right.

—Is she still stunning?

—She's aging gracefully.

—Does she still look like your girlfriend?

—Come again?

—Remember? You told me people mistook her for your girlfriend when you guys went out together when you were a teenager.

—Yeah, she still looks younger for her age, if that's what you meant.

—Are you guys still close?

—Yeah.

—You know, I'll give you Julia's e-address. She would love to hear from you.

She meant her mother. Dorit again:

—That way I don't have to relay everything to her. She really does ask about

you all the time.

—Is that right?

—I'm not kidding.

—Hmm.

—Frankly I wonder whether she has the hots for you.

—Oh come on!

—What do you mean, come on. There's no generational gap between you guys. She's only ten years older than you.

—I've forgotten about that. How old is she again?

—Do the simple math: I'm thirty. You're thirty-eight. My mother was eighteen when she had me.

—Which makes her forty-eight. Only forty-eight and she's a chief surgeon?

—She's smart. And very attractive.

—I remember that.

—Is she with someone?

—Are you kidding? She's too busy for one thing. And fiercely independent for another.

—So she has no time for guys.

—She might have time for you.

—Is that right?

—E-mail her and ask her out. Actually you should add her name to your e-address group. If she gets one of your group postings, she'll get a kick out of the fact that your e-address group reads like the Jerusalem White Pages.

—Really?

—Really.

—OK.

—OK what?

—I'll ask her out.

—Wouldn't that be a hoot? You going out with my mom?

—Are you really trying to set me up with her? Or are you testing me again?

—Holy Toledo! I'm only kidding. You know that, don't you? Or are you serious?

—I can't tell with you.

—Are you interested in her?

—I might be. I see a lot of you in her.

—You and I were an item for God's sake.

—So we were.

—I'll kill you if you ever get together with her romantically.

—Do you think she would even consider doing that with me?

—Who knows with her? She always tells me she wished she had an African-American or African boyfriend.

—Really?

—Really.

—Doesn't she have the opportunity to meet blacks at Mount-Sinai?

—Not there. But she volunteers at Harlem Hospital, where she has the opportunity.

—I thought that was closed.

—You're right. It's just a clinic now.

—Of course I would never be involved romantically with your mother. What do you take me for, a pervert?

—I don't know . . . you spent a whole year in Montana with all the other kooks: the Unabomber; the Freemen; the guy who shot the Capitol cops in DC after shooting several cats days before in Montana. This wacko shoots up a bunch of cats at his parents' house in Montana and then travels to DC the next day to shoot a couple of cops at the US Capitol. I can't recall his name off the bat.

—I can't either. Jacob Westling? Westin? Something like that.

—You were in Montana when it happened.

—Yeah but he lived east of the Divide. Missoula is west. No rednecks there.

—That's what you think. Anyway, like I said, you might have picked up some peculiar habits while you were there. After all, you got together with Katya.

—Oh come on.

—Oh come on yourself! You told me she was a sex fiend. And I told you that she might even be a sexual addict. You also told me that you fucked her countless times during the nine months you guys were an item.

—She *is* a sex fiend, but maybe not an addict. And yes, I fucked her countless times, except for the last two weeks.

—Here I am. Poor little me. All I have is my mother.

—Frankly I'm puzzled why you're not with anyone.

—For one: Do you know how difficult for someone like me to find a guy who'll accept me for what I am? An attractive woman with brains? I scare men off.

—I suppose. I can understand that. Men feel threatened by intellectual women, we know that too well. I'm not threatened by you though.

—I know. We were romantically linked for a year, remember?

—I'm attracted to intellectual women in fact. I'm not the kind of guy referred to in the retro lyrics of "100 Ways to Lose a Man."

—What are those lyrics?

—Quote—a splendid way to lose a man. Just throw your knowledge in his face. He'll never try for third base—Unquote.

—You've got the base wrong. It's second base. You don't even play baseball.

—So you know the lyrics. You were just testing me.

—And for another reason I'm not with someone: my friend Eliane in Paris, the filmmaker. Emilie's friend also.

—Yeah. She makes features and documentaries. She lives in the Sixteenth Arrondissement, so she must be loaded.

—She e-mailed me the other day. She said in contemporary world culture, but especially in the Western Hemisphere, in those areas that have high-tech saturated societies, romantic relationships between straight, lesbian, or gay couples are mostly impossible.

—And why is that?

—People don't know what they want anymore. It's especially rough among straights. I hate to echo Freud here: Women especially don't know what they really want. Women know what they *don't* want, but they don't know what they want.

—Do you suppose technology, and the way we're plugged into it, is reconfiguring human desire?

—I'm positive. It's very complicated. It goes something like this: Technology develops by continuing to . . . splice the human body into . . . cybernetic and teletopic circuits, by continuing to incorporate human . . . sensorium into . . . disembodied systems.

—Human sensorium. I like that. Can you explain it?

—Technology is an extension of our nervous system. Telephone is an extension of the ear, which feeds remote—meaning *tele* , as in teleport—sound—meaning *phonè* , as in phonetic—into our brains. And the television camera is an extension of the eye.

—Of course, of course. Please tell me more.

—Television, your own industry, projects distant images into our own vision. The worldwide web, what Marshall McLuhan had the prescience to call global village, is nothing but one gigantic nervous system.

—I like that. I like it!

—Thanks. So you see, all of this ongoing machine-human loop is bound to affect the way we feel and desire. I think desire is also becoming disembodied. And that's why it's difficult for partners to be attached for long durations, like our parents. Love seems impossible in this time of silicon.

—Very good. That sounds like Paul Virilio.

—I got that from him in fact.

—A friend of mine in Missoula, Rob, who owns an Internet company that develops applications for moving data from databases to web sites, once told me that he's nothing more than an interface.

Dorit, laughing:

—Very clever. A web site itself is nothing more than an interface. Rob must be a web developer who uses one of those languages, like Visual Basic, to move data from its storage in a database, like Access, onto a web site. He probably then uses dynamic HTML to build the web site so that the data there can be updated every ten minutes, like at NY Times dot-com.

—Thanks for that primer on web development. But you know I know that stuff quite well. You don't need to show off.

—I'm not showing off.

—Getting back to Freud: How about you? Do you know what you really want?

—I would like to meet a literary divorced guy with kids. But he lives in Utopia, in a very different zip code from 10019, where I live, where you have lived, and where you probably will live in the future.

—Are you talking about me?

—I don't feel like going there, or talking about you-living-in-Utopia.

And we didn't. At least not last night. We talked and drank until around 3 AM, then I took the subway back.

Francette is bound to show up any minute now. If her flight landed at 2:30 PM as scheduled, the cab ride from La Guardia should take about an hour or so. Pre-rush hour traffic should be light over the Brooklyn-Queens Expressway, so by my strict calculations, she should have been here ten minutes ago.

At this point I feel intensely at the vortex of my life. I need to reflect on my life that drifted throughout these 90s. How I got to this point, and in which directions I need to conduct my life in the few years. I tell myself I'm a writer. I'm under contract to write about culture and politics with MSNBC-NBC. And I just finished revising the manuscript of my first novel. According to my original contract, the novel was supposed to have been released last month—shipped from the printer to the warehouse, with advanced copies mailed out to reviewers the month before. The books are supposed to be in bookstores by now. I'm supposed to be signing author's copies after a reading at The 92nd Street Y. Instead, I've just mailed two hard copies of the manuscript, with corresponding floppies, to my publisher. I had to deal with floppies in this case because my small literary publisher never downloads files.

What can I show for my life up to this point? The finished manuscript of a novel. Fifty articles of various lengths on politics and culture in assorted journals of opinion, print and online, as examples: *The New Republic*, *The Nation*, *Slate*, and *Salon*. And I have published about thirty "action reports" and news analyses at the web-sites of the Independent Media Center and the Direct Action Media Network, highly political web-based multimedia news services that came into existence in recent years. I have an ex-wife and a kid, a three-year-old daughter who lives with her mother, Sarah, in Minneapolis. We had a house in Minneapolis that Sarah and I got rid of in a fire sale after we split up. I was strapped for cash then. And In fact I'm strapped for cash now. I've always been strapped for cash. To quote Dorit: My wallet is always thin. I've got to do something about that at some point. I have an apartment here in the city I'm subletting to Dorit. I've been involved in only one serious relationship since my divorce three years ago: Katya.

What have I done with my life? And how can I account for it? One thing is clear: I'm not afraid of anything anymore, and I'm not afraid to die. In the mid-90s I lost too much: wife, job, and house. I experienced all the major stressors. I've "been around the block," as they say, and I've managed to "come through the other side," as they also say. Much more about all this later.

To repeat: I currently work for MSNBC-NBC, broadcast network news, which, as my friend Jon Katz—who used to work for CBS—told me recently "is basically a corpse that hasn't been announced yet." The moribund—in my opinion also—broadcast network news media (specifically ABC, CBS, and NBC, and also the cable "news" networks CNN and Fox) are currently and ferociously driven by market-economy and by the relentless pressure of daily ratings. The network news divisions are increasingly expected not only to be profitable (which was definitely not the case in the days of Eric Severeid and Edwin Murrow), but also to compete successfully with entertainment divisions. And correspondents and reporters are encouraged to make themselves the news rather than investigate and report them.

As an example: *Brill's Content* (the monthly that monitors the media for "accuracy, labeling and sourcing, conflicts of interest, and accountability) recently did a feature on Alex Kuczynski, the media reporter for *The New York Times*, (titled "Smart Alex") saying that she is the new breed of journalist who is her own brand, who gets into the gossip columns, and who prefers personality-driven pieces over hard-core business stories (the article highlighted her as "the reigning 'It' girl of media coverage, with her high-profile social life and hip writing, the face of a changing *Times* . . . "). And the current head of ABC News was recently reported to have told his correspondents and panelists to ratchet up their social lives—"to entertain more, to get into the social columns, and to create buzz." Consequently, the broadcast networks have contributed significantly and implicitly to lowering the level of public discourse in the US about itself and about the world in general. ABC, for instance, has closed so many of its overseas bureaus that its correspondents must cover events in vast areas stretching from Moscow to Johannesburg by relying on satellite uplinks instead of first-person reports.

(By cutting their overseas staff, the broadcast networks created a lucrative void that Reuters and Associated Press—which in recent years decided to supplement their print and photo businesses with full-fledged video operations—rushed to fill: Ironically, the broadcasters then started paying in excess of $1 million a year for footage from Reuters or Associated Press Television News (APTN), and *The New York Times* online started relying more and more on Associated Press's overseas news dispatches to the point of creating a sublink for AP on its web-site.)

Especially after the end of the cold war, interest in foreign coverage among the networks simply evaporated. As another friend who works at ABC pointed out to me: In the ABC newsroom the running joke about "World News Tonight" is that "it's not the world, and it's not news. It's just tonight." And most daily print media usually report the obvious these days. Consider the inept headlines that follow from various newspapers (some of them major) around the US:

*Low wages said to be key to poverty
*Affluent top list of political donors
*Dean wants students to take required courses
*Research finds lawyers are overpaid
*Dysfunctional families said to affect children
*Revival of death penalty paves way for more executions
*Plot to kill officer had vicious side (Chicago Tribune)
*Commission cuts will hurt stockbrokers, analysts say
*Religions have varied views on redemption
*Teenage girls often have babies fathered by men

Officials say only rain will cure drought
House cleaners find careers in homes of others
Life bleak for men in chains
Malls try to attract shoppers
Survey finds dirtier subways after cleaning jobs were cut (New York Times)
Larger kangaroos leap farther (Los Angeles Times)
Police finds more tolerance lowers crime
Study finds sex, pregnancy link
Obese should make diet top goal, study says
Homicide: Makes you feel violated
Harmfulness of violence can no longer be denied
* Infertility unlikely to be passed on (Montgomery Advertiser)*

And so on.

Now for the death-knell for network broadcast media: A whole generation of young journalists with considerable talent are moving into web-based new media, especially the noncorporate "indy" multimedia networks split-up into radio, video, and print "teams."

I've got to seriously think about what I want to do for work in the future. The new-media sector clearly appeals to me, since it combines my love of writing, editing, and engaging ideas with my technical knowledge of the Internet. Another friend of mine who helped to organize the Independent Media Center has been telling me about these new networks, hoping that I'd join one of the "teams" as a "staff writer." These are things I have to reflect on for the new millennium.

But for now, before Francette shows up, I want to get back to Missoula, to the conversation I had with Jacques about Bryn the Sunday after I met her, after she dropped me off early afternoon.

Missoula: Sunday, August 23, 1998

Jacques and Christine had had another one of their big fights that Sunday before I got back to his house. Christine had accused him of lusting after Janice. Christine was just leaving when Bryn and I pulled up late afternoon. After Bryn left, he told me their split-up was imminent, the same dull-drone I had listened to for the previous three years. Jacques was a tiresome—and tireless—plaintiff: Over the years I'd gotten used to his rants and raves about a number of his perennial "problems": Christine; his departmental colleagues (all of whom, with one or two exceptions, he thought were morons); academia; bourgeois women; Republicans; Montanans; and American culture in general. In this latter category, I was often compelled to defend the culture, even to stake out positions I wasn't invested in myself. I'd tell him time and again that because he has lived only in New York; the midwest; and the northwest during his entire tenure in the US, his assumed understanding of American culture was limited at best. He made the most outrageous statements that his friends and colleagues led slide. Sometimes I simply tuned him out. And sometimes I challenged him. Some remarked that we were like an old married couple. And ever since my divorce he'd taken a special interest in my subsequent relationships, sometimes playing matchmaker.

Bryn's case was no exception.

Jacques to me:

—Bryn is quite a beautiful young woman. Unusual name.

—It's a unisexual name. I once knew a male Bryn ... in New York.

—What's her last name?

—Asselstine.

—Unusual too. What name is that?

—I don't know. It might be Jewish.

—You once told me you're an expert on Jewish names.

—So I did.

—So did you fuck her?

—No. But we slept in the same bed.

—What's wrong with you? How many times do I have to tell you to get down with these women!

—Many times, Jacques.

—That woman is ready to be fucked—and molded. She's in need of some guidance, some father figure. Good God! I'd do it myself if not for Chris.

—How do you know that Bryn's in need of a father figure? Or that she's ready to be fucked? Did she tell you all this?

—Of course not. But I know the type. Trust me.

—Is that right? Two weeks ago you wanted me to fuck Katya. Now you want me to fuck Bryn. Whom do you want me to fuck next? Make up your mind.

—I've changed my mind. I select Bryn, for sure.

—Do I have anything to say about it?

—It's your life. I'm only trying to help, as a friend.

—I appreciate it. Look, my friend, stop trying to control other people's lives. Why don't you focus your energies on straightening out your own mess with Christine first?

—You know it's more complicated than that. Breaking up with someone you've had a relationship with for five years is a process, sometimes a long one.

—I guess. Have you talked to Katya?

—No. Why?

—I think she's definitely pissed. I'll call her. I feel a little bad about how things came down at the party. I should have paid more attention to her. She's new in town after all. She doesn't know anyone. And you're no ideal host either, leching after every skirt on sight.

—Katya is a big girl. Why should I be her babysitter? I took her to the party didn't I? I'll introduce her to people. It's up to her to develop things. I'm not going to do that for her.

—You don't understand.

—What don't I understand?

—Let's drop it.

—I agree. Let's talk about Bryn.

—What about her?

—I'm planning a dinner party here for next Saturday. Why don't you invite her?

—Sure. What's the occasion?

—What do you mean? Since when do I have to have a reason for having a party? I'll invite Katya and Janice as well. The whole gang.

—Is Kathyrn joining the community?

—Yes, yes, for sure. She's an interesting woman. A writer.

—Another Missoula writer?

—She hasn't published anything yet. She's trying to sell her manuscript.

—Is that right? What kind of manuscript?

—It's a novel.

—About what?

—Some kind of mystery.

—I see.

—In fact, I told her she should talk to you.

—About what?

—How to go about getting published.

—Listen dude, I wish you would stop doing that.

—You have connections.

—Is that right? Well, they're not for everyone. How do you know her stuff is any good? Not every writer deserves to be published.

—With all the crap that your New York publishing friends have already published? Her stuff, from the two pages I've seen of it, needs to be out there. She's broke and has an aversion to normal work.

—OK, OK. She can talk to me. But I need to read more than two pages of her stuff first before I tell her anything. And I certainly do not have the time for that.

—Can you do it as a favor to me?

—Are you planning to fuck her, Jacques?

—What do you think?

—I think you're planning to fuck her, if you haven't done that already.

—When would I have had the time to do that?

—Did you go home with her or with Christine?

—Chris spent the night here.

—Did you spend it here with her?

—I took Janice home, then I came back here.

—Where does she live?

—In an old school bus at the edge of town. She lives on the fringe, literally and metaphorically. And I'm attracted to women who live on the fringe.

—Is that right? Where's the school bus?

—It's parked in the backyard of a friend's house, in the no-man's land between Missoula and Fort Missoula. She uses the bathroom of her friend's house and then sleeps in her school bus.

—So you're planning to fuck her in her school bus?

—Why not? Better there than here. You know how Chris sometimes drops in unannounced.

—Speaking of Christine. How about her?

—What about her?

—Will she be at the party?

—I don't give a fuck what she does. If she wants to come, fine. If not, fine.

—You're setting yourself up for some real trouble, my friend, totally, as Bryn would say.

—That's OK. You know I like to do that. The more ingredients, the better. More grist for the mill.

—I really feel bad about Katya.

—Well, call her then.

I called her. She wasn't home. I left a message on her voicemail. Two hours later she called me back. Jacques picked up the phone. Usually she would chat with him for a while. This time she simply said hello to him and asked for me. I had a hunch that he felt somewhat slighted as he handed me the phone. She suggested we meet for lunch Monday. I said sure. That whole exchange—and the context with Jacques—more or less set the stage for the unpleasant drama that would unfold during the nine months from September 1998 to June 1999. And of course I really never had the chance to read Janice's magnificent manuscript, especially after

I got involved with Katya. On one of our weekend hikes on various mountains within a twenty-mile radius of Missoula, Janice told me at length about that manuscript when we fell behind the group (normally I'd be ahead but I had a hangover that morning). The manuscript as she described it to me did sound as interesting as Jacques had opined.

*   *   *

10

Paris: Saturday, July 3, 1999

Francette and I just got back from registering at the conference, which formally starts on Monday the 5th instead of tomorrow the 4th, in deference to American participants. The conference is at the University of Paris-7 at Jussieu, in the 5th Arrondissement.

It's great to be in Paris again. My last time here was two years ago, visiting Emilie Deleuze, Gilles's distraught filmmaker daughter, whom I had met in 1985 when I spent a whole academic year studying with her father at the University of Paris-8 at Vincennes, at the southeastern edge of the city. That was basically his last year of active teaching before he "retired." Emilie and I had developed a cordial, warm, close, and near-filial relationship over the years, and I had gone to Paris mainly to visit her almost a year after her father committed suicide on November 5, 1995, by jumping out the window of his apartment on avenue Niel in the 17th Arrondissement. I was in grief as well, as he was the only person I could ever claim honestly more or less as an "intellectual father." So I was also—obviously to a much lesser degree than Emilie—in need of consolation. And so therefore my last visit here had been invested emotionally, and was somewhat traumatic. But since Francette and I have been here, I've not experienced any traces of that cathartic trauma that attended almost every moment of my two weeks in October 1996.

We flew into De Gaulle Airport Thursday morning, around 9 AM. Francette's gay roommate, Michel, picked us up. Quite generous of him. She said some weeks he makes his own hours at the clinic. He's a family physician working at a state-operated clinic in the 6th Arrondissement, something of a paradox, since the 6th is a rather ritzy quarter of the city. Michel drove to 7 rue Fénelon. Francette had packed a lot of luggage (I always travel light), so we had to lug several heavy pieces up four flights of stairs to her apartment on the fourth floor, as there was no elevator. Half the number of apartment buildings in Paris have elevators, especially if they were built after mid-century, but not this one.

Her apartment, as it turned out, is huge. Exactly how she had laid it out for me: You walk into the living room right away, big enough for a grand piano, three sofas, and several bookcases. The formal dining area—with a table big enough for eight diners—was off toward the balcony, which itself was accessible through French windows.

(The balcony has stunning views, to the right, of the shops and supermarkets at the intersection of rue Lafayette and boulevard Magenta, and to the left, of the statues that adorned the upper half of the Eglise St Vincent de Paul.)

Francette's room is to the left of the living room, with a bathroom adjacent to it. A door separates both rooms from the living room, so in a sense Francette has her own self-contained quarters. A hallway leads to all the other rooms: the kitchen to the left; another bathroom to the right; then Michel's room to the right, and the guest room to the left; the room-cum-study stood at the end of the hallway.

I stayed up all day Thursday till midnight, trying to beat jetlag. After the so-called continental breakfast—which Michel fixed—Francette and I made the rounds of a few cafés: Rostand; l'Industrie; Cluny. Then we went out to dinner at the café on the top floor of Virgin Megastore on Les Champs Elysées. Shortly after midnight I dropped off to sleep in my room, completely relaxed, after Francette gave me a massage. Michel went to work after breakfast Thursday morning and didn't show up until Friday night—last night. Francette said he had a rich lover he sometimes stayed with. I suppose he wanted to give us some space.

Friday I essentially stayed here while Francette went to visit some friends. I watched some television, played some CDs, and tried to read some newspapers and magazines piled up on the coffee table. But I stayed away from my laptop.

This morning, after breakfast, around 10 AM, Francette and I walked down four flights of stairs to rue Fénelon, turned right, went down the steps of St Vincent de Paul, through Place Franz Liszt to rue Lafayette, turned right again and walked to Métro Poissonnière, and took the same train all the way to the campus of the University of Paris-7 on rue Jussieu, and back here—going through Chatelêt, the big hub—without having to change trains. Quite convenient.

Francette is out on some errands. She wanted me to come along, but I wanted to stay here and begin writing again. I need to continue the probing of my relationship to Missoula, and of the intersection of my life with Katya, especially the last nine months I lived there.

In New York before we flew here, I more or less gave Francette a sketch of those nine months. During our peregrinations around Paris Thursday, Francette introduced the topic of Katya. As usual, she spoke to me mostly in French.

—I somehow have this feeling that if you hadn't broken up with
  Katya you wouldn't have come to Paris with me.
—I'm not sure that the two were mutually exclusive. I really wanted
  to come. But I surprised myself by the fact I was nonetheless
  shaken up by the split-up.
—You must have gotten over that. Because from Tuesday since I've
  been with you I haven't felt any negative Reiki energy coming
  from you. In fact when I walked into your friends' house I felt
  a good aura.
—That might have more to do with my friends than with me.
—Oh give yourself some credit. Don't be so hard on yourself.
—I'd forgotten that you're into all that New-Age stuff.
—It works for me. You know I also give massages. That's what you
  need. I'll give you a good massage.

—Oh oh.

—Why do you say oh oh?

—A massage is risky, if you know what I mean.

—No I don't know what you mean.

—I mean it might be sexual.

—Don't worry. It'll be nonsexual. I'm very professional about it.

—Good.

—Relax. I don't have any expectations from you on this trip. Whatever you want. I'll leave you alone.

—Good.

—But I want to ask you something.

—Shoot.

—In your novel your alter ego, the narrator . . . I'm sure he's your alter ego . . . mentioned the type of woman he's attracted to.

—Yes?

—He said that his type of woman must speak French and wear black most or all the time; and must be: thin; into art; Jewish; from New York; and into Deleuze.

—You have adumbrated correctly.

—Adumbrated?

—Listed the attributes correctly.

—Well, I don't mean to be presumptuous, but I have most of those attributes. I'm French; I'm thin; I wear black most of the time; I'm definitely into contemporary American art; I'm into Deleuze and others. I'm not Jewish. But I'm not typical French Catholic either. I'm a Protestant, in the minority. I'm not from New York but from Paris.

I raised my eyebrows at this point. And also at this point we were sitting and sipping kirs at Café de Cluny at the corner of boulevard St-Germain and St-Michel, a tourist hotspot in Paris, and as the season was just heating up (this is July!), the café was packed and humming with tourists, who were humored and waited on by waiters (all male) dressed up in silly medieval garb. In spite of this touristic atmosphere, I took Francette there to attempt to savor the many moments Emilie and I had spent there years before. The Cluny was Emilie's favorite place. She was friends with two of the waiters, whom she introduced me to, and who have treated me with the same affection that they accorded her. I went back there alone without her a few times during my sojourn. Back to my conversation with Francette.

—Francette: What are you driving at?

—I guess what I'm trying to say is that I qualify as your love interest.

—Whoa! Wait a minute here. Are you serious?

—I'm half-joking. You're take things too seriously. Relax a little.

—Don't confuse literature with life.

—Oh come on. You know better than that.

—I'm sure *you* would confound literature and life, since you're now trying to write in the currently fashionable memoir genre.

—Trying to write? I am writing.

—Sorry. Unfortunate choice of words.

—Are you going to give me feedback on the chapters I e-mailed you?

—Of course.

—I'm counting on you. I respect your judgment and your talent.

—Don't worry: I'll give you feedback when we get back to the States. Maybe even here.

—Don't count on that. You'll be quite busy. You'll see the full schedule tomorrow.

—So will I get to meet the famous Jesse Jackson?

—He's coming for sure. My father confirmed it. He better come. They were going to give Madame Mitterand the award ... then Jackson got the GIs released and they changed their mind the last minute.

—I've never had the honor of meeting the man.

—I'm surprised you've never met him, given the rarefied circles you move in.

—Well, I *have* met a lot of famous people.

—Didn't you me you met Ehud Barak in Jerusalem last spring?

—Yeah. So I told you. My friend Debbie Sontag introduced us. He was not the prime minister then but a candidate. I doubt that I'd have the opportunity now to meet him again. Mossad will see to that.

—Who is Debbie Sontag?

—She's the Jerusalem Bureau Chief for the *New York Times.*

—My my. I'm impressed. How did you meet her?

—We media types manage to find one another. And Israel is a very small country. Not many people know that. Eight hours drive from northern tip to the south. Two from west to east. That's it. Israelis don't have enough space. Now in a country that small, the press corps is small enough so that everyone knows everyone.

—I didn't know that Israel is that small.

—That's why this peace with Palestinians business has been so difficult. Don't get me wrong. I think Palestinians deserve their own space and state.

—You have to tell me all about your experiences in Jerusalem at some point.

—I will.

—It's getting to be 8:30. I'm starving. Are you?

—Yes, yes.

—Let's go then.

—Where do you think?

—Let's go to the bistro on top of the Virgin Megastore. I like it up there. I'll treat you of course. You're broke, right?

—Yeah.

—You can pay me back by telling me more about Katya.

—I'll be glad to tell you my side of the story. Delicious French cuisine beats a ramen-noodle meal anytime.

—You eat ramen?

—Yeah. When I'm broke.

—But you're always broke. You eat it all the time?

—OK, then. When I'm extremely broke. You can't beat a meal for twenty-five cents a packet.

—That shit is really bad for you. It's full of monosodium glutamate.

—Oh well. I like MSG, which, BTW, is what most people call it.

—What is BTW?

—By the way in Netspeak.

—I see. Anyway, I'll feed you well tonight. Then I'll give you a massage when we get back home.

—Are you sure that's a good idea?

—I told you I'm a professional. Trust me.

She gave me a massage after we got back. I had never had a massage before. For the first time in my life, I completely surrendered my body to a woman, although in a nonsexual way. She kept her hands away from my crotch, and even though I felt relaxed most of the time, I never had an erection, which to my mind logically meant only two things: Either I'm not physically attracted to Francette. Or I'm not quite recovered from Katya as I thought I was or as I'd like to be.

*   *   *

11

Paris: Sunday, July 4, 1999

Francette is out visiting some friends again. After she gets back, we're both headed for a party later, a 4th of July party at the American Embassy at 4 PM, to which most of the conference participants were invited. Francette's father, a former member of the French National Assembly, is a good friend of the current US Ambassador, a Clinton appointee and a Francophone, who in his previous life was a financial analyst at Lazard Frères in New York. Right now I wish to get back to Missoula and Katya.

Missoula: Monday, August 24, 1998

I met Katya that Monday for lunch in Missoula at Food for Thought, a restaurant frequented mostly by students and faculty, given its location on the corner of Daly Street and Arthur Avenue at the edge of the campus of the University of Montana. For the first time since I met her she was wearing all black: a T-shirt, tight jeans, boots, and a beret. We ordered some food, somewhat average: What one might expect from a student-faculty food joint. We sat by a window.

Katya:

—Is that all you're having?

—Yeah.

—Aren't you hungry?

—Of course I am.

—You need to eat. Order anything you want. My treat.

—Really?

—Really. I know you don't have much money.

—How did you know that?

—Jacques told me.

—He is such a motor mouth.

—That's an expression I never heard before. It's good though.

—Thanks.

    I ordered more food. I:

—You're wearing all-black! What's the occasion?

—Do I need an occasion to wear black? I have a collection of black clothes. I just don't like to wear them all the time, like some people I know.

—I grew up in New York, and black is the only color for that city.

—I see.

—I've been wearing black since high school.

—I see.

—You're dressed up just like Bryn. Is it a coincidence?

—What do you mean? You and Bryn don't have a monopoly on black clothes.

—Of course not.

—Well, it's pure coincidence. I just was in the mood for black today.

—If you say so.

—You don't believe me?

—I believe you.

—How's Jacques?

—He's all right. He and Christine are fighting again.

—Tell me what's new. Why doesn't he just dump her?

—Jacques finds it very very difficult to let people and things go. As far as breaking up with Christine, he keeps telling me: It's all a process, and it takes time. Well, the process has been going on for five years.

—I see.

—He's a little miffed at you for being abrupt with him on the phone yesterday.

—Miffed?

—Angry.

—He is, is he? I didn't feel like talking to him. I called *you*. In fact,
   I was calling you back.

—Indeed.

—Speaking of Jacques, isn't his film conference on Tuesday a week
   from tomorrow?

—Yes indeed.

—Are you ready?

—For my presentation you mean?

—Yeah.

—I'm still putting my paper together.

—I see. On *Blade Runner*?

—Right.

—That's one hell of a dystopic film.

—I disagree. When that film came out it was *way* ahead of its
   time.

—When did it come out?

—1982.

—I was still in Moscow at the time ... What do you like about
   the film?

—Everything.

—Can you be more specific?

—Of course. The film demonstrates what Deleuze said about
   cinema.

—What did he say? I haven't read him.

—Deleuze said that cinema, as a technology of time-and image-
   movement, now demands an epistemology of the image.

—I see.

—*Blade Runner* articulates precisely such an epistemology by
   showing how, through the conquest of time, technology and
   capital produced Los Angeles as a digital city subvented by
   visual regimes.

—Oh man! You're so theoretical! I'm not into theory the way you
   are ...   I just know literary theory.

—I'm not into what you're calling theory either. You wanted me
   to be specific. I'm a journalist, remember?

—But you sounded just like Jacques just now, the way he parrots Deleuze.

—That's hardly surprising, considering that we both studied with Deleuze in Paris.

—I see.

—I'm currently tracking capital and technology, the way they've been working for each other. And I love *Blade Runner*. So when Jacques asked me to give a presentation, the paper clicked together in my head.

—But you haven't written it yet.

—In a manner of speaking, I have.

—But I thought you said . . .

—The material is in my hard drive. I just have to cut and paste it into the paper, so to speak.

—That's clever.

—Thanks.

—I have an idea. I've seen the film only once. I'd love to see it again. Why don't we rent it tonight and watch it at my place? Do you have any plans for tonight?

—No. The only thing I'm looking forward to is listening to Jacques rant on and on about Christine and his colleagues.

—Oh really. Does he talk about us?

—Most certainly.

—What does he say about us?

—Everything. About you: He's not sure about your politics.

—You mean he doesn't think I'm a marxist.

—Precisely.

—Well I'm not.

—What are you?

—I'm not Jacques's idea of a marxist . . . of the ineffectual French kind.

—Is that right?

—He should live in Russia for a while. Then he can tell me what he thinks of marxism.

—I'm confused. You're not a French marxist. But are you a Russian marxist?

—No.

—What are you? You're not a marxist. Are you a leftist?

—It depends on what kind of leftist you mean. In Moscow I was a dissident. In Israel I was definitely anti-Zionist.

—The marxism in Russia is actually Lenin's idea of marxism, isn't it?

—Oh man. You American intellectuals amaze me.

—I'm not an intellectual. I'm a journalist.

—You're an intellectual.

—OK. I stand corrected. Totally, as Bryn would say.

—Do you like Bryn?

—I think I do. Jacques thinks I should start something with her.

—Let's stop talking about Jacques. Come to my place for dinner and we'll rent the movie from Crystal Video.

—We don't need to. Jacques has a copy of it.

—Then we can borrow it from him.

—Why don't *you* come over to Jacques's. I'll tell him to cook dinner. You know he likes to cook. Then we'll watch the movie.

—No no no. Let's have dinner and see the movie at my place. Let's leave him alone with Christine tonight.

—Yeah, right. As if he's dying for her company.

—So it's settled then? For tonight?

—It's settled. I'll get the tape. You'll have to pick me up at Jacques's. The buses stop running at 6.

—I'll pick you up.

—Then we're set.

—You don't mind seeing the movie again?

—Not at all. I've seen it maybe fifteen times. I can never tire of it.

—Great. I can see the movie again so it'll be fresh in my mind. Then when I come to your presentation I'll know what you're talking about.

—You're coming to my presentation?

—Of course. Of course. I won't miss it for the world! I want to see how your mind works.

—You mean you don't know already?

—I have a vague idea. I want to see it at work specifically and discursively.

—Why?

—Let's just say that I am *very* curious.

She said this with an impish grin on her face. To me now with benefit of hindsight, the semiotics of the conversation that Monday afternoon, of the vestimentary codes and words and gestures exchanged, began to fray a path that more or less led to where I am today, barely a year later, in Francette's huge apartment in Paris, by way of Missoula.

*   *   *

12

Paris: Tuesday, July 6, 1999

The first day of the conference at the University of Paris-7-Jussieu went well. The keynote presentation was by Slavoj Zizek, a Croatian cultural analyst who heads the Slovenian School of Psychoanalysis, and who frequently jets to the US to give workshops and seminars— sometimes as a visiting professor—at universities on the Northeast corridor. The point of his presentation—well-taken by most of the audience including participants—was that although Milosevic's attempted "genocide" of Kosovar Albanians was outrageous and reprehensible, the US (or more specifically the Clinton Administration) more or less produced this monster, and now feels, aided by NATO, compelled to destroy him: all of this notwithstanding the Serbian foundational myth of victimhood that also fueled the atrocities.

Thursday I get to meet Jesse Jackson when he gets his award. That should be interesting, although I'm not sure what I would say to the man. I'm not even sure what I really think of him and his "accomplishments." I guess he's an effective lightning rod but not really a great "leader." He sometimes picks wrong battles and chooses wrong targets. An example: a few months ago he led a verbal assault on Silicon Valley for not hiring minorities. Now the high-tech industry, which I know intimately because I'm also somewhat technical, happens to be virtually postracial and postnational. As they say, "on the Internet nobody knows you're a dog." (Of course, I don't mean to equate minorities with dogs.) A close friend of mine, an African-American woman of Creole heritage from Louisiana, is a highly skilled software engineer and platform developer who won a scholarship to MIT and started out her career with Apple. She was then wooed after three productive years by US West and subsequently by Microsoft—where she still is. And if my sources are accurate, only 40 percent of Microsoft employees in the US and overseas are American. In any case, Silicon Valley responded to Jesse Jackson's attack by saying he picked the wrong target, and that he should focus instead on the Los Angeles public school system and work to "correct" the way it has poorly served the local community. A few weeks later, Tamar Jacoby, a friend who used to be the editorial writer for *The New York Times*, responding to Jesse Jackson's "issue," wrote a very thoughtful article in *The New Republic* analyzing the phenomenon of the dearth of minorities in the high-tech industry. But I'm digressing here once again. I would like to focus on certain developments involving Francette and me that happened yesterday after the last session of the day at the conference.

Around 9 PM, Francette and I walked out of the campus onto rue Jussieu. As it was still quite light out and warm, we decided to forgo the Métro and walk, heading for Café de Cluny, even though we knew we had to negotiate our path through tourist-choked streets. We took the scenic route: We turned left on rue de Boulangers, to rue Monge, then turned left on rue des Ecoles and stayed on all the way to boulevard St-Michel, turned right, and finally got to the café, on the northwest corner of St-Michel and boulevard St-Germain. Francette was clearly in the mood for "self-disclosure," and she startled me with some information.

—Did you know I'm bisexual?

—Nope. This is something of a surprise. Are you actively bisexual?

—Yes. My most recent relationship fizzled at the end of April.

—With a woman.

—Correct.

—You don't look lesbian.

—Correct again. I'm what is called a lipstick lesbian.

—Is that right?

—You know what that is?

—Of course. Another bisexual woman friend explained that to me years ago.

—You're not shocked . . . just surprised?

—Why should I be shocked? Your sexual orientation is your own affair, not mine.

—Good. I have a community of bisexual, gay, and lesbian friends here in Paris that I'd like to introduce you to. Do you wish to meet them?

—Sure. Are they all French?

—No. Two of them, actually a couple, are American.

—Is that right? Women?

—Yes.

—Interesting.

—I told them about you. They're looking forward to meeting you.

—When will this august event take place?

—How about Friday afternoon? They meet at a café every Friday afternoon.

—That's fine with me. What about the conference?

—I'm sure we can duck out of the conference for an hour or so.

—Fine. What do your friends do?

—Various things. Designer. Math professor. High-school teacher. Film editor. Student. Investment banker.

—No physician? Is Michel not part of your community?

—No. He has his own, but some of his people know mine. I mean, we are roommates, after all.

—I see. A motley crew of bisexuals, gays, and lesbians. Interesting indeed. Totally interesting, as a friend of mine in Missoula would say.

—You mean Katya?

—No, I mean someone else.

—My last lover was a woman.

—So you said.

—Now I wish to shift to a man.

—Is that right?

My radar suddenly activated.

—Yes. That's right. I haven't been with a man since I divorced my husband.

—I keep forgetting you were married.

—For ten years. I told you this. To a French lout.

—So you did. But I don't remember the lout part.

—He was a lout and a lazy fuck, in all respects.

—But you stayed with him for ten years.

—That's because I had affairs all during that time. With men and women.

—Oh wow.

—He didn't know how to fuck. French men in general don't know how to fuck.

—Is that right? And you know this—existentially?

— Of course. I've sampled quite a few Frenchmen. Here and in the US.

—Oh wow. You've been pretty active. Americans also?

—All kinds. Africans, African-Americans, Asians, Jews, Latinos, a motley . . . to use your expression . . . crew of international men and women.

—Oh wow.

—I could teach you a few things.

—Really? But Francette, you promised we would never be physical.

—We were already physical.

—Yes, but not sexually.

—You weren't aroused during the massage?

—Nope.

—Well, I was.

—Is that right?

—I certainly was. I masturbated that night before I fell asleep.

—Oh wow.

—I was really turned on. It's been a long time since a man turned me on. I get a lot of chakra and sexual energy from you.

—What do you want to do about this situation? Since I'm not
     aroused?
—I want to act on my fantasy.
—Which one?
—The one I developed about you after that night.
—Pray do tell.
—I want to fuck you in the ass while I'm wearing a dildo.
—What? You're a . . . New-Age pervert!
—Thanks. That's a badge I'm willing to wear proudly.
—You're really a piece of work.
—I'm an art-form. Have you ever been fucked in the ass?
—Nope. I'm not gay.
—I didn't think you had been fucked in the ass. I have. And I can
     tell you that coming in the ass is the most pleasurable of all.
     Much more than genital.

At this point we were passing College de France on rue des
Ecoles, by Place M. Berthelet. I thought this coincidental and
interesting, as Michel Foucault's last teaching position was at this
institution, before he died of AIDS in 1984, and as Francette and
I were talking about anal sex. I said nothing. Francette again:

—What do you think? Will you let me fuck you in the ass? You
     don't have to do anything. I'll do all the work.
—Is that right?
—That's right. Are you a good fuck?
—I think so.
—Are you really? Didn't you tell me you and Katya had prob-
     lems?
—Yes but that was my choice.
—Your choice?
—Yes.
—You mean you kept yourself from being aroused by her?
—Most certainly.
—That's amazing that you can do that. I can't.
—Yes indeed: I can do that.

—Is that what is happening right now with me? Is that what you did the night I gave you the massage?

—To be honest, no. I didn't even think of it. I just wasn't aroused, that's all.

—For now. You're not aroused because you're not free.

—What do you mean?

—You must still have Katya on your mind. Your psyche is still in escrow with her.

—Now that's an interesting way of putting it. But you might have a point there.

—Well, I'll have to cure you. In fact, my goal on this trip is to cure you of Katya.

—Since when have you had this goal? Before we left New York?

—Since the night I gave you the massage. Before that I absolutely had no intention of seducing you.

—Good luck.

—Don't underestimate me. Think very seriously about staging this fantasy. It'll open up new worlds for you, make you a better lover.

We were on St-Michel at this point. Then we drifted to other topics. The cure for Katya. What a proposition. So now back to Katya.

*   *   *

13

Paris: Thursday, July 8, 1999

Missoula: Monday, August 24, 1998

That Monday night in August, Katya picked me up in her Subaru at Jacques's at 7 PM. We stopped at Bilo's 24-hour supermarket on 39th Avenue (which becomes South Higgins as you head toward downtown) to pick up some groceries and a liter of cheap red wine, all of which Katya paid for.

When we got to her place—on Daly Street between Hilda and Helen Streets—I sipped some wine and watched MSNBC (of course!) while she prepared dinner, an "Katya special" that I've delightfully foisted on friends since: A truly delicious rice-and-sausage dish loaded with peanuts and garlic and other spices, some hot, cooked in microwave, a somewhat simple recipé that required complicated cooking intervals—all within twenty-six minutes.

We had dinner and then watched the videotape of *Blade Runner,* the director's cut, the one without the narrator's voice-over. By the end of the film I had drunk most of the liter of red wine. The film's narrative unfolds in a post-apocalyptic Los Angeles "sometime in the future." Four "highly dangerous" replicants (slave-robots designed to be almost human, complete with virtual memories of their "pasts") have escaped from the Off-World, a slave-labor planet, and are now nomads on Earth. Deckard, a retired Blade-Runner, a sort of policeman-hunter played by Harrison Ford, has been reactivated to find and kill them. The replicants have escaped to Earth to seek out Tyrell, their "architect," because they're looking for answers about who they are and how long they have yet to live—questions we humans also would like answered. The film's narrative works out these issues and their complications quite effectively, with lots of verve. Katya was still convinced that the film was "dystopic." She certainly had several questions for me about the film.

—So the film is about capital and technology?

—Yes indeed. The film's Los Angeles is dominated by a visual regime that enslaves everyone.

—I see. It is certainly very violent, especially when Deckard guns down the female replicants.

—You're right there. Notice how monitors are everywhere.

—Monitors? You mean television?

—I mean monitors. I say monitors to emphasize the complete convergence of computers and television. Both the computer monitor and the TV monitor will soon be completely fused into one. Web TV is the first generation of this development.

—Oh boy. You've really thought this through.

—I didn't need to think it through. It's already here. We already have this in broadcasting: TV is interactive. And high-quality audio and high-resolution video can already be streamed through the computer monitor. It's just that this technology is not yet available for consumers.

—Now you're sounding just like Rob.

(By Rob she meant one of Jacques's community of friends who owns an Internet company in downtown Missoula—more about him later.)

—Rob is deep into this business. Did you know he wrote the source-code for Microsoft Word when he worked for Microsoft?

—No I didn't know. What's a source code? No no, don't answer. Let's get back to Earth, to the film.

—Vision in the film is part of the system of Capital.

—I see.

—Neon lights and commercials dominate the Los Angeles of the film. Corporations have figured out how eyes work and mass-produce them. Remember Chew, the eye-maker?

—Yeah, the Oriental guy.

—Remember he wears a crazy goggle contraption to do his work?

—Yes, yes.

—And people on the streets wear glasses with flashing lights. Also Roy, the replicant Rutger Hauer plays, teases J.F. Sebastian with a pair of glass eyes.

—Yes.

—Vision is sacred for the replicants. In a grisly act of revenge, Roy seeks out Tyrell in his apartment and bursts his eyeballs with his thumbs. And remember in one of the powerful moments of the film, how Roy, near death, describes the myriad wonders he has seen?

—Yeah I remember the scene, near the end, after he rescues Deckard from falling to his death.

—He said: quote, I have seen things that you humans wouldn't believe. I have seen dazzling lights reflected on the gates of Tenenhaus. I have seen attack ships on fire off Orion. All those moments will be lost in time . . .   like tears in the rain. End quote.

—You remember all that? Just like that?

—I've seen the film about sixteen times, counting tonight. And I've read the film-script.

—Interesting. How come there are no blacks in the film?

—Very good question. A most curious blindspot indeed, given the film's visual capture of nomadism and multicultural blends.

—As you say, a curious blindspot. But there are plenty of Asians.

—Indeed. My presentation will analyze the two main visual machines in the film.

—Which ones?

—The Voight-Kampff machine that appears in the opening scene with Leon and Holden and is later used to discover that Rachael-Sean Young is a replicant. This machine is a menacing allegory of the way we see: It reduces the eye to a purely physical object, to be comprehended completely by science and examined for what it can reveal about one's thoughts.

—That's one machine. What's the other one?

—The Esper is the other, which Deckard-Ford uses in his room to
   mobilize Leon's photograph the same way the cinema mobi-
   lizes

   images into what Deleuze called time-movement. The Esper
   dissects the photograph for Deckard's investigation. Remember how he inserts it into a slot, and it appears on a screen
   within a grid? With voice commands, he dissects it, zooming
   in on one section, revealing details ever more minuscule.

—Fascinating.

—Grids are a function of visual technology, a mapping of the space
   inside the frame onto itself. In *Blade Runner*, reality is
   compartmentalized and looked at through a screen of horizontal
   and vertical lines (which are likewise implied by the borders of
   monitors). The grid concretizes visual regimes.

—Awesome. You sound really awesome.

—I won't bore you anymore with all this. Just come to my
   presentation.

—I can't wait. The paper sounds brilliant.

—Thanks.

—Is this the kind of stuff you do at MSNBC?

—Nothing this fancy. By the time my frames end up on air, the
   material is diluted.

—Your frames?

—My intellectual frame. My story frame. My background frame.
   All those frames form the core of what I do. The research, the
   writing of cultural and political stories. That's what I do. I'm a
   content-provider.

—What a fantastic job!

—Let me give you a concrete example of what I do. Jane Pauley
   did a one-hour program of Castro's Cuba about a year ago.

—Yes.

—Anything she had to say about Cuba's writers and intellectuals
   came from what I gave her.

—Now I understand. They must pay you well.

—I guess.

—Then how come you don't have any money now?

—I'm on a nonpaying one-year leave of absence, as you know.

—We call that a sabbatical in academia.

—I know. But I'm not in academia. And even though I hang out with academics I'm not an academic.

—Don't be so sensitive ... Don't you have any savings?

—No.

—I see.

—I have a funny quirky relationship to money.

—Tell me more.

—I simply piss off money. In fact, I think money is an overrated commodity.

—Is your family rich?

—Middle class. Middle-class immigrant family in New York.

—Nigerian immigrants.

—Yes. My brothers and I were born in New York.

—What does your father do?

—Did. We lost him in 1987.

—Sorry.

—That's okay. He was more or less old. Seventy-five.

—What did he do?

—He was at the UN. Then he stayed on here. My mother is still a grade-school teacher in New York.

—I see. What an interesting background.

—You seem to have an interesting one yourself.

—Not as interesting as yours though.

—Let's not compete on backgrounds.

—I'll have to tell you more about mine sometime.

—Tell me something now.

—What?

—Do you have a main squeeze?

—A main squeeze? You mean a boyfriend?

—Yes.

—I have a boyfriend.

—You do? Here?

—No. In South Carolina.

—South Carolina?

—South Carolina.

—Why down there?

—He lives down there. In Columbia.

—How did you guys meet? Did you used to live there?

—No. We met in DC.

—Yeah?

—He was one of my students last spring when I was teaching at Georgetown.

—You seduced one of your students?

—The relationship began after he stopped being my student.

—You and Jacques have something in common.

—Yeah? What is that?

—You both fuck your students.

—That's sounds crude. Glen and I are very much in love.

—Is that right? Is he a native of South Carolina?

—Yeah.

—So you're in love with a cracker from the south.

—*He's not a cracker!*

I, somewhat startled by her yelling:

—I'm sorry I didn't mean to upset you.

—No I'm sorry. I shouldn't have yelled at you like that. I'm sorry. But Glen is not a cracker.

—Sorry.

—I'm really in love with him. But sadly, the relationship has no future.

—What do you mean?

—He comes from an old aristocratic southern family.

—Indeed. With plantations, no doubt.

—And they will never accept me.

—Why won't they accept you?

—I'm a Jew from Russia by way of Israel.

—Yeah, OK. I understand.

—The whole thing is sad. But I don't know what to do about it.
—How old is he? He must be young.
—Twenty-three.
—How old are you?
—Thirty-five.
—Interesting. Twelve years.
—He's great fuck too.
—Is he?
—He is.
—But Katya, that's too much information than I need right now.
    I again:
—Have you been married before?
—Yeah, to another Russian Jew.
—Where is he?
—DC.
—Any kids?
—One daughter. Fifteen. She lives with her dad.
—Interesting. So you were twenty when you had her.
—Yeah. So I'm divorced with a daughter. Just like you.
—How did you know that?
—Jacques told me. He told me about Sarah and your daughter.
—I bet Jacques has told you everything about me.
—Not everything.
—How come he told you anything at all?
—I was asking him questions.
—Why?
—Because I'm curious about you. You fascinate me. I've never met
    a Nigerian before.
—An American. I'm American. I was born here.
—Okay: I meant an American of Nigerian heritage.
—And I've never met a Russian Jew before.
—You were married to a Jew.
—An Ezskenazi Jew from New York. Jacques really has been talking.
—He has. He also told me you have a thing for Jewish women.
—That bastard.

—You know, he startled me in the department the other day when he came up with a racist joke.

—Jacques came up with a racist joke? I don't believe it. In what context?

—I forget. But it was racist, I assure you.

—Well tell me.

—He said: Who's dumber than a dumb Frenchman? I shrugged. Then he said: A smart Algerian.

—No he didn't.

—Yes he did. Your friend Jacques. He told me that joke.

The whole exchange at Katya's that August night foreshadowed the psycho-sexual drama that was to unfold between us for the nine months between September 1998 till June 1999 when we broke up. For one thing, Jacques more or less functioned as Banquo's ghost anytime Katya and I were together.

Now back to Paris, to Francette.

*   *   *

14

Paris: Friday, July 9, 1999

This afternoon I get to meet Francette's gay-lesbian and bisexual friends. We're meeting at Café de Flore on boulevard St-Germain, near St-Germain-des-Prés, a café I rarely go to, tourist trap that it is, thanks to Jean-Paul Sartre and his existentialist drinking buddies. I agreed to meet her friends after all that happened between us last night.

I listened to Jesse Jackson ramble for almost two hours yesterday afternoon after accepting his peace award. Somehow he managed to work the domestic US racial situation into his talk (which was actually little more than a loose series of statements), a move that I thought highly inappropriate for the venue: an international audience of writers and intellectuals assembled to discuss the NATO-Kosovo debacle that involved Serbs, Kosovar Albanians, and homeland Albanians, with its multiple ramifications for Europe, particularly Central Europe (which now includes a rudderless and economically crippled but still nuclear-powered Russia, with its broke and unpaid nuclear engineers now freelancing for Iraq and Libya, and its resentful old communist operatives and apparatchiks frustrated and angry over the Soviet exit from history), and the ambiguous and multivalent function of the United States (its government and culture and economic habits) in an increasingly global-capital (that is to say, increasingly American) post-cold-war world wired for absolute speed.

More to one point, however, that Jesse Jackson missed completely in his rambling "presentation," and that he should have taken the golden opportunity to tell these people at the conference, was that the US is an excellent example of a multi-ethnic and multicultural regime, with a high-tech industry and an all-volunteer military operating in a society where the international media and the entertainment industry have more power and influence than the national political class. I mean, the state apparatus "beyond history," as it were, cannot even protect its own citizens: witness the shootings at Columbine and similar incidents. And one does not have to read a lot of psychoanalysis to understand that as state power wanes with the day-by-day sensational media coverage of the performance of various stock exchanges (New York-Dow Jones, New York-NASDAQ, Tokyo-Nikkei), specific state agencies, notably law enforcement, would vent their frustrations of impotence against members of ethnic and cultural minorities: witness the police shootings of African-Americans in New York and elsewhere.

The other point that Jesse Jackson missed (and that Zizek also missed, I might add) was that currently, Europe is struggling with its own identity, in light of the massive presence and continuing influx of immigrants from the third world: the empire come home to the motherland to roost, as it were. The fact that NATO rushed into the war in Kosovo, where the Christian Serbs turned against the Muslim "ethnic" Albanians is certainly a symptom of this identity crisis.

Europe is also currently attracting more asylum seekers—mostly from the third world—than is the United States. In 1998, only 30,000 people applied for asylum in the US, down from 127,000 in 1993. Whereas 365,000 did so in the 15-nation European Union. This shift is troubling to a Europe that tends to see more problems than promise in "alien" blood. But its causes are not about to disappear. The collapse of the Soviet Union has opened up new land routes to Europe from Asia and transformed once-closed cities like Moscow and Kiev into nodal points of migrant travel from Afghanistan and China directly to points in Europe. And so an opulent Europe, even one with high unemployment (as an example: France's unemployment has hovered around 12 percent for some years now), glimmers as a land of opportunity. More than 70 million migrants are said to be on the move at any one time. And on the whole, Europe looks relatively accessible to them than does the US, which is more expensive and more remote to get to, given the expanse of the Atlantic Ocean. Plus: the European Union has now eliminated most of its internal borders, making Athens to Amsterdam a passport-free passage. Yet this Europe is profoundly uneasy about its emergent role as a haven for the world's dispossessed. Unlike the US, no mythology embraces "your tired, your poor, your huddled masses." A "migration expert" at London University was recently quoted as saying "No European country has voted for a multicultural society, or thought of itself as such, yet we are now told we live in one."

Germany is struggling with its perennial Turkish *geisterbeiters* (so-called "guest workers"); Austria: Turks and Vietnamese; Switzerland: also the Turks and recently Serbs and Croatians; Italy: Chinese and West Africans; France: perennial Algerians, other North Africans, and Francophone sub-Sahara Africans; Spain: Latins Americans attempting to reverse Pisarro and Cortes's Great Conquest, and Moroccans. Ironically, only the United Kingdom of Great Britain and (for now) Northern Ireland seems, at the time of this writing, to consciously, socially, economically, and politically accommodate (albeit with occasional incidents of racism) its sizable population of Pakistanis, Indians, Sri Lankans, Saudis, and Anglophone Africans—perhaps because of its highly complicated history of the Raj and the ambiguous commerce with the Africans. Perhaps also, because its colonial history is not as violent as those of the other imperial machines. Certainly, one symptom of this productive cross-fertilization is that what is erroneously referred to as "English literature"—when they mean "British literature"— but which should really be called "literature in English," is now being revitalized by first-and second-generation immigrants from the Empire: From the mid to late 90s, nonwhite writers in the

English language won the Booker Prize, Britain's highest annual literary prize.

My apologies for the long digression: Back to Paris-Jussieu: I tuned out Jesse Jackson after an hour. And I almost left the main auditorium at the Jussieu campus, but decided to prolong my torture when I realized that almost everyone would notice my leave-taking (we sat in the middle of the crowd), which would then be interpreted as rude by the mostly white audience, sufficiently ironic with an African-American as perpetrator. I was however irritated— at least visibly to Francette.

Francette, in English, as we emerged from the campus onto rue Jussieu around 7 PM:

—You could have at least disguised how you felt.
—Was I that obvious?
—You were huffing and puffing throughout his lecture.
—You call that a lecture?
(She was still speaking in English, which was unusual, since for
    the most part, she speaks to me in French.)
—What do you call it?
—It was more like a rambling and loose series of statements.
—You were so disrespectful.
—Sorry.
—I was starting to feel embarrassed.
—My apologies if I embarrassed you.
—That's besides the point. He's a great guy.
—He's an opportunist and a phony baloney.
—Yeah? Give me one example of that.
—Well, after Martin Luther King was shot in Memphis in March
    1968, your hero Jesse Jackson faked being the first person on
    the scene by staging his discovery of a bloody handkerchief ...
    that he'd planted himself minutes before.
—This was never reported. How do you know this?
—I'm in the media, remember? I saw some archives. Besides, *The
    New York Times* reported this again a few years ago.

—So?

—What do you mean, so? By doing that he was setting himself up
    as the rightful heir to King's work, giving that shift some kind
    of emotional grounding. It was shameful and disgusting.

—You're being too hard on the guy.

—You can't be too hard enough on someone like that.

—Still, you were disrespectful. This was an important occasion.

—I said I was sorry!

—All right all right. You don't need to be upset all over again.

—You are getting under my skin about this. (She then switched
    to French.)

—Oh come on. You need to relax. You're pretty pissed.

—What do you feel like doing tonight anyway?

—We need to have dinner.

—And?

—We could catch a movie afterward.

—What's playing?

—Let's pick up *Pariscope* over there, at the newsstand.

    We crossed Place Jussieu to the newsstand and picked up the
    weekly *Pariscope*, which lists all the weekly goings-on in Paris.
I let

    Francette peruse it, since she suggested seeing a movie.
Francette:

—*Bound* is playing at Odéon UGE.

—What's *Bound* ?

—A movie.

—I know it's a movie, Francette. What's it about?

—I've seen it before. I like it a lot and won't mind seeing it again.

—What's it about?

—Here, I'll read *Pariscope* 's description of it. I don't want to talk
    you into it with my own bias.

—What you're about to read is someone else's bias who just hap-
    pens to get paid writing copy for *Pariscope*.

—Oh come on, don't be a wise guy with me. OK, here goes: In this American movie, a tough female ex-con, Corky, and her lover, Violet, design a scheme to steal millions of stashed mob money and pin the blame on Violet's crooked boy friend, Caesar.

—Ah ah, a lesbian movie.

—A lesbian thriller, to be specific. And it has some steaming sex scenes in it too.

—So then: a steamy, lesbian sexual thriller.

—That's it. Maybe you should have written the copy for *Pariscope*. The copy here is more discreet.

—Maybe. Although the French are not really known for holding anything back on matters of sex. When did it come out?

—1996.

—I missed it. It must not have had a successful box-office run in the States.

—I think it had a limited release in theaters. Then it became a cult movie when it came out in videotape.

—A cult movie within gay-lesbian circles?

—I think in straight circles too. You know that straight men are turned on by lesbians making love.

—It depends on what the lesbians look like. Who's in the film?

—Gina Gershon plays Corky, and Jennifer Tilly plays Violet.

—Whoa. They played lipstick lesbians then. Unless they were completely made over for their roles.

—I think their love scenes will turn you on.

—I first saw Gina Gershon in *Showgirls*, which bombed at the box-office. Now that's one film I rented several times in video.

—Because of Gina Gershon?

—No. Because of Elizabeth Berkley. I would fast-forward and then rewind to see Kyle MacLachlan fuck her again and again in the swimming pool.

—Now who's the pervert.

—I met Jennifer Tilly once, at a party in New York.

—You go film parties?

—Not really. A close friend of mine, Kathryn Bigelow, you know, the director, *Strange Days, Blue Steel,* had the party and invited me.

—Does Jennifer Tilly really speak like that in real life?

—You mean with that voice that seems to have nodes in it?

—Yeah. She always sounds as if she's on her last breath.

—That's her screen voice. She doesn't speak like that at all.

—Wow. She's so good!

—Who's the director?

—The Wachowski brothers. It says here they also wrote the original screenplay. Their directorial debut.

—Andy and Larry. They're really good. OK. That clinches it. Let's see the movie. When is it playing?

—There's a show at 8.

—Let's go to that and eat afterward. Unless you're really hungry.

—No that's fine. We'll have a late dinner.

—Is it a long movie?

—The standard two hours, as I recall.

We took the Métro from Jussieu, Direction de Pont St-Cloud, straight to Odéon, emerged from the station, and walked across Carrefour de l'Odéon to watch the film at Odéon UGE Cineplex.

In *Bound,* Corky-Gina Gershon, a lesbian ex-con hired to work in an apartment as a plumber, meets neighbors Caesar-Joe Pantoliano—who launders money for the Mafia—and his girlfriend Violet-Jennifer Tilly. The two women soon begin a passionate love affair and decide to steal the 2 million dollars that Caesar-Joe Pantoliano is holding in custody for Mafia boss Gino-Richard Sarahfian. After twists and turns—tired clichés of the genre—the women successfully set up Caesar-Joe Pantaliano as the scapegoat. The two love scenes with Gershon and Tilly did turn me on. But the film essentially impressed me as a lesbian fantasy of male-bashing to some extreme: all the male characters are either stupid, besotted by Tilly, careless, or misogynist, or all or some of these combined. The film's attempt at being raw and gritty fell short, in my opinion. In one scene, after socking and kicking Gershon, foiling her attempt at escape, Pantaliano grits his teeth and yells at her: "Get up! Get up, you fuc-king dyke!" And in one of the last scenes, before blowing Pantaliano (who spent most of the film telling himself to think) off with a gun, Tilly tells him: "You don't know jack shit, Caesar!" After the film and before we sat down to dinner at Les Balkans, I gave Francette my impressions.

Francette, responding in English as we walked on boulevard St-Germain and turned left on rue Danton on the way to Les Balkans on rue de la Harpe:

—Oh come on, you're speaking from heterosexual privilege!

—What the fuck is that?

—See? The fact that you don't even know what that is quite revealing. You know what a lipstick lesbian is but you don't know what heterosexual privilege is. You have serious gaps. I need to educate you.

—Pray do tell me what it is. I have an idea though.

—I'll give you an example instead of a definition. See that couple walking in front of us?

—Yeah, what about them?

—Notice how they have their arms around each other?

—So?

—So they're bathing in heterosexual privilege without even being conscious of it.

—I see.

—You weren't even conscious of it, were you? A lesbian or gay couple would never dream of having their arms around each other like that in public. And if they did they would be doing it very consciously, making some kind of political statement, at their own risk, depending on the particular environment they happen to be in.

—I get your meaning. The key is being conscious: You assume heterosexual privilege when don't think about assumed practices. And you can apply this paradigm to race, gender, and class privileges.

—That's good! That's very good. You're a good student. By the time
   I'm done with you, you'll be a completely different sexual being.
—Yes, ma'am.

We got to Les Balkans. Francette ordered a couscous marguez
and I couscous d'agneau. I'd always liked Les Balkans ever since I
was a student in Paris. At that time, in the early to mid 80s, I had
little money, and for 21 French francs I had a great three-course
dinner with a half-carafe of red wine. Now in these late 90s, I've
retained the habit of frequenting Les Balkans, and 45 francs will
buy you the same delicious dinner.

Francette, in French, which I was now learning to interpret on
this trip as an index that she was feeling relaxed with me:
—Do you want to hear my own impressions of the film?
—Of course, of course.
—Bound is a product of perfect casting, innovative cinematogra-
   phy, an excellent script, wonderful acting, simple yet power-
   ful set design, amazing direction, beautiful lighting, and per-
   fect music.
—My God! You sound like one of those commentators on the
   Yahoo Movie web site or the Internet Movie Database. Are
   you sure you don't want to consider writing movie-publicity
   copy as an alternative career?
—Wait, wait: I'm not done yet.
—I'm all ears.
—It's a movie that immediately grabs you into the story, pulls you
   to the edge of your seat, and holds you there to the very end.
   I love the way each of the characters does a complete turn-
   around from the stereotype.
—Bull! The movie is completely stereotypical.
—It would be stereotypical if you're a square heterosexual.

—Look, some of us might be straight but we're not quote unquote squares. We are also hip. We drink café latte and Chilean red wine. We eat Sri Lankan, Peruvian, Korean, Ethiopian, and Moroccan cuisines. We read *Spin* and *ArtForum*. We listen to the music of Cesaria Evora and Salif Keita. We watch foreign movies with subtitles. We speak different languages: Portuguese, Hindi, Yoruba, Mandarin, Arabic, Hebrew. We work on our laptops in various cafés in the boho sections of big cities in domestic US and overseas. We spend our vacations in Sai Gon or Santiago. We roam the world with our e-tickets and boarding passes. At airports we spend our layover time looking for outlets for our laptops. Some of us are born Muslims or Jews or agnostic. Some of us are biracial, even multiracial. Some of us are foreign-service or army or missionary brats. Some of us have, reluctantly or willingly, assumed waiter or dot-com or media roles. Some of us have gone into mainstream broadcast media to make money. And some of us are in new media to change human life on the planet.

—In the name of God! Take it easy! What brought all that on? Was it something I said? Listen, my friend: Most of you are corporate hipsters, goat-cheese-and-shiraz bohemians, limousine liberals,and Viagra radicals. Most of you are closet readers of *The Economist* or *The Wall Street Journal*. And I bet most of you speak only English. Besides, you don't speak Portuguese do you? At least you never told me you did.

—I don't speak it but I understand it. Viagra radicals? I like that, but what does it mean?

—Oh come on, you know what I mean: short-term radicals, fake radicals, virtual radicals.

—OK, OK, I get it.

—*Esse mundo ê fôlse. Ca bô vivêl por atacóde cheio d'ironia mim jam' curtil.* (This world is bitter. Don't live in a rush. Take it calmly and with humor.)

—I didn't know you speak Portuguese.

—My ex-husband and I lived in Lisbon for a year.

—I see. I have a sense of humor! Give me a break.

—You could have fooled me.

—Well . . .

—I think it is Jennifer Tilly's best role to date. She is convincing, cool, manipulative, and smart.

—I agree with you there. I wanted to jump in there with her and Gina Gershon.

—I'm sure you wanted to. Do you feel like jumping into bed with me tonight?

—I beg your pardon?

—You're so tense. I think you need another massage.

—I guess I could use another massage.

She ordered more wine.

—Drink up. I think the combination of couscous and red wine is an aphrodisiac.

—Oh oh. An aphrodisiac? I thought this will just be a massage.

She didn't respond.

We finished dinner and took the Métro back to 7 rue Fénelon. Her roommate Michel wasn't home. She gave me one-hour deep massage in my room. I was so relaxed, with help from almost a whole bottle of Côtes du Rhone red wine, that, according to Francette, I dozed off for about thirty minutes. When I woke up she was still in my room and now lying supine beside me panting. I wondered what was going on until I realized that she was masturbating.

—You're masturbating!

She said in-between pants:

—Oh, you're awake.

—So I am. I've never seen a woman masturbate before.

—You are seeing one now. I do it to relax.

Her pants increased until she came to a climax. She then rolled over on top of me and kissed me on the mouth. Probably because I was groggy and still in the subconscious realm, I did not resist and slid my tongue into hers. We kissed and licked each other for perhaps twenty minutes. Then I pulled back.

Francette, in French:

—Oh, come on.

—I don't feel like it tonight. Maybe some other time.

—I feel like it tonight. As you can see, that film really turned me
     on. I feel hot and I am hot.

(She employed the two French tenses for the body's experience of the [weather] temperature and the heat of sexual desire.)

—Ah ah. Desire filtered through the film-text.

—I'm tired of all your textual shit. You've got to put your dick
     where your mouth is. At some point all theory-talk has to
     stop.

—Stop for what? What do you have in mind?

—The foreplay is over. I feel like fucking you in the ass tonight.

—Francette . . .

—Shut up! I'll go get my dildo. I want to fuck you in the ass. I
     want to fuck those theory brains out.

—That's scary, Francette . . . dick, ass, and brains? You're mixing
     up the organs . . .

—Sex is scary and painful and pleasurable. And I'm not mixing
     anything up. One is anatomical, the other metaphoric: When
     I'm
       fucking you in the ass, that's all I want you to think about
     with your brains.

—You're a real pervert.

—Don't fight me! You'll like it. Like I said, it'll make you a better
     lover. Trust me.

Somewhat helplessly and seemingly paralyzed, I lay there and
watched her strap a dildo to her crotch. She lubricated the dildo
with a skin moisturizer, then rolled me over and rammed it into
my ass. She stroked, at first gently, then pumped hard for about
ten-fifteen minutes before I yelled at her to stop. I felt a novel
combination of pain and pleasure, and I'm not sure what my body
would have experienced if I hadn't stopped her. But my body was
definitely beginning to spasm.

Francette, in French:

—You're afraid, aren't you? What are you afraid of?

—You were beginning to hurt me.

—Liar. You were also enjoying it. You're afraid to let go. You coward.

—My ass hurts.

—You would have come in another five minutes. I could feel it myself.

We lay there for another hour. I let her perform fellatio on me. I came three times, then eventually fell asleep for the rest of the night. I woke up this morning and felt Francette's body next to mine and her arm around my chest. She had stayed in my bed all night.

This instance of sexual desire and act mobilized by the film-text recalls a somewhat similar—but not identical—experience that I had with Dorit Levin in New York about nine years ago.

*   *   *

15

Paris: Friday, July 9, 1999

New York: Wednesday, September 12, 1990

Coincidentally, before I started this entry, I opened and read a 15K-size e-mail from Dorit, responding to my own posting to her two nights ago. I promise to cite her e-mail in its entirety at the end of this entry. But I want to deal first with the film-text transformed into desire.

Almost a year after I met her, Dorit and I went to see a movie, *Hiroshima Mon Amour*, at the (then) newly opened Angelika Film Center on Houston and Mercer Streets, before we going to dinner at Time Café (where the big clock prominently displayed on the wall was set to run rapidly backward) on Lafayette and Great Jones (shibboleth Third for natives) Streets.

In addition to *Blade Runner*, *Hiroshima Mon Amour* is easily, for me, one of my most favorite films to date.

In the film, a nameless Parisian woman played by Emmanuèle Riva is in Tokyo acting in a film dedicated to peace. In the one week she's in Tokyo, she meets and has a brief affair with a nameless Tokyo architect played by Eiji Okada. On their last night together, at a tearoom in the small hours of the morning, she's haunted by her memories of the affair she had, during World War II, with a German soldier in her hometown of Nevers, in France—and of the town's subsequent ostracization of her and her family. These memories are spliced into the poignant leave-taking scene unfolding in the tearoom. The film delicately juxtaposes the bombing of Hiroshima with the German occupation of France.

To cite exchanges from the film relevant at this point in my narrative:

Riva:

—How could I have known that this city is made to the measure of my love? How could I have known that you were made to the measure of my body? You know the art of seeing has to be learned? . . .

Okada:

—Hiroshima was the beginning of a new unknown, of a new fear.
—What do you do in life?
—I'm an architect. But I'm also involved in politics.
—Ah, that's why you speak French so well. . . .

Okada:

—I like lying and also telling the truth. I have a problem with morality. My own morals are rather dubious.
—Nevers is the one city I dream about the most, but also the one I think about the least.
—You give me the longing for love.
—It's all about these chance encounters.
—I'm a happily married man.
—I'm also a happily married woman.
—It's never that simple.

Riva:

—I'm just now getting to know you, among the other thousand things in my life. . . .

Riva:

—The Loire is a very beautiful river with no navigation. The light around it is so very soft. At Nevers, sleep comes at dawn.
—Does it ever rain? . . .

Riva:

—I begin to see you again. I remember our happiness and our love. I remember my life. I remember your death. I see that the shadows now get longer. I see the ink. I see the text. I see my life going on and on. And I see your death going on and on.)

That September night in New York with Dorit was the tenth time I saw the film. And it affected me the same way it always had: The images of love and death renewed in me the desire to love and to travel. I remembered again and again the opening shot of the naked bodies interlocked, Eiji Okada's impeccable French and Emmanuèle Riva's intense face, the tumescent sound track, the soft-focus shots of Nevers (the town in the middle of France that the nameless Riva character said she dreamt about the most) and the banks at the edge of the Loire river, and the incredibly poignant scene at the tearoom at dawn with the *bal-musette* music from the jukebox. The film reminded me again that desire conjoined with memory comes from death, like the illusion of the impossibility of forgetting, like the cornflowers and gladiolas and morning glories and day lilies that sprung from the ashes in Hiroshima with extraordinary vigor fifteen days after the bombing. The film reminded me again that love was like madness or intelligence: One couldn't understand it; it simply flooded one's body completely.

After a two-hour dinner at the Time Café, where Dorit and I consumed two bottles of wine between us, I invited her for the first time to my two-bedroom coop apartment on East 3rd Street where for the first time we made intensely passionate love for several hours, spliced with intervals when we sipped one and a half bottles of Côtes du Rhone between us.

Before that night, we had simply been casual friends, seeing each other at book parties around Manhattan and exchanging semi-intellectual pleasantries. Within a week after the movie and love-making in my apartment, we became "an item" for a year until Karyn Ross captured my heart and mind almost a year later. In fact during that year, Dorit and I developed a habit-in-tandem of watching a movie (either VCR or [art] theater), and then existentially duplicating the essential experience articulated in the movie: As an example: We once watched Nagisa Oshima's *In the Realm of the Senses*, also at the Angelika, in which the two protagonists, a woman and a man, more or less made love for the two-hour duration of the movie. Then we went back to my apartment and more or less did the same. That same night, we both made a mutual discovery. After we made love, Dorit was checking out the books on my bookshelf while sipping some merlot. Suddenly, while browsing the theory section, she yelled:

—Hey, you've underlined the same passages in *L'Anti-Oedipe* that
    I underlined when I read the book!
(She meant Deleuze's *The Anti-Oedipus.*)
—Is that right?
—Yes in fact that's right! I can't believe it!
—When did you read it?
—1987.
—The same year my dad died. I read it in 1979.
—Eight years earlier. Isn't that something?
—Yeah, isn't that something.

So that discovery was the first indication of the Prussian mind meld that we shared.

During our one-year romantic relationship, in January 1991, Dorit and I went to Guadeloupe: What for me was a trip of a lifetime before I went to Chile. We took an American Airlines flight from JFK to Pointe-à-Pitre. We then rented a car for a twenty-minute drive to Gosier and stayed at PLM-Arawak, the near-paradaisical hotel-garden of cabins by the Caribbean Sea.

We stayed at a charcoal-brown cabin overlooking the turquoise sea, with a balcony where we sat every night, after an elaborate dinner of creole cuisine (rice and fish and chicken in spicy-hot tomato juice) and many glasses of merlot and Amarrone, sipping vanilla-colored cocoa-punch (that putative aphrodisiac power-drink fueled with rum) while we watched the blue-white full moon's quivering reflection in the water. And then after that, we went into the cabin, where made intensely passionate love that the cocoa-punch fueled. In the morning, we got up around 10 AM or so and went for a seven-eight-mile run together, the longest we could run in those first few days or so, because of the humidity, which was so dense that our bodies needed at least four days to adapt. After the runs, we took showers together and sometimes made love in the shower, and then sometimes we had indolent drawn-out Parisian-vintage lunches. One day we packed a picnic and drove to Sainte-Anne on Grande-Terre and ate on the beach. Another day we took the ferry to the island of Marie-Galante and saw the Vieux-Fort, where slave ships carrying Africans landed, before the slaves were dispersed to other islands in the Caribbean. Another day we took another ferry to Désirade Island and spent all day seeing incredibly exotic mineral landscapes that might well have been located in distant planets in the galaxy.

One day we were simply mundane instead and drove to the luxuriant, lushy lower wing of Guadeloupe (the island itself is shaped like a butterfly with two wings), called Basse-Terre, the windward part of the island, which got so much rain and sun, where the light was so soft, and sought out an empty, virgin beach at Pointe-Noire, where we had a picnic and drank wine and napped a bit, and where we made love again. Later, at Basse-Terre, we drove all the way up to the defunct volcano, La Soufrière, after lunch, and hiked on the arid terrain around it. And then after-ward, we went to the little town of Trois-Rivières and took one of those tour-boats where we watched all kinds of tropical fish through the glass panels installed on the floor of the lower decks.

After ten days in Guadeloupe we flew back New York, back to the concrete jungle. Karyn Ross picked us up at JFK. Two months later, at the beginning of spring in New York, Karyn derailed my relationship to Dorit. Karyn Ross more or less functioned as Banquo's ghost during my relationship with Dorit—a role that Dorit also played in my subsequent relationship with Karyn.

And as I said in a previous entry, Jacques more or less functioned as Banquo's ghost anytime Katya and I were together. So then on to Missoula with Katya and Jacques, before getting back to Paris and Francette. But before all that, the following is Dorit's e-mail that I had promised to reproduce in its entirety:

*   *   *

Dorit's e-mail:

Yo, Bro! My apologies for my delay in responding to your posting, which I enjoyed quite a bit. Now I'm the point that I can type and post you this e-mail, imiliar un emilio, as we say in cyber-Spanglish. In fact, your posting was definitely a tonic (spiked—as you would say, although I'd say laced—with a little gin) to my spirit: Its timing couldn't be more perfect. So here we are again on the Internet, el Internet, as we also say in cyber-Spanglish. Somehow your posting reminded me of the way our romantic interlude began in 1990, and how it was conducted. In 1990, in its infancy in the old days of pine, before Tim Berners-Lee invented the World Wide Web, writing the world's first browser and then releasing its software as an open-source code in 1991 the Internet was a high-tech tool that permitted us to connect with each other in an old-fashioned way. Remember what I told you then, that many of the world's greatest romances began and were sustained through the written word?

The way our bodies connected after we saw *Hiroshima Mon Amour* was sustained through pine—Bitnet to be exact—and in a sense our exchanges online were charged with and enhanced by the tremendous sexual energy unleashed from that inaugural love-making.

Like I said, your posting was quite timely. I've been in a rotten mood lately, especially this week. I don't know exactly where my life is going. I tell myself I'm a staff writer at THE NEW YORKER. I have several essays under my belt. But what next? I don't want to go another magazine. Besides, there's no where else to go. As far as

I'm concerned, THE NEW YORKER tops the list. And how higher up can you go at THE NEW YORKER than a staff writer, except as the editor? I most certainly DO NOT want to be the editor. I'm not an egotistical masochist.

I suppose I could shift industries all together, go into the dot-com world. Now that's an expanding and exciting industry. After all, I've always been interested in those technical things. Remember that I taught myself dynamic HTML and Visual Basic. I'm the resident techie at THE NEW YORKER, no contest there: Most of the writers there are either outright old-fogey Luddites or analog curmudgeons who would mistake GUI for a small country in the South Pacific or dBase for a military installation. With my French, Spanish, and Portuguese, I cover vast areas of the Northern, Southern, and Western Hemispheres.

But seriously, I would like to write a couple of books before I die: one fiction, the other nonfiction. I have several ideas for these books. The nonfiction would be easy to write, since I have extensive notes and my own essays to feed off on.

The book I'm thinking about writing will dovetail with your own work somewhat: how women, already subjected to other regimes and at conflict with legal, political, and economic institutions, figure in the new regimes set up by capital and technology. More narrowly, I want to examine how women figure in all respects in the new technology and media industries.

For instance, I'm fascinated by what you've told me about your friend Donna Auguste, the African-American woman who was raised in New Orleans and went on to MIT on a scholarship, and who's worked at Apple, US West, and is now at Microsoft. It's quite fascinating that in an industry with few blacks and few women, she's being courted by everyone in the dot-com business. She will be one of my case-studies. I promise to pick some of your brains on her, but I'll do my own research. But enough about this already, which might well turn out to be wishful thinking.

My apologies again for the delay in responding. I've been buried in myriad and annoying and sometimes stupid little deadlines, including dealing with upstart Jane Kramer-wannabe interns, and I wanted to clear the time to respond appropriately.

What a day! A drunk almost threw up on me on the D-Train on the way home. When he finally did threw up, a real stinker, I had to go to the next car. Normally I just walk home, but I was feeling quite beat and uninspired. I did my usual six-miler on the loop this morning in Central Park, but I did repeat hills on the Harlem Hill, six of them, so I was feeling sore all day. In fact, I'm still sore. And I can feel some cramps coming. It's getting to be that time of the month, if you know what I mean.

I began my formal training for the New York City Marathon this morning. I'm lifting off a base of fifty miles a week, going up to about eighty. I'll be doing 12 miles a day, two loops around the park, one in the morning, the other in the evening after work. And there goes my social life.

I can't meet anybody after work. It's either that or I do the two loops in the morning and get it over with. But as you know I need to deal with my networks in Europe and points east in those early hours instead of pounding the loop in Central Park.

You know I'm a night owl like you. And I don't necessarily have to go into an office, but I sometimes want to, for the discipline. Besides, the NEW YORKER library is quite handy for my research. I mean, I could go to Donnell Library on West 53rd, just a few blocks away, but a lot of perps have been hanging out there lately. The last time I was there a bum proposed to me. "I want to marry you. Will you marry me?" he proposed. "No I don't want to marry you. I can't marry you. You're a drunk, and I don't want a drunk for a husband." I responded, risking his explosion. But I felt secure because the security guard was keeping a watchful eye on things. Besides, this somewhat loud exchange raised the eyebrows of a few users.

I really want to break 2:40 this year. I'm definitely ready for it. I feel great. Over the winter and spring I did 24-milers every Sunday and felt strong. I needed only two days to recover. Next week I'll start doing speed intervals at Bakers Field at Columbia. Are you running New York this year? It'll be great if you are, because then I'll try to hang with you for the first ten maybe fifteen miles. I know you usually take it easy for the first twenty miles, then race the last ten kilometers. I'll never forget what you told me about your marathon-racing strategy: That when you're racing you carry the image in your head of being chased by cops. When I told a girlfriend that recently she laughed herself into stitches.

I can only dream of your personal best of 2:23 and change. I know you missed Boston because you were in Jerusalem. If you weren't planning on New York you should reconsider. I'd love for you to pace me. We can even train together when you get back to New York. Now that would be fun. We haven't run together since 1990. Do you remember all the long runs we did together on Sundays? Four loops around Central Park? I used to look forward to them a lot. I also enjoyed them a lot. For three hours, I would listen to your breathing and get high from all the oxygen. Also, I would get quite wet, and not just from the sweat, if you know what I mean. I really believed then, that running together for us was love-making continued by other means, to twist Carl von Clausewitz's formulation about war and politics. Oh well.

I saw your name in the credits after a "Dateline" program on Channel 4 the other night. The show was on cities that are changing in America. You never told me you did the background research and writing on that. Jane looked good, as usual. I enjoyed meeting her and Garry that one time we went to dinner at their place.

I just finished dinner. And now I'm sitting by the desktop, drinking red wine, and feeling calmer after my ordeal with my boss at the office this afternoon. Don't worry: I won't bore you with details. I'm listening to Cesaria Evora, PETITS PAYS, the cut "Tudo dia e dia,"

> "Every Day Is a New Day,"
> "*Vivé más devagar*
> *Ca bô tem pressa*
> *Esse mundo ê nôsso* ..."

(Live more easily
Don't be in such haste
This world is ours ...)

I could listen to Cesaria for hours at a time. In fact I have listened to her for hours on end.

I liked very much what you said about living in the imaginary. I also liked your sense of having lived several lives in one lifetime. For me, there are also so many "Been there, done thats." There's always this question of the saturation of experience. (I remember well the conversation we had about all this one afternoon at MICHAEL'S PUB at 55th and 3rd.)

This brings up two points as far as I'm concerned: These days I get bored very quickly with things around me. (This has gotten— slowly but progressively—worse since we were "together.") The other point is that, as you know, I relate completely to your sense of having lived several lives in one lifetime. For the past three years especially, I've lived really really intensely, and especially in the imaginary, for someone who's only thirty. I've been through zones of intense experiences, some of which were completely hellish. This is why I feel isolated and disconnected from the rest of the world these days.

You're lucky you have Shoshana to ground you at this point, to keep your life—which has been somewhat adrift—from drifting away completely. Lucky, or unlucky, who knows. One of the reasons I panicked and left Rick, apart from his drug problems, was that I was afraid of that kind of grounding. I was afraid of what seemed to me (at least at that point) as an end instead of a beginning. I was afraid of that kind of stability. I never told you the details of how I felt after I broke up with Rick, but I was a disaster. I lived almost completely in a metaphoric and delirious bubble.

Now back to having experienced several lives: I (throughout the past year that I've been living at your place—who knows how motivated this fact is or not?) have had the acute sensation that I have lived several lives, that I was moving back and forth between lives, revisiting all these previous lives. At certain points these revisitings became somewhat hallucinatory.

Some nights I had terrifying nightmares where I'd wake up completely covered in sweat, trembling all over. But I never really got scared. In fact, I experienced moments of ecstasy or rapture from time to time. I had an intense love affair with myself, even with the nightmares.

During these revisitings I also released some of my childhood terrors, and so there were moments when it seemed that I was physically transformed into Dorit-when-she-was-five. And so I would relive that psychological state of a child, of pure innocence and wonder, and when the terror came, I could manage it because I experienced it through adult eyes.

Now since I've read almost all of Freud and Lacan and Deleuze, I had some idea of what was going on, and so I kept my cool and let myself ride and experience these waves fully. I allowed myself to feel in a way I'd never felt before, and trusted that any particular state would soon be transformed into another state. And in fact I indulged myself by enjoying it all.

I disagree with you said about your life: You've accomplished so much. For me, I've lived far too much in the imaginary. All those zones of intensities were totally solipsistic.

Now, and especially this week, I feel quite acutely, in a way I've never felt before, my own biological clock ticking, literally, at night when I'm in bed. I'm not speaking metaphorically: Some nights I can actually hear the clock ticking from inside my body. Really scary. I'm thirty. I want kids. A woman's body is programmed to have kids, and so I want my cells to fulfill that program. I know I have time. But most of my close friends are married, believe it or not, and they have kids.

I went to see a show the other day that I think you'll like. It's something called HUMAN/NATURE at the Caren Golden Gallery in Chelsea, on West 26th Street between Tenth and Eleventh Avenues. The exhibition was organized around the old nature-culture binary. The show featured the works of thirteen artists, but only few really caught my eye. My favorite: Marguerite Kahrl's funny "Conversation With a Luddite" ensconces a little reproduction of your friend the Unabomber's Montana cabin in a papier-mâché tree, with an audio of a woman sprouting forth a confusing discourse about anti-modernist theories, much like Ophelia's fractured discourse of "botched thought" that others cut to fit into their own imagined coherent discourses. Roxy Paine had magical-realism cow pies from which psychedelic mushrooms sprout. Nina Katchadorian had her photographs also of mushrooms colored with rubber patches. And Austin Thomas also had photos of ordinary-looking stones with odd typewritten diaristic stories attached to each. I don't know what really made me think of this show now. Maybe because I was telling you earlier about the Luddites at THE NEW YORKER.

Anyway, I can't believe how much I just wrote.

I'm glad you're enjoying Paris but sorry to hear about your tensions with Francette. Be careful with her. Even though she seems to be wonderful and unusual, she sounds screwed up and deluded. You have to take care of yourself with these women. Remember what happened with Karyn. Remember what happened with Sarah. And remember what happened with Katya. I know you're ever the existentialist who needs to experience things first before you come to conclusions. You know well that I'm almost the exact opposite, that I come to conclusions first and then experience events the way I expected, and this might be the only difference between us. I know you too well, probably more than you know yourself. In fact, as I told you many times when we were involved, we two seem to have a Prussian mind-meld. And this scares me.

Now I better go.

Cesaria Evora is till on, so I want to close with her lyrics as I'm listening here. She's singing the cut "Doce Guerra" (Sweet War)

> "Bô qu'ê nha dor mas sublime
> Bô qu'ê uh'anguista nha piaxiao
> Nha vida nascé

Dum desafido di bô clima ingrato
ontade ferro pô na peito
Gosto pa luta pô na nhas braços
Bô qu'ê nha guerrs nha doce amor

Estende bôs braços
Bô tomá nha sangue
Bô regá bô tchom
Bô flori
Pá terra-longe
Bem cabá pas nôs
Bô cu mar céu e bôs fidgos
Num doce abraço di paz "

(You are my most sublime pain
You are my most anxiety and passion
I was born in a challenge to your arid climate
In my heart a will of iron
In my arms the love of fighting
You are my war my sweet love

Open your arms to me
Take my blood
Water your soil
And we make it bloom
So that exile
Comes to an end
With you, your sea, your sky
And your children
In a soft embrace of peace . . .)

*　　　*　　　*

I will engage Dorit's e-mail at some point. I suspect it signals a shift in the odd relationship that we've had since Karyn broke us up several years ago.

"I remember well the conversation we had about all this one afternoon at Micheal's Pub at 55th and 3rd." Dorit wrote in her e-mail, referring to the sense of living several lives in one lifetime. I remember this conversation well, as we were finishing off two bottles of fine French Amarrone between us at Michael's Pub on September 14, 1990.

New York: Friday, September 14, 1990

Dorit's and my romance was just two days old. We had made love for the first time the previous Wednesday. As planned that Friday, she had picked me up at the CBS Broadcast Center on West 57th Street, and then we walked to Michael's Pub to see Woody Allen play his clarinet, also as planned. We had arrived early so we could talk. We were talking about the saturation of experience.

Dorit, as she sipped her glass of Amarrone:

—Well, then. How about you? Do you cultivate joy? Do you like your life?

—I do for now. I have my moments. I can't really complain about my life, all things considered. I feel as though I've had many lives in one lifetime.

—Really?

—Yeah. I feel that I've accumulated a host of intensive experiences.

—As examples?

—I feel as if I've been everywhere and done everything in quality, value, and intensity. I mean, sometimes I feel that it doesn't matter where I am: Paris, New York, London, or Los Angeles. It would still be this café where I work on my laptop and read, or drink latte or wine, meet that woman.

—Meet that woman, eh?

—Well . . . It would still be this city where I go to that dinner or cocktail party fueled by nicotine and alcohol and engage in discourse about politics and culture. Lounge on this beach or browse this museum with well-known paintings and sculpture. Or sample fine cuisine in this restaurant during a four-hour layover in some airport on my way to that continent. Or run by that river or in that park.

—You've just executed a montage shot of a hip body moving through contemporary spaces and experiences.

—Well . . .

—This all reminds me of James Dean.

—*Giant! Rebel Without a Cause. East of Eden.* What of James Dean?

—He said quote Live fast, die young, and leave a beautiful corpse. End quote.

—Well put.

—I've forgotten that you're a runner.

—I haven't forgotten that you told me you've run seven marathons. All New York.

—Do you run marathons?

—Yes, yes, Ms Levin.

—How many under your belt, if I may ask?

—Around thirty, by my last count. Mostly New Yorks. A few Bostons.

—Holy Toledo! Can I ask your personal best?

—Yes you may ask. It's 2:23 and some change.

—Holy Toledo! I'm trying to break 2:50!

—Then you've done 2:50?

—Yeah. 2:50:49

—That's moving pretty fast. 6:30 pace.

—2:23. Let's see . . . that's about 5:28 per mile.

—Pretty good. You're a math genius to be able to figure that out that fast.

—Don't let me fool you. I have those tables that *Runners World* published that has your pace figured out from your times.

—Ah ah.

—Do you feel as if you've lived all your lifetimes then?

—I guess. There's a cartoon in a recent *New Yorker* that showed a middle-class couple in a restaurant looking at the menu. The man says to the woman somewhat annoyingly: Let's go. There's nothing here that we haven't had before.

—That's just saturation of life. Too much living. It's sad in a way.

—And then I think that one day might be a fine time to die. I'm always amazed to see what constitutes life for some people. You know, there's a TV commercial for one of those geriatric drinks that's supposed to keep death at bay. The tag line at the end of that commercial says something like: "This drink may not add years to your life. But it will add life to your years."

—I like that.

I poured myself another glass of Amarrone and gestured to Dorit:

—Can I fill your glass?

—By all means, please. The other day I read a list, in one of those glossy magazines, of the twenty things one must do in a lifetime.

—Do you remember any of those twenty things? I'm curious to see if I've done any of them.

—Sure I remember all the twenty things. I have a great memory.

—Well, then. Adumbrate.

—Let's see what each of us has done on that list.

—OK. Shoot.

—Number one: Visit the country your ancestors call home.

—Piece of cake on that one. I came to the US from the country of my ancestors. What about you?

—I'm not sure what they call home. Germany? Israel? In any case, it's yes to both.

—Two?

—Two: Leave a dollar where a kid will find it.

—I've done that one too. Two out of two ain't bad so far.

—So have I. Three: Fly over the Grand Canyon in a helicopter.

—Strike out on that one. I don't even know how to drive.

—Now I've done that! Four: Lend money to a friend without expecting it back. I've done that one too.

—I've definitely done that one many many times.

—Five: Have a suit made by a Saville Row tailor. I definitely haven't done *that* !

—Nor have I. I never wear suits, at least, not conventional ones. And British suits look odious to me. Even if, as someone once told me, Charles the Third invented the prototype of the suit as we know it.

—Did he really? Six: Ride in a gondola down the Grand Canal in Venice.

—Now I have done *that* . With a girlfriend when I was in college.

—Oh, wow, honey. That must have been really romantic. I've done that also. But with my mother.

—It sure was romantic. We did that at night. It was also fabulous: in the original sense: the stuff of fables. What's seven?

—Teach a class.

—Obviously I did that as a TA at Columbia. Quite boring. I hated standing in front of three hundred undergraduates and laying down the law.

—I was never a TA. Now you'll really impress me if you've done eight.

—I can't wait.

—See the sun rise over Machu Picchu.

—I've never done that.

—I have. My mother took me to Peru when I was a junior.

—Wow! I'm impressed!

—Nine: Plant a tree.

—I haven't done that.

—I have. In Connecticutt. Ten: Fly on the Concorde.

—Can I impress you? I've actually done that. Once, thanks to CBS. I flew on A British Airways Concorde from London to New York in all of three hours and some change. You get to relive the same day twice.

—That's one thing that I really like to do sometime.

—It's quite an experience, I can tell you that. You're so high up there that you can see the curvature of the earth.

—That must have been an experience. You were straddling the atmosphere.

—Yeah. I remember thinking: What if something extraordinary happens and we just drift into space?

—One of those *Airport* movies had a plot like that. The flight drifts into space and was rescued by NASA. Let's get to eleven: Stand on the Great Wall.

—Nope. I've been to Hong Kong, but never to mainland China. Have you?

—Never been. Neither to Hong Kong nor to China.

—What's number twelve?

—Make your own beer.

—I haven't done that either. I like beer though.

—I don't like beer and I've never made it. Thirteen: See an opera at La Scala in Milan.

—Now that's one experience that would definitely kill me. I hate operas. Nietzsche was right: Opera is the bastardization of the two art-forms of music and theater. I have been to Milan, however. Do you like operas?

—No. Now I know for sure you've done fourteen.

—I'm dying to hear it.

—Learn to speak French.

—Oh well, oui . . .

—Fifteen: Take a balloon ride over the Serengeti.

—Never been to Tanzania. You?

—Nope. Sixteen: Hang up on a lawyer.

—I've never done that. Have you?

—I've never hung up on any lawyer. Oh wait a minute. I once hung up on my brother. Once when I was really mad at him. In fact, when he won't let me check out his online girlfriend, the one who lives in New York.

—There you go.

—I'll be surprised if you *haven't* done seventeen: Kiss someone passionately in public.

—Most certainly. I've done that with *all* my partners.

—Now none of my partners like to do that.

—Including Rick?

—Including Rick. Now I'll really be surprised if you've done eighteen: Play the Old Course at St. Andrews.

—Dear God! Maybe in another life. Golf is not even a sport. And most certainly I've never been to Scotland.

—I've been to Edinburgh—the film festival. And most certainly I've never played golf. Nineteen: Shoot the rapids on the Snake River in Idaho.

—I've never even been to Idaho. Hemingway and militia country.

—I've passed through Idaho. Cour d'Alene to be specific.

—Oh no. That's where the Save the Aryan race people camp out.

—Well I didn't see any of them. Not that I was looking. It is pretty country, however. I know you haven't done number twenty: Drive the new BMW 7-series.

—Most certainly not, since I don't drive.

—You and Jack Kerouac are the only American males I know who don't drive.

—Kerouac! How ironic. The guy who wrote *On the Road* spent his life in the passenger seat.

—I know a lot of women who don't drive. They also grew up in New York, like you.

—Right. Oh now I know.

—Know what?

—Now I get it: That list must have been an ad for the BMW.

—You're really smart. What's the score? Who won?

—I wasn't keeping score. I don't care who won.

—I don't either.

And that was that at Michael's Pub that September evening in 1990.

"Remember what happened with Sarah," Dorit also wrote in

her e-mail. I remember all too well what happened with Sarah Guggenheim, the woman I was married to for two years, the woman who is the mother of my daughter, Shoshana.

I met Sarah in New York in 1992—February 14, 1992, to be specific, Valentine's Day—almost a year after Karyn and I split up, at an art-opening party for the exhibition of Jeff Koons's paintings that an artist friend had invited me to, at the Forum Gallery on Fifth Avenue and 57th Street.

Since 1992 is quite significant in my life—when I met the only woman I married, and since I'm a journalist whose areas are culture and politics, following is a chronicle of the significant events that happened that year.

*   *   *

1992:

In the former Yugoslav republic of Serbia, the bloodiest European conflict since World War II began when Serbia began a brutal campaign to annex parts of the republic of Bosnia and Herzegovina. (Ethnically divided Yugoslavia had already come apart at the seams: Slovenia, Croatia, Bosnia-Herzegovina, and Macedonia had already established their independence.) Bosnia was—and is still—a patchwork quilt of ethnic and religious groups: 41 percent Muslim; 31 percent Serb; and 17 percent Croat. In any case, the Serbs began subjecting Bosnia to "ethnic cleansing" by consigning civilians to a routine of rape, torture, and slow starvation in concentration camps, foreshadowing more brutal and ghastly events in Kosovo against ethnic Albanians in 1997-1998 that then provoked the NATO war with the Serbs in 1999.

In the former Soviet Union, civil war broke out within the former southern Caucasian republics of Georgia, Armenia, Azerbaijan, and Tajikstan.

In Somalia, George Bush sent troops to restore order among local warlords, and food supplies to a "nation" more or less in anarchy: the Western media had reported and displayed scenes of mass starvation and feuding warlords (between the Hawiye and Darod clans) hijacking incoming food supplies. The US escapade in Somalia hastened the latter's current state: no government, borders, or valid currency. Thousands of Somalians are now refugees in the US, most of them in Minneapolis. (A friend of mine who lives in Minneapolis but was born in Mogadishu told me recently that the largest Somalian population in the world outside Somalia lives in Minneapolis. He also said that one of his favorite hangouts in Minneapolis was the East African Restaurant on the West Bank [a neighborhood on the west bank of the Mississippi River], which, according to him "looks like Mogadishu"—the city that he came from nine thousand miles away.)

In the United Kingdom of Great Britain and Northern Ireland, Queen Elizabeth declared the year as an *annus horribilis* for the royal family, apparently because of: public attacks on the Queen's tax-exempt status; a catastrophic fire at Windsor Castle; and marital troubles between Prince Andrew and Sara Ferguson, Princess Anne and her husband, and Prince Charles and Diana. Updates on these three royal couples have been played out ad nauseam in mainstream and tabloid media to merit any repetition here.

In the US:

In Los Angeles, an all-white jury's acquittal of four white police officers in the apparently savage beating (captured on amateur videotape and widely played on all TV broadcast and cable networks) of African-American motorist Rodney King triggered a "civil unrest" that spread from mostly black south-central Los Angeles to other parts of the city, which involved other hyphenated Americans.

(In New York that Friday of the riot in LA, on a cab around 2 PM on 5th Avenue at midtown heading downtown for an appointment, when, unaware of the LA riot, I saw several midtown store-owners pulling down their shutters. These people are really early for their weekend leave-takings, I thought. The person I had the appointment with downtown then told me about the riot and also about the rumor that had seized New York that afternoon:

Macy's was on fire as well as other unspecified stores in Manhattan. The rumor led mothers to pick up their kids from school—and people to leave work—early. Of course most New Yorkers seemed to take everything in stride that day. I personally saw only a few traces in New York of the virus of the events in LA. Later on that day, in early evening, Sarah and I were on Bleecker Street, on our way to see a mutual friend who is a jazz singer perform at the Bitter End: on the sidewalk, broken glass from shattered storefronts and restaurant windows. After our friend's performance, Sarah and I ducked into the (then) Minetta Bar on MacDougal Street for drinks. The first thing we saw, to our amusement, was a couple passionately kissing on the bar stools, completely oblivious at that moment to the huge TV monitor in the background displaying an apparently anguished Rodney King saying: Why can't we all just get along?)

* * *

Now back to Sarah and me at the Forum Gallery on 57th and 5th. More specifically, we were introduced by our mutual artist friend (the same one who had invited me to the opening), literally—so inscribed is this meeting in my memory—as we stood by Koons's *Woman in Tub* (1988) that was on display. She was then an associate curator at the Dia Center for Contemporary Art on West 22nd Street, and also an artist in her own right: a talented collagist who mated painting and sculpture by means of idioms common to both. The Museum of Modern Art at that time had acquired two of her pieces for its permanent collection.

Sarah and I became an item almost immediately after that opening. Her appearance made a deep impression on me that night at the gallery on West 57th Street: Frizzy-jet-black shoulder-length hair, olive skin, high-cheek bones, highly attractive intense and energetic face, average height, lean tight-muscled body packed in black clothes and boots, and definitely semitic-looking. Look: We all have our types when it comes to being attracted to partners. I might as well profess mine: all the attributes I've just assigned Sarah, plus those attributes that Francette—during our discussion in an earlier entry—adumbrated from my first novel, *In the White City* : She must be from the Northeast corridor; Francophone; into high theory; and connected somehow to the art world. Now why each of these attributes? And why this particular combination? I'll be honest: I have no explanation. I could try to explain, maybe flirt a little bit with psychoanalysis, but what's the point?

I want to confine the narration of my relationship and marriage to Sarah to only one entry, which will consist of: our important trips together—first to Algeria, which was the foundation of our relationship, and second, to Venice for our honeymoon; the party in Minneapolis that Mimi Roth, the director of the Walker Art Center, had at her house by Lake of the Isles to welcome Sarah to the Walker and to Minneapolis, the party where I was privy to some interesting—bordering on comical—art conversations; three crucial exchanges that we had in mid-January 1997, during the last week of the marriage; and two humiliating events that I experienced within six months after my divorce.

My four-and-a-half-year relationship (which included our two-year marriage) with Sarah—from 1992 to 1997—was intense and tumultuous in all respects. With her I experienced the space "between dog and wolf," to cite a French expression. "Between dog and wolf" means dusk, the hour that every being becomes its own shadow, and thus becomes other than itself. Dusk is the hour of transition from day to night, the hour of metamorphoses, when people anticipate with half fear and half hope that a dog will (not) become a wolf. So that living with Sarah for me was always living in that liminal unfamiliar space where I was never sure whether— or not—the dog would be transformed into a wolf. In other words, I could never tell with her what was coming next. I suppose at first I found all that exciting and erotic. But then: At some point it became a senseless marriage to me. Reflecting on all this now, I realize that the only redeeming and wonderful product of this marriage was our daughter Shoshana.

*   *   *

16

Paris: Friday, July 9, 1999

Sarah grew up as a Jewish Brahmin in New York, born and raised in a six-bedroom apartment on Park Avenue on the Upper East Side. She's distantly related to the famous Guggenheim clan of the art world. And in fact, she benefitted, I thought, from that affiliation, since she functioned fully in that world as well. People typically assumed she was a close relation, and she never denied it. At a small wedding ceremony that her mother had organized, she and I got married on September 17, 1994, in the same apartment where she grew up, a little over two years after we met at the Forum Gallery.

Since I got married to Sarah in 1994, I wish to chronicle the one significant event that happened that year.

*　　*　　*

In 1994, Los Angeles police announced that O.J. Simpson, football celebrity, movie actor, and telegenic corporate pitchman, was a suspect in the twin brutal murders of Nicole Brown Simpson, his white ex-wife, and Ronald Goldman, her friend. Nicole Brown Simpson and Ron Goldman had been found awash in their own blood outside her townhouse in the affluent Brentwood section of Los Angeles, just after midnight. On the day the police set out to arrest him, Simpson took flight in his white bronco with his longtime pal Al Cowlings, and thousands turned out on freeway overpasses to cheer him (with chants of "Go OJ, go go!" as if he were on a homerun for the Buffalo Bills, his team when he was still active) as he led a phalanx of police cruisers on a bizarre live network-and-CNN-televised low-speed highway chase. Eventually, he surrendered to the police, followed by the long process of trying him in criminal court. The trial unfolded for a whole sensational year—by the hour—on CNN and Court TV and occasionally on other networks. Briefly, the highly complex chronicle touched on more or less all the issues plaguing America at the end of the twentieth century: racism; classism; careerism; sexism; obsession with the legal system; sports superstardom; domestic violence; and media-saturated situations. Just about every American had an opinion about the volatile case, but response to the verdict (the jury—mostly African-American women—found him not guilty on all counts, although I personally think he was guilty, given all the media files I read) a year later pointed out the bitter racial divide in America. Most white feminists especially had their race consciousness put to the test. (One of them, a friend I had known for some ten years, astonishingly—and ironically—told me that she "will never trust a black man again" [!].) The media significantly became extremely obsessed with the case and chronicle: a trauma that could only be repeated again and again, occupying as it did, the deep structure of the nexus of race and gender in the American psyche.

                    *   *   *

In 1994 I was working for CBS as a writer-researcher for "60 Minutes," assigned to Ed Bradley's staff, the only prominent African-American male in the media in the early 90s.

The first two years of the relationship Sarah and I traveled extensively, within domestic US and overseas, to Europe (France, England), to the Caribbean (Guadeloupe, Martinique), to South America (Brazil, Peru), and to Africa (Morocco, Algeria, Nigeria, and Kenya). On some of these travels, Sarah joined me whenever her schedule allowed when I was on assignment for CBS. When we were in New York, we lived the yuppie life, surrounded by our equally yuppie friends. In 1993 Sarah moved into my two-bedroom coop apartment on East 3rd Street, the same apartment where Dorit and I made intensely passionate love for the first time after we saw *Hiroshima Mon Amour.*

So then, the narration of the trip to Algeria that grounded our relationship romantically:

Paris: Friday, October 15, 1993

Sarah and I took the eight-hour train ride from Gare de Lyon in Paris to Marseilles, before we got on the boat-ferry to Algiers. It was my first time in Marseilles. We had a three-hour layover there. We walked around the Vieux-Port, the old section of the city, and had bouillabaisse at a restaurant that a friend of ours had recommended. Then we got on the ferry (called *Tipasa* after an Algerian town on the coast, the one Albert Camus had written about in a lyrical essay called "Nuptials at Tipasa") and settled into a twin cabin—a high Japanese-style partition separated the two cabins for two couples. That night, the couple (an Algerian man and a French woman, it seemed to me) in the other cabin kept us awake with their lovemaking, as the woman's ululatings mixed with the sound of the Mediterranean outside the potholes.

At some point Sarah said:

—Those two are it again. They're sex maniacs. Her vagina must be in shreds by now. Imagine getting fucked like that.

—I think they're butt-fucking on this round. She's simply too loud for the conventional stuff.

—Damn. Maybe *we* should fuck to counter all that.

—I really don't feel like it.

—Okay, okay. I might go out for a walk on the deck. You wanna come?

—Good idea.

So we went onto the deck. After about an hour on the deck, I decided to go to the bathroom but found no toilet paper. I got hold of one of the boat's officers (who looked Algerian to me) and told him there was no toilet paper. He laughed and said in French: —Use your hands and water. It's better.

Then I remembered the Muslim practice, groaned, and made a note to myself to warn Sarah for the surprise. I went to the bathroom. When we eventually got back to our cabin, the other couple were still at it. We managed to drift off to sleep. And they sounded still at it when we woke up in the morning.

The next day, we picked up Spanish-language TV stations as *Tipasa* went by the islands of Majorca and Minorca. Then we got to Algiers. Even before we landed, we could see the Atlas Mountains behind the city. I couldn't help thinking and musing about the first sailors who first crossed the Mediterranean to North Africa, about what they must have thought when they saw those mountains.

We got to Algiers and the first week stayed at the Casbah with friends. The Casbah made a deep impression on me, with its near-narcotic smell of spicy couscous combined with that of piss, and the loud Muslim calls to prayer at dawn that blasted through the exterior speakers attached to houses. I was somewhat disoriented around the city.

In the Algiers we saw in 1993, the women's bodies were covered with cloth, their faces with the *chador*, and they were not at the bars with men, but at home with their kerosene lamps and oilcloths and meager furniture: which precisely described the modest house in the Casbah we stayed in. At dusk, scores of Algerians gathered near the quays (to which they had no access unless they had tickets) and gazed at the Mediterranean in the direction of France.

The following week we went to Blida, a small town south of Algiers, at the edge of the desert, with our friends and we all stayed at the house of their relatives. We spent a lot of time in the desert, especially at night. At the end of the week, we passed through

Algiers, went directly to the quays, and got on *Tipasa* to sail back to Marseilles.

Throughout the trip we ate a lot of couscous and lamb, and drank extremely strong Algerian red wine.

That was our foundational trip to Algeria. The rough times we experienced glued us together, I thought, for the next three years.

Then, the honeymoon trip to Venice after our wedding.

Venice: September 24-October 7, 1994

Sarah and I went to Venice for our honeymoon. This honeymoon trip was our wedding present from Sarah's parents: the fare, a generous stipend to cover myriad expenses, and the two-week stay in the empty villa of a business partner of my new father in-law. We spent most of the time at various cafés at Piazza San Marco, decompressing from the intensity of the wedding events. We also spent some time cruising the canals on gondolas, and some nights, sitting on the porch of that villa at the edge of Europe, I dreamt of Istanbul on the other side of the Adriatic.

I remember well that Sarah and I made love all night our second night in Venice, animated, perhaps, by the Chianti we had consumed at the dinner we had earlier that evening with the two American women (from New York in fact) we had met that morning. I also remember well that all four of us talked at dinner about Venice and decay, about death and desire, and about making the most of the gift of time on earth.

After two weeks in Venice, we rented a car and drove to Rome, where we took the flight back to New York's JFK.

Throughout that trip, we consumed a lot of pasta and Chianti.

About a year after our wedding, on September 22, 1995 to be exact, Sarah and I moved to Minneapolis. We sold our cooperative apartment in New York and bought a urban-type townhouse in Minneapolis, on Milwaukee Avenue in the Seward neighborhood. We bought this three-bedroom house with straight cash from the killing we made on the East Village apartment on East 3rd Street, which we sold for three times the amount I paid for it in the late

80s because of the considerable gentrification the neighborhood had gone through since then, especially since the real-estate market was quite low the time I bought it.

In any case, we moved to Minneapolis because Sarah had an offer she couldn't refuse: to be the chief curator at the Walker Art Center. Mimi Roth, the director of the Center, made Sarah the offer sometime in July. Mimi, also a New York Jewish Brahmin, had known Sarah from the New York art scene of the 80s, when Mimi was director of 20th-century painting at the Museum of Modern Art. (Mimi in fact was the one who acquired two of Sarah's pieces for MOMA's permanent collection.) I could afford to move to Minneapolis and still work for CBS because I mostly worked online, even at the time. The only condition my boss (a woman who reported directly to Ed Bradley; more about her below) imposed on me was to be in New York one day a week to attend to production matters. (By the way, that was when I began to rapidly accumulate the countless frequent-flyer miles I have banked with Northwest Airlines.)

For about six months before Shoshana was born, Sarah and I continued the yuppie life we led in New York—in Minneapolis, also with our equally yuppie friends, a few of whom were New York transplants like us. Our New York transplant friends in Minneapolis had something in common: They either had kids, had just had them, or were planning to have them. There was no way they were going to raise these kids in the big bad gritty city. The friends developed an allergy to New York City when they were living there, and they did not want to expose their kids to this allergy. They (and some of them willfully downsized their careers) wanted to move to a mid-size American city where everyday transactions were civil and hassle-free, where, as a transplanted New Yorker pointed out to a reporter in a *Newsweek* cover story on these kinds of cities, "you could be downtown one minute, and after driving in a car on a freeway for ten minutes you could be in the countryside, fishing in a pristine lake." They wanted to move to a city (preferably one that had a symphony orchestra, a reputable museum, one or two art-house cinemas, and a night club attuned to "cultural diversity") where they could afford a house, preferably a big three-or four-bedroom house in a "nice" neighborhood, where they might even afford to pay straight cash (from the two-bedroom coop they might have sold in Manhattan perhaps) for the house without having to take out a mortgage. They wanted to move to a city with a "good" public school system, so that they could send their kids there instead of shelling out 15 thou a year for each kid for a private school in Manhattan.

In fact, Minnesota by that time had gained a reputation as a halfway-house recovery haven for the walking wounded of all sorts and substances (it had acquired the moniker "Minne-sober), either megalopolis-fatigue-syndrome refugees (like our friends) from the Northeast corridor, specifically, from the island of Manhattan, or refugees from failed marriages or careers, or refugees who needed to recover from any number of psychic and-or physical ailments. Minnesota's reputation was confirmed in an article that the *New York Times* ran in its magazine section one Sunday in 1993.

As for Sarah and I, we settled into our urban-type townhouse in the Seward Community, on historic-landmark Milwaukee Avenue. This community baffled real-estate agents because homeowners are highly educated but have low incomes: These homeowners were a mixture of countercultural professors, drop-out grad students, community activists, old and retro hippies, artists, freelance writers and designers, and mostly Somali and Ethiopian immigrants. Sarah and I fit right in.

I remember well the party—in October 1995—that Mimi threw at her house for Sarah when we first moved into Minneapolis. She had invited the whole art world of Minneapolis to that party, it seemed to me. Before that party she and I had met in New York only a few times but had never spent any time alone together. Mimi was an outspoken and highly energetic woman. That night she told me how she saw and ran the Walker.

Mimi told me at some point that she was not interested in "art that sits on its ass" (obviously quoting Claes Oldenburg) and that her plan was to open up the Walker to a number of issues in the community instead of having "the same five thousand (mostly white) rich culture-vultures perennially coming in and out of the revolving doors of the Walker."

Minneapolis: Saturday, October 22, 1995

The party at Mimi's that night was not that remarkable in itself, although my close friends Coco Fusco and Guillermo Gómez-Peña—who were visiting the Walker from New York when the party was held—entertained us with witty aperçus of their experiences from their performance pieces throughout the US, South America, Europe, and Australia when they were commemorating what they called "The Year of the White Bear": their moniker for 1992.

———————

In 1992, Coco Fusco (of Cuban heritage) and Guillermo Gomez-Peña (of Mexican heritage), performance artists who lived in Brooklyn (Fort Greene to be precise) at the time, were in Minneapolis as guest-artists at the Walker Art Center. They had been invited to participate in the celebration of the opening of the new sculpture garden at the Walker with their ongoing "cage" performance marking the 1992 "counter-quincentennial" of the "Discovery of America" by Christopher Columbus (Cristóbal Colón) five hundred years earlier—and to supervise the installation of their exhibit "The Year of the White Bear" in one of the Center's galleries.

———————

The party guests that night at Mimi's were asking Coco and Guillermo about what they did in 1992. Coco and Guillermo took turns answering the questions:

—What do you think of Christopher Columbus?

Coco:
—You mean the first illegal alien in America?
—Who does Queen Isabella remind you of?

Guillermo:

—Margaret Thatcher, of course.

—Who are you guys anyway? Are you with the Walker Art Center, that bastion of high, elegant, and decent art?

Coco:

—No. We're artists. I'm a multi-culti art semiotician from Nueva York, and he's a post-Mexican performance artist who lives with me.

—What do you think of NAFTA?

—What else? Free salsa and free tequila, of course.

—What was it like when you first saw white people?

—Oh, it was so nice! They gave me free mirrors, which empowered me to participate in the new global economy.

—Now come on, you two, don't you think it's about time you junk all that anger?

—You mean that we should forget about history altogether?

—Look, we're all the same these days, you know, if you really think about it. With the new global capital and media, we all consume and love the same things: art, food, information, technology, clothes, the environment, and sex.

—Look, and then you listen: we need to confront our complex history first of all if we all want to live in a truly multicultural society.

—Yes, but that was then and this is now.

—Quite dead wrong. In 1995, even as we speak, the state machine in Washington and the capital machine in New York are both using the same tactics as the Spanish Inquisition in 1492. Don't you know this? Or don't you even have enough brains to figure that out?

And then, once again, that night at the house on the edge of Lake of the Isles, I was subjected to the kind of art-talk that was typical of—and ones that I learned to get used to during my tenure with Sarah in Minneapolis—not only the parties at Mimi's house but also almost all the art parties.

Some of the art-conversations were erudite, and some bordered on the inane, in my opinion. As examples:

—So tell me a little bit about your city-graffiti series. You had described them as, like, anemic. What exactly did you mean by that?

—Anemic was a reference to Duchamp's anemic cinema. I was probably thinking of a failed chronicle, a fault line between the architecture of display and the information displayed.

—Architecture by nature is, like, static and immobile. So that your work, by injecting itself within this setting, acts as a disruption.

—Definitely.

—How has your concept of anemic display been transformed in the context of your recent projects in Europe and South America?

—My new projects are more surgical than those early bus shelters.

—Like, how so?

—They have touched more directly on the social implications of the sites in which they were situated. Looking back on this importation from an American to a European context, it was probably more natural that my work would tighten up.

—What do you think the role of the artist is in an urban setting? How has living in New York affected the nature of your work?

—New York is simply where I always come back to recuperate. I travel a lot working on projects, which means I spend a lot of time on planes, so it really doesn't matter where I live anymore. All these cities are more or less alike anyway, in my opinion.

—Oh yeah? How's that?

—London, Paris, Berlin, New York, San Francisco, even Santiago: They're all starting to look the same to me. There's always a boho section where everyone wears black, boots and all.

—Hm. Like at this party. Like you and me. The art uniform.

—Every one consumes the same music, movies, and books— including the same cuisine and drinks in the same sidewalk cafés. The conversations in art and literary circuits sound the same.

—Like also at this party, even though we're in the upper midwest. This town also has a boho section where everyone, or least almost everyone, wears black and drinks latte. It's called uptown, where I live.

—And Citibanks and ATMs are everywhere. Even a small town in the south of Chile has an ATM.

—Right. People say you don't even need travelers checks anymore for domestic and international travel. Just carry your cash card.

—Exactly. And you certainly get the best foreign exchange rates when you use your ATM card. You get the stock market rate for local currency, no bank commissions. See, technology makes capital work for you.

—Amazing. Have capital will travel. Maybe it's capital that makes technology work for you.

—They work for each other.

—Like Janus, the monster with two heads.

—You can even read the *New York Times* and watch CNN and *Star Trek Next Generation* in any of these places.

—Interesting point. I've been to most of these cities, and I guess I know what you mean.

—Virilio said it: It doesn't really matter where our bodies are anymore. Our bodies simply emit or zap signs wherever they are.

And another:

—Let's talk about public art within public spaces.

—I really don't know what a public space is. And I don't know exactly what public art is. After all, isn't all art personal exploration?

—Yes, but the meaning of art is experienced by the viewer, not the artist.

—Well, as far as I'm concerned, one essential question is: Is art for the self? For the educated few? For all people all the time? Another essential question: primarily, should the art fit the space of its display, or should the space of display fit the art?

—I know your work has been about testing what public space and public art are all about. So what do you *really* think public space is?

—A place that's accessible without effort, like Loring Park. But I really hate the way public art has been bought into by institutions like the Walker.

—Public art has been institutionalized even from its origins. But don't let Mimi hear that.

—I really think the last thing these institutions want is art, especially pubic art, to be brutally honest. Mimi's fantasy notwithstanding.

—Did I just hear that? *Pubic* art? Ah, sexist too. You're not being a good guest. You're at her house, for Christ's sake.

—You mean I'm not being a good house nigger. Fuck her. She won't even display my work. None of her curators are interested in my stuff.

—Shh. Now come on, don't be a naughty boy tonight. There are some important white Twin Cities people here tonight. Mimi is expecting some big money from these people—to keep her dream projects alive.

And another:

—I have taken my work to serious potential venues and was rejected by all. It's so frustrating. I'm just not good at marketing myself.

—I'm not good at marketing myself either. And yet I never have any problem getting my work displayed.

—What are you trying to tell me?

—Nothing. Just the facts, m'am.

—I once walked into a gallery in Soho to see their stuff. The guy at
the desk yelled at me that they've stopped taking on any new
artists for an indefinite time to come, that their stable was
quite full.

—Did you tell him you were an artist?

—No. But maybe he just smelled something or didn't like the
way I looked. But I just wanted to see what they had.

—What kind of stuff do you do?

—Cows.

—*Cows*?

—Animals in rural spaces. My work really moves people, people
who are not art-sophisticated. People seem to see their own
memories in my work all the time. I like to think I paint psychic events.

—Art is just decoration, m'am. Either the art-piece works as that
or it doesn't. Most of the time people buy art just to fill the
wall space in their homes.

—Speak for yourself. I disagree. I also disagree with Cézanne when he
says that art creates order out of chaos. On the contrary, good art
creates chaos out of order, and that moves people. That kind of
art unleashes in the viewer emotions of which he or she is unaware. That piece of art creates a bit of a quake in their lives. It
moves them in directions they never even imagined. Isn't it of
interest, for instance, that people whose homes were destroyed
by a volcano or quake always rebuild in the same spot?

And so on. Look: A decent, feel-good, risk-free, Disneyland
multicultural time was had by all at the party at Mimi's house
that night. At those kinds of parties in Minneapolis, I learned that
it was easier on my lean system *not* to mix with people I didn't
know, and to mix with people I already knew, like for instance the
few artists and writers and academics I had met before in New
York, and with some art demimonde people whom Sarah
superficially courted and cultivated to legitimize to herself and
others her self-constructed semi-bohemian origins in New York.

*   *   *

During the six months before Shoshana arrived, when I was in Minneapolis and not at some other US city or overseas on assignment, we spent a lot of time eating egg ramekin or piperade basquiase for breakfast at places like Sobas on Lyndale and 26th Street, or gyro sandwiches for lunch at the Trieste Café at the Lumber Exchange Building downtown at First Avenue and 5th Street, or having squid and *empanadas* for dinner at Machu Picchu's at 29th and Lyndale Avenue. We also spent considerable time in the Loring Park area (for Sarah conveniently close to the Walker Art Center), at the Loring Café with our friend Jason McLean—who owned that weekend pickup joint—and at the rooftop terrace of Joe's Garage, a restaurant that had several imported beers that I sampled.

We listened to the sweet Woloff lyrics of Baaba Maal and the voodoo rhythms of the Haitian thumpers, Boukman Eksperyans, at First Avenue downtown on 7th Street and First Avenue. We sipped wine around 5 PM at Gallery 8 at the Walker Art Center by ourselves to catch up on intensely personal matters. We spent several exuberant hours sipping more imported and locally brewed beers with dear yuppie-friends at the Bryant-Lake Bowl on West Lake Street.

After Shoshana arrived on a bright spring dawn on March 22, 1996, I continued to travel as usual. My daughter was certainly the "light of my life," to resort to a worn-out cliché. I would have liked to have cut back on my travels, but I couldn't. Sarah and I began to develop two separate lives from that point on. She soon had her own circle of friends in Minneapolis, and I had mine in Minneapolis and also in New York. But we continued to share the friends we had in New York when we lived there together as a couple. Then one night in January 1997, Sarah dropped the other shoe.

Minneapolis: Monday, January 13, 1997

On that snowy Monday night in January 1997, on Martin Luther King Day, a few hours after I got back from a four-day weekend conference in Toronto, and after we put Shoshana to bed, Sarah said to me, as I was watching Brian Williams read the news on MSNBC and sipping merlot:

—We need to talk.

—Can this wait till tomorrow?

—No it can't. It has to be tonight.

—It's that urgent?

—It's that urgent. And, like, pretty serious.

—Is it about Shoshana? Work? Your parents?

—Neither.

—I'm all ears.

—I've been seeing someone.

—Holy fuck! That explains things. You've certainly been emotionally distant the past couple of months. I thought maybe you were just going through one of your periodic retreats.

—No, not at all.

—It's that serious? Jesus, Sarah. We have a nine-month-old daughter..

—Whom I'm raising alone while you jet around the world partying with friends.

—Is that what this is all about? My traveling too much?

—Yes. I've felt so lonely and abandoned while you've been living what you like to call your quote unquote nomadic life.

—Traveling is integral to my job, Sarah. You've always known that from Day One. It's damn if you do and damn if you don't.

—Yes, I've always known that. But things are different now. We have a child. People change. I certainly did.

—But your job doesn't involve the kind of traveling I have to do.

—Yeah, like the traveling you did to Paris for two weeks to spend time with Emilie Deleuze instead of staying here with me and Shoshana?

—Oh come on, Sarah. I had to go to Paris on business and took the opportunity to grieve with her for our loss.

—Emilie had to grieve for the loss of her father. Gilles Deleuze was *her* father, not yours.

—Gilles Deleuze was my mentor. You went to grad school. You should know how strong those relationships can be. It seems to me that you're trying to devalue the one I had with him.

—I'm not trying to do that. But you should have gotten over it sooner, moved on sooner. Did you have to go to Paris for two weeks last October, one year after he jumped out the window, to grieve with his daughter, whom you had a thing for anyway? How did you think I felt about that? Did you ever stop to think how I felt about that?

—I had to go to Paris for a project. It was an occasion for me to see Emilie.

—What project was that again?

—The one about Gorée Island. All those records I had to check at the Bibliothèque nationale.

—Bullshit. You could have done all of what you had to do online, from here. What do you think I am, stupid? Puleeze! Give me a break! That trip to Paris was nothing more than a love-fool's errand. Let me ask you something about that while we're at it.

—Sure. Go ahead. Ask me.

—Why have you spent all these years dancing around Emilie? Getting together in Paris, dining together. And all the furtive e-mails to each other when you're in the US. Why haven't you done me a favor and spared me all that pain?

—What pain? What favor?

—Why haven't you just fucked her? Or have you done even that already?

—As I've told you ad nauseam, we're just close friends.

—Bullshit. You never stop talking about her. It's Emilie this and Emilie that.

—Let's not argue about this. I don't want to talk about it.

—Okay don't. I was just curious. Right now it's a lot of water under the bridge.

—So you resent my traveling. You especially resent those weeks I spent in Paris. But you never brought it up until now.

—I guess I didn't see the point then. As for professional travel: I could be spending a lot of time in Europe shopping for art for the Walker. But I'm not. I made special arrangements with Mimi instead. In fact, she does the traveling for me.

—Well, I don't have that option. How long have you been seeing this guy?

—Two months.

—Are you fucking him?

—Yeah I'm definitely fucking him.

—Oh Jesus! Anyone I know?

—I doubt it. His name is Ken, and he just moved here from New York.

—Is he an artist?

—Yeah. He's a sculptor.

—I should have guessed. Are you in love with him?

—Hell no. It's purely physical—for now.

—For now? I see.

—Yeah for now. Who knows? It might develop into something else.

—What do you want to do?

—I don't know. What do *you* want to do?

—I have to think about it. Sweet Jesus, Sarah! This is bad.

—I guess you can say that. Although I don't know.

—What are doing to me? Damn it, Sarah!

—I'm sorry. But lower your voice. I don't want you to wake up Shoshana.

—I should have seen this coming. Any fool would have seen this coming. I'm devastated. How many people know about this?

—Just Jacques. I told him yesterday.

—You told *him* before you told me?

—I had to tell someone.

—It had to be *him* ? This will be all over the goddamn academic community in a week!. Our friend doesn't do drugs, he does information. He needs to know, and he needs to know that people know what he knows.

—I'm sorry.

—Damn it! Someone should throw a blanket over me. This is so humiliating.

—Just which part is humiliating? The fact that I'm fucking somebody else besides you or the fact that Jacques knows about it?

—Both. How can you do this to me—with Shoshana?

—I'm really sorry. But really, is that what all this is to you? What I'm doing to *you*? What about what you've been doing to *me*?

—Let's not get into any of that right now. What do you think I should do?

—I really don't know. It's up to you. This might just be a phase I need to get through. I doubt it. But I don't know.

—I don't know either. Jesus, this hurts. But I'm thinking about Shoshana.

—Shoshana is important, I know. But you also need to think about yourself. We can't just stay together because of her.

—Is it splitsville for us then?

—You know when you're about to take off on a plane, when the flight attendants are going through the safety instructions?

—Yeah? What are trying to tell me?

—They tell you to put your own oxygen mask on first before helping anybody else with theirs. I need to breathe.

—*You* always think about yourself. I ask you again: You want to split up?

—I don't know. I really don't know.

—Goddamn it. I need to sleep on this one.

—Fine. I just wanted to get it off my chest tonight. I'm really confused. I'm not really sure whether I'm still in love with you or not.

That was the first crucial exchange. The second happened two nights later.

Minneapolis: Wednesday, January 15, 1997

Sarah to me, again when I was watching Brian Williams and sipping merlot, and again after we had put Shoshana to bed:

—We need to talk.

—About Ken?

—Yeah.

—I should have guessed.

—I have a proposal for you.

—Just what is it this time? What's next? I've already been humiliated enough. Almost everyone I know here and probably in New York must be talking about you and Ken fucking each other all around Minneapolis. I feel like Emma Bovary's husband.

—Whoever might be talking about us must be busy bodies who don't have anything better to do. And what's this Emma Bovary shit? I'm not a housewife in Yonville dreaming of Monsieur Léon and Paris and distant places and adventures while sitting by the living-room window. I'm an artist and the chief curator at the Walker.

—Look, let's not make things more difficult than they already are. What's this proposal that you said you had?

—I don't want to end the marriage because of Ken. But I also want to continue seeing him.

—Come again? Am I hearing you correctly?

—Yeah. I want to stay in the marriage with you. But I also want to continue to fuck Ken.

—Does my name spell moron, m-o-r-o-n?

—You tell me, does it?

—This is really incredible. I can't believe what I'm hearing.

—I'm saying I want to continue to fuck you and Ken.

—Are you serious? Has moving to Minnesota does something to your brain?

—You tell me.

—Look Sarah: Are you out of your fucking mind? What have you been smoking?

—You tell me.

—There's no way I'll be part of a triangle. Has this Ken-fuck dick-
   head turned you on to some stuff? This is incredible. What
   the fuck is going on? You're gonna share this guy's erection
   with mine? Are you nuts?
—No I'm not. In third-world cultures, men have several wives.
   Why can't a woman have more than one husband?
—This is the fucking US of A.
—Jacques said one of his women friends in California is doing the
   same thing. And she's American.
—What same thing?
—She has two husbands. They all live in Berkeley.
—Is that right?
—Yeah that's right.
—So you want to practice polyandry?
—Yeah.
—And you think this will be good for Shoshana?
—Welcome to postcontemporary times, as you would put it. Kids
   grow up these days under stranger circumstances.
—Jacques gave you *this* idea? Since when did this guy start run-
   ning my life?
—No one's running your life. You run your own life.
—Let me tell you something: No triangles. And fuck this third-
   world bullshit.
—You sleep on it. Now let me tell *you* something. I will continue
   to see and fuck Ken, no matter what you do.
—You can't be serious.
—Oh yes I am.
—This is simply incredible. I can't believe this is happening. You're
   really fucking me over, Sarah.

Reflecting on all this now, here in Francette's apartment in
Paris two years later, I'm not really that surprised by Sarah's moves
in January 1997. She called all the shots, even up to our third
crucial exchange two days after our second. It seems that at that
point I had lost complete authorial control of my own life (I became,

in a sense, "The Fourth Stooge"), and, understandably, felt completely degraded.

On to the third exchange on Friday, two days after the second.

Minneapolis: Friday, January 17, 1997

Sarah to me, again under the same conditions—Shoshana in bed, Brian Williams, the glass of merlot:

Ken and I have decided to live together. So I want a divorce.

—Fine. I've been giving this a lot of thought myself.

—I'm sorry.

—I need to be put out of my fucking misery. It's been the wintry week from hell. How should we go about it? Do you have a lawyer?

—Not yet. I'll get one. But I don't want a legal battle.

—I don't want one either.

—We should have joint custody of Shoshana. I want you to be very much part of her life. She's biracial after all. She needs her father.

—That's good.

—You can have the house. Can you buy me out?

—No, I can't. And if I could I won't. I'll just move back to New York. There's absolutely no reason for me to stay here if we split up.

—Not even for Shoshana's sake?

—It's too fucking complicated. I'll be a separate parent in Minneapolis? And my job is in New York?

—Haven't you always told people you could live anywhere and do your job?

—Well . . .

—Shoshana would certainly miss her daddy if you go back to New York. Although, on second thought, maybe it won't make that much difference, since you were hardly ever around in Minneapolis with us anyway.

—How can you be so fucking cold about all this? You've just pulled the rug out from under me and Shoshana. I've been royally fucked over, and it really burns me up.

—I'm so sorry . . .

—How the fuck did I let myself get to this point?

—You tell me.

—Why did we ever get married?

—That question has also been on my mind lately.

—Did we get married to get divorced?

—I don't think anyone gets married to get divorced.

—Why then did we have a kid together?

—We both wanted one We both love kids.

—Heterosexual marriage and divorce? Who fucking invented this?

—You can write about it.

—Fuck you!

—I'm truly sorry. I'm just trying to be rational under the circumstances. Things are, like, bizarre enough as it is.

—You can say that again. You're being rational? What a fucking joke! Let's talk about the nitty-gritty of *the* divorce.

Look, I'll be quite brief: The divorce was not contested. We went through mediation and what is commonly—and stupidly in my opinion—called "an amicable divorce." We both agreed on joint legal and physical custody of Shoshana, although Sarah has been the sole physical custodian by default, since indeed I did move back to New York six months after the divorce. During that time, I rented a two-bedroom apartment in Minneapolis instead of moving back to New York right away. (The reason for this delay will become clear when I narrate one of the two humiliating events I mentioned earlier.) I have always had access to Shoshana anytime I've wanted to, and I've made efforts to see her at least once a month, and during summers when I am in fact in New York, Shoshana sometimes has been there with me for two weeks at a stretch, even when I have been at Al and May's in Park Slope. When I was in Missoula, I took advantage of Northwest's cybersavers to see Shoshana in Minneapolis as a frequently as I could.

But now I want to narrate these two humiliating events.

When I was at CBS, I had the misfortune to have Devorah

Smith as my immediate supervisor. She was a putative "marxist" white feminist who liked me more than I liked her. One immediate problem with this was that she interpreted any professional disagreement I had with her as a form of betrayal. Before and during the time I was married to Sarah, Devorah made several suggestive comments to me about a possible physical involvement (see samples below). After my divorce, Devorah stepped up the pressure. Of course I was in no shape to be sexually involved with anyone at that time, and even if I were I was never attracted to Devorah because she was in no way my "type." She was a Goyem white woman—and from my standpoint, even worse: an Anglophile— who grew up in Westfield, New Jersey, went to Middlebury College in Vermont, and got into journalism after that. With only a BA in Russian, she went up the corporate ranks quickly at CBS, as she told me at some point, "sleeping her way to the top." Within three years at CBS she became one of the associate producers of "60 Minutes," reporting directly to Ed Bradley. She was also an only child who desperately wanted to be liked by everyone but she never succeeded in that objective. She could be crass and crude: for one, whenever we alone together at various bars and restaurants in Manhattan, ostensibly discussing "60-Minutes" projects over countless glasses of wine, she had the habit of scratching her crotch, sometimes quite vigorously. Three samples of some of our conversations follow:

*   *   *

Devorah (D): What is going on with you?

I: I've been so tense this past week. You might have noticed.

D: I certainly have. I've been so concerned about you.

I: I know.

D: Do you need a back rub?

I: Oh no, thanks.

D: I'm known for my back rubs. Are you sure you don't want to take advantage of me?

*   *   *

D: What will you drink? My treat.

I: Merlot.

D: I should have known. How was your day?

I: Very productive. I think I'm about to nail that interview with Pat Moynihan.

D: Fantastic. Listen: If you nail that we'll have to celebrate. When will you hear from him?

I: He said he'll call me around ten tomorrow morning.

D: If he says yes you should come to the apartment on Saturday for dinner. Do you have plans?

I: I might. I'll have to check my book.

D: Richard will be away. I'll be disappointed if you don't come.

*   *   *

D: How are you today?

I: Not so great. I didn't sleep much last night. I dreamt a lot.

D: Sorry to hear that. Did you dream about me?

I: No.

D: You know, I really like you. Do you know that?

I: I've noticed.

D: I'm definitely attracted to blacks.

I: Really, some kind of fetish, then?.

D: I know you're into psychoanalysis, but that's not it at all.

*   *   *

In any event, things came to a head one Friday afternoon in New York at the CBS Broadcast Center on West 57th Street—March 15, 1997 to be precise—when she yelled at me to get of her office. The following Monday, instead of flying back to Minneapolis as I usually did, I stayed in New York an extra day and filed a sexual harassment complaint against her with the New York Equal Rights Commission.

The local media jumped on this development of events. During those post-OJ times, a sexual harassment case—within the media industry itself—by an African-American male against his boss, a white woman, definitely made for great news bytes. The *New York Times* and the *Village Voice* ran pieces. WABC (Channel 7) and WNBC (Channel 4), the local CBS and NBC stations respectively, did "spots" on it during their Eyewitness Evening News. I got calls from several print and electronic reporters that I had to refer to my lawyer—a Jewish woman. The upshot of this state of affairs was that CBS bought out the rest of my contract and fired Devorah. I put half the amount from this settlement in a trust fund for Shoshana, and used the rest first to rent a two-bedroom apartment in Minneapolis, and then later when I moved back to New York that summer, to buy my current two-bedroom coop on West 57th Street that Dorit is subletting. To escape all the media publicity, I decided to hole up in Minneapolis instead of heading back right away to New York in the wake of my divorce and the event with Devorah Smith. I started writing my first novel, *In the White City*, during this period. I fell into depression, and all I could do was write. I also began to see a therapist because I could do nothing else but write. My therapist referred me to a psychiatrist, who prescribed Zoloft for me. I spent a lot of time online, communicating with friends and relatives all over the world. Not that surprisingly, Sarah more or less implied that the business with Devorah—who had been shamelessly courting her friendship when we were in New York—was probably complex, and that in fact I might have been implicated as well: Sarah never said that I fabricated the whole story with Devorah, but that the question of "what happened" in a sexual situation is always highly complicated affair. In other words, she "doubted" my version of events.

I also spent considerable time with Shoshana. But most of the time when I was alone, I felt paralyzed. I spent days on end in bed, listening to the BBC World Service. (In fact, my therapist told me that BBC was my lifeline during this period, that even when I was in bed I was still traveling around the globe, thanks to reports from BBC correspondents at far-flung places like Djakarta and Tierra del Fuego.) I felt "normal" when Shoshana was with me, but I fell back into my "surreal" bubble when I was alone. Dorit called me from New York everyday to ask how I was doing, sometimes talking to me on the phone for three hours. I also had cash-flow problems, since I paid my rent in advance for the six months I stayed in Minneapolis after the divorce with the cash that wasn't tied up from the CBS settlement. Now on to the second humiliating event.

I was extremely cash-strapped especially around May 1997. I had no food in the refrigerator. Within a week I had eaten all the ramen noodles that I had in storage within a week. Desperate, one day, I called Sarah and told her I was hungry and broke: Could she share some of her groceries with me? She responded: "Go to a food shelf. There's one near you." A week after this, as we were discussing a change of schedule apropos Shoshana, she said to me: "I'm always returning your serves." Late that summer, in New York in my new apartment, as I was watching the US Open Tennis Championship on TV, as I was wont to do every year, I suddenly had an epiphany about the entire metaphorics of Sarah's remark about serves. You return a serve to your opponent, whom you're in competition with on the court while playing tennis. Your opponent is your competitor. From Sarah's perspective, I was her opponent and competitor throughout our relationship. She was competing with me all the time. This epiphany further deepened my depressive grieving.

In August 1997, through the help of my union, the Writers Guild, I signed my contract with MSNBC-NBC. In September 1997, I pulled up stakes in Minneapolis and flew back to New York, after closing on my two-bedroom coop apartment on West 57th Street.

Now I have accumulated enough knowledge about myself so far to recognize and realize what my relationship and marriage to

Sarah was all about. The relationship was stillborn: We never had a chance. Sarah was not only a rebound from Karyn, as Dorit said: Sarah was more than a rebound, which, as Dorit also said, was bound, as it were, to fail.

Sitting here in Paris in 1999, I realize that I was attracted Sarah from day one because, in a sense, she represented art to me: not only because she was an artist as well as a curator, combining, as it were, both theory and practice, but also because the name Guggenheim was a cultural signifier for twentieth-century modern art. Also, her work articulated a certain critical aesthetics to me, one that she was able to animate and mobilize in her work.

I realize all this now because I also know that there is currently no foundation that grounds knowledge, so that everything is more or less adrift and anarchic, and that some people I know, including myself, are looking to aesthetics to work out the next foundation. Now, certain epochs have a privileged mode of expression: in the classical epoch it was mythology; in the medieval, theology; and now, at the end of the Second Millennium, it may be aesthetics. In other words, the community style of the fin-de-millennium might well be aesthetic.

So that, in a sense, I think my attraction to Sarah was more or less a deep yearning for that foundation of knowledge that had been lost in the drift of human history, from its Nilo-Saharan origins, through its Judeo-Christian phase, to the Middle Ages and the Renaissance, down to these postcontemporary times.

So it was not really fair to either of us that we got together because I did it in bad faith, because all through the relationship Sarah represented critical aesthetics to me, and so I simply caught fugitive concrete glimpses of her-in-her-body in the metaphoric fog-paradigm of an epistemological foundation. So, to quote Kafka, "there was hope but not for us." Hope was never our business for the whole time we were together.

The liminal space between dog and wolf that I mentioned earlier, in which our relationship unfolded, makes sense: Since Sarah was a metaphoric paradigm to me, I never knew who she really was in her body. I never knew what she was all about concretely, and so all my experiences with her unfolded in an equally metaphoric and unstable space between dog and wolf. I know all this now at the edge of the millennium, sitting here in Paris in Francette's apartment. And to repeat: Shoshana—whose eyes when she was born opened a bright morning on my life—is the only positive production of the relationship and marriage Sarah and I had, the wonderful combination of our respective DNAs. Since our divorce, I've struggled to confine my exchanges with Sarah to the business-like coordination of our schedules relating to my access to Shoshana.

My profuse apologies for this lengthy digression about Sarah, but I wanted to dispense with this period of my life in the mid-90s—what seemed to be a bizarre but understandable aberration—so that I can get on with the main elements of my research at the moment, which seem to cluster around Katya and Jacques and Missoula, and Francette and Paris.

"Remember what happened with Karyn," Dorit wrote in her e-mail. If I ever get to an appropriate point later on in these entries, I promise to narrate what I need to remember about Karyn Ross.

"Remember what happened with Katya," Dorit also wrote. Now I need to get back to Missoula and Katya, and to more film-texts mobilizing desire.

*   *   *

17

Paris: Saturday, July 10, 1999

Missoula: Wednesday, August 26, 1998

That Wednesday evening, around 6:30 PM, Jacques and I were sitting in his living room chatting after dinner. Christine had also dined with us but had left to run an errand, and it wasn't clear whether she was coming back. Jacques and Christine had had a rapprochement after their fight the previous Sunday. Jacques was telling me about the dinner that he had planned for the following Saturday, whom he was inviting, whom he wasn't. He was inviting Katya of course, and her neighbor, a German woman who was also a colleague, but not anyone else in the department. He then seguéd into his usual rant about his colleagues in his department. Just at that point the phone rang. He picked it up.

—It's Katya for you.

He gave me the cordless receiver.

I:

—Katya, what's up?

—I feel like doing something with you tonight. Have you had dinner yet?

—Jacques and I just finished dinner.

—Oh that's too bad. I was going to invite you to Shadow's Keep. It's a great night, and the view from up there is bound to be lovely.

—You can still invite me up there anyway. You can have dinner, and I can work on an appetizer and some merlot.

—That sounds wonderful. And then after dinner I was also going to invite you to see the new *Psycho* with me.

She meant the new remake of Alfred Hitchcock's masterpiece by Gus Van Sant that was then playing at the Wilma Theater downtown.

—OK, you're on. You want to pick me up?

—I'll pick you up right now. Ten-fifteen minutes.

Jacques, after I hung up the phone:

—What's up? You and Katya are going somewhere?

—Yeah. We're going to Shadow's Keep and then we'll go see *Psycho*.

—Really? Shadow's Keep? She must be loaded. That's an expensive restaurant. Like all the restaurants in this stupid town, the food isn't that good, but the view is great up there if you sit outside.

—Yeah I know. Are you forgetting that you told me that last week when you and Christine had dinner there and I couldn't go with you guys because I already had dinner plans with Bryan and Dee?

—No I haven't forgotten. So you and Katya have been spending some time together lately.

—So we have. We're getting to be friends, that's all.

—That's what you think. She's looking for a boyfriend.

—She already has a boyfriend.

—Glen?

—Yeah, Glen.

—She told me she's going to dump him. He's too young. She said their relationship quote unquote doesn't have a future.

—She told me the exact same thing, using those same words.

—I know she's looking. And you seem to be the candidate.

—I doubt it. I'm not really that attracted to her romantically. She sort of intrigues me through. She's from the other side of the diaspora. She's the first Russian-Jewish woman I've met.

—I see. If you want my advice: Stick with Bryn instead. Bryn is young and bright. A fresh young thing. An artist ready to be fucked and molded.

—You're starting to repeat yourself, Jacques. That's a bad sign.

—I say go with Bryn instead of Katya, who's divorced with a
    daughter.

—Bryn isn't interested in fucking me. She told me so herself.

—And you believe her? You're so fucking naive.

—Look, let's not get into that again tonight, OK?

—OK, OK. Katya can only be trouble. Don't say I didn't warn you.

—Look, we're friends. Nothing more. Incidentally, did you talk to
    Katya recently about Frenchmen and Algerians?

—Frenchmen and Algerians? I don't know what you're talking about.
    Why would I be talking to her about Frenchmen and Algerians?

—Maybe you were giving her a colonial history lesson.

Katya showed up in her Subaru. The front door was open but we
could see her through the screen door. She came right inside without
ringing the door bell. She said hello to Jacques, then to me:

—Are you set to go?

Jacques, to both of us, but it seemed more to Katya:

—Can I come along? I want to see *Psycho* also.

Katya:

—No Jacques. There's something I want to talk to him about alone.
    Why don't you go see it with Christine?

—She and I have been fighting. I'd rather see it with you guys.

—Well, you can't.

—OK, then. Have fun you two. I have work to do anyway. I have
    to finish my paper for the conference next Tuesday.

Jacques again, to me:

—Have you finished writing yours yet?

—No.

—Will it be written by then? I'm counting on your contribution.

—It's almost a week away. I have bits and pieces of it in my hard
    drive, as I told you.
Katya to me, somewhat impatiently:
—Come on. Let's go.

I then noticed for the first time that she was all dressed up.
She was wearing a long black dress, with the top lowly cut to
reveal the upper cusp of her breasts. She wore a black lipstick and
two huge gold hoops—bigger than mine—on her ears. Her high-
heeled shoes made her look taller than five-five. And she had her
sunglasses on. For the first time since I met her, she impressed me as
somone who could easily fit into the boho art-world of New York.

We had dinner at Shadow's Keep in South Hills, outside on
the terrace overlooking the golf-course and most of South Missoula.
I had three-four glasses of merlot and some chicken wings, and
Katya had steak and rice—also with two glasses of merlot—after down-
ing two shots of vodka for an apcritif. We then drove to Wilma on
North Higgins by the Clark-Fork River to see Gus Van Sant's *Psycho.*

I'm not sure exactly why Gus Van Sant *really* made the film,
which completely matched Hitchcock's shot by shot, with some
interesting—and curious—variations. (He had said in interviews
that he made the film as a homage to Hitchcock.) The remake is in
color, for one. And before Norman Bates (Hitchcock's Anthony
Perkins, Van Sant's Vince Vaughn) commits his two murders, he
has hallucinations, which were not in Hitchcock's. Gus Van Sant
also has Marion Crane's sister, Lila Crane (Hitchcock's Vera Miles,
Van Sant's Julianne Moore), as a lesbian. And then the most curious difference of all: Before stabbing the Marion Crane (Hitchcock's
Janet Leigh, Van Sant's Anne Heche) in the shower, Bates watched—
through a basement window—Marion undressing in her motel
room, and masturbated in the process. Now, I've read enough psychoanalysis to know that this scene in Van Sant's version is egre-
gious vis-à-vis Hitchcock's signifying matrix. If Norman Bates can
masturbate to Marion Crane's denudement, then he wouldn't
need—or have—to fatally stab her while she's taking a shower.

If he can masturbate, then he would be a mere neurotic and not the psychotic that Hitchcock clearly meant him to be.

Now, during the crucial—and ghastly—shower scene (which Hitchcock said contained forty-seven film shots in his classic!), Katya buried her head in my chest, and at that point I had my arms around her. I made that gesture reflexively, but Katya's own gesture was definitely calculated. She told me months later that she also knew I would put my arms around her after she buried her head in my chest.

(Lest I forget: that was also the night Katya told me Bryn was a retard, the exchange that I narrated in Entry 6: New York: Saturday, June 26, 1999.)

On the subject of a woman with calculations, I have to get back to Francette in Paris at this point.

* * *

18

Paris: Saturday, July 10, 1999

Yesterday afternoon, around 8 PM, I met Francette's gay, lesbian, bisexual, and transsexual friends at Café de Flore. Francette and I got there late, so ten people were already sitting around a huge table when we arrived, sipping wine or beer and eating crêpes. Francette apologized and introduced me to everyone, with names all of us knew I'd never remember right away. I felt somewhat awkward. I sat down and ordered red wine. Francette sat down also, but next to a woman, whose name I can't now recall, and to whom she started talking immediately. Everyone continued the discussion that our arrival had interrupted. Francette seemed to have no trouble joining the discussion, as the topic, which I also cannot now recall, must have been familiar to her. From time to time Francette caught my eye and smiled at me. I felt left out and abandoned. At some point I got up and went to the bathroom. Then I sat at another table. Francette was the only one who registered my move. I ordered another glass of red wine and dinner, as I was getting hungry. I then opened my laptop to review some essays I was working on. An hour later Francette came over. She said, in English:

—What's going on?
—Nothing. I felt like an appendage, so I decided to come here and do a little bit of work. You guys don't need me around.

—Oh come on. You're just pissed because you're feeling ignored.
   You have to make an effort to join the conversation. So you
   have enough money to order wine and dinner? You told me
   you were broke.
—I have a little. I'm broke, but I can still eat something.
—I see.
—Listen, I'll split soon. You can stay as long you want. But I'll
   leave in another thirty minutes.
—OK, then. You do whatever you want.

She then went back to sit with her friends at the big table. I took
   the Métro—direction Porte de Clignancourt—from St-
   Germain-des-Prés to Gare du Nord. Then I walked south on
   Boulevard Denain and got back to 7 rue Fénelon at 10:15
   PM. Michel was not around, as usual. I watched TV for maybe
   two hours and drank a whole bottle of Côtes du Rhone from
   Francette's well-stocked collection. I opened another bottle of
   Côtes du Rhone. I then booted Francette's desktop machine,
   logged on to My Yahoo, and responded to Dorit's posting
   while drinking half of the newly opened bottle of wine. I must
   have been online for at least an hour writing to her, since I
   went to bed right after I logged off at 1:40 AM. Francette
   never came home.

*   *   *

19

Paris: Saturday, July 10, 1999

I woke up at around 10:00 AM with a headache, went about my ritual ablutions, had continental breakfast, and booted Francette's machine to find Dorit's response to my posting last night, a 10K e-mail. Her OneBox mail date read: Sat, 10 July 1999 09:33:35—0500 (EDT). Since New York's time-zone is six hours behind Paris's (the -0500 [EDT] indicated Eastern Daylight Time [EDT] minus six hours Greenwich Mean Time [GMT], which is always the standard reference for the time of all e-postings: Paris time-zone is one hour ahead of GMT), the OneBox date indicated that she composed her mail right after she read my own posting. Before I proceed with my narrative of Francette and Katya, I again reproduce Dorit's e-mail below in its entirety, because at this point I want to engage what appears to be a shift in my relationship with her.

*   *   *

Dorit's e-mail:

Yo! That was quite a tome you posted to me. Really, I'm quite moved by everything you said. Are you all right? I hope you are. I'm genuinely worried about you but I also know that you're strong.

I think you should come back to New York right away after this conference instead of staying another week as you had planned. But I'm sure you'll want to be in Paris for Quatorze Juillet. I can actually see you on July 14 sipping a few kirs at CAFE DU L'INDUSTRIE near the Bastille itself. When you get back I promise I'll treat you to fine French cuisine for dinner. I'll to take you to LA CARAVELLE, on 55th and 5th, a French restaurant of the old school that's just a few blocks from here, and that I've been frequenting lately. The food there is to die for. I can have the poularde Marat (stuffed boneless chicken), and you the boeuf à la mode de la rue de Valois (beef stew with vegetables), since you love beef and I love chicken.

Or maybe we should instead go to HELL'S KITCHEN, which my mother took me to the other day. It's a nuevo-fangled "multicultural" cantina on Ninth Avenue and 47th Street: a gritty quaint café that's a colorful and candle-lit oasis in the neighborhood surrounding it. When you look at that neighborhood through the café's floor-to-ceiling windows, the cabs and the motley crowd outside play like a distant movie. It's hip in there, and so's the food. The chef's crunchy chayote-and-portobello-mushroom roll in chipotle sauce is to die for. As is the ancho-marinated shrimp with coconut rice that seems imported from Thailand. Of course you can't have that since you're allergic to shrimp.

You have to decide which one of these restaurants you're in the mood for. and then I'll treat you.

I got up this morning with a headache and read your posting. I was out last night late with some friends, including my close friend Jenny Feder, who owns and runs Three Lives Bookstore on Waverly and 10th. I'm sure you've met her a few times. We went to two spots: one uptown, the other downtown. First, we went to SYMPHONY SPACE at Broadway and 95th to listen to Abdelli, the Berber mandola player and singer. Do you know him? He's Algerian-born and now lives in exile in Belgium, and was making his New York debut last night. His music blends South American influences and traditional North African instrumentation to produce hypnotic rhythms and rich exotic textures, a perfect blend for me. I have his CD, something called "New Moon," that I'll play for you when you get back. If you've never listened to him before, I'm sure you'll like him.

The second place we went to after SYMPHONY SPACE was

MOOMBA, a nightclub on Seventh Avenue South and 10th Street, where multiracial hipsters hang out. We took a very crowded Number 1 train all the way down from Broadway and 96th to Christopher Street-Sheridan Square. Going there was not my idea but I ended up having a gas. I was exposed for the first time to that cheesiest of art-forms, karaoke. The karaoke session was MC'ed by a tomboyish woman who told me "Get them drunk enough, and anybody will sing." When we entered, two buxom blondes were leading the crowd in a cheer of "Get Laid."

We even espied some celebrities there: Lisa Ling, TV talk-show personality; media-proclaimed "celebrity" Taye Diggs; actors Liev Schrieber (Jon Favreau's buddy in SWINGERS) and James Van Der Beek; and models Yasmine Bleeth and Christy Turlington. I said hi to Christy. She also went to NYU where she majored in comparative religion and philosophy. Did you know that? A model with some brains. Do you think I look like her? My cousin Barbara Stein (you've met her: She's the cultural attaché at the US Embassy in Rome, remember dinner at ODEON sometime late 1990?) thinks Christy and I look alike.

At MOOMBA we witnessed ample evidence of disposable income: One guy to my left put out his cigarette in my drink and offered to buy me two more. Toward the end we listened to a soulful version of "New York, New York." It was 4 AM when I finally got back here.

I have a headache, as I said, but I'm responding to you right away before I head off for my long run this morning in the park. I'm running twenty-four miles with my friend Carol Tisch, who is an associate producer at CBS, and whom I'm sure you've heard me talk about before. I just got off the phone with her. In another five-ten minutes she'll head out the door of her apartment on East 83rd Street between York and First Avenues, and jog her way through the streets of the Upper East Side to pick me up here, and then we'll head into the park. That gives me enough time to write · and dispatch this. Carol (who was also with us last night) and I hope the long run will sweat off the alcohol, which we all indulged in copious amounts.

You wanted to know about Rick, about why I really broke up with him, aside from his drug problems. My radar tells me that what you want me to tell you about all that is important to you.

Before I begin, I want to tell you about an object lesson I'm sure you already know: Any human relationship defies (cartesian) logic, and therefore one should never second-guess what makes a relationship "work" and what doesn't; the way a relationship looks from the outside, and even from the inside, is not at all what it *seems* or *is* , either through the efforts of the members of the couple themselves or through whatever other people who know them (again because of their own investments or insecurities) might wish to see or project into that relationship; any relationship, no matter how (seemingly) harmonious, contains seeds of farce and tragedy; and as long as we are alive *anything* is possible. So here goes.

Let me begin by saying this: Rick's drug situation was just part of the problem: Things are more complicated than that, as always. I'll try to tell you all this in a way you can understand.

I rejected Rick's body. One day, all of a sudden, I just didn't— and couldn't—feel sexual feelings toward him anymore. Everything about sleeping with him horrified me. And right after we broke up, men's bodies repulsed me, especially those that betrayed signs of aging, reminding me of my own.

Now I never told you this: Three weeks after the split-up, I suddenly had the craving for the bodies of younger men in their early twenties. I had intense serial sex with five men, each for one-week duration. They all had tall lean beautiful hairless bodies. Of course they were lean: They were all fast marathoners, yuppie-wannabe-Frank-Shorters I had picked up in the park. You know how easy that is for me, given that men are easily attracted to me. A couple were alpha-males, not really my type for a long-term relationship.

One of them was a stockbroker who tried to impress me with his killings in the market, and who definitely impressed me as someone who thought with the head of his dick. Another was a dot-com guy whose start-up had just gone IPO and was telling me about his windfall. Another was a corporate lawyer bent on telling me the megadeals he'd put together. And yet another was an aspirant writer of fiction who was a trust-fund baby and had been "working on a novel" for seven years. He told me that his "day job" during those seven years consisted of putting his plastic bank card into ATM machines. The fifth guy was also in the tech industry: magnetic media. He manufactured "magnetic media," as he put it. Do you know what magnetic media is? I didn't, and so I asked him. Magnetic media is simply the industry term for tapes and disks of all kinds: audio, video, floppies and zip disks. Magnetic because that's the element in all those media that enables data storage. I wanted to tell them all—but didn't—that I wasn't impressed in the least with any of that, that I just wanted to fuck them, that their bodies were simply sexual hardware to my psychic software. Now here I hope you don't think I'm providing you with more information than you need: All five of them were really great fucks in their own ways.

I hope you don't find this crass, and that I'm not alienating you. I hope I'm not. I really want to be up front with you right now. I'm just being honest, letting everything out, having a clear slate with you.

This frenzied period lasted for five weeks. Then I reverted to my previous state of revulsion, which has ameriolated somewhat considerably over the years. I've had flings here and there that never amounted to anything. One guy accused me of "mindfucking" him. I supposed he was right. Then I simply stopped going out with men all together. I didn't want to hurt men any more.

But my problem with physical intimacy lingers just a little bit. Sometimes I really believe that it is my life itself that is fucked in general (as distinct from the specific fucks I might have had with men), and I have trouble seeing myself with a partner again. I mean, you might not suspect this, but I'm more likely to pick up

the first edition of the Sunday *New York Times* at 10 PM on Saturday
night instead of heading out to THE KNITTING FACTORY to
listen to Marc Ribot y Los Cubanos Postizos (my current favorite
performers). In other words, I prefer, as Nietzsche said, *actio in
distans.* OK, OK, last night was an exception. I figured I better get
out, otherwise I'd go crazy, especially in light of the week I had.

Which brings me to my next item: the silent transaction of
desire that occurred this past week between two apartment
occupants (yours truly and a guy) on the respective twenty-eight
floors of the two highrises on West 57th Street across the Ninth
Avenue divide. Again, I hope you don't think I'm getting weird on
you. You know how my—I'm sorry, your—entire living room is
completely within binocular distance of the living room of the
apartment across Ninth Avenue. You also know that I had set up
my desktop machine right by the living room window, so that
when I'm working I'm completely visible to whoever is in the living
room of the apartment across the street, assuming he (or she) has a
pair of binoculars or a telescope.

In any event, Monday and Tuesday nights, I worked from
midnight till 3 AM, and I suspected that someone was watching
me from the living room across Eight Avenue those two nights. In
fact I saw the curtains there move a few times. Well, for the rest of
the weeknights this past week, I worked on my desktop machine
during those same hours (midnight till 3 AM) wearing only my
underpants, and nothing else, on purpose. I hoped that the guy
was jerking off, turned on by a semi-nude nubile woman tapping
on the computer keyboard. In a perverse way, I suppose he got
turned on by watching me sexually phase into my Windows-
platform machine. In a sense, I transformed my keyboard into
someone's (I'll die first before I tell you whose) penis, or, depending
on my psychic frame, into an extension of my clitoris. That's crass,
and I'm sorry. But I'll bet you're not shocked. I've read your stuff,
and I know you have this thing about the erotic (and spiritual)
possibilities of new technologies.

I should tell you what happened to me last November while

you were in Hong Kong. I met an older guy. He told me he was fifty-two. And he looked fifty-two. He's a successful famous writer: I will not disclose his identity to you at this point. We spent a wonderful two weeks together in New York (he lives in New York). He was great. I thought: Finally, here's someone who can take care of me. But then things got really nasty when we took a trip out of town to visit some of his friends.

Oops, my intercom is buzzing. Carol must be here. I've got to go. More to come. I promise I will finish telling you about this guy

this afternoon, while I recover from four loops around the park. In fact, I want to finish telling you about this guy. I don't want to leave you hanging like this. But I gotta run—literally.

If I know you, you'll read this mail I'm about to click your way—in the morning in Paris—probably right after you get out of bed. Unless, of course, Francette has already complicated—and altered—your lifestyle considerably. Who knows? Anything can happen in this world. You're fond of telling me that "as long as we're alive, anything is possible." I'm not going to tell you what I'm thinking about you right now. It scares the living daylights out of me. In fact I my never tell you.

I hope your lifestyle hasn't changed, and that you're reading this in the morning in Paris while sipping a café crème in Francette's apartment, without her looking over your shoulder. More to come later.

Love.

*   *   *

20

Paris: Saturday, July 10, 1999

In all fairness, before I engage Dorit's two e-mails to me in Paris so far, I should reproduce below my own posting to her last night before I went to bed, the one I composed while I was drinking one and half bottles of red wine—the one she responded to that you just read. I click on Folders to the left of My Yahoo Mail, then click the Send box to pull up my posting. I'm surprised by its huge size: 18K.

*　　*　　*

My e-mail:

Yo Dorit! How could our flesh be composed of suns that might burn us through the various days and nights of our lives, perhaps blazing the royal road to the unknown, to the other scenes in the sand written by desire that could be decoded perhaps only with a Rosetta Stone?

Does desire not transform the body into an overheated factory where the human face explodes and organs burst from every pore? Does desire not always scramble frontier limitations? Does desire not introduce a wave of shit into a complacent socius? We spend the days and nights of our lives trying to figure out what we want to do with our lives, and then one day or night we die. So that when in one of those days or nights, one of us recognizes a moment condensed with desire, should one not speculated on—and exploit—it like gold? I mean, was anyone born Hamlet?

Dorit, I had a shitty experience tonight with Francette's gay-lesbian-bisexual friends. She wanted me to meet them, so she introduced me to them at CAFE DE FLORE. They completely ignored me. Francette was so insensitive about it. I got really pissed and came home by myself. I'm going through another bottle of expensive Côtes du Rhone from Francette's collection as I'm writing this. I already finished a whole bottle earlier while watching TV.

I feel shitty all over. And I'm in a strange mood. Dorit, I feel as if I want to die. I know how easy it is to die, either psychically or physically. After Sarah and I split up I wanted to die. My body simply shut down, and for almost nine months my life became a long Ingmar Bergman film. I'm not the suicidal type, as far as I know. My parent's Yoruba heritage militates against that.

No matter how depressed I was or how hard I tried, I could never bring myself to hate this life. But I thought, that if that desire seized me at certain moments then it could happen to anyone. Dorit, may you (or anyone you love) never walk where the road waits, famished. You see, I will tell you what I've never told you before: After Sarah and I split up (which, by the way, was *her* idea, not mine), I became simultaneously a spectator and a participant in my own life: It was as if I was living someone else's life, not mine. Because you see, my identity, the one that was tied up in the relationship with Sarah, had dissolved in Minneapolis, and the one that was at that point emerging after I got back to New York, was as yet unknown, even with the new job I had with MSNBC. My psyche went completely south those months: concretely and metaphorically.

In fact, you remember that in January 1998, consciously riding the two metaphors of "going south" into "the unknown," I risked a concrete voyage into the unknown, my first trip to the southern hemisphere: I went to Chile for three weeks to visit Ethan, who was there for a year on a Fulbright. He had invited me down there to come and see him as a way of cheering me up. We spent some time in Santiago, where he was based, but we took trips to Viña de

Mar, Isla Negras, Valdivia, and all the way down to Punta Arenas and Patagonia.

I've already told you about this trip in detail in face-time, but really the only point I want to make here is how closely that trip mirrored my psyche: in the southern hemisphere, just like the antipodean seasons (winter in the north; summer in the south), the familiar constellations were reversed, and even the water flowed the wrong way (counter-clockwise) when flushed down the toilet. I flew back from the tip of the Andes Mountains (from the trip of a lifetime) and crashed into the valley of the Hudson River.

Anyway, Dorit, back to Paris: I saw a film in New York at the Film Forum before I came to Paris: something I also saw in New York when it first came out: *Leaving Las Vegas*, (which you might have also seen) in which Nicolas Cage plays a script-reader in Los Angeles who, before the narrative time of the film, had just lost his wife, and then when the narrative opens, loses his job, and then after that, decides to drive from Los Angeles to Las Vegas, where, as he had planned to do, he more or less drank himself to death, in spite of the vague promise of being redeemed by a prostitute-with-gold-heart Elisabeth Shue.

It's a movie, I know, but scary nonetheless. Because you see, the film followed the logic of its narrative to its bitter end (absolutely no Hollywood upbeat ending), to the point of sobriety, pardon the inappropriate (for the film) but unavoidable (for my own narrative) metaphor. Really scary, also, because John O'Brien, who wrote the novel the movie was adapted from, also committed suicide very shortly after writing the novel.

But then Dorit, I guess some of us survive, and some of us do not, and the will to live or die has little to do with intelligence or with how many books we've read: No amount of theory will save us from the abyss. I've never heard a résumé read aloud at the three funerals I've attended. I went to my father's funeral in Lagos, Nigeria, in 1987, for instance, and no one read his résumé aloud in a very hot sun in that land of sad oranges.

Dorit: I know I'm flitting about here: But let me tell you

something: I think a lot of people will freak out in the year 2000; the people who are already on the edge, on the fringe of the millennium, will definitely go over the edge. Your aunt might already have told you about this, since she lives in Jerusalem, but just the other day, I read *The Jerusalem Post* online about the "Jerusalem Syndrome," which afflicts religious fanatics, who are then subsequently seized with the urge to go to Jerusalem to observe the "Second Coming" of Christ at the point of Ascension on Mount of Olives. Dreading a deluge of tourists into Jerusalem, Israeli authorities are already screening visitors for traces of this affliction.

And some of my sources tell me the authorities are also bracing themselves for the mass suicide of a considerable number of the afflicted, who might well be extremely disappointed when (and not even if) Christ doesn't show up. The proprietor of the modest-looking Mount of Olives Hotel, raised as a Muslim in Detroit, and who described himself as a "material pragmatist," sent multiple faxes to several churches around the world telling parishioners about the great view from his hotel of the Church of Ascension on Mount of Olives, so that pilgrims can personally witness the "Second Coming."

If possible, Dorit, I wish to be Rip Van Winkle and sleep through the year 2000 and wake up in 2001; I wish to skip "the end of the millennium" all together. I really don't want to be around for the party.

Again, Dorit, I'm definitely in a strange mood. And tonight, here in Paris, getting drunk on Francette's exquisite Côtes du Rhone, I feel compelled to multiply memories, texts, bodies, and desires in the myriad narrative spaces of my life, all of which, for me, represent the forces of rebirth, and most of which, for me, as far as I know, are not merely mirror-figures from my imaginary.

Because Dorit: What really does a person see and feel and experience that can then be recollected and narrated from memory? Are we talking about other bodies and objects or just so many self-reflections from our encounters and experiences? And can we ever traverse the limits of our bodies and perceptions? What really is the link between body and language?

It's interesting, isn't it, for instance, that an organism that begins its life as a bundle of nerves and instincts, can, through the play of genes, be transformed into a machine of language and reflection.

First the bodies, then the texts. Cyberflight to my worldwide web of filiations, spanning far-flung time-zones. It's now almost 1 AM, Paris Time, Saturday early morning. This translates into 7:05 AM. Saturday morning in Hong Kong. According to My Yahoo weather, online, it will be 75 degrees Fahrenheit there today— well tomorrow. My friend Eva Man Pang is probably online at the moment, and perhaps has been for about two-three hours. She's married to another friend Michael, a Hong Kong urban architect with whom I'm collaborating on that screenplay I told you about.

Eva likes to get online as soon as she gets up to read newspapers around the world and to check and to respond (or not) to her e-messages before she heads off to a story location or to the newsroom at the *South China Morning Post*, where she's a reporter and features writer responsible for the cultural beat. (She also works on Saturdays. As you know too well, in the media there is no distinction between weekdays and weekends.)

I remember once sending her an e-mail from New York around this time (which would translate to 6 PM Friday evening New York time) and getting her response within minutes. It's 9:05 AM. in Tokyo, also Saturday morning. 65 Fahrenheit. My brother and his wife, Nigiste, are probably at home. In Santiago, 6:05 PM, Friday evening. My Yahoo says it reached 74 F there Friday, pleasant and dry. If I remember Clarice's routine well (assuming she's even in Chile at the moment; she might be in Bulgaria with her long-term partner with whom she has a commuter relationship, and with whom and where I can't even presume to guess her routine). She might be anywhere at this time. But I know that around midnight when she's in Santiago she usually heads out with friends to a café in Plaza Nuñoa or on avenida O'Higgins to inaugurate the evening's events, which might extend till 3 or 4:30 AM.

So there: alone in my body, here in Paris, I can invoke a small sample of my worldwide cyber-community.

But let me ask you this, Dorit: Are we all condemned to live alone and die anyway—in spite of our illusion of community and filiation? Here is how La Fontaine, mixing metaphors, describes loneliness: like a flower dying in the desert; like the oyster turning itself over and over again, with nowhere else to turn.

But then, seizing on solitude as a desirable state,

Samuel Beckett at some point said "Our allotted time on earth is not long enough to be used for anything other than ourselves." And a chronically distraught friend of mine once told me that the only things he wanted to do with his life was just sleep, dream, wake up, eat good food, drink fine-vintage wine, maybe watch a cable movie on TV or read a novel, masturbate, go back to sleep, and dream again, and that doing anything else was useless. He said that in fact all the work in the world was useless, made no difference in people's lives, and that, aside from medical research, all the work in the world was designed simply to keep people busy and obedient, like the blood in our veins obeying its blind circuit.

Beckett (again) had a similar version of my friend's desired mode of life: All I really want to do is sit on my ass and fart and think of Dante. And Dorit, it seems apposite here to compound the literary references by recalling Nietzsche's observation that some of us were born posthumously.

You know something? At first I wasn't really sure exactly what he meant by that. But then do you remember when you once asked me, shortly after we met, why I always wear black, and I responded, because I'm in mourning for my life? So perhaps I was already dead when I was born.

Yet, Dorit, I seek anchor in a community, but what good is an anchor that turns out to be lethal? A friend told me sometime ago: Take the plunge, take the risk, straddle the edge. It's called life. The future is unknown.

I remember shortly after Sarah and I split up, and I was in mourning, I told a friend that my future was unknown. My friend said: All of our futures are unknown. It's just that when you were married to Sarah you thought you had a future *with* her: Everything seemed planned and assured and certain. But in fact what you had was the illusion of a future. You know, best-laid plans.

I also remember telling another friend at that point that my only country appears to be that of words. But there is *no* exclusive country of words. Any country of words is a textual space, but not all spaces are textual, and the act of will that tries to transform the everyday space of lived visceral experience into the space of the textual seems to become more difficult by the day.

For some other folk, days become only the space of waiting for time to pass so inevitably, and the nights come too quickly, producing only the possibility of many more useless (and hopeless) days and nights to come. These are people who are passengers in and not navigators of their own lives. These are people who are just waiting to die.

And Dorit, the possibility of something does not necessarily produce it. The possibility of love does not necessarily produce that love. And in fact, like you, it also seems to me in these fin-de-millennium times, that love's possibility now appears so remote, like a phantom glimpsed briefly on the horizon, like those excruciating sunsets at the edge of the Loire Valley that leave the sky redolent with emptiness.

Dorit: A while ago, in New York, before I went to Missoula, someone asked me what I was working on. I responded, Historical analysis, and I'm at the point when Emmett Till encounters Virginia Dare." "Whassthat? He asked. A paradigmatic encounter obviously, you dodo. I told him.

As I'm sure you know, but then one can never assume: Till was a black teenager from Chicago who in 1955 was lynched while visiting relatives in Mississippi for whistling at a white woman. Dare was the first white person (a woman) born in the United Statesin 1585, at Roanoke Island, what became the Lost Colony.

You see, Dorit, the ramifications of that historic" encounter are still being worked out in fin-de-millennium America, even as I write this tonight in Paris, as racial incidents between civilians and civilians, and between civilians and the police—multiply by the day, especially in New York.

The police have been shooting blacks in cities all over the US: They shot Amadou Diallo in the Bronx while he was standing at his doorstep. They shot a twenty-one year-old African-American woman in Riverside, California while she was passed out drunk in her car. She had been startled when she saw the police trying to break into her car: The police then shot her when she reached for what they thought was a gun. They shot Patrick Dorismond in Manhattan on his way home after he had finished his night shift. So you see, that encounter between Till and Dare produced tremendous meanings without number.

Dorit: I feel really strange and lost. I wish you were here with me in Paris. Speaking of the paradigmatic interracial couple— Emmett Till and Virginia Dare—brings me, in a sense, to a crucial question: Do actual interracial *marriages* (as distinct from couplings) ever work? Sarah and I split up after only two years of marriage, for instance. But enough.

Tell me Dorit, what really happened between you and Rick? You seemed well-suited for each other. What really happened? Pray do tell.

Love.

*   *   *

So I wrote to Dorit in my e-mail:

"I went to my father's funeral in Lagos, Nigeria, in 1987, for instance, and no one read his résumé aloud under a very hot sun in that land of sad oranges."

Since 1987 was another significant year in my life, and so I want to chronicle the significant events that happened that year.

*   *   *

1987. New York. My year in the Chinese horoscope: The Year of the Rabbit. Such a momentous year for me. Please indulge me this chronicle of world-events.

In Sao Paolo, Brazil: President José Sarney announced that Brazil was suspending interest payments on its $108 billion debt, and creditors in the so-called G-7 nations (the US; Canada; Britain; Japan; France; Italy; Germany) shuddered. The creditors knew that Latin America's biggest debtors (Brazil, Argentina, Mexico, Venezuela) together owed $284 billion. If the others followed Brazil's example, financial institutions in the West could be seriously damaged. Several major US banks, forced as a precaution to divert capital to their bad-debt reserves, posted losses for the year.

In Tokyo: A released Japanese study of American economy cited mismanagement and poor labor relations as the causes of a slide that threatened to reduce the US to a "hamburger-stand economy." By contrast, Japan was then (in contrast to currently) the world's leading manufacturer and creditor. President Reagan's response was to impose a 100-percent tariff on some Japanese imports—as retaliation for what he called "unfair Japanese trade practices."

In France: Klaus Barbie, former Gestapo chief of Lyons, stood trial in person and faced charges of having ordered 842 deportations to Nazi death camps. Barbie had long been untouchable. After the war, like many ranking Nazis, he had gone to work for US Army counterintelligence, running operations that snooped on communists and far-rightists in Germany and elsewhere. His handlers shielded him from arrest by French and US authorities, but he was eventually tracked down in Bolivia by Nazi hunters and extradited to France. "The Butcher of Lyons," as the media dubbed him, seldom appeared in court during his two-month trial. His lawyers trivialized the Holocaust, harping on France's war crimes in Algeria and America's in Vietnam. The jury found him guilty, but since France had abolished the death penalty in 1981, Barbie was sentenced to life in prison.

In West Berlin: Rudolph Hess, Adolf Hitler's first admirer and closest friend, strangled himself to death with an electric cord at Spandau Prison. Hess, who was 93, had been in custody since 1941, when he mysteriously flew to Britain on an apparent peace mission. Convicted of war crimes at Nuremberg, he was sentenced to life imprisonment at Spandau, where he outlived all of his fellow inmates.

In Rome: Primo Levi, Italian writer and Holocaust survivor, died on sidewalk impact when he fell out of the window of his apartment. Speculations still abound about whether his death was an accident or a suicide.

In St-Paul-en-Vence, France, in the house he bought after he left the tiny top-floor apartment at 56 rue Jacob, where he had lived for several years, the writer James Baldwin died of "natural causes."

In the US:

In New York, pop-artist Andy Warhol died, like my father, in a hospital during a (what-was-supposed-to-be) routine prostate surgery.

In New York, Bob Fosse, choreographer and filmmaker of the *All That Jazz* fame, died of AIDS.

In New York, on Monday, October 19 (now known as Black Monday), the Dow Jones Industrial Average plunged 508 points. It was a 22-percent drop, almost double that of the 1929 crash that set off the Great Depression. Some $870 billion in equity values simply evaporated, resulting in fluctuating prices, major downsizings, and mortgage foreclosures. The carnage soon spread to jittery markets around the world. Stock prices fell in London, Tokyo, Hong Kong, and Paris. The causes of the global downturn were numerous, but analysts pointed to one factor above all: the deplorable state of US economy. My friend Al had a very busy week, as prices fluctuated wildly in record heavy trading. And most analysts agreed that the market had been seriously overvalued and · was now due for "a correction."

In Washington DC, after a bitter debate, the Senate narrowly rejected the nomination of conservative appellate court judge Robert Bork to the Supreme Court. Reagan had nominated Bork, who had carried out the "Saturday Night Massacre" for Richard Nixon in 1973 during the Watergate affair. Bork's opponents, notably Edward Kennedy, successfully depicted him as "a dangerous extremist." Reagan's next nominee, Douglas Ginsberg, was also dismissed after he admitted to having tried marijuana as a student years earlier.

In Washington DC, Gary Hart, the leading contender for the Democratic presidential nomination, dropped out of the race when his extramarital affair with model Donna Rice was exposed. (In a moment of hubris typical of certain Washington politicians and operatives, he had dared the media to expose his reputed marital infidelity.) *The National Inquirer* later published a picture of him and Donna Rice on a huge sailing yacht appropriately named *Monkey Business.* Hart briefly reentered the race later in the year, but questions about his judgment soon forced his retirement from politics. He later retreated to his gulch ranch-house in Colorado to write novels before he became a globe-trotting "businessman." Hart's case blazed the trail for the spate of politico-sexual scandals that have littered the US political landscape in recent years.

In North Carolina, televangelist Jim Bakker resigned as the head of the $100-million-a-year Praise-the-Lord ministry after his tryst with church secretary Jessica Hahn came to light. Bakker's wife, cosmetics buff Tammy Faye, initially remained loyal but eventually divorced the fallen minister after he was sent to prison.

In Islip, Long Island, the town ran out of space for the dumping of industrial waste. A local entrepreneur named Lowell Harrelson then had a late-night brainstorm: He'd ship Islip's trash to North Carolina and sell the methane gas emitted by the rotten trash for profit. The problem was: North Carolina didn't want the 3168-pound fetid waste. Thus began the 162-day 6000-mile odyssey of the garbage badge *Mobro.* After being turned away from five states and three countries (including two West African ones), the rancid *Mobro* finally went back home to New York, where its cargo was incinerated. The bizarre incident highlighted America's waste-disposal crisis, which the Environmental Protection Agency said would reach a critical point within ten years, when half the country's municipalities would run out of landfill space. Americans suddenly became obsessed with how they disposed of their waste, and mandatory recycling programs were inaugurated all over the country.

In New York, at Sotheby's auction house, Australian beer tycoon Alan Bond bid an astonishing $53.9 million for Dutch impressionist Vincent Van Gogh's vibrant *Irises*, which he painted in 1889 after his breakdown. The record sum pushed up the ever-rising ceiling for art prices to a heretofore unheard-of level: an exemplum of the extreme commodification of the New York art scene of the 80s. *Irises'* s record was to be broken three years later, when in 1990, *Portrait of Dr. Gachet*, which Van Gogh painted the year he died, in 1890, was sold to a Japanese industrialist, Ryoei Saito, at Christie's New York for $82.5 million, an amount that remains, at the time of this writing, the most expensive art-work to sell at auction.

The fact that Van Gogh's piece blazed the trail for the art-commodifation that began in the 80s was itself ironic. The narrative of his life also exemplified the vagaries and vicissitudes of an artist's life and body sacrificed to art and posterity. Please indulge me this narrative of Van Gogh's short but interesting life, as follows:

Vincent Van Gogh was born in 1853. Despite a reputation for antisocial behavior (the episode of the amputated earlobe looms large), Van Gogh was a people person. He was an avid talker and letter writer, fluent in four languages. Early in his short life he held a number of face-time jobs: apprentice to an art-dealer; school-teacher; and evangelical preacher. Later, as an artist in Paris, he met practically everyone in the avant-garde.

The child of a middle-class Dutch-Reformed minister, at sixteen, he landed a position in an art gallery in The Hague. Shortly thereafter, he was transferred to the company's London branch. In London something went wrong: He fell in love, was rebuffed, and got morose. He then moved to a down-and-out Belgian mining village, where he taught gospel, nursed the sick, and drew portraits of the miners. After a run-in with the church, he channeled all his energies into art.

In his late 20s, Van Gogh returned to The Hague to begin a new career in art. With no money for professional models, he asked elderly pensioners in the city to sit for him. He had been looking at all kinds of art for years, from the Dutch old master paintings to English popular engravings. He crash-educated himself as a draftsman by copying pictures from student manuals and as a painter by drawing figures from life.

Van Gogh soon went to Paris, where a new kind of art was being produced. He stayed there for two years, met many painters— Gauguin, Toulouse-Lautrec, Suerat, Pisarro—and learned from all of them. He also began the series of self-portraits that formed the bulk of his work.

Badly strung-out, in 1888, he left Paris for Arles in the south of France. Joined by Gauguin, Van Gogh experienced his golden age there. His art opened up. The richest concentration of his portraits date from 1888. But his stay in Arles ended in disaster: mental collapse, self-mutilation, and a rupture with Gauguin. In 1889 he was whisked off to an asylum in nearby St-Rémy, where he turned out some awesome paintings (ironically, for instance: *Irises*, which sold around a century later for the record $53.9 million at Sotheby's in New York), but the path was downhill. Further breakdowns brought him to Dr. Gachet in Auvers, near Paris. The denouement came quite soon, in 1890: Alone in a field, he shot himself and died two days later. But before he died that year, he painted the record-breaking portrait of his doctor, *Portrait of Dr. Gachet* , which in 1990, sold at Christie's New York for $82.5 million, and which—again quite ironically—remains, at the time of this writing, the most expensive art-work to sell at auction.

Van Gogh's reputation not only survived him but grew tremendously. Art theorists have demonstrated his influence on figurative painters from Matisse to Chuck Close. Van Gogh gave us the first complete visual record of a body disintegrating in public.

Through several contemporary exhibitions of his body of work, we watch his paintings again and again, like a documentary video of a disaster. He was our first celebrity martyr, the patron saint of our contemporary cult of disability, which culminated in the record-sum 1987 New-York sale of his *Irises,* then in the record-breaking (again) New York sale of Portrait of Dr. Gachet. David Norman, the head of the Impressionist and modern art department at Sotheby's, described the art market for Van Gogh as "incredibly compressed" because he painted for less than a decade, and only in the style for which he was best known for two years before his death. "The sky is the limit, even for his minor pieces," Mr. Norman said.

*   *   *

My apologies for the indulgent Van Gogh digression.

OK: now finally getting back to Dorit. I'm genuinely confused about her. I was definitely in love with her in 1990. When I saw her recently in New York before I flew to Paris, my body felt those dull aches I felt when I was in love with her. She looked stunning to me that night at the Zinc Bar on West Houston, as we talked and listened to Afro-Caribbean and Brazilian music. She was wearing night-crawler clothes as usual: tight black Levis tucked into high black double-buckle boots, a black silk shirt that exposed her chest, a black straw hat, two huge hoops on each ear, and tainted glasses. And her green eyes dazzled me as they refracted through those glasses.

That night I also felt those rapid heartbeats anticipating what she would say next. I had erections when I read in her e-mail that she made serial love to those marathoners. And before I drifted to sleep last night, in my mind's theater while listening to BBC World Service on Francette's portable short-wave radio, I ran graphic scenarios of her making love to all those men. I suspect I'm growing somewhat attached to Dorit again. One definitely can't police desire. Now my question: Am I falling in love with her again?

Who knows whether she and I might end up together again?

This is of course assuming that she would want me. Anything is possible as long as we're alive, right? I mean, how many combinations can there be in a deck of cards that some sleazy guy is shuffling in the back of a sleazy joint?

My experiences with Francette since we've been in Paris have certainly been extraordinary, even for me. These experiences have thrown my psyche off kilter, and might point me to new unsuspected directions. Like Dorit, I've been in a strange mood lately myself. Almost everyone I know is having major changes in their lives right now. Someone told me in New York recently that "the universe shifted" a few months ago. I'm not sure exactly what *that* means. I'm not sure what anything means anymore. Maybe it's the fin-de-millennium. Some of my friends who have Ph.D's are burning countless hours reading *The Book of Centuries*, a huge tome by Michel de Notre-Dame, better known as Nostradamus, for interpretations of events that have happened on this planet in the past few years, specifically in this last decade of the millennium, and for clues about what might happen in the future. As for me, the more I read and hear and see, the more I realize the vast extent of what I don't know. I find it more and more difficult to figure out what's going on.

I have to continue to probe my life that's drifted to get to this point. Here I am in Paris, in Francette's apartment, alone. Her gay roommate has more or less disappeared ever since we got here. I haven't seen Michel since the first day when he picked us up at De Gaulle and made breakfast for us. And Francette is probably with one of her lesbian or bisexual lovers—this latter could be a man or a woman—to get back at me for what she thinks was my bad behavior last night. Last night I got drunk on her expensive Côtes du Rhone and spilled my guts online to Dorit. My research into my life that's adrift now has to get back to Missoula: that is to say to Katya, and—to a lesser but crucial extent—to Jacques.

*   *   *

21

Paris: Saturday, July 10, 1999

Missoula: Saturday, August 29, 1998

Dinner that Saturday night at Jacques's house on Highwood Street in South Hills. Jacques told people to show up around 8 PM. The whole community of friends were there: me; Katya; Christine; Casey, college professor in the English department; Janice, wannabe writer who lived in an old school bus parked in her friend's backyard; Rob, cyber-entrepeneur who owned his Internet company; Rob's wife Laura, aspirant painter who had a day-job teaching art in continuing education at the university; Bryn; Trish, theater teaching specialist who gave the party where I met Bryn; and Sigi, German woman and adjunct professor in the department of foreign languages and literatures, and also a next-door neighbor of Katya's on Sixth Street between Helen and Hilda Streets.

I had met Sigi only in passing—in the department hallway when I went to see Jacques—but had never spoken directly to her before that night. Katya had told me she lived with her husband Sunil, who was born in India, and who was a musician and children's book writer; they live with their five-year-old son Praha. Jacques had invited the whole family, but only Sigi came. Sunil supposedly was nursing a cold and wanted to spend quality time with Praha. I was disappointed, as I was looking forward to meeting Sunil especially because of his background and because of what little of his history Katya had related to me.

The family had lived in Washington, DC before Sigi got the

job at the university. She was hired about the same time as Katya, and also on a three-year contract. In Washington, Sunil had worked with the Human Rights Watch while Sigi was finishing graduate school at Georgetown University, where Katya was also freelance teaching. Both of their tenures there had overlapped, but their paths never crossed.

I'm dwelling somewhat on Sunil because he and I spent a lot of time together the last month I was in Missoula, when Katya was in Moscow. He played music and was a highly talented writer of children's books, and during the time we spent together I helped him secure contacts in juvenile trade book publishing in New York so that he could successfully get his manuscripts published. But I'm getting ahead of myself again. Back to the dinner.

Jacques had a expansive dining table that could sit ten people quite comfortably. He did all the cooking, and for kitchen support-staff, he deployed me and Christine, who had made up with him—at least for then—and who had arrived hours early to help. For this dinner he had bought several bottles of red wine of various sorts: shiraz, Beaujolais, merlot, cabernet, a couple of Côtes du Rhone, and three whites: a white burgundy, a sauvignon, and a chablis—the latter surprised me.

Jacques made red snapper broiled with olive oil and seasoned with herbs du Provence, tarragon, and cilantro; brown rice; wild mushrooms (which he picked himself while hiking on the mountains around Missoula—he knew quite a bit about mushrooms) sautéed in garlic; and steamed broccoli, also with garlic.

The guests walked into the living room to the sound of Mozart's "Six Haydn Quartets," specifically, to Quartet No. 14 in G Major, K. 387, played by the Juilliard String Quartet. Jacques had had me and Christine set the dining table, light the candles, carefully place the vases with fresh flowers at strategic locations on the table, and also place name-tags that he had made for everyone—with the tag-lines he designated for each person: I was "postmodern nomad"; Katya, "Slavic-Jewish Princess"; Bryn, "free-spirited nymph"; Janice, "cutting-on-the-edge writer"; Rob, "cyber-warrior." I don't recall how Jacques designated Christine or anybody else.

Laura and Rob were the first guests to arrive. They walked into the house and sauntered over to the dining and kitchen area. Laura handed me a bottle of Concha y toro red wine they had brought.

Laura:

—Wow, Jacques, you've really outdone yourself this time. This all looks so wonderful.

Jacques:

—Oh, Laura. This is nothing. Just a simple meal made for dear friends.

I:

—Jacques is being modest. He spent most of the afternoon preparing all this stuff himself. Christine and I did nothing. We were just the kitchen help.

Laura:

—It all smells so good.

I:

—We eat like this every night. I've always told Jacques that the best restaurant in Missoula is right here, in this kitchen and dining room in South Hills.

Jacques:

—Well ... What do you guys want to drink? There's everything. Wine, beer, créme du Cassis for kir, gin, scotch, bourbon, pernod for calvados.

Rob:

—I'll take scotch.

Laura:
—I'll take red wine.

Jacques:
—The one you guys brought?
—It doesn't matter. I'll take whatever red you have open.

Minutes later, Jacques, Christine, Rob. Laura, and I were all sitting in the living room with respective drinks, waiting for the others to show up. Katya and Sigi arrived next—together, in Katya's car, as I was told later. By 8: 50 PM, everybody had arrived. Bryn arrived last. Jacques introduced people who didn't know each other. I had more or less met everyone before. Soon, everyone was milling around the living and dining area, drinking, eating Doritos dipped in salsa or guacomole, and making the customary small-talk preamble to dinner.

Everyone was making small talk, except Rob. At that point of my sojourn in Missoula, I was just getting to know Rob gradually. I first met him at the Missouri Club (or "Mo" Club, as the natives called it), a small bar in downtown Missoula, a couple of blocks from 201 South Main Street, which is on the corner of Main and Ryman Streets, where Rob's Internet web-development company is based. Jacques and Casey and I were drinking at the bar one afternoon in early August when Rob walked in, and Jacques introduced us.

Rob then sat with us, and for the next two hours we all drank and talked about the wonders of the Internet. He told me he had seven employees (five men and two women) in his company (let's call it DragNet from now on), whom he paid six figures to do various things, from programming to software development to simple web-site design.

Rob explained to me then, that he and his team were working to transform DragNet into a leading global digital network service provider for consumers all over the world. He said DragNet wanted to enable anyone with an Internet connection to use their browser to send huge digital files—within highly secure encrypted bandwidths—and have DragNet track or store whatever information they were transmitting. He said he started the company with another friend (now his co-director) in his garage (how more clichéd can you get?) as a business-to-business Web-based service that transmitted, tracked, and stored encrypted digital information—graphics, images, data, audios, videos, text, codes—for multinational corporations to anyone anywhere on the Internet. Rob said DragNet's business-to-business digital network transmitted huge files (terabytes in minutes!) that couldn't make it through the regular ways of Internet transmission for all sorts of reasons: for instance, narrow bandwidths, busy signals, and dropped lines—Netscape's famous "broken pipe" error messages.

After that afternoon at the "Mo" Club, Rob invited me to visit his office, and said I could drop in from time to time to use his machines for high-speed Internet access. My laptop 56-kbps modem usually choked—and my monitor sometimes froze—after I did my e-mail and visited only two web sites, so I began to spend three to four hours each weekday at DragNet to do my online work.

The atmosphere at DragNet's office (which captured so exquisitely the spirit and passionate technophilia of the e-decade) was most certainly something out of central casting for Net-Head geeks working for a cyber company. I was getting to know his employees. Two employees (a man and a woman) telecommuted mostly from home and came into the office only for the routine weekly meetings. The ones who came in everyday had flex-time. The refrigerator in the office kitchen was stuffed with Diet Coke, Pepsi, Doritos, and frozen pizzas. When they are in town, Rob and his co-director often walked around the office speaking into small microphones attached to their shirts—and wearing earpieces connected to the cell phones in their shirt pockets—while holding their Palm Pilots. I said when they're in town: They frequently flew around the US and sometimes to Europe on business.

More about Rob later. Now back to Jacques's dinner party that Saturday night. While everyone else was making small-talk, I heard Rob tell Casey:

—History is gone, man. Every molecule now stretches toward the future. It seems really freakish now to look backward. The very notion of reflecting on what has happened, rather than what will happen, seems to violate the laws of physics. Listen: History is now a luxury that only the underexposed can afford. And I thought: oh boy, this will be some evening.

At some point Jacques took Janice and Bryn, first-time guests at his house (unlike everyone else), down to his basement to show them his books: about (I swear) ten thousand titles. He liked to show first-time guests his book collection, the repository of his psychic and libidinal investments of his life in Missoula. He once told me he bought that house for his books.

When Bryn came back upstairs, she was gregarious with Janice for several minutes. They must have bonded downstairs while scanning Jacques's titles. Then I saw Bryn sneak out to the porch—off the kitchen at the back of the house—to smoke a cigarette. (An occasional smoker himself, Jacques didn't permit smoking inside the house.) Bryn was dressed exactly the same as the night I first met her. But that dinner night she looked especially stunning. I slid open and shut the glass door to join her on the porch. I don't smoke, but I wanted to see again the great vistas from the porch: the red streak of the sunset over the remote mountains where sometimes you could see several weather systems from the distance.

Bryn and I were on the porch for about ten minutes. Katya came out, saw us, gave me a sheepish smile, and hightailed it back inside. Bryn and I went back inside a few minutes after that, into a group discussion about Jacques's peculiarly furnished house, especially his living room and kitchen.

A few comments about this aspect of Jacques's house: His living room walls looked like collages, filled with posters of paintings from all periods—from classical, through baroque (by his own admission his favorite period), to contemporary. The walls had contemporary originals donated by his former students turned aspirant painters. And the furniture was a mixed bag of odd-looking couches and a couple of funky armchairs. His kitchen looked French classical: cluttered with pots, skillets , spices, dried fruits, hung hard sausages and garlic heads, jars of dried mushrooms, and bottles of white and red wines for cooking and consumption.

Around 9: 25 PM, Jacques abruply told everyone that dinner was ready. He then personally sat everyone down next to their name-tag. And almost everyone was amused by how Jacques designated them. Almost everyone—except Katya. She winced at me as she sat down. Her gesture did not bode well for the rest of the evening.

I have to interrupt this: Francette just came back, and she says she wants to talk to me. I sense trouble. I'll continue narrating that August dinner evening at Jacques in Missoula tomorrow.

*   *   *

22

Paris: Sunday, July 11, 1999

Missoula: Saturday, August 29, 1998

I have some interesting (and quite unexpected) items to narrate about what transpired between me and Francette last night, but I had promised to continue talking about Jacques's dinner party that Saturday night.

At first, for about ten-fifteen minutes, everyone at the dinner table was consuming red snapper and broccoli soaked in garlic, brown rice, and red and white wine. Then, somewhat abruptly and suddenly, as far as I can recall, Jacques started talking about World War II and Germans and Jews and concentration camps, one of his favorite topics at that time. I sensed impending trouble but felt powerless to deflect it. For one, Jacques was hard of hearing in all respects physical and metaphoric. For another (related), he was stubborn and highly opinionated, so that once he embarked on a specific discursive path he took no prisoners.

He began talking for almost ten-fifteen minutes about the distinction between concentration and death camps, between Auschwicz and Dachau. He deployed the historical authority of his father for this distinction, saying that his father was with the French Resistance, was captured with several Jews and thrown into Auschwicz, and was later luckily rescued by a German soldier who had recognized him from the prewar years in Toulouse. Jacques said German in fact was his second language, and launched into a few German phrases to prove his point, while looking at Sigi for confirmation. Sigi did not respond, and no one challenged him about any of his claims.

No one, except Katya:

—Hey Jacques, your distinctions don't hold water. You don't know what you're talking about.

—What do you mean I don't know what I'm talking about.

—Those distinctions are blurred. They might have functioned at the beginning of the Holocaust, but they became blurry during the pogrom.

—My father told me all this. He was there. You don't know what you're talking about. Were you there?

—I wasn't there, but you're forgetting I'm Jewish. I grew up with friends whose parents were Holocaust survivors.

As Katya said this, she glanced at Rob—who also had Russian-Jewish heritage—for some form of corroboration. Rob said nothing.

Sigi then piped in:

—Katya is right, Jacques. The concentration camps eventually became death camps.

Jacques:

—I'm surprised to hear you say that. You're German. You should know better.

Sigi did not respond. She instead reached for her wine glass. Things were getting a little tense. Jacques had raised the stakes. And I was trying to figure out what to do. Katya did not press things further. But Jacques was on a war path. He turned to Katya:

—Have you spent any time in Europe? You emigrated directly from Moscow to Jerusalem, then directly to the US. You don't know very much about Europe or its history. You've never lived there. I am European. I grew up in Europe.

Katya:

—I've lived in Paris.

Jacques huffed and puffed:

—When? You lived in Paris? I don't believe you. What were you
doing there? And for how long?

I intervened:

—Jacques, what reason do you have for not believing her?

He did not respond to me, but he continued to interrogate
Katya:

—Where and when did you live in Paris?

—Near the Arche de Triomphe. In the mid-80s

—The mid-80s? Which Arrondissement?

—I don't remember.

—Ha!

Then, somewhat inexplicably in my opinion, he switched to
talking about the swastika:

—You know, the other day, I had a discussion with Chernow about
the swastika.

(He meant Sara Chernow, his department head, whom he
reviled with extreme prejudice, and whom he always referred to by
her last name. And the exchange that followed was mostly between
Jacques and me.)

I:

—And?

—I told her the swastika should be redeemed from the sins of the
Nazis.

—Why?

—Because it was a good luck symbol all over the world before the
Nazis adopted it and transformed it into a powerful icon of
racial hatred.

—Yeah, so what? I know that the word swastika comes from the
Sanskrit word *svastika*, which means well-being and good
fortune. But all that can never be recovered after what the
Nazis did with it. Period.

Rob:
—He's right.

Jacques was not to be deterred:
—Navajo blankets were woven with swastikas. Buddha's footprints
were reported to be swastikas. Synagogues in North Africa and
Palestine were built with swastika mosaics . . .

I, in French:
—Jacques, *Attention*!
(In French, this expression means "Watch out, pay attention"
and/or "Danger, be careful!")

He seemed to heed my point. He then shifted the topic, and
to Sigi:
—Do you like teaching in the department?
—Yeah, I do.
—Really?
—You disappoint me. How could you like teaching in that stupid
department with all those morons? How about you, Katya?
—I like teaching there also.
—Now I'm really disappointed. And depressed.

Jacques looked at me and shrugged. I said nothing. All the
other guests also had said nothing during this entire transaction.
They preferred to play the captive audience. Bryn especially was
looking at me constantly, I suppose wondering if and when I was
going to do something to end all what must have seemed to her
somewhat bizarre. I hadn't explained to her before that evening
my peculiar relationship to—and my strategy with—Jacques.

A few minutes later Jacques expanded his domain-target of the department of foreign languages to include the whole of the University of Montana. He said the university was garbage dumpy and third-rate, and that he would be "getting out" as soon as he could. He said he simply needed to finish and publish a couple of book manuscripts he was working on. Then he said he'd write his ticket to either coast, maybe to California or back to New York, where he went to grad school. Casey mumbled one or two lame comments that implied that he agreed with Jacques's views about the university. Casey said the English department was no better than foreign languages and literatures.

I:
—Jacques, you're deluded. You'll have a harder time getting out of here than you think.

He then said to me in French, lowering his voice:
—Listen, do me favor. Let's agree to disagree tonight. OK? We each know, implicitly, what we and the other person are talking about.

I got his message and shifted to Rob.
—So, Rob, what do you mean, history is gone. I heard you earlier.

Of course I knew what he meant. He and I had touched on the topic briefly—but surgically—at DragNet one afternoon. But I simply wanted to change the subject and the tenor of the evening so far.

Rob, after sipping some red wine (the following exchange was confined to just me and Rob):
—You know about e-Bay right?
—Yeah, the new e-commerce site.
—It simply mediates transactions between sellers and buyers all over the world. A seller in Australia can sell something to a buyer in Beijing.
—Yeah, I know that.

—These transactions go on continuously all over the globe, without regard to time-zones or borders. Just on that level of commerce, capitalism works twenty-four hours a day.

—There is another level, of course. On the level of information, Capital assures complete mobilization from daybreak to sunset.

—Yeah, and only recently, the New York Stock Exchange and
NASDAQ announced that they will stay open during evening
hours—their closing hour now is at 4: PM New York Time.

—I know, Rob. I read about the new hours they're proposing.
Given the new regimes of Capital, I was surprised that it took
this long for these primary US stock exchanges to stay open in
the evening.

—It's only a matter of time before they're open for all of twenty-
four hours. Listen: The stock market, which right now is frag-
mented into different exchanges and time-zones, will soon be
one big global market when all these exchanges merge. NYSE,
NASDAQ, Tokyo-Nikkei, Frankfurt, will all soon merge. Trust
me on this one.

—So just like e-Bay, the stock market will make transactions twenty-
four hours a day.

—You got that right. Human bodies will sleep of course, but at
their own peril, since the machines of Capital will stay awake
for ever.

—Right on, Rob.

—Capital operates with speed and overexposure, history—
including what subvents it, memory—is more or less elided.
In fact, history becomes a luxury that only the underexposed
can afford. That's what I was telling Casey.

Bryn at this point:

—The underexposed? Who are those?

Rob, looking at her as if she was from another planet:

—The poor and the unskilled, period.

He then sipped some more red wine.

Bryn again:
—The poor and the unskilled are underexposed? To what?

Noting that Rob was still sipping his wine, and that he glanced at me at that point, as if handing me the baton, I responded:
—To the machines of Capital. To technology. Briefly, to computers, to the Internet. In other words, the poor and the unskilled are not online.

Bryn:
—Ah! The digital divide. Awesome! Totally awesome.

At this point Jacques raised his wine glass, trying I suppose to do damage control to his own discursive contributions so far to this evening at his house:
—Let's drink some more wine. To Capital! Long live the machines of Capital!

Everyone raised their wine glasses and yelled:
—Long live the machines of Capital!

Everyone, except Katya. And that was when I concluded that Jacques's gesture was too little too late.

There were no more "incidents" (or as the French say "interventions") at Jacques's house for the rest of that evening. By about 1 AM everybody was more or less drunk. I spent more time with Katya than I did with Bryn. Bryn and Janice talked to each other almost exclusively for the rest of the evening. Bryn told me later that she gave Kathyrn a ride back to her school bus. And Katya told me later that Sigi told her on their way back to their respective neighborly homes that she (Sigi) had a great time but would never set foot at Jacques's house in South Hills again.

Back at the party, people drifted off one by two. We listened to more music. I played a few CDs from my collection: Alla, playing the ûd, "Improvisations III, IV, and V," "Le Foundou";

Dexter Gordon, "For all We Know" ; Baaba Mal and Mansour
Seck, "Lam Toro," "Loodo"; Cheik-Lo, "Né la thiass."

At about 2:30 AM, I left Casey and Jacques and Christine,
who was cracking up the other two with her raunchy blue-grass
and blue-collar jokes (as she was wont to do when drunk) in the
living room and went into my bedroom to go to bed. As I was
wont to do before I drifted to sleep, I tuned my portable radio to
National Public Radio, which (as it was wont to do from 11 PM
till 5 AM Mountain Time every night) was then transmitting the
BBC World Service.

Now back to Paris, to Francette.

*   *   *

23

Paris: Sunday, July 11, 1999

Yesterday late afternoon, around 5:30 PM, Francette came back home as I was using her desktop for my entries into this narrative. Normally I use my laptop for my writing, but because I was online retrieving Dorit's and my e-postings for this narrative, I simply got offline, opened up Word 6.1 on Francette's desktop for convenience, inserted my floppy disk, and clicked open the backup copy of *Love in This Time of Silicon*—rather than turn off her desktop to then boot up my laptop. So these were the first words she said to me, in English, after I left her at Café de Flore Friday night:

—You know, you have ask my permission to use my computer. It *is* my computer, after all.

—I'm sorry. Since you've been very generous sharing your things and space with me, I thought it was OK. I have to use your machine to get online. My little laptop chokes after five minutes online.

—I share everything with you—but my computer is sacred. It's personal. I don't want you prying into my e-mail, for instance. That's really private stuff.

—I didn't pry into your e-mail! Come on. Don't you trust me? I was online posting a lengthy e-mail to my friend Dorit.

—Dorit? Who is Dorit?

—I never told you about her? She's subletting my apartment in New York. She's a close friend, someone I've known since 1989.

—No, you never told me about her. But it doesn't matter. I suppose you wrote her to complain about me.

—Not necessarily. I told her I was upset, which is true.

—I was upset too. You have no idea how upset I was. Especially after you left like that.

—Well, I left because I felt completely ignored. Your friends shunned and therefore dissed me. I guess they had no use for a straight bird like me.

She raised her voice:

—That's not fair! They actually blamed themselves for you leaving.

—Really?

—Yeah, really. They agreed with you that they had ignored you. And they felt shitty about it. They regretted what happened.

—Is that right?

—Yeah, that's right. And in fact the whole incident made us look at ourselves as a group. We looked at how we interact with outsiders. We questioned whether we were being too defensive. We discussed the situation for several hours. My friends want to meet you again.

—I don't know about that.

—Oh come on. They've invited us to a big party they've planned for Wednesday Quatorze Juillet. Three nights before you head back to the US, which is on Saturday, right?

—Right. Well, we'll see about all that. I'm surprised actually. When you didn't come home I figured you were too pissed at me to see my face. In fact, I was thinking I should probably head back to New York early, skip the end of the conference.

She switched into French:

—Oh come on. You don't have to go back to New York early. I want to apologize for last night. It was shitty the way we treated you. I didn't come home because Sylvie and Anne wanted me to come home with them. They wanted to calm me down. They said it'll be bad aura here if I came back.

—I guess.

—So I went home with them. We shared a lot of Reiki energy. It
  was great Shakra.

—Who are they?

—You met them. Don't you remember them? I was talking to
  Sylvie
  most of the time you were there. Anne was sitting two seats to
  your right.

—I guess I remember them. Anne is the one with cropped hair.
  Sylvie is quite attractive. Long black hair. Very French-looking.

—Yeah. She's a very French-looking long-haired lipstick lesbian.

—So they're a couple?

—Yeah. They've been together for one year now.

—Did you get it on with them?

—Yeah. Sylvie and I used to be an item for two years until I
  terminated it. Then she met Anne, and I've been close with
  both of them ever since. I try to spend a lot of time with them
  when I'm in Paris. They've visited me in LA twice. Making
  love to them is wonderful and relaxing.

—That's nice. It must have been something. A three-way lesbian
  fucking.

—Do I sense some jealousy here? Are you jealous?

—Me jealous? Why? You and I are not an item.

—I think you're jealous. And I think jealousy also had something
  to do with the way you behaved Friday night.

—Really? You flatter yourself.

—You've had me mostly to yourself since we got here. Friday was
  the first time you had to share me with my friends. For the
  first time I wasn't giving you all my attention. I was paying
  attention to other people, and you couldn't stand it.

—That's not true. I told you I felt ignored.

—I agree you felt ignored, and for that I apologize. But you were
  also jealous.

—Look: I've shared you with Michel.

—You don't feel threatened in the least by Michel. You know that
   I know that. And I know that you know that.

—I was not jealous. I am not jealous.

—Admit it. Come on. Your posturing doesn't fool me. I'm starting to have an effect on you. I'm growing on you. Admit it.
   It'll make you feel better. It'll free up your psyche.

—I'm somewhat closer to you on this trip, that's true. But I'm not
   romantically attracted to you, I can tell you that.

—That's what you think . . . I want to make up to you for Friday
   night.

—How?

—Let's do two things tonight: have a nice expensive dinner on me
   and also take in a movie. Do you have any plans for tonight?

—Not yet.

—Good.

   Then I lied:

—But I was thinking about calling Emilie.

—Your intellectual father's daughter? That's incestuous. Don't call
   her. Go out with me.

—The possibility of incest is tempting. Where do you want to go
   for dinner?

—I was thinking about going to a movie first. Then we can go to a
   cabaret afterward.

—A cabaret sounds nice. What movie do you have in mind?

—Spike Lee's *Summer of Sam* is playing at Danton, on boulevard
   Saint-Germain.

—That's already playing in Paris? It was just released in the States.

—Spike Lee is big in Paris.

—I definitely like to see that. It deals with the summer of 1977. I
   was a teenager in New York that summer. A sixteen-year-old
   high-school student. That was some summer.

—What happened that summer?

—A lot of things. There was the son of Sam for one. David Berkowitz. He shot several women and their boyfriends in Queens and one woman in the Bronx. All the women had some things in common: black hair, attractive, and all were shot while making out with their boyfriends in their car at night. He claimed that a neighbor's dog told him to shoot all those people.

—What else happened?

—There was a blackout one night for several hours. A lot of people in the city were without power. Several people were trapped in elevators, some overnight. There was widespread looting by blacks all over the city. In Manhattan, in Brooklyn. Some neighorhoods in Brooklyn, like Flatbush, never recovered from that night's looting. That summer was also especially hot and sizzling. The thermometer reached 103 Fahrenheit one day. Now that's a record. And the Yankees won the World Series. Reggie Jackson became forever known as "Mr. October" after that summer when he had three home strikes in a row, giving the Yankees the series.

—I didn't know you followed baseball.

—I don't. Except that every New Yorker follows baseball when the Yankees are in contention. They also won in 1996. And in 1998.

—You're right. That must have been some summer.

—From what I've read, Spike Lee's film deals with all that somewhat. He used the son of Sam's mayhems as a membrane to capture the unease and psychic anxieties that plagued New Yorkers that summer. I'm curious to see whether he pulled it off.

—OK then. We'll go. There's a show at 7:30. We can go to that and then to the cabaret.

—Ah, the cabaret? And where are we going for that?

—Something called Alcazar de Paris on rue Mazarine, in the Sixième. It's very close to Danton. We'll walk there and have a nice dinner and listen to great music and watch some great dancing.

—Who's performing there tonight?

—Two shows. *Pariscope* said a French-Indian quartet called Mukta
   is playing. And a Suzana Baca is singing. I don't know who
   they all are.

—Suzana Baca? You don't know who she is? My friend Dorit took
   me to listen to her one night in New York.

—Well, who is she?

—She's is a Lima, Peru native whose sensual music is a sumptuous
   mix of Spanish, Andean, and African influences.

—Do you anything about Mukta?

—No. What does *Pariscope* say about them?

—Just that their music is a blend of Indian sitar and jazz.

—Sounds fantastic.

—We'll have a great time tonight!

—Sounds like an ideal evening to me. I'm broke, you know that,
   right?

—Yes yes I know that. As you've told me many times. I told you
   it's my treat. Don't worry about it.

I will narrate the rest of the Saturday evening's experiences
and events with Francette, but I need to share Dorit's next e-mail
to me that she wrote last night (New York Time) and that I read
this morning (Paris Time) on Francette's desktop—while she was
still in bed, so I didn't have to ask her for permission. Dorit's e-
mail continued where she left off the one before that.

*   *   *

24

Paris: Sunday, July 11, 1999

Dorit's e-mail:

————————————

Date: Sat, 10 July 1999 21:08:09 -0500 (EDT)
From: Dorit Levin <doritlevin@onebox.com> **Add Block**
Subject: My Electra Complex, etc
Message: Yo again. Now I can finally sit here and finish telling you about this fifty-two-year-old famous writer I met when you were in Hong Kong.

The long run this morning with Carol was fantastic. Normally I do my long run on Sundays but some weekends I do it Saturday if I feel guilty about how much I drank and ate Friday night.

It's Saturday night, and instead of going out on the town again I went out to pick up the *Times* and I'm sitting at my desktop drinking merlot and writing to you. My voyeur friend across Ninth Avenue must not be home, since his lights are out. Or maybe he is home and by his window watching me right now. Don't worry, I have some clothes on. Specifically, I have my running tights and a running T-shirt on. But one confession: I'm not wearing any underpants. I chafed from my running shorts during the long run, so I'm keeping that area warm and cozy. I'm also listening again to Cesaria Evora, this time *Cabo Verde*.

Anyway: the first two weeks after I met this guy were fantastic. As I told you, I said to myself, here's someone who can finally take care of me. I think I have a fully developed Electra complex.

Perhaps I'm attracted to older men because I'm looking for my father in men.

In any case, after those two weeks, he suggested that we drive to Vermont Brattleboro to be precise to visit two of his close friends, a couple, who had worked as Wall Street corporate lawyers in New York but who got out of the rat race and moved up to Vermont to run their own bed-and-breakfast place.

We were supposed to visit with these friends for a long weekend that he had dreamt up. In hindsight, I'm sure he had told them he was bringing up his latest conquest, a twenty-nine-year-old foxy Jewish chick who just happens to be a staff writer for THE NEW YORKER.

The whole trip with him was awful, simply awful. Brattleboro in Vermont is about a six-seven hour drive from Manhattan, including the one hour or so in the city on a Friday afternoon trying to get to the Thruway. So we drove up, or I should say I drove up. You know I like to drive. I drove you and I around in the rental when we were together. This was not a problem by itself.

But while I was driving us up there, his true personality came alive. He became mean and bossy all of a sudden. He became a complete ogre, and got really mean. He basically treated me like a servant, or worst still, his nursemaid. He literally asked me to wait on him: I gassed up the car, and got the cooler out, poured him his chardonnay, spread out the chicken and rice, and all that.

I was fuming. You know me: He might be a famous writer, but I do not suffer fools gladly. In fact, I surprised myself by letting him get away with all that for that long. I went along with it for about two-three hours. Then when we were going through Massachusetts, around Northampton and the South Hadley area as I recall from seeing the Mass Turnpike signs, I let him have it. Boy did I let him have it.

I lit into him. He seemed shocked. Maybe he wasn't used to women talking to him like that. I mean, he might be a great writer he's even won the National Book Award but he was an asshole and a 404 (you know this means clueless, don't you? named for those

404 error messages you get in Netscape when you're looking for a web-site that doesn't exist). By the time we got to Brattleboro we were barely speaking to each other. There was no way I was going to spend the weekend with him and his friends up there.

So when we got to his friends' bed-and-breakfast house I told him I was peeling off to visit my own friends in Burlington. I drove him to his friends' place and drove to Burlington. I took the car because I got the rental in New York. We didn't even say goodbyes. I dropped him off in front of the bed-and-breakfast and high-tailed it out of Brattleboro. I did not even wait long enough to see his friends. I had a great time the rest of that weekend with my friends in Burlington.

I haven't heard from him since. Now I ask you: What was all *that* about? For a week I was really hard on myself. I blamed myself for the whole experience. I should have known better, I told myself. Was I attracted to him because he is a famous writer? And then I agreed to go with him to Vermont after knowing him for only two weeks? The sex was great, especially for a fifty-two-year-old, but that's also besides the point.

The interesting thing is this: The week after that I felt a real loss. Before that trip I was starting to trust him. I was starting to let my guard down with him.

But the one object lesson I took away from that experience is that people have to communicate very clearly about their expectations before they embark on something like that together. I was really baffled about what he had wanted and had expected from me. For a while there I wanted to e-mail him to try to clear things up at least for my own sanity.

It would have been interesting to hear his side of the story, which he never shared with me.

In any case, on to a very important thing I need to tell you. This afternoon after I came back from my run, my boss at THE NEW YORKER called me and said he wanted me to go up to Montreal for two months to research and do a story on the elections in Québec that people up there are all riled up about. He also wanted me to do a profile of Lucien Bouchard of The Bloc Quebecois, one of the conservative candidates running against the separatist Parti Québecois.

All of which could turn out to be interesting. My boss seems to think that our readers would be interested in the elections in a Canadian province looking to break away from Canada. Maybe he believes the rumors floating around that Quebec wants to be financially linked to New York state.

I've got to find an apartment in Montreal for two months August and September. Anyway, my point is: You can certainly stay in your apartment during that time. In fact, when you get back to New York this coming weekend you can stay here. We'll overlap by about a week, but I don't have any problem with that if you don't. You can sleep on the sofa-bed. Or I can sleep on the sofa-bed. It doesn't matter. Hey, then I can treat you to that French restaurant I told you about LA CARAVELLE. We'll just have a nice walk over there for dinner.

But then maybe Francette will object. Hell if I know what you guys have really been up to in Paris in spite of what you've intimated to me. Hell maybe you guys are now an item. That city has a way of doing things to people. I know about this from first-hand painful experiences. That's where I met Rick after all, and where I fell in love with him.

So anyway, think about all this. You can stay at your place instead of being one of the bridge-and-tunnel crowd when you get back. I certainly have nothing against Park Slope. Some of my best friends live there. And I really like Al and May. She's such a sweetheart and he's so sardonic. I love that combination in a couple.

Oh before I forget: I met a young British writer, Zadie Smith, last week. She's black, and waiting for her first novel to come out. It's something called WHITE TEETH. She lives in London, and was in New York visiting her American agent. She's really cool. Her novel is about interracial marriages in an ever-changing London. A fresh voice from England! There's always a sense of romance and intense energy in discovering new voices in literature. New voices keep us in touch with the hope that as the world changes there are people around who will understand it and capture it well enough to allow us to continue seeing it. I had a two-hour lunch with Zadie, and she seems to me to be one of those new voices. I think you'd like her. After talking to her for two hours, I had the sense that in her fiction, she used her own psyche as a delicate radio station tuned to different channels of the outside world.

Now I better go. I want to visit some web-sites and see about an apartment in Montreal. I have some addresses I pulled out with my trusty meta-search engine, Metacrawler.

Please, my dear, respond to me right away about your apartment. I hope you're feeling better.

I'll close out with some lyrics from the Cesaria I'm listening to right now, the same CD *Cabo Verde*, from the cut The Sea is the Home of Nostalgia:

> *Mar é mrada di sodade*
> *El ta separá-no pa terra longe*
> *El ta separá-no d'nôs mae, nôs amigo*
> *Sem certeza di torná encontrá*

> *M'pensá na nha vida mi sô*
> *Sem ninguem di fé, perto di mim*
> *Pa st'odjá quês ondas ta 'squebrá di mansinho*
> *Ta trazé-me dor di sentimento*

> (The sea is the home of nostalgia
> It separates us from distant lands
> It separates us from our mothers, our friends
> Unsure if we'll see them again

> I thought of my lonely life
> With no one I have faith in at my side
> I watched the waves gently dying
> Sentiment came over me)

Dorit Levin Staff Writer
THE NEW YORKER
Condé Nast Publications
4 Times Square
New York, NY 10036
Voice/Fax: 1-212-421-8774
e-mail: doritlevin@onebox.com
Website: http://www.newyorker.com

*   *   *

Now back to Saturday night with Francette. We took the Métro
to Odéon and walked to the Danton UGE Cinéplex to see Spike
Lee's *Summer of Sam*. I had actually met Spike Lee once at a party
at my friends Al and May's townhouse in Park Slope. This was
when Spike Lee was still living in Forte Greene before he moved to
Westchester. As I recall him at that party, he was quite obnoxious,
arrogant, and full of himself, but he managed to entertain the
guests with a self-deprecating sense of humor. Sounds contradictory, I know, but he pulled it off. He could also be quite charming.

Summer of Sam used David Berkowitz's (played in the film by
Michael Badalucco) mayhems during the summer of 1977 in New
York to capture the general psychic anxieties that gripped New
Yorkers that summer and to chronicle significant events that
happened that I have already adumbrated to Francette.

Specifically, the film focuses on a group of Italian-American
friends who live in the Throg's Neck neighborhood of the Bronx
and their exploits on the pier butting into Eastchester Bay, where
they hang out daily—drinking beers, taunting outsiders, and ar-
ticulating and acting out their various prejudices. These prejudices are also somtimes intra-group: when they turn on Tony (Joe
Lisi), who tries to sell them the broken lobsters he pulls out of the
Bay, or on Bobby (Brian Tarantina) who is gay, or on Ritchie (Adrian
Brodie, in a stellar performance), who has gone punk and sports a

mohawk and funky sunglasses and leather jacket and a phony Cock-
ney accent.

More specifically, the film filters most of its somewhat
fragmentary narrative through the eyes of Vinny (John Leguizamo),
the priapic protagonist, a hair dresser who cheats on his wife Dionna
(Mira Sorvino) with her visiting Italian cousin Chiara (Lucia Grillo)
and with his boss Gloria (Bebe Newirth). Vinny's "identity"
progressively disintegrates in the course of the narrative as he loses
his wife, his job, and the respect of his friends, culminating in his
betrayal of his best friend Richie. Lee (who appears in his film as a
local TV newsman John Jeffries) uses the various displacements
within Vinnie's psyche and identity to also track the shift in New
York's music culture between the waning days of disco (worked
out in scenes at Studio 54), and the emergent punk scene (worked
out in scenes at CBGB's, where Vinnie and Dionna go to watch
Richie and his girlfriend Ruby [Jennifer Esposito] play in their
punk-rock band).

I thought one of contemporary cinema's most dramatic—and
exhilarating—moments came when the ghost of David Berkowitz's
neighbor's dog, long dead, reappears in his room to tell him (in
John Turturro's voice) to go out and kill some more people in Brooklyn and the Bronx.

And I also thought that one of contemporary cinema's most
steamy sexual scenes came when Vinny was plugging Chiara from
behind in his car while ostensibly taking her home from the bar,
where his wife was expecting him to bring her back a sandwich.
Vinny and Chiara had decided to make out in a quiet spot, right
in the middle of David Berkowitz's predator-territory, and by a
stroke of luck, narrowly escaped being blasted by him. Berkowitz's
car headlights interrupted Vinny and Chiara's lovemaking, and
they had to hustle quickly out of the area. As she was pulling on
her pants, Chiara made some remarks in Italian that the French
subtitles didn't translate, and so after the film while walking on
rue d'Ancienne Comédie toward Carrefour de Buci on our way to

the cabaret Alcazar de Paris on rue Mazarine, I asked Francette, who spoke Italian, what she said.

—She said: Asshole! Why did he have to show up when I was just coming?
—I have to tell you, that scene really turned me on.
—You know something?
—Yes?
—That film sort of reminds me of why I like American culture.
—Why do you like American culture?
—I like American culture because it's barbaric, exotic, erotic, and psychotic. The sex scene in the car really turned me on too, really turned me on!

She looked at me intently as she was saying all this. And I'd seen that look before, also in the eyes of a woman: Katya, when she rushed to hug me tightly after I gave my presentation on *The Blade Runner* at the Five Rivers Film Festival in Missoula in September of 1998. We'll get back to Paris and Francette and *Summer of Sam* and the Alcazar de Paris cabaret and 7 rue Fénelon, but now let's go to Missoula.

*   *   *

25

Paris: Monday, July 12, 1999

Missoula: Tuesday, September 1, 1998

The Five Rivers Film Festival ran for three days in Missoula. The festival had two components: an "academic" segment, with several presentations on various topics that Jacques had organized around the topic of narrative and technnology. He had invited top film scholars in the field, including our dessertation adviser, William O'Brien ("Boston Billy," as we called him because he ran marathons, mostly in Boston) who gave the keynote speech on Stephen Spielberg's *Saving Private Ryan*, which had captured the box office that summer.

"Boston Billy" was an athletic jockhead (also played handball in addition to marathoning) Bostonian with two doctorates (one in French and the other in art history), who liked to mix the Renaissance and Montaigne with Derrida and Foucault, and who also liked to mix—in the context of intellectual and aesthetic production—the sixteenth and nineteenth centuries with the twentieth.

Harvard University, which since the early 90s had been aggressively recruiting top scholars in their respective fields, even if they have doctorates from non-Ivy League schools, had just recruited "Boston Billy" the previous academic year, in what must have been a crowning achievement for him at that point in his career. It seemed that Harvard was preparing itself for the twenty-first century by recruiting intellectuals known for their pioneering work.

In any case, William O'Brien's keynote speech on *Saving Private Ryan* was mostly incomprehensible (to me in any case), as were

Jacques's own fragmentary comments on "the figure of desire in postmodernity." The audience for the academic presentation was, not surprisingly, a mixture of faculty, students, and film production students. Since the other component of the festival focused on the so-called "below-the-line" aspects of filmmaking, the film production people must have been curious about what the academics were up to.

As always when I gave papers at academic conferences, I took great pains to demonstrate that I was in no way an academic but a cultural and political journalist, and that even though I was trained in the academy to be a professor, in fact I never taught and had left the academy for the media as soon as I was done with my doctorate, and that I had gotten the academy and its disciplinary habits completely out of my system. I also liked to point out to people at these conferences that my doctorate was mostly useless, and that the only thing of value that I took out of graduate school was the significance of research. Then, more siginificantly, I also took great pains to make sure that my presentations were free of Latinate and obscure jargon and as clear as possible, even when analyzing debates and issues that have their origins within academic circles.

Therefore, I was not in the least surprised when, after my own presentation (which was the last that first day of the festival) analyzing in *Blade Runner* the visual regimes that capitalism and technology had set up, I got a number of questions about the film, which it seemed almost everyone in the audience had seen, and was also told—by several people who rushed up to me after the Q and A—that my paper was the most comprehensible they had listened to all day. This latter might be because of the strong effect that *Blade Runner* often had on viewers. For one, the idea that we might all be replicants, complete with memory implants, signified by the film's suggestion that Decker-Harrison Ford himself might be one, might be quite threatening to most people. For another, the Los Angeles of 2010, where the film's narrative unfolds, was · not all that different from the Los Angeles of 1982, when the film was released. The best science-fiction films, in my opinion, were

those whose worlds have familiar elements, punctuated throughout
by unfamiliar ones.

After my interlocutors dispersed, Katya rushed to give me a
very tight hug and a kiss right smack on the mouth. She then
congratulated me on my presentation. Bryn was right behind her.
Again, that late afternoon, Bryn was dressed all in black, high
boots, Levis, shirt open to reveal part of her chest, and a Hoqey
like mine. She was wearing sunglasses, and she also complimented
me. Then she said, quickly, abruptly, and somewhat authoritatively:
—Let's go to The Old Post and get something to drink.

Katya looked at me, somewhat stunned, and as if Bryn beat
her to the punch. Katya wanted to say something but wasn't quite
sure what. Then she looked at Bryn somewhat disdainfully. Bryn
seemed nonchalant and even ignored her, fastening her eyes on mine.
I hesitated somewhat, not quite sure how to respond, then said:

—Sure, let's go.

At The Old Post, Bryn treated me to two glasses of merlot. She
ordered imported beer for herself. While I was nursing the first
glass, she said:
—I really loved your paper. You're a very good writer.
—Thanks.
—But you're totally theoretical.
—I agree. I've been trying to work away from that. You have no
    idea how really theoretical I was, say, ten years ago, and how
    far I've come since then.
—Not far enough. Let's spend some time together. I will intro-
    duce you to the underbelly of Missoula. The experience can
    only help your writing.
—You want to spend time with me?
—I want you to spend time with me. I'll introduce you to a few of
    my activist friends. You already know Vanessa. She's a tree-
    hugging activist.
—What have you and friends been active about?

—Totally saving the environment for one.

—Is that right?

—One of them, a really close friend, is also in the media. I've been meaning to tell you that ever since we met at Trish's party.

—Really. What media? Here in Missoula?

—Right here in Missoula.

—What kind of media?

—Public access television.

—Really?

—Yeah, really. Missoula Public Access TV is not too far from here, near the library. I can take you to the station later this week. I have to introduce you to Mirta. She's totally cool. I think you'll like her.

—Mirta. That's a nice name. What's her background?

—You mean where is she from?

—I meant her educational background.

—She's getting a masters in journalism and also works full-time at the station. Her parents were born in Cuba.

—Ah ah.

Then she told me about the campaign to save the environment she and Mirta had been involved in for about a year: how for instance, she and her friends spiked some trees to thwart loggers; how they chained themselves to trees; and how they built tree houses and camped on trees for weeks at a time to prevent them from being cut. And how Mirta had recorded all these activities on video and audio, with her narrative voice-over.

Then she told me more:

—You know, I lived on the Rez.

—The Rez. You mean the Indian Reservation.

—Yeah. I lived there totally for six months with my friend Pemina Yellowbird.

—That's her real name? Yellowbird?

—Yeah. Don't you know anything about Native American names? I guess you're from New York, so you wouldn't know.

—There are Native Americans in New York—the Iroquois, the Algonquins.

· —I know that. I meant New York City. The Native Americans are Upstate.

—You certainly know quite a bit about New York for someone who's never been there.

—I'm very active politically, so I make a point to know about different places.

—I noticed. But you're wrong about Native Americans in New York City. They're in the city as well. They built all those skyscrapers.

—Yeah you're right. I totally forgot about that. They were used—I guess totally exploited—by construction companies because they're not afraid of heights.

—Precisely. Which Rez did you and Pemina live on—Flatheads north of here?

—Yeah.

—Why?

—Why what?

—Why did you live there?

—My friend Pemina's idea. She's a writer also, of short stories. She's a protegé of Sherman Alexie.

—The guy who wrote the original screenplay for *Smoke Signals* ?

—Yeah. Have you seen that?

—No.

—I have. We can go see it. It's still playing at The Crystal.

—Bryn: Tell me about your parents. Your last name: Where does it come from?

—Asselstine. I think it's made up. Sounds Jewish, right?

—Yeah.

—It ain't. My father told us he was second-generation Swiss. But he could have lied. He was a carpenter who left my mother when I was ten. He now lives in California with his wife.

—He could be right about being Swiss. And your mother?

—She's a drunk and a registered nurse who still lives in Olympia, Washington, where I grew up.

—How did you end up here in Missoula?

—I followed my heavy-metal boyfriend here four years ago. He's an Olympia native.

—Bryn: You're really full of surprises. You lived on the Rez? What did you do there for six months?

—That'll have to wait for another evening. Do you want another glass of wine?

—Sure.

—Are you hungry? You want to eat here? I can totally buy you dinner.

—Let's finish our drinks and head over to Jacques's. He's having a welcome dinner party for the conference participants. Trust me: There'll be plenty of food there.

—You think it's totally cool if I come along?

—Totally cool.

—Is he going to go on and on again about concentration camps and swastikas?

—Who knows? With his mentor around, he might be on his good behavior tonight.

—You mean the Harvard guy who talked about *Saving Private Ryan*?

—Yeah. Boston Billy.

—I totally disagree with his take on that film. At least, the part of his presentation that I could follow. I didn't know what he was talking about most of the time.

—You know what?

—What?

—Neither could I. I also disagree with his take on the film. He thought the film was retro reactionary, and that Spielberg was exploiting quote unquote the last good war for his own preachy conservative ideology.

—Spielberg is conservative? The same guy who directed *ET: the Extraterrestrial* and *Schindler's List*?

—I'm sure Billy thinks those films are conservative also.

—I saw Jacques nodding his head from time to time during Billy's
    presentation.

—He must have understood every word of Billy's paper.

—Maybe they share a secret language.

—Perhaps. Jacques admires Billy.

—Jacques seems to totally worship Billy.

—Jacques likes you though.

—He does?

—Yeah. He thinks you and I should get together.

—Really? He wants you to get together with me romantically?

—Yeah.

—I thought he was trying to set you up with Katya.

—He was, until he met you.

—I feel honored. But honestly, where does he get off setting people
    up? He should let people get together to do their own fucking.

She drove us up to South Hills, to Highwood Avenue, where
Jacques's house was teeming with guests. This time Jacques used
the conference money for a catering service.

Aside from conference participants and straggler-graduate
students who usually showed up at Jacques's loosely structured
dinners parties for free food, the whole community of Jacques's
friends were there. People talked mostly about the day's
presentations. I got a few more questions about *Blade Runner*. One
of the questions was also, like Katya's, about why blacks were absent
from the film. As always at these academic post-session informal
dinner parties, there were a lot of posturings: graduate students
trying to impress the academic "stars." And of course the stars
trying impress the students. So then Boston Billy had a circle of
people around him throughout the party. And even Jacques was
caught up in the charade. Even though he was the host and made
sure that everything was more or less happening according to
expectations, from time to time he managed to find himself in
orbit around Boston Billy's Harvard star.

I had the impression that Katya wanted to talk to me during

the party, but I spent most of the time with Bryn instead. When we walked into Jacques's house, Bryn and I mingled as a tandem with the crowd in the living room and the kitchen, eating and drinking. She seemed glued to me. She might have been intimidated by the critical mass of academics. As we were talking to each other between bites and sips, I noticed Katya sometimes circling— or looking at—us, trying to catch my eye. But she never directly approached us. And then Bryn insisted on smoking, and so because Jacques had loudly designated the porch for the evening's smokers, we adjorned to the crowded porch of smokers for most of the evening at that party.

Bryn:
—The food is good, and the booze too, but what a zoo!
—Have you ever been to these so-called informal academic parties before?
—Nope. I've been to Trish's parties, but those are totally different.
—Trish doesn't consider herself an academic, even if she teaches at the university.
—You're totally right. From what I've seen at those parties and from what I know of her, she's not at all an academic, if I understand how you're using that term in this conversation.
—An academic is someone who is tied to disciplines, who believes that knowledge is divided into disciplines, and who, in some quote unquote disciplines like literature and art history, also believes that knowledge is divided into centuries.
—You're totally funny and knowledgable.
—Thanks. You want to know where disciplines come from?
—Please enlighten me.
—Disciplines are a construct, one of the frightful legacies of the Roman Empire. The Romans invented disciplines in order to colonize knowledge by storing it in legitimate boxes and establishing authoritative protocols.
—Authoritative protocols? What do you mean?

—Disciplines establish proper ways of talking about the knowledge stored in them, and also of the ways of doing research in
them.

—You mean someone in sociology talks and does research in a
certain way, and someone in history talks and does research in
another way?

—Exactly. I couldn't have put it more clearly myself. And it also
means that someone in sociology cannot talk about history
with any kind of authority.

—I never thought about it that way.

—Disciplines are bullshit in any case. I don't believe in them.

—They don't sound cool.

—They're not, totally. Anyway, these kinds of parties are full of
students
trying to impress their professors, professors trying to impress
their students, and all forms of pretensions.

—That's a world I don't care about.

—I know you don't.

—You do?

—Yeah. You're an artist. You're not an academic. And there's no
reason you should care about what's going on in that world.

—You know all that in the short time you've known me?

—Of course. I know enough about you by now to say that. I
happen to be a good judge of people.

—Tell me what you think about me so far, totally.

—You seem kind. Free-spirited. Talented. Attractive. And young.

—Those are great compliments. Thank you.

—What do you think of me?

—I think you're one of the most intelligent people I've ever met.

—Oh come on! You can't be serious.

—I am. You're too fast for me. I struggle to to keep up with you.
I'm totally serious. You're highly intelligent. And sensitive.
You're not arrogant, like . . .

—Like who?

—Like Jacques. Or Rob. Jacques likes to control things. Events and people. Rob is simply an arrogant bastard.

—Hey, you're a great judge of people too! You're dead on the money about those two.

—Thanks.

—But if you continue to tell me how intelligent I am I'll start believing it myself.

—I'm saying it because I totally believe it. And because I think it's the truth.

As she said this, dragging a cigarette, with patches of the Rockies behind her in the distance, and with her hair that was not tucked underneath her Hoqey beret blowing in the crisp September mountain air that was now descending into Bitteroot Valley, where Missoula was nestled, Bryn looked absolutely sexually desirable to me that night, and I couldn't help what I said next:

—Bryn, I want to go home with you tonight.

—You can if you want. But why?

—I want to fuck you.

—Why?

—I'm attracted to you.

—I'm attracted to you too. But not in a sexual way.

—Why not?

—I don't know. Maybe just the chemistry. I really want to be your friend though.

—But you won't fuck me?

—No. I'm sorry. But please don't take this personally. My impression is that you're extremely attractive to women. I can see that and I can even see why. For instance, I can tell that Katya would totally love to fuck you. Women can sense these things.

—But I don't feel like fucking Katya. I feel like fucking you. Tonight.

—You're not listening to me. I just told you that I don't want you to do that, and I also told you that the first night we met. Remember that I told you that that first night at Trish's?

—I remember it well. But I thought you were just being prudent.

—Prudent? Do I totally strike you as the prudent type?

—No.

—I don't feel like fucking you. Or anybody else for that matter.

—Why?

—Look. I'll tell you something, OK? Like I said, it's not personal with you. About a month before we met, I ended a five-year relationship with a guy.

—Really? What happened?

—He totally abused me.

—How? He beat up on you?

—Not like that. He was more subtle. I was totally in love with him but he used me.

—How?

—He totally took advantage of me for his own hangups.

—Was he an older guy?

—He was my age.

—So what happened?

—We had an intense relationship. He was a musician. I was totally in love with him. The first adult love of my life. I got involved with him when I was eighteen.

—So what happened?

—The only sex he ever had with me was anal.

—What do you mean?

—I mean the only fucking he ever did with me was in the ass.

—You mean you both fucked each other through the ass?

—I mean he fucked only my ass. He never fucked my vagina. We never had what what you call missionary sex. I really wanted that sometimes, but he never wanted to. And I always went along with what he wanted. The other thing: He never once kissed me. Our physical contacts were totally confined to butt-fucking.

Just at that point I had an erection made visible through the bulge in my pants that I immediately concealed with both hands. My id wanted to jump on her right there and then and pin her lean gamine body against the wooden railings on the porch and make love to her. Instead, my superego said:

—How weird. And you went along with that for five years?

—I told you: I was hopelessly and totally in love with him.

—But you finally broke up with him.

—I had to. My ass was so sore all the time. He would totally ram his dick in there when he butt-fucked me. I finally had the strength to break it off.

—I'm sorry you had to go through that.

—Well. The guy had some serious problems. I think he was a closet-gay. When we were together, I had short hair.

—So you're saying he took you for a surrogate guy?

—That's exactly what I'm saying. I could look like a guy if I wanted to. I wear pants and shirts all the time. And with my short hair. . .

—Yeah. Yeah I can see that.

—Listen: Like I said: I don't feel like being romantic or sexual with anyone for a while.

—That's too bad. What happened to you I mean. Is the guy around? Have I seen him?

—No way. He and his band moved to Colorado after we broke up. It was either him or me. If he hadn't moved I would have. This town isn't big enough for both of us.

—Did you see a therapist after all that?

—Nope. I couldn't afford one.

—Couldn't you get one through public economic assistance?

—Nope.

—Why not?

—I don't make enough money to afford a therapist, and I make too much to get medical assistance for psychotherapy.

—That's too bad. What kind of music does he play?

—Heavy metal.

—That figures. Oh wait: Is he the guy you moved to Missoula with?

—Yeah. I followed him here.

—As I said, I'm sorry this happened to you.

—It's all right. I'm feeling much better already. And I'm glad I finally got to tell you about all that. I totally want to be your friend. There's so much you can teach me.

—I totally want to be your friend also.

—And something else.

—What?

—I want you to totally trust me.

—I will.

—You can still come home with me if you want.

—Really?

—Totally.

—But we won't fuck?

—No. We won't fuck. We'll sleep on the same bed. Like we did before.

—Well . . . I'll go home with you.

—I was hoping you would say yes. Are you sure?

—Yeah I'm sure.

—Because if you really want to get laid tonight you can go home with Katya. All you have to do is just ask her. She'll be totally obliged I'm sure.

—I don't want to go home with Katya. I don't feel like fucking her.

—Why not? She's totally attractive and intelligent. Why aren't you sexually attracted to her?

—I don't know. Maybe it's just the chemistry—as you would say.

—Funny. I like your sense of humor.

—Thanks.

—In fact, you know something?

—What?

—You beat me to it.

—What are you talking about? Beat you to what?

—I wanted to ask you to come home with me tonight. But I might not have asked.

—Why?

—Because I think all you would want to do is fuck me.

—Oh Bryn, I'm not like that. I'm not like Jacques.

—I know that. But I wasn't sure. Not many men will sleep in the same bed with a desirable woman without wanting to fuck her. Actually, not many women will either, for that matter.

—I'll go to your house with you.

—Great! I'll get us more wine at Bilo's on the way.

—You feel like leaving now?

—Do you? I don't care. Don't you want to spend more time with these people? You speak their language.

—Are you kidding? I speak their language all right. But I've had too many evenings like this one to last several lifetimes. Let's get out of here.

—Sure. Listen: Let's also stop at Crystal Video after Bilo's to pick up a tape.

—Of what?

—*Blade Runner*. I feel like seeing the film with you, especially after I listened to your presentation this afternoon.

—We don't need to stop at the Crystal for that. Jacques has a tape of it.

We left for Bryn's place after I cut my way through the sycophant-crowd glued to Boston Billy in Jacques's living room to grab the videotape of *Blade Runner*. Two people visibly noticed our leavetaking: Katya, who gave Bryn a New-York-style dagger look; and Jacques, who winked at me. I chuckled, and for the rest of my tenure in Missoula, I never disabused them about whatever "conventional"—and logical—assumptions they might have had about what Bryn and I might have done at her place later that night. What Bryn and I really (and as she would say, totally) did later that night before going to bed, and without making love, was watch Jacques's videotape (the same videotape that Katya and I watched at *her* place) of *Blade Runner* on Bryn's VCR, while we drank more wine and while I explained the film to her scene by scene. "That woman is ready to be fucked—and molded," Jacques told me apropos Bryn in my Entry 9: New York: Tuesday June 29,

1999; Missoula: Wednesday, August 26, 1998. Well: He was right about only the latter and not the former. So he assumed wrongly.

Speaking of assumptions, and also of anal sex: Let's get back to Paris and Francette. Francette certainly had several assumptions about what *we* would do at *her* place last Sunday night as we left Alacazar de Paris.

*   *   *

26

Paris: Monday, July 12, 1999

Paris: Sunday, July 11, 1999

    After listening to the exquisite music of the French-Indian quartet called Mukta and hearing Suzana Baca sing with the dreamy power of a warm sea breeze at the Alcazar de Paris, Francette and I walked to the Carrefour de Buci, then turned left onto rue St-André des Arts, heading for the St-Michel Métro. We took the train, direction Porte de Clignancourt, changed trains at Chatelet and got back to 7 rue Fénelon. Michel was not home, as usual. As soon as we walked into her apartment on the top floor, Francette said:

—Let's sit out on the balcony for a little bit. It's really nice and breezy. I'll get a bottle of Amarrone that I've been saving.

We drank about half the bottle on the balcony.
Then she said:
—Listen I want to ask you for a big favor.
—What favor?
—Remember I told you I was completely turned on when Vinny was fucking that woman in the ass in the car?
—Yeah, I was as well. Vinny-John Leguizamo plugged Chiara-Lucia Grillo in the ass.
—I want you to fuck me in the ass like that!
—I don't know, Francette . . .
—Oh, come on! Please. I've been like a bitch in heat since I saw that scene.

Suddenly, I surprised myself. I superimposed Bryn's face onto Francette's as the former appeared to me on Jacques's porch the · previous September. And I also transformed Francette's balcony into Jacques's porch. I suddenly pulled Francette into her bedroom and flung her on her bed. For about twenty minutes I think, we kissed, rubbed, licked, and sucked each other. Then I positioned myself and, seconds later, rammed her from behind, and the mingling of her screams with the street noises blasted through my ears. We were both exhausted after thirty minutes.

Francette, in French:
—That was superb. Just superb and great! Do you want some more wine? I have another fine bottle of Amarrone. In fact I have several fine bottles.
—Yeah sure.
—Did you enjoy it?
—Yeah I did, but you know something?
—I know: That was your first time fucking someone in the ass.
—Yeah. I always fantazised about doing it.
—Well, my dear, you can act out your fantasies with me anytime.

She got the bottle and we adjorned to the balcony again. I quaffed two glasses within ten minutes as I gazed languidly at the stunning views, to the right, of the well-lit shops and supermarkets at the intersection of rue Lafayette and boulevard Magenta that hadn't opened for business yet—and to the left, of the statues that adorned the upper half of the Eglise St Vincent de Paul. A splendid dawn was breaking over the exquisite rooftops of Paris. And for the first time during that trip to Paris with Francette, I seemed at peace with myself. I coincided with the moment. In other words, I felt completely within my body, at one of those rare moments in one's life.

Francette:

—I feel like doing it again!

—I'm exhausted, Francette. I don't even know if I can get it up. That session knocked me out.

—I have something that will help you.

—What ... Viagra?

—Yes yes!

—You can't be serious!

—Oh yes I am.

—You keep that around?

—I got it in LA. I wanted to test what they were saying ... that it was also good for women.

—And?

—I tried it, but it made no difference. To my body anyway. So?

—So what?

—Will you take it and fuck me in the ass again? I read that it will give you an erection for at least an hour. And that's okay with me ...

—Well, sure, why not? This is a night for first-time experiences, after all.

And so I took *sildenafil citrate*, commonly known as Viagra, for the first time in my life. We went back into the bedroom, where I plugged her from behind. Francette screamed for another hour and a half. On this second round of chemically aided anal sex, I didn't fantasize about Bryn: I was "totally" with Francette. I must have passed out after that second session.

When I got up at noon today, after my ablutions, I booted the desktop of a still-sleeping Francette, logged on to My Yahoo, saw the red text that told me I had thirty messages, then clicked e-mail to find Dorit's stunning and completely unexpected (at least to me) 2K e-posting, which I reproduce below.

––––––

Date: Sun, 11 July 1999 23:18:29 -0500 (EDT)
From: "Dorit Levin" <doritlevin@onebox.com> **Add Block**
Subject: Coming to Paris!

Message: Yo! You'll never believe this! I'm coming to Paris! I should arrive Tuesday morning at De Gaulle. I have to look at some documents at the Bibliothèque national for a week! The material is rare and not online. THE NEW YORKER is paying for the whole trip. I need to research some historical material for the stuff I'm developing on Québec. It has to do with how France actually ceded Québec.

BTW, I found an apartment in Montreal that sounds gorgeous, in a neighborhood called Plateau Mont-Royal. I'll have a roommate, but that sounds okay. She's an artist and she sounds interesting. I'll have to tell you all about it. I can't believe I'll be seeing you in Paris tomorrow!

I'm staying with Emilie. Listen, please respond and give me Francette's voice number. I'll call you from De Gaulle. My flight arrives at 9 AM Paris Time.

> Cesaria Evora:
> *Nha fé nha esperança*
> *E di bai pa longe*
> *E di bai pa terra grande*
> *Terra di felicidade*
>
> (I have waited for you in vain
> But I have always had the faith and hope
> To go far away, toward a big country
> Toward better ground)
>
> I better go. I'll talk to you tomorrow!
> Love.

––––––––

Dorit Levin—Staff Writer
THE NEW YORKER
Condé Nast Publications
4 Times Square

New York, NY 10036
Voice/Fax: 1-212-421-8774
e-mail: doritlevin@onebox.com
Website: http://www.newyorker.com

*   *   *

Dorit had developed a friendship with Emilie independently of me ever since I introduced them to each other in 1991 when Emilie was visiting New York. For one, they had a mutual friend: Eliane, the documentary and feature filmmaker who e-mailed Dorit about the impossibility of relationships in the contemporary world. Eliane had written Dorit that in contemporary world culture, but especially in the Western Hemisphere, in those areas that have high-tech-saturated societies, romantic relationships between straight, lesbian, or gay couples are mostly impossible. What Eliane had written Dorit might explain what happened between Katya and me in Missoula for nine months—from September 1998 to June 1999.

So let's get back there. Specifically, to the day after Bryn and I left Jacques's house-party together and went to her house on Spruce Street, where I spent the night.

*   *   *

27

Paris: Monday, July 12, 1999

Missoula: Wednesday, September 2, 1998

The second day of the Five Rivers Film Festival. The first day was devoted to the academic component of theoretical presentations about narrative and technology, which Jacques was in charge of. The rest of the conference consisted of the production component of so-called "below-the-line" people involved in film production, below the line, that is, of director and producer when credits are being scrolled at the end of a film. This component comprised a series of film screenings and workshops.

Early that morning, Bryn drove me back to Jacques's. Then she picked me up around 11 AM and drove me to the Missoula Public Access TV station and introduced me to her friend Mirta Gonzales. All three of us went to lunch at Hobnob Restaurant in downtown Missoula. I took a liking to Mirta immediately: She definitely looked like a Latina, was lively, quite energetic, seemed as free-spirited as Bryn, and had some interesting news for us that afternoon. She announced that she just found out that she was pregnant. She knew who the father was (also a graduate student), was definitely looking forward to having the baby, had no plans to "marry" the father, but he would participate in raising the child. She was elated in fact at all the prospects.

After lunch, Bryn had to go to work at Wordens. Mirta went back to the TV station. I attended a few workshops in the afternoon. Katya was nowhere to be found in any of these workshops. Then, in the evening, there was a free buffet dinner for all the participants at the highly expensive Red Bird Restaurant, also in downtown Missoula. Bryn had a prior engagement. But Katya showed up. She seemed genuinely glad to see me. She smiled at me broadly and made a beeline for me.

—Good to see you! Bryn released you, I see.
—That she did.
—Where is she?
—She's out with friends.
—Did you two have some fun?
—That we did.
—I told you she wanted to fuck you.
—That you did. Let's drop all this.
—OK, OK. Don't be pissed at me.

She rubbed my cheek and continued:
—Let's sit down and eat. Are you hungry?
—I'm ravenous.
—Just have a seat. I'll get us both plates of things. You want everything, right?
—There's only chicken and rice, right?
—Right.
—Then I want everything. Red wine too.
—Of course. Of course.

She came back with a tray of two full plates and two glasses of merlot. Jacques and Christine joined us for about thirty minutes or so, but most of the dinner Katya and I were alone. She said to me at some point, out of the blue it seemed:
—You know I like your hands.
—How do you mean?
—I like the way you gesture with your hands when you're speaking.
—Thanks.
—Those hands really turn me on when you gesture with them like that.

—Oh oh.

—What do you mean, oh oh. You turn me on through your hands. And I think I'm in love with you.

—You can't mean that. We just met.

—What does that matter? I realized I was in love with you after I listened to your paper yesterday.

—What about your boyfriend?

—I told you that has no future. Do you love me?

—I like you.

—What's the problem? Is it Bryn?

—No. Bryn and I are close friends.

—That's all?

—We're developing a very close friendship.

—I think it's interesting that we met when we did.

—How do you mean?

—Both of us found ourselves in Missoula by chance. Two months ago neither of us could have predicted that we would be here. And here we are. And then we met.

—The way you say that makes it sound fatal.

—Maybe. We were destined to meet.

—Missoula is such a small place. We would have met anyway.

—Yes. But not in the manner we did, through the intimate party of your friend.

—Do you have a proposal?

—I want to be in a relationship with you. You really turn me on sexually. Are you attracted to me at least?

—Somewhat. You intrigue me.

—How?

—You're from the other side of the diaspora. A Russian Jew who emigrated to Israel, then to the US.

—What do you mean the other side of the diaspora?

—When people think of diaspora, they think of the third world.

—So?

—Your origin is the recently dissolved second world, dissolved into the first world. The former Eastern and Central Europe is now simply Europe. Although Russia's situation is quite ironic at the moment.

—What do you mean?

—In 1917 the Revolution stopped a natural historical development. I'll explain: The Revolution stopped the development of a bourgeois civilization. That's why there is no middle class there. And that's also why a transition to democracy will be difficult.

—Yeah? Why is that?

—There has to be a considerable middle class in a country for democracy to flourish there.

—And why is that?

—It goes back to the Enlightenment.

—Oh?

—It's too comlicated to explain. But this leads me to my next point, since the French invented the Enlightenment. If Napoleon had succeeded in capturing Russia in the nineteenth century, then there would have been a middle class instead of what Russia has now.

—Russia has an upper-class elite who live in dachas, and a considerable lumpen agricultural lower class who live the drab sections of Moscow, Kiev, and St Petersburg. In other words: sizable portions of Russia fall into the third-world. In many ways Russia is actually a third-world country with nuclear weapons. Which makes Russia exotic to me.

—I'm exotic to you then?

—You can say that.

—That's good.

—Yeah?

—It's good that you find me intriguing and exotic. Because I also find you intriguing and exotic.

—That's the norm. What is not is that I find *you* exotic. I've never been involved with a Russian Jew before.

—Here's your chance.

—You seem convinced that this is going to happen.

—I'm an only child. I usually get what I want. And what I want is
   to have a romantic relationship with you. But first things first:
   I want to fuck you. Tonight.

—Yeah?

—Let's go my place.

—Now?

—Yes. Why not?

We left the Red Bird for her place on Sixth Street between
Hilda and Helen Streets. I drank two more glasses of merlot and
she drank some vodka. Then we made love for about two hours.
She must have come about three times. I'd never seen a woman
come as easily and effortlessly as Katya. The first time she came I
did not even penetrate her. I was simply licking and sucking her
breasts. I ended up spending the night at her house.

Now I need to get back to Paris and Francette and Dorit, to
narrate a few interesting events that closed out my trip there. But
I'm getting ahead of myself.

*   *   *

28

Paris: Friday, July 16, 1999

I'm flying back to New York's JFK tomorrow at 9 AM Paris time. Some incredible events have happened. I'm still at Francette's, alone. Michel is not here as usual. And until I leave, Francette is staying with her lesbian couple friends Sylvie and Anne at 4 rue de Rocroy, the street parallel to rue Fénelon, just two blocks away. Dorit is staying at Emilie's as planned, at rue Bizerte in the Seventeenth Arrondissement, until she flies back to New York next Wednesday. But I'm seeing her tonight. Following is what happened.

Paris: Tuesday, July 13, 1999

Dorit called me from De Gaulle around 10 AM, after she cleared French immigration and customs. Emilie was there to pick her up. Dorit could have waited until she got back to Emilie's to call me, but she kept Emilie waiting while she called me from a pay phone. Francette and I were having breakfast when the phone rang. She picked up the phone. In French:

—Allo?

Francette again:
—He's here. Who is speaking?
Then she handed me the phone, still in French.
—It's your little friend. She's here.

I:

—Hi there! You're here.

—My plane landed about thirty minutes ago. I would like to see you.

—I'd like to see you too. How was the flight?

—Smooth all night. And I slept like a baby, thanks to the booze flowing freely on trans-Atlantic flights.

—Let's see: American Airlines?

—Good memory. That's my carrier all right. Gotta keep those frequent flyer miles up.

—Welcome to Paris. What are your plans for today?

—Emilie, Eliane, and I plan to spend sometime together. Then I've got to go to the library. Gotta get going right away. We can meet for some apéritifs, then dinner.

—Sounds good.

—I want you all to myself. Will Francette approve?

—There's nothing for her to approve. There's nothing between us.

—Where do you want to meet?

—How about I pick you up at the library? Rue de Richelieu. Métro Bourse.

—Thanks for telling me where it is. Just kidding. I remember where it is. You'll pick me up there then—in the ornate lobby?

—Deal. 5:30?

—See you then.

Francette obviously overheard my side of the conversation. In English:

—So you're getting together with your little friend?

—She's not little, Francette. She's five seven.

—Oh excuuuse me!

Ever since Monday when I told her about Dorit's unexpected Paris junket, Francette had been teasing me nonstop. And now it was wearing a little thin.

—We're going to dinner. Any recommendations?

—Am I invited?

—No.

—When am I going to meet her? I like to meet her!

—You will. Tomorrow maybe.

—Remember, we're getting together with my friends for Quatorze Juillet.

—Yes I remember. Your friends want to make up to me. Where are we getting together again?

—You've forgotten. I told you: At Anne and Sylvie's.

—Where do they live?

—4 rue de Rocroy. About two blocks from here.

—Do they have a big place?

—Huge. Much bigger than this one.

—They must be loaded. At least one of them must be.

—You're right. Sylvie is. Her parents bought it for her when she was still a student at the Louvre School.

—She went to Louve School of the Arts?

—Yeah.

—Back to Quatorze Juillet. You can meet Dorit then.

—She's not invited.

—You're kidding.

—No.

—You're not kidding.

—No I'm not. But you can invite her to the big conference close-out party on Thursday night.

—Yeah you've been talking about that. A lot of people—mostly participants—will be there, right?

—Right.

—Where is that party taking place?

—At Anne and Sylvie's again. They've been very generous donating their apartment for the occasion.

—It must really be a big place.

—It is. Wait till you see it tomorrow.

—OK. Back to my dinner tonight with Dorit. Any suggestions? ·

—Depends.

—On what?

—On whether this will be a romantic dinner or not.

—It doesn't matter. Just a place where we can talk.

—How expensive?

—I don't think that really matters either.

—She must be buying.

—She is. She always buys.

—Lucky you. You have all these women buying for you.

—I'll pay all of them back when I come into money.

—All of us you mean. Don't forget me. I've sponsored your fine trip to Paris all the way. Plane ticket, lodging, and meals. The whole works.

—You're right. You're absolutely right. I'd never really realized it like that.

—Don't you forget what dear Francette has done for you.

—I won't. Any recommendations?

—Is she hip?

—Of course.

—I'll go easy on her wallet.

—Thanks.

—She can thank me later. If you guys want a place that's hip where you can talk, and where the food is relatively good for the price, then you can't beat the café on top of Virgin Megastore on Les Champs Elysées. The same on we were at.

—Thanks.

During that conversation Tuesday morning, Francette had mentioned one of the two events that was to be crucial in clarifying my respective relationships with Dorit *and* Francette. But I'm getting ahead of myself.

I picked up Dorit at the Bibliothèque nationale. We went to Café Rostand at Place Rostand and rue Soufflot, across the street from one of the entrances to Luxembourg Gardens, for a few kirs before dinner. She was looking great, dressed in black as usual, except for a red beret. "When in Rome ... "

We talked nonstop there, and later at the Virgin Megastore

Café, mostly chewing over the events we had written about during our e-exchanges. One of the possibilites Dorit had mentioned became somewhat clarified that evening:

—So I'll be back in New York next week.

—When?

—Wednesday. July 21st. Then Friday I leave for Montréal for two months, till the end of September. Like I said before, you can stay at your place. We'll overlap by two days, but you can handle that, can't you?

—That sounds very tempting. I'm always welcome at Al and May's.

—But that's all the way in Park Slope. Bridge-and-Tunnel. You'll be stuck taking the 2 or 3 or D trains, more the latter if you're going to NBC at Rockefeller Center. In Manhattan you can just walk there.

—As I said, it's tempting. At Al and May's the food will be free, and I don't have to pay the mortgage.

—So that's what you're worried about? The mortgage? Don't worry: I'll continue to pay the mortgage. I still plan to live there when I come back. Assuming it's OK with you.

—Of course it's OK. I can't afford the mortgage right now.

—You will when you win the lotto, or if you sell the film rights to your novel. Or if the screenplay you're working on with your friend in Hong Kong becomes a hit. You have several opportunities to strike gold.

—We'll see about all that.

—Just stay there when I'm in Montréal.

—OK. I will. I'll take the cab from JFK to West 57th Street on Saturday.

—I think you've made the right decision.

The full ramifications of her remark were to emerge during the second event Francette mentioned during our conversation that Tuesday morning—the big conference party at 4 rue de Rocroy that took place last night. But again I'm getting ahead of myself.

The first event Francette alluded to, the Quatorze Juillet,

happened unremarkably at 4 rue de Rocroy: drinks; dinner; an
excursion to the crowded quays by the Seine to watch fireworks;
· then more drinks at a café on rue Dauphine, close to the Seine.
Let's immediatly leap to the crucial event last night.

Paris: Thursday, July 15, 1999

Dorit came by 7 rue Fénelon around 8 PM. She walked up
four flights of stairs to Francette's apartment after punching the
code that I gave her on the phone to open the front door of the
building. I introduced her and Francette to each other. At first
Francette was frosty. She invited her to stay a little bit for some
wine and then gave her a tour of the apartment. By the time we
got to Anne and Sylvie's around 9 PM, they had warmed up to
each other. Or so it seemed to me. In any case, the apartment at 4
rue de Rocroy was packed when we got there.

As I alluded to in an earlier entry, the conference participants
were an interesting admixture of international writers, academics,
and media people. I was impressed—again—with all the European languages and some African ones drifting through my ears
that evening. As soon as we got inside the apartment, Francette
disappeared into the crowd. A buffet dinner table had been set up,
and Dorit and I had something to eat before we went out to the
balcony. The balcony was somewhat similar to Francette's but bigger, and on it one could see the intersection of boulevard Magenta
and rue Maubeuge. We could even see the roof lights of Gare du
Nord in the distance.

Once again, the rooftops of Paris looked magnificent to me
that night, as car headlights wound their way around various intersections and streets. As we sipped red wine and gazed at the
scene, Dorit said:

—Perfect night. I can't believe I'm here, with you, on this balcony,
  tonight, gazing at a neighborhood of Paris. If anyone had told
  me a week ago that I'd be doing this with you I'd have thought
  they were looking at the wrong crystal ball.
—I can't believe you're here either.

—Let's seize this moment. Let's embrace this gift of time at the
edge of the millennnium.

I had no idea what she was talking about, until she spoke next.
Again, Dorit:

—Why are we dancing around all this? Let's get married.

—What did you say?

—I said let's get married. I've never stopped loving you. I've never
let you go for the past ten years. Even when you were married
to Sarah. Listen, I'm the only one who understands you.

—This really doesn't surprise me. I've been thinking about you and
us as well. Ever since your first e-mail to me after I got to Paris.

—It's been a strange summer for me.

—I'll say. For me too.

—Maybe it's the millennium bug. I feel like changing my life
radically.

—As do I.

—Look: I don't really know what love is, but what we have comes
the closest, in my opinion. We don't have to explain ourselves
when we talk to each other. We understand each other per-
fectly. We admire and respect each other intellectually and
emotionally. We think alike most of the time. We care for each
other deeply. At least I know I do for you. And the sex was
great between us when we combined our DNAs several years
ago. We like to wear black. We're both addicted to the Internet,
where we both like to type in Palatino. We're the closest to a
perfect couple.

—You're absolutely right about everything you've just said. I think
I'm in love with you also, ever since that night at the Zinc Bar.
It's always been a question of the untimely between us ever
since we broke up.

—I'll bet that if that bitch Karyn hadn't derailed us in 1991, we
would have been together all through the 90s, sparing you all
the shitload of painful experiences you had to go through
throughout the 90s.

—Oh one never knows. Maybe I was meant to go through all that shit-cargo of experiences.

—Will you marry me?

—Is this a proposal?

—Yes it is.

—I'll marry you, Dorit.

—Fantastic! This calls for a toast.

—No champagne? With red wine?

—Why not? How appropriate for Paris! And the day after Quatorze Juillet.

We clinked glasses and had our sips.

I:

—When should we do the honors?

—You pick a date. Just give my mother two weeks to organize things.

—No problem with that. I have a logical date for us.

—When is that?

—January 1, 2000. It's my birthday and it's also the first day of the millennium.

—Perfect. I can't wait to tell my mother. She'll be thrilled to death.

—And I can't wait to break the news to my mother, relatives, and friends when I get back to New York. I can't wait to tell Emilie. And I can't wait to break the news to Francette right here.

—Oh boy. I wonder how *she'll* take the news.

Just at that point Francette showed up, glass of wine in hand, smiling and saying in French:

—Oh, there you are you two. I was wondering where you've been hiding out.

I:

—We have some good news to tell you.

—What?

—Dorit and I are getting married.

—*What* ? Is this some kind of joke?
—We're getting married on January 1st, 2000.

Then, of course, Francette switched into English (and of course Dorit said almost nothing during the following exchange, except for her intervention):
—You can't be serious.
—We're very serious.
—When did you decide to do this?
—Just now. In the last few minutes.
—Isn't your decision a little hasty?
—Not really. We've known each other since 1989. This has been brewing for a while.
—Why didn't you tell me about her before?
—There's been no reason to. It's all been a question of the untimely.
—The untimely?
—Yes, the untimely, in a Deleuzean sense.
—Fuck Deleuze. You bastard. After what we've both been through together the past two weeks?

Dorit at that point looked at me with some consternation, and almost yelled:
—*After what you've both been through together*? What is she talking about?
—She simply meant after all the experiences of our being together most of the time the past two weeks. With me staying at her place and all that.
Francette at that point threw her wine in my face:
—You bastard!

Honestly, I had expected her strong reaction to the news, but definitely not that display of raw emotion.
Francette dashed back into the apartment. Dorit followed her

inside to fetch a glass of water to wash the wine from my face. Then Dorit said:

—I feel like splitting pronto. Can we just leave?

—Yeah sure. Let's get out of here.

We left immediately and found ourselves on rue de Rocroy. I suggested:

—Let's go a café on boulevard Denain, near Gare du Nord. There are a lot of cafés on that street as you head for the station. Let's go to one of them.

—Sure. What are you going to do later?

—Go back to her place.

—Are you sure that's a good idea? After what just happened?

—Yeah. I want to do that. I owe her an explanation.

—You can come with me back to Emilie's. There's enough space.

—I want to go back to Francette's.

—OK, fine. But promise to call me if something goes wrong. You can then come to Emilie's. I'll warn her.

—OK, I promise.

Later, as we sat at the café, appropriately named Café du Gare, Dorit said:

—You can move all your stuff back into your apartment on West 57th before I get back next Wednesday.

—That'll be easy, since I really don't have that much stuff.

—Your nomadic days are over.

I didn't respond.

Dorit again:

—I'm excited. Are you excited?

—Are you kidding? Is the Pope Catholic?

We spent the first two hours of that revived romantic relationship drinking wine, making plans, and reminiscing. Those moments seemed to me outside the narrative of time itself. I'll narrate a sample of our conversation Thursday night at the Café du Gare, about a block from Gare du Nord, which I saw for the first time in my life in 1991 when I went there to take the EuroStar to London, where I was headed also for the first time in my life. I was then taking a journey into the unknown.

In 1991, I was headed for London in the United Kingdom of Great Britain and Northern Ireland, the first new country I was visiting in five years. As I sat there at that café near Gare du Nord with Dorit that night, talking about plans for our marriage, I couldn't help noting one irony of my full circle that spanned the decade of the 90s: I took that train journey to London in 1991 barely a week after I left Dorit for Karyn Ross.

Because 1991 was the starting point for that incredible circle, I want to chronicle the one significant event that happened that year.

*   *   *

In 1991, in vitriolic and highly dramatic hearings, the Senate Judiciary Committee examined allegations by Anita Hill, a law professor at the University of Oklahoma, that Supreme Court nominee Clarence Thomas had sexually harassed her ten years earlier. Hill, who had worked with Thomas when he headed the Equal Opportunity Employment Commission (the federal agency responsible for, among other things, policing sexual discrimination), accused her former boss of pressuring her for dates, boasting about his sexual prowess, and describing the content of pornographic movies.

Thomas, a conservative lawyer who had since been made a federal judge, denied the charges and played a racial wild card (both he and Hill are black) by calling the televised hearings a "high-tech lynching." (Editorializing, the CNN camera was trained on Thomas's white wife, Virginia, who sat a few seats from him, at the exact moment [which turned out to be quite defining for the whole hearing] that he made his accusation.) A rapt television audience all over the US (and CNN's Europe and the Pacific Rim) watched the he-said-she-said debacle. Republican senators defended Thomas by assailing Hill as a liar, tramp, or psychotic spinster. Somewhat lost in the furor was Thomas's apparent underqualification to be a Supreme Court Justice. He was later confirmed in any case. The hearings (and subsequent media dissections) touched on major issues at America's fin-de-millennium: classism; racism; careerism (and the recognition of the existence of a black professional middle class engaged with all these three issues); the legal system; and myriad permutations of the identity politics of race and gender.

*   *   *

Now to the sample of the conversation between Dorit and me on Thursday night. Dorit:
—You know, my mother told me to propose to you.
—She did? Really?
—Last Saturday she took me out to dinner, to Circus.
—Circus?
—A Brazilian restaurant on Lex and 62nd.
—I don't know it, obviously.
—The food there is great. I should take you there sometime.
—So what did you have?
—I had something called *picadinho*.
—What is that?
—Beef sautéed with wine and thyme, topped with a poached egg and accompanied by rice, beans, and cooked bananas.
—Yum yum. Sounds like a Nigerian dish that my mother might have made.
—That makes sense, since the chef told us that that dish specifically comes from Bahia, the Afro-Brazilian province of Brazil.
—Yeap. You're right about the province. And they speak Yoruba there.
—I even know that!
—So Julia encouraged you to propose to me?

—I had been talking to her on and off about you ever since you
   and Katya broke up. OK, I'll come clean: I've been wanting to
   reconnect with you romantically since then.
—I suspected all that from your e-mail. Perhaps unconsciously I
   was wanting that too.
—So my mother was right!
—Right about what?
—She was guessing that you would probably want that too.
—She was?
—Remember that night at the Zinc Bar?
—Of course.
—The day after that I told her about our conversation, especially
   the part about how I was encouraging you to go out with her.
—No you didn't!
—Yes I did.
—And?
—Well, she was in stitches. And that was when she said she had a
   hunch you might still be in love with me after all these years.
—I think maybe she was right.
—So over the past two weeks she needled me to propose. She was
   convinced you'd never do it.
—Your mother said I would never propose? I wonder what gave
   her that idea? She doesn't know me that well.
—She thinks she does.
—You know, our respective friends and relatives will be very
   surprised by this move. We haven't been together in about
   nine years, and now we're leaping into marriage.
—Let them be surprised. I know what I want.
—Which is . . .
—To be married to you. No question about it. It was meant to be.
   And marriage is a serious proposition for me.
—For me also. I don't think I would have left Sarah. She left me.
—I know. I was there in spirit and sometimes in body.
—So now you want to marry me, in spite of my baggage?
—We all have our baggages.

—My own full disclosure: I'm not sure whether I'll ever find another soulmate like you.

—I *know* I'll never find a guy like you. At least some one I'd like to marry, to spend the rest of my life with.

—How can you be so sure?

—Some philosopher—I forget who—said that for each of us on earth, there's only one person, only one, and that's it. I strongly believe that. And that one person is you.

—Wow. That's heavy stuff. But then you're always heavy.

—That's right. I'm always heavy. That's me, Ms. Heavy. I wanted to marry you even when I was depressed after you dumped me for Karyn. I was grieving but I was also pining for you. But I've forgiven you.

—I was completely to blame for all that, as I've told you many times. I should never have believed from the beginning what Karyn told me about you.

—You mean to tell me now that you don't think I'm lesbian? And that I made a pass at that bitch?

—That was just so stupid.

—Yeah it was stupid. And senseless. I was so depressed. My mother told me then that no amount of intellect will ever cure a body steeped in depression. She said depression is not only psychic but quite physical. You also know that from your own experience. You've said as much to me in your e-mails.

—I know that well. Low serotonin and nuerotransmitters and all that. And that's what scares me. We can never will ourselves out of our depression, no matter how smart we think we are or how many books we've read.

—What scares you?

—I don't think I can survive another divorce. I almost died that time. I never *ever* want to go through that again.

—I will never divorce you. I can never divorce you.

—How can you be sure about that?

—Listen, you're the only person I've wanted to marry. You're the only person I'll ever marry.

—What if we break up in the future?

—I don't know why you say that at this point. You were the one who dumped the first time. I would never do that to you.

—Remember: Anything is possible as long as we're alive.

—That's one of your favorite aphorisms.

—But what if we split up? You'll never marry again?

—I repeat: You're the only person I'll ever marry. If this marriage fails, then it's a mistake. If my marriage with you fails, then it'll fail with anyone else. I never repeat my mistakes.

—I know that about you. I also know that you're not afraid to make mistakes.

—You know me too well. That's why I want to marry you. And another thing.

—What?

—I want to have kids with you. And I can never divorce you if we have kids. I know the effect of divorce on kids, after what my brother and I went through. If we have kids, I can never do that to them. And there's no way I'd let *you* divorce me easily. I'm warning you. I want to tell you something else. And I want you to listen very carefully to what I'm about to say. I want this to sink in with you tonight.

—I'm listening . . . very carefully.

—Remember our conversation about how the human-machine interface is reconfiguring human desire?

—How can I forget?

—Let me ask you a question.

—Do you know what the first code is?

—Let me think. This is tricky . . . is it . . . the genetic code?

—Yes, yes, the human genome, the real source code, the source of human life. This first code comes before all the source codes that the geeks play with in all their dot-coms. It's special, and must be protected at all cost.

—I like that. But why are you telling me this?

—You're my first code. And I want you to trust that I'll be your first code. In a way, the person I am right now, the person you will marry, began to live in 1974.

—Now you have to explain. Weren't you born in 1969?

—Yes I was.

—Then what do you mean, you began to live in 1974?

—My formative years began in 1974.

—What happened in 1974?

—That's when my father divorced my mother. I was five years old at the time. And I remember promising myself then that I would never ever marry someone who was the enemy of my enthusiasm. I promised myself that I have to really be extremely careful choosing a lifetime partner.

—Enemy of your enthusiasm. I like that.

—So I've chosen you.

—I guess 1974 is really a significant year for the both of us.

—You've got that right.

So that's a sample of what we talked about during the first two hours of that revived romantic relationship, as we drank wine, made plans, and reminisced at Café du Gare on boulevard Denain, near Gare du Nord in Paris. Before we get back to another revived romantic relationship, to Missoula and to Katya, I feel the urge to chronicle significant events in 1974.

*   *   *

1974. I promise I'll be brief.

In the United Kingdom of Great Britain and Northern Ireland, British physicist and cosmologist Stephen Hawking smashed established ideas about the universe when he asserted that black holes emitted radiation. By the accepted definition before his assertion, black holes (hypothetical collapsed stars whose gravitational pull is so extreme that not even light can escape) emitted nothing. Hawkings managed to integrate relativity with quantum theory, a feat that Albert Einstein and others had attempted without success. Hawkins's equations helped explain how the universe had expanded in some 15 billion years from a point to an immensity, and how it could (Lord help us!) shrink back on itself in a so-called "cosmic crunch."

In Ethiopia, radical military officers first forced Emperor Haile Selassie to replace his rubber-stamp cabinet with one headed by a "liberal aristocrat" (whatever that might be). Then the officers arrested government ministers one by one. Then the officers nationalized the Emperor's thirteen palaces. Finally, after Selassie failed to turn over the $10 billion that he had stashed in foreign accounts, the officers placed him under house arrest. The military junta, called Derg (the shadow) for the anonymity of its members, eventually shot Selassie and fifty-nine officials later that year.

India detonated its first nuclear device, becoming the sixth country (after the US, Britain, France, the Soviet Union, and China) to possess nuclear weapons. The fact that Indian scientists had constructed the bomb from "peaceful" materials (whatever those might be) was considered "especially disturbing" by the leaders of the other five countries.

In the Soviet Union, communist authorities sent the writer Aleksandr Solzhenitsyn into exile. He settled in rural Vermont for several years before eventually returning to Russia after the collapse of the Soviet state machine.

West German sculptor Joseph Beuys arrived at Kennedy Airport wrapped in felt and placed in a stretcher. He was then brought by an ambulance to the René Blok Gallery in Manhattan, where he lived with a coyote for three days and nights before being wrapped in felt again, then transported back to the airport in an ambulance. This piece of performance art was titled *I Like America and America Likes Me*. In his work, Beuys often evoked his memories of World War II (he was shot down by the Allies, and later rescued by nomadic Tartars who treated his wounds with animal fat and wrapped him in felt to keep him warm) and other traumatic events through sculpture, graphic arts, and "actions" (as he called them) involving highly unusual media. He was a key figure in Fluxus, a

1960s art movement that rejected professionalism and permanence in the fine arts.

In the US:

In Philadelphia (the birthplace of the Episcopal Church), in defiance of official church policy, four Episcopal priests ordained eleven women to join their ranks. The House of Bishops declared the ordinations illegal but endorsed the *principle* of women priests.

In August, Richard Nixon resigned in the wake of Watergate. "I have never been a quitter," he told the nation. "To leave office before my time is completed is opposed to every instinct in my body. But as president, I must put the needs of America first."

At Berkeley, newspaper heiress Patricia ("Patty") Hearst was abducted at gun point from the campus apartment she shared with her fiancé. Her captors called themselves the Symbionese Liberation Army (SLA). The kidnappers demanded that Hearst's "fascist-insect" parents distribute $2 million free food to the poor in the Bay Area. After the family complied, a tape-recorded message arrived, along with a photo of Hearst toting a machine gun. "I have chosen," she said, "to stay and fight." Taking the nom de guerre Tania, Hearst took part in an SLA robbery and freed two comrades caught shoplifting by spraying a storefront with bullets. Later that year, four hundred police and FBI agents shot all the occupants of an SLA hideout in Los Angeles. In her communiqué after this event, Hearst denounced her fiancé as "a pig" and eulogized the dead, who included her lovers, a Chicano "guerrilla" named Cujo and SLA's African-American [or black, in that epoch's parlance] leader "Field Marshall" Donald "Cinque" DeFreeze. (Hearst was later apprehended, tried, and sentenced to seven years in prison. After twenty-two months, President Carter commuted her sentence. After her release, she married her bodyguard, a former FBI agent [who according to unconfirmed sources I saw in the media files, was among the agents who shot up the LA hideout], and settled down as a suburban homemaker in Orange County.)

Streaking hit campuses everywhere. Students shed their clothes for nude campus dashes. Streaking soon overflowed the campuses into several American spaces: Hawaii's statehouse; the Academy Awards; sporting events; state dinners; and Webster's Dictionary. Both genders partook, but male streakers outnumbered female. Cultural pundits read the practice as "the ultimate expression of the sexual revolution."

And Roman Polanski's *Chinatown* was released in theaters near everyone everywhere. The film's premise (that society was rotten to the core) seemed to resonate with a Vietnam-vanquished, Watergate-weary nation. Set in 1930s Los Angeles, the movie articulated the venality—in politics, real estate, and personal relations—that powered the city's development from desert to film-industry Xanadu and capital of the American Dream. Robert Towne's script added freshness, wit, and incest to a very tired detective-movie template: a street-smart white private "dick" on the job; a shady broad; a monstrous millionaire; and a mysterious murder. Reports claimed that Towne wanted an upbeat ending, but Polanski (who appeared in the film as a diminutive thug switching a blade up the private dick's nose) insisted on a final burst of nihilistic bloodbath.

*   *   *

Now let's head back to the September of 1998, to Missoula and Katya, to the first few hours of another incipient romantic relationship.

*   *   *

29

Paris: Friday, July 16, 1999

Missoula: Thursday, September 3, 1998

Around 2:30 AM. Katya and I had just finished making love for about two hours.

I:
—I don't think this is going to work.
—Why not?
—You have a boyfriend.
—I told you the relationship has no future.
—But you're currently with him. Do you plan to tell him about me?
—In time.
—When are you planning to leave him?
—In time. Please be patient with me. I want a future with you, not with Glen.
—I refuse to be part of a triangle.
—Please be patient with me. I swear to you: I will leave Glen.
—I have a definite hunch that this Glen thing will be a problem.
—It won't, I promise. Now I want to ask you something.
—What?
—I've seen all these women in Missoula going after you. Which one of them have you fucked? I want to know who my competition is—besides Bryn.
—You're competing with Bryn only in your head. She and I are getting to be close friends, as I've told you time and again.
—So who else have you fucked in Missoula?

—Trish.

—Trish? *The* Trish?

—She and I had a one-night stand at her place after a party that Rob and Laura gave at their house.

—Just a one-night stand?

—Just a one-night stand.

—Are you attracted to her?

—Somewhat. She's an interesting woman.

—And a loser.

—Why do you call her a loser? She's not a loser.

—She's a divorced woman.

—So are you.

—She's twice divorced, from abusive alcoholic husbands. She's a drunk herself. And look at the way she lives. Her house is a mess.

—True enough. But how did you know all this?

—Jacques told me.

—I see. She's a nice woman. And she's focused on her job and her students. She might be a victim, but she's in no way what you called a loser.

—Look: I won't compete with her.

—With Trish? She's not your competition.

—And I won't compete with that retard Bryn neither.

—Bryn is not a retard. Can you do me a favor? Don't ever call Bryn a retard to my face again. She's my friend. You just have to accept that, period.

The drift of this exchange a few moments after Katya and I made love should have been a red flag to me. It certainly set the tone and pace for the period of the relationship.

For the rest of September 1998, Katya and I started spending progressively more time together—at her place. And consequently I was spending less time with Jacques—and also less time at his house in South Hills. In fact at that point I started to develop a weekday routine in Missoula that turned out to be more or less operative for me for the rest of my sojourn there.

At Katya's I would get up at 9 AM after she had left to go teach on campus, which was just a few blocks away. After my ablutions, I'd drink coffee while listening to the BBC World Service for an hour. Sometimes before I drank coffee I'd run up the "M" on Mount Sentinel behind the campus. Sometimes I would get online on my laptop to check only my e-mail. Then I would cross the bridge over Clark-Fork River to go to DragNet, where I did all my web-site work on one of Rob's super-networked machines.

Circa 5 PM, I would walk back across the Clark-Fork Bridge to Bernice's, the coffee-house on West Third Street South, for another two hours, where I would work on my laptop with material I'd downloaded from various news web-sites, or simply continue the manuscript work on *In the White City*, the original reason after all, that I was sojourning in Missoula. Sometimes, the women-workers at Bernice's would flirt with me or me with them during the breaks from my laptop. (Katya was to become more and more jealous of this segment of my routine as our relationship "progressed." She would keep asking me why I don't work "at home," meaning her place, instead of going to Bernice's, "to flirt with the blonde women there.")

I very quickly became an icon in dowtown Missoula. Bus drivers of the Mountain Line would sometimes honk at me while I was walking on Higgins Avenue—since I took the 12 bus from South Hills toward downtown on those mornings when I'd spent the night before at Jacques's house.

About 7 PM, Katya would pick me up at Bernice's, and we'd walk back to her house, where she would make dinner. Sometimes after dinner we'd watch a tape we picked up at Crystal Video. After that we'd talk and make love until 1 or 2 AM. Then she would fall alseep. Sometimes I'd then get online for another hour, finally drifting to bed while listening to the BBC World Service. That was my weekday routine—with a few variations.

My weekend routine was a little different. I still got up late. Or sometimes Katya would wake me up and make breakfast. Then I'd go for a run. After I got back, she and I would go "shopping" at the South Mall. Or we would go to Albertsons or the Orange Street Food Farm for groceries. Then after that she would go to her office on campus to work on her manuscript, which was her dissertation on Pushkin and Dostoyevsky that she was trying to transform into a book manuscript for Edwin Mellen Press, a vanity academic publisher in upstate New York: the usual requirement for tenure in US academia. From time to time, she would ask me to look at some of her manuscript pages and help her with her writing in English. On Saturday nights, we would go to Charlie B's, the so-called "writers bar" on Higgins Avenue, where Katya would delight in telling me that she attracted her students, a few of whom would come to talk to her as we were drinking by the bar.

For me during my sojourn in Missoula, it was quite magnificent, for instance, at Charlie B's, amid its funky interior decor, to observe personally the wreckage of Rousseau's fantasy of the "Noble Savage" on the faces of the teeming beer-guzzling barflies, fastened to each other or to the pool tables. For at that point in the contemporary history of Missoula that was rapidly unfolding, the contemporary Missoulian who was still yoked to a nostalgia for myth and history was being transformed in New York nanoseconds—and in front of my eyes—into a relic in a museum by the new cyber-culture frontier that Rob and DragNet represented. And the new technology that was producing these tranformations was dissolving the topological boundaries of Missoula in all registers, and most significantly, was exploding the figure of the Pioneer and the Cowboy in the dude ranches of Montana that were never real— that is to say that were virtual—to begin with. A short digression here about Missoula's demographic.

When I was there, Missoula residents could be classified into three economic categories: university faculty and staff (like Jacques and Katya); telecommuters (like me or Rob); and minimum-wage slaves (like Bryn or Janice). Some people traversed two categories (like Bryn, who was also an artist). And there were number of minimum-wage slaves trying to earn either undergraduate or graduate degrees or who had already earned graduate degrees.

And indeed, a lot of minimum-wage slaves in Missoula were highly educated.

As in many American college-towns, Missoula had a robust labor force of perennial and professional students and nature-loving graduates eager and desperate to be slaves in order to earn the privilege of living in a town surrounded by mountains and hiking trails. To belabor my point: Sarah told me that in Minneapolis, where the landscape was flat—albeit with lakes—but where the labor market was tight and unemployment stood around 2 percent, workers got paid $10 an hour to flip hamburgers. Whereas in Missoula when I was there, writers got paid $7-8 an hour at a local editorial sweatshop to summarize the content of web sites.

So that when I was there, Missoula, and by extension the state of Montana, was once again at another frontier, which I could call cyber: the transition—and transformation—from a minimum-wage slave economy into the ether economy of cyber technoculture. I witnessed this transformation. Missoula's slave economy was already shrinking. Families—with kids—who could not afford rising housing and living expenses began to move out to the trailer parks in the outskirts of town. Consequently, enrollment in public schools dropped precipitously, resulting in the closing of two schools, since the young dot-com people moving into town did not have kids yet.

But back to Katya and my routine.

After Charlie B's Katya and I would walk back to her house and make love for two to three hours. The point is this: If everything was up to her, Katya and I would make love every night. But I simply was not up to that, and I told her. On Sundays, when Katya and Jacques were still on friendly terms, we all—including a few more members of the community of friends—would go for the long hike followed by dinner, which I mentioned in an earlier entry. As I said in the earlier entry, Katya froze out Jacques within those first few weeks for the duration of our relationship. Katya and I had a conversation about this later that month.

Missoula: Thursday, September 17, 1998

Katya and I were sitting in her living room. We had just finished the dinner she prepared for me: rice and chicken sautéed in
garlic and tomato sauce. I was finishing the bottle of cheap red
wine that she had picked up at Albertson's on Brooks Avenue.

Katya:
—I think Jacques is trying to sabotage our relationship.
—Why do you think that?
—Whenever he sees me in the department, he keeps telling me I
    don't have to spend so much time and money on you.
—What do you tell him?
—That I spend time with you because I want to spend time with
    you, not out of any obligation.
—I wonder what his problem is.
—I think he's jealous.
—Why?
—I think he's a closet gay. Maybe he's in love with you, who
    knows?
—Oh come on. He's an old old friend. Maybe he's just anxious for
    me. He wants to make sure I'm in good hands.
—You know what Casey told me the other day?
—What?
—He said quote Jacques is mad at you Katya unquote. When I
    asked why, he said quote Because you stole his girlfriend un-
    quote.
—Casey meant me?
—I don't know who else he could have been referring to.
—So now the people in your department are feminizing me?
—Casey was making the point I've been trying to make.

About a week after this conversation, I brought up the whole
topic with Jacques during one of my increasingly rare evenings at
his place. I was beginning to spend only one or two nights a
week at his house, although most of my stuff was still there.

But before I engage that conversation, I have to wrap up this

entry because I'm running short on time. I have to get out of
Francette's apartment and take the Métro to Café de Cluny, where
I'm supposed to meet Dorit for drinks and dinner and who-knows-
what-else. And I have to tell you about what transpired between
Francette and me when I got back to her apartment late last night—
or should I say this morning.

Paris: Thursday-Friday, July 15-16, 1999

I found a tearful Francette around 12:45 AM when I got back
to 7 rue Fénelon—after Dorit and I had said our goodbyes when I
walked her to the Métro at Gare du Nord so she could take the
train back to Emilie's at rue Bizerte, and after we had made plans
to meet later today so that we could spend my last night in Paris
together.

Francette in French:

—How could you do this?

—I'm sorry if I hurt you. But I had no idea you thought there was
   something between us.

—You bastard. After everything I did for you? How could you not
   think that?

—I'm sorry, Francette.

—Look, under the circumstances . . .

I didn't let her finish.

—I know. I know. I can't stay here.

—I didn't say that. I was going to say something else. I can't stay
   here until you leave.

—But this is your place.

—Yes, but . . . No problem. I'll just go back to Anne and Sylvie's.
   They're expecting me back. In fact, they didn't even want me
   to come back here tonight.

—Bad aura and chakra.

—I'm not in the mood for being teased tonight.

—Once again, I'm sorry.

—I told them I'd come here briefly, to get a few things I need to
stay at their place, and also to say goodbye to you. I still want
us to be good friends, but I think it's best if we say goodbye
now, and then try to mend things when I get back to the US
at the end of the summer.

—I very much wish to stay friends with you too, Francette. You
mean so much to me. My experiences with you these past two
weeks have been really swell, and have probably changed me
forever and helped me.

—I wish you and Dorit the best of luck. I mean it.

Then in the next minute she simply lost it. She burst into
tears. And I felt so much tumescence that I also burst into tears.
And that's how Francette and I said our goodbyes. She collected
herself and walked out of her apartment, after telling me to leave
her house-key under the carpet by the front door on Saturday
morning, on my way to De Gaulle to catch my flight back to New
York-JFK. I tried to kiss her on both cheeks French-style as she was
leaving. But she turned her face away and walked down the stairs.

After she left I felt somewhat spooked out, and so I helped
myself to three-quarters of a bottle of her Amarrone red wine, and
sat on the balcony, gazing at the rooftops of Paris and at the well-
lit shops at the interesection of rue Lafayette and boulevard Magenta, and at the now dwindling headlights of the cars winding
their way around the streets.

*   *   *

30

New York: Monday, July 19, 1999

I'm back in my apartment on West 57th Street and Ninth Avenue. It looks both familiar and unfamiliar. Dorit's stuff is all over the place, but arranged neatly. And she's altered the arrangement of the furniture somewhat and added a few of her own. I can see the desktop by the window that she wrote me about. And I can see the window across Ninth Avenue where the voyeur might have been spying on her while she was working at the desktop—with only her underpants on.

Paris: Friday, July 19, 1999

Dorit and I spent my last night, that Friday night, in Paris together after drinks, dinner, and more drinks, at Emilie's apartment on rue Bizerte—in Emilie's bed. Emilie generously let us use her apartment that night while she camped out at Eliane's swanky apartment on rue Pergolèse in the Sixteenth Arrondissement, promising to come back in the morning and drive us to De Gualle so I could jet back to New York. Saturday morning, as we lolled in bed before we all mobilized for De Gaulle, Dorit whispered that having sex with me was much better for her in many subtle ways since our last session in 1991. And she wondered where—and how—I had picked up the new knowledge and experience.

New York: Monday, July 19, 1999

While I was in the shower this morning I looked at my face in the mirror. And I asked myself: Is a mirror frozen or flushing water? Is a mirror a deep cold spring with sealed memories or lukewarm water to be flushed down the toilet? And then I thought: How many people have looked at their faces in this mirror? And then I said to myself, maybe if I looked for a while I'd see wet and naked ghostly figures, wrapped bodies of turds: mirrors and mummies.

Quite strange to be back here. Dorit gets back on Wednesday. There are many things I could consider about my moving back here with Dorit, about my psychic state at the moment, about how I feel about everything that's happened to me since I left Missoula and Katya and Jacques barely three weeks ago—June 24, 1999 to be precise. It's as if I now live in a completely different galaxy from the one I left back there.

For these reasons, and because once Dorit gets back on Wednesday I'd have less time to write these entries for a while, I feel quite anxious to dispense with my narrative of events in Missoula, in order to begin to think concretely about my future with Dorit. Therefore, my next few entries will be devoted to the rest of my sojourn in Missoula, after which I never wish again to have to dwell on that town in these pages.

Missoula: Thursday, September 24, 1998

After dinner at his house that Thursday night, Jacques actually broached with me the subject of Katya putting him on ice:

—Katya is saying less and less to me these days. I even think she's
     hostile. Did you say anything to her about me?
—No. What would I say to her? You're the one who's been talking.
—What do you mean?
—You're the one who's been telling Katya all kinds of things.
—About what?
—About me. About Trish. And about who knows who else?
—What did I tell her about Trish?
—That she's a loser, for one.
—I never told Katya that Trish was a loser. I just told her that Trish
     has been divorced twice. And that her ex-husbands were drunks
     and junkies who beat her up. I never called Trish a loser. Katya
     must have made that up.
—Well, look: You talk too much. And to the wrong people.

The drift of this exchange should also have been a red flag to me, a clue to what I was to experience with Katya for the nine months we were an item.

*   *   *

31

New York: Monday, July 19, 1999

I had interrupted writing these entries to take a break. I had to run two short errands. For the first errand, I went to the Carnegie Deli a few blocks away to pick up a sandwich. It's still lunch break in New York, and so I had to negotiate the lunch crowd and the tourists on 57th Street to Seventh Avenue and back. And when I got back I went online to check my messages.

Before I left Paris and Dorit—or rather before I left Dorit in Paris—she gave me her password for Internet access from her desktop so that I can go online. And generally when I'm online I try to check for my e-messages every ten minutes. And so then when I got online after my first errand I read the following e-posting from Dorit from Paris:

———

Date: Mon, 19 July 1999 19:30:09 +0100
From: "Dorit Levin" <doritlevin@onebox.com> **Add Block**
Subject: Hello from Paris!
Message: Yo from Paris! How are things going?
Interesting reversal: I'm now e-posting you in New York from Paris, when just last week you were e-posting me from Paris to New York.

Did you find everything OK? Did you move your stuff in yet? I hope the apartment is not too much of a mess? I hope you're not too upset that I've rearranged the furniture a little bit? Is Carlos the doorman being nice to you? I forgot to tell you about him. He just started two months ago.

I want to apologize for the delay in e-mailing you. But it's been a social whirlwind with the girls since you left on Saturday. After we dropped you off we met up with some more people and went to the restaurant in the Louvre for a nice leisurely lunch, and the social calendar never did let up for the rest of the weekend.

Anyway, it's 7:30 PM right now in Paris, and Emilie, Eliane, and I are headed out for a nice night on the town. I don't know exactly where we're going. Eliane is treating us, and she said it'll be a pleasant surprise. Emilie is not back yet from a shoot. And I just got back here after another gruelling and tedious day at the Bibliothèque. They need to do something about those dreadful reading rooms. I thought they would be nicer in the new buildings, but they're just as bad as the old ones. Anyway I should stop whining. I wanted to dash this off to you before Emilie gets back, since we have to leave right away to meet Eliane, and since in fact she's late.

How are you? I miss you already and can't wait to get back to New York, and to you, on Wednesday. I spoke with my mother yesterday. When I gave her the news and she said I told you so. I told you she'd be thrilled. BTW: She wants you to call her so she can take you out to dinner. Will you promise me you'll call her? Like right after you finish reading this? Maybe you guys can go out on a date together. No one will ever guess that you're not a couple.

She's promised us a very nice wedding present one that we will both really appreciate. Obviously it'll be a surprise wedding present. She also wants you to give her a list of the people you want to invite to the occasion. You and I had talked about maybe 75 people, the number that will fit comfortably in my mother's apartment. She's got about five months to prepare. But you know how the holiday season between Thanksgiving and New Year's gets sucked into a black hole. So that in reality she's got only three and a half months.

Emilie just got back, so I have to get offline. But listen, dear: Can you do me a favor and check my mail right now for anything from THE NEW YORKER? If it looks like a check, please open it and help me deposit the check in my bank, Chase Manhattan, the branch just two blocks, on Seventh Avenue. I'm running out of cash and will need to use my cash card for the ATM. My checkbooks are in the bottom-left drawer of your desk. Can you then please confirm this to me one way or the other? If the check hasn't arrived yet, e-post me also.

Now I better go. I love you.

——————————

Dorit Levin Staff Writer
THE NEW YORKER
Condé Nast Publications
4 Times Square
New York, NY 10036
Voice/Fax: 1-212-421-8774
e-mail: doritlevin@onebox.com
Website: http://www.newyorker.com

*   *   *

I got offline and checked her mail. And sure enough: There was the check from *The New Yorker*. I then got online to e-post Dorit about her check. Then I had to go back out to mingle again with the lunch crowd and tourists to run the second errand at Chase Manhattan.

And now I'm finally back here to write more entries. As I said before, I need to dispense with these entries about Missoula and Katya before Dorit gets back on Wednesday. Apropos of which: The last time I more or less paid attention to somebody else's mail was during those first few weeks when I was staying on and off at Katya's house on Sixth Street in Missoula—when, that is, I would sift through her unopened mail to see whether there was anything from Glen, postmarked from Columbia, South Carolina.

For this next entry, I'll narrate what I consider to be representative samples of my everyday-and-night experiences in Missoula—mostly with Katya, but also with Bryn and Mirta, and to a lesser extent, with Jacques and Rob—during those few weeks of what I've chosen to call the pre-Hong Kong period of my tenure in Missoula, that is, the period before mid-November, before I left Missoula for Hong Kong on a freelance-writing assignment for my friend Michael Pang, a Hong Kong urban architect, whom I had to help on his project on the everyday uses of public spaces in Hong Kong, and who is the husband of another friend of mine, Eva Man Pang: and this latter I've already mentioned once in these pages in an earlier entry—when in my e-posting to Dorit from Paris, I was telling her about my cyber-flights to my far-flung worldwide web of friends.

Missoula: Thursday, September 24, 1998—Sunday, November 15, 1998

Katya and I would be sitting in her living room after the dinner she prepared. I'd be watching television while sipping a glass of merlot that Katya had paid for at Albertson's on Brooks Avenue. She might be watching televison as well, or trying to talk to me while she was reading a book. The phone would ring and she would pick it up. (Even though she never asked me not to, I never picked up her cordless phone when it rang, out of protocol.)

She would say:

—Hello? Oh, hi, Glen.

Then she would take the phone into her bedroom and shut the door. One or two hours later she would emerge from the bedroom, reset the phone on its base, and snuggle up next to me on the couch, somewhat sheepishly, where I had been sitting all that time, fuming with raging jealousy, and pretending to watch television.

So she would snuggle up next to me, knowing that she'd done something that didn't feel quite right, and knowing that I knew, and that I knew that she knew. She would mumble something irrelevant. I'd mumble something back. Then she would pull me into the bedroom, where after first feigning reluctance, I would then seize—and tear into—her small body with the frenzy and fury of an animal, still raging with jealousy and seeking to settle the score with rough sex. And a piercing scream would emanate from this body again and again—until she came, also again and again. These love-making sessions, which sometimes left both of us sore with muscular pain, would last at least one-and-a-half or two hours, sometimes until 2 or 3 AM, even though she had to get up in time for a 9 AM class she had to teach. I'm positive that Glen called every night that I was there, and that this sexual sequence afterward was repeated each time.

(Katya and my sexual sequences recalled to my mind episodes of *StarTrek* when Klingon couples, after drawn-out love-making sessions, would report to sick bay with broken bones.)

Sometimes I'd be so angry at her for putting me through this ordeal that I'd fight the impulse to simply get up from the couch and walk out of her house, never to come back again. I was never able to act out this fantasy. Instead some nights I'd get up from the couch and tiptoe to her bedroom door and put my ear to the door, trying to catch snatches of conversation behind it. Sometimes I'd catch a word or two in English and try to reconstruct the conversation. Other times I'd catch a word or two in Russian, and would have no clue. Glen was fluent in Russian, by Katya's admission.

On those nights when we went out to dinner or went out after dinner, say to Charlie B's or to a movie at the Crystal or the Wilma, these sequences were also repeated—that of Glen's phone call, sometimes coming as late as 1 or even 2 AM, and of the love-making, sometimes lasting till 4 or 5 AM depending on when Glen called.

And on some nights after dinner at her house, to forestall the fresh agon of the first sequence—Glen's inevitable phone call—I'd have arranged for Bryn to call me at Katya's, where she'd pick me up. Some nights Mirta and-or Vanessa would be with her, and all three-four of us would cruise the bars in downtown Missoula or the more seedy dives on Brooks Avenue, following Bryn's script about turning me into a "real" American writer whose writing "from the guts" would feed off his "real" experiences to make his work "authentic." When all three women were with me, I'd always get curious stares from male locals anytime we walked into any of the downtown bars or the watering-hole dives on Brooks Avenue. On these nights I felt a sense of emanciption from the Katya-Glen agony, only to sink back into it the next night. I never told Bryn about these sequences of my Katya-Glen nights. But I e-posted Dorit about them. Following is one of her responses:

Date: Thur, 22 October 1998 23:30:09 -0500 (EDT)
From: "Dorit Levin" <doritlevin@onebox.com> **Add Block**
Subject: My Montana Friend's Idea of Love
Message: Yo! What have you gotten yourself into in Montana? Are you sure this woman is in love with you? And are you sure she's not a sex addict? It sounds like she's got you by the balls. So you have to ask yourself whether she has you in sexual bondage of some kind, and whether at this point, you're thinking only with the head of your dick, which is quite unlike you.

If she loves you she'll drop that Glen like a hot tamale.

You have to ask yourself: What would a future partner of yours think about all this if she knew? Will you get the respect from her that you certainly deserve? I know you've been through very difficult times.

I've always wished you well. But honestly, this woman doesn't sound right for you. And you will soon realize it.

Please call me if you wish to talk.

un abrazo.

Dorit Levin—Associate Staff Writer
THE NEW YORKER
Condé Nast Publications
4 Times Square
New York, NY 10036
Voice/Fax: 1-212-421-8774
e-mail: doritlevin@onebox.com
Website: http://www.newyorker.com

*   *   *

Katya would be jealous in her own turn of these Bryn-Mirta nights, and she'd accuse me of using them "to get back at her" because of Glen. Sometimes I'd disagree with her. And sometimes I would not respond, confident that she would interpret my silence as a tacit agreement of her accusation.

During those long weekends when I took advantage of Northwest's cyber-savers to be with Shoshana in Minneapolis, and stayed with my New-York transplant friends, Katya would call me at night, talking to me—as she did to Glen—for one-to two hours. When I got back to Missoula, I'd peruse her phone bills to discover that sometimes she had—or would have—talked to Glen for the same period of time after—or before—she called me, and for the same period of time. For her, it seemed, Glen-me functioned like an on-off switch, and I marveled at her psychic ability at modulation.

And so my nights would alternate between Katya-Glen and Bryn-Mirta, sometimes just Bryn. On the just Bryn—or even on the Bryn-Mirta—nights, Bryn would either drop me off at Jacques's house quite late, when he would inevitably be asleep (and so I never saw him at night when I slept there—and he'd be gone to campus by the time I got up in the morning), or she would drive me back to her house on Spruce Street, where again we would sleep on her bed without making love.

During this period I also saw Jacques and Rob, but less frequently.

I met Jacques only for lunch, usually at Food for Thought. We talked about Katya less frequently, focusing instead on discussions about politics and culture, those staple topics that had glued our friendship solid over the years. And I caught Rob in glimpses at DragNet when I went there for my high-speed Internet access. A few of those glimpses spun out into lengthy impromptu discussions about the Internet and the high-tech industry. And indeed I also picked up some technical knowledge at DragNet, thanks to Rob.

This insufferable and psychically exhaustive routine—with Katya, a remote Glen, Bryn-Mirta, Jacques, and Rob—went on and on, forever it seemed to me, until one overcast November Sunday afternoon (Missoula had been overcast for almost a week), when I took a Northwest flight from Missoula "International" Airport into the sun, first to Minneapolis (where, incidentally I had a two-hour layover and saw Shoshana and Sarah at the airport), then to Detroit, then after one hour there, to Tokyo's Narita Airport (where my connecting flight was so tight that I couldn't even call my brother), and finally, to Hong Kong—for the second time in my life.

Michael Pang's freelance assignment (which he had introduced to me when I was still in Missoula in the form of a lengthy e-posting with an attachment) sprung me from the first phase of my Katya-Glen miasma, and therefore terminated the pre-Hong Kong period of my tenure in Missoula.

I have to stop typing all this. I need to mobilize myself, since I will call Julia Stein (she reverted to her maiden name after Dorit's father divorced her). And in fact, since I'm broke, I'm looking forward to being treated to a delicious dinner in some swank Manhattan restaurant tonight, as I know too well she'll all be too happy to do. I'll resume this typing tomorrow.

I'm anxious to meet my own deadline (self-imposed for psychic and cathartic reasons): dispose once and for all the Missoula segment before Dorit gets back. And since she arrives in New York around 3-4 PM Wednesday, I have to finish it tomorrow, as I might not have time to type on Wednesday. Therefore, I'll do whatever I can to accomplish this, even if I have to get up quite early and work all day, with breaks in-between here and there to fulfill other obligations, like running in Central Park and going to the liquor store on the Upper West Side to get a few bottles of merlot.

*   *   *

32

New York: Tuesday, July 20, 1999

I woke up this morning at 6 AM, with a hangover, to the sound of Bob Edward's voice on National Public Radio's "Morning Edition." Then Carol Van Damme read the news, with more coverage of John F. Kennedy's plane going down over Nantucket Sound.

Julia Stein took me to dinner last night. I told her I was in the mood for some Spanish cuisine, as a break from the heavy dose of French and North African I got over the last few weeks. She suggested that we meet at a Meigas, a relatively new Spanish restaurant in South Village on Hudson and King Streets. Meigas, in a former industrial building, is huge with very high ceilings, and its beachy color scheme of sand and aqua made me feel that I was in a giant bathhouse. I had paella and countless glasses of sangria it seemed. Julia had rabbit loin surrounded by sauteed scallops, pearl onions, scallions, and garlic outfit, and fewer glasses of sangria. I'm positive that we went through two pitchers of sangria. We had a great time, and I felt completely relaxed. We ate, we drank, we talked, and we laughted for about three hours. At some point she called me her "favorite future son-in-law." There was one comical moment after Julia paid me this compliment, when our fortysomething waitress told us that we "looked good together." We thanked her, did not disabuse her of her assumptions, and cracked up after she left our table. Around 1 AM, Julia hailed a cab that dropped me off at West 57th and Ninth Avenue first, before continuing on to East 87th between York and First Avenues to her place.

But let's proceed to Hong Kong, which turned out to be a welcome respite from my Katya-Glen abyss in Missoula.

Hong Kong: Monday, November 16, 1998—November, Tuesday, November 24, 1998

Michael Pang's project that I was in Hong Kong to help him write was a first-person "study" of the uses of "open," "public," and "private" spaces of the island-nation-city-state. I had to be there in person for three weeks (when he did his field-work) to help him turn this project into a filmscript for a documentary, which he had received a grant to develop. His project had two functions: first, a study that the Hong Kong government could use to engage all the problems of how these spaces are used—Hong Kong was so condensed into Hong Kong Island and Kowloon that space was highly contested by the day (as I was to discover); and second, the draft of a filmscript of a documentary film of everyday life in Hong Kong. I had to be out in the streets with him to help translate his Mandarin-influenced English, in turn filtered through his Mandarin consciousness and perceptions filtered through Mandarin, for the English-language world market.

After the first week on the streets with Michael, I soon discovered that in Hong Kong "public" and "private" spaces were not that easily defined, either on paper or in practice. I found out, for instance, that not all the streets in Hong Kong belonged to the government: some were privately owned, as in long alleys between— and at the back of—buildings. A few "public" spaces have restricted public access, like Kowloon Walled City Park or the Shatin Bicycle Park in Kowloon. And a few "private" streets have public access, like Fu Shin Street in the Tai Po district in the northeast corner of the New Territories of Hong Kong (which the Chinese leased to the British July 1, 1898). Michael and I were to spend considerable time on Fu Shin Street during my visit.

I had been to Hong Kong before, for three days, in 1993, while passing through on my way back to New York from Tokyo, where I was visiting my brother and sister-in-law. At that time I was also visiting Michael and Eva, friends I had met in graduate school at Columbia University. And at that time they had picked me up at—the old—Kai Tak Airport, right in downtown Hong Kong. For me that first time, just landing at that airport by was itself worth my whole trip there. We flew within binocular distance so close to the buildings as we approached the airport that I actually saw into apartments and offices in skyscrapers, and Michael and Eva told me later that pilots had to be specially trained to fly that route.

On this second visit, Michael and Eva picked me up instead at the new Hong Kong International Airport on Lantau Island—on Monday November 16, 1998, a little over a year after the Handover of Hong Kong from the United Kingdom to China. We crossed the bridge from Lantau Island into Kowloon, then drove for a while on West Kowloon Highway, took the Jordan Road exit onto Jordan Road, then turned right to their place on Woosung Street, a neighborhood straddled by Yau Ma Tei to the north and Tsim Sha Shui to the south, two districts in the southwest of Kowloon.

During my first week there, Hong Kong seemed the same to me after the Handover. For twenty-four hours, the streets still teemed with too many people, buildings, cars, and objects for its size. The food was still so delicious. And my hosts were still as delightful as ever to be around. And during that first week, I got only one e-message from Katya—my very first from her:

––––––––––

Date: Wed, 18 November 1998 01:20:39 -0800 (MST)
From: Katya Brodsky <kbrodsky@selway.umt.edu> **Block**
Subject: (no subject)
Message: Hello Sweetie. How are you? I'm fine here. I've been very busy teaching and working on my book. I miss you, Sweetie. Please write me soon. Hope you're having a great time. I love you. Bye bye.

––––––––––

Katya Brodsky Assistant Professor
Department of Foreign Languages and Literatures
University of Montana
Liberal Arts Building
Missoula, MT 59801
E-Mail: kbrodsky@selway.umt.edu

*   *   *

The tone and length of this e-message was clearly typical of all the e-messages I ever got from Katya during our relationship. At some point she told me that she really didn't believe in cyber-communication. She said although she does not consider herself against technology, she was more invested in face-time.

During the first days of that first week, Michael introduced me—during the day while Eva was out on assignment—to all the streets and parks we would be "researching" for the project: Fu Shin Street, mentioned before; Market Park, also in Tai Po; several parks on Public Square Street in Yau Mai Tei; and the two bridges that link Hong Kong Polytechnic University and the Hunghom Kowloon Railroad Station, known in local parlance as "Poly U Bridges."

The first night of those few days, Michael, Eva, and I took the green-and-white Star Ferry from Tsim Sha Shui across Victoria Harbour to Hong Kong Island and headed for City Hall, a fantastic dim-sum restaurant in the Central District, Hong Kong's "downtown" if there was one. Then after dinner we went to Soho, a neighborhood so named because it was south of Hollywood Road, and cruised the trendy bars on its narrow streets, then settled at the cozy Petticoat Lane.

The following few nights, a few of their friends joined us for more adventures in Soho, where we cruised more bars. Like Michael and Eva, these particular friends had also gone to graduate school in the US and were now back home teaching at various Hong Kong universities.

As I implied before, I was both so relaxed at night and distracted during the day by Hong Kong's density and frenetic pace during that first week—that I never responded to Katya's first e-posting to me. Missoula and all its heart-wrenching psychosexual agonies felt quite distant to me geographically and psychically—with one exception:

Because all of a sudden, at the beginning of my second week in Hong Kong, pseudo-hallucinations of Glen making love to Katya—and her habitual screams during love-making—started to haunt me, made more acute by the realization that she must still be speaking to him on the phone every night, and made even more acute by my own fantasy that Katya might have taken advantage of my absence from Missoula to invite Glen to visit her—to make love to her some more. Then the specific memory of one night in Missoula with Katya at her place invaded my consciousness.

Missoula: Wednesday, November 4, 1998

After dinner Katya and I were sitting on the couch in her living room, as usual. I was watching Brian Williams on MSNBC, drinking cheap merlot that she had picked up at Albertson's, and she was drinking vodka and trying to read some novel in Russian, as usual. The phone rang, as usual. She sprung up from the couch, picked up the phone, said something in Russian, then made a beeline for her bedroom with the cordless and shut the door. I was livid with rage and jealousy, as usual.

By the time she emerged from her bedroom two hours later, John Seigenthaler was on MSNBC with Special Edition. Katya snuggled up to me, as usual. Then she asked:

—What are you watching Sweetie?

I didn't respond.

Katya again:

—You're mad at me.

Again, I said nothing.

Katya again:

—Why are you mad at me, Sweeetie?

—You know precisely why I'm mad at you.

—Please be patient with me.

—Look, this has gone on long enough. I'm taking myself out of this stupid triangle.

—Please be patient with me. I'll break up with Glen.

—When? You've been saying that now for weeks.

—I'll find the right time to do it. Please don't be mad at me.

Suddenly, at first she buried her hand out of sight behind her butt, scratching—it seemed to me—the area between her anus and her vagina, for what seemed to me to be a minute and a half. Then that hand emerged, and she then used it to scratch her vagina, at first gently, then quite vigorously, for what seemed to me to be another two minutes. I slowly developed an erection during this whole operation, and I couldn't help saying what I said next:

—Let's go into the bedroom and fuck!

—I thought you'd never ask.

For the next hour I was like an animal. I rammed her hard, first missionary position, then as she rolled on top of me, I plugged her mechanically and swiftly from the bottom, fueled by the agonies and anger of the hour before. Her typical screams and moans further roused me to plug her again and again, causing her to scream and moan again and again. Afterward, she gasped as she lay on her back panting, as she said:

—You really wasted me that time.

—So I did.

—And I know why. You're jealous about Glen. And this egged you on. I feel sore all over. My body is trembling.

I said nothing.

Katya again:

—But listen: I enjoyed it immensely.

—You do?

—I like it when you're rough with me. I like it when you waste me like that.

—You like it rough?

—I want it rough. Most of the time. I love it when a man fucks me like that. I like a hard male animal.

I surprised myself: I had an erection again as she was saying this. I then pounced on her almost immediately and tore into her for another thirty minutes. As I pounded her, she blurted in spurts, in-between screams and moans:

—I . . . I want you . . . I want you to fuck me . . . to fuck . . . to fuck me . . .. I want you to fuck me as you've . . . as you've . . . as you've never done before . . . I want you to fuck me . . . fuck me . . . ah . . . ah!

* * *

33

New York: Tuesday, July 20, 1999

I just came back from a short walk around the southern loop of Central Park. It's supposed to climb up to 92 F late this afternoon in the park. I had to get out of the apartment to clear my head and to reflect a bit about my life again. My mind was getting really crowded writing all that material about my agonies with Katya, and even now, here in New York, I was beginning to relive the psychosexual agony I went through during that relationship, and also to experience the traces of grief that flooded my body, even if unconsciously, in the wake of the breakup. In a sense, my leaving for Paris right after I quit Missoula (albeit with a brief respite in New York), delayed and masked the grief that, in all honesty, I have to acknowledge at this point.

I went for that walk in the park because I had to remind myself again that I'm now getting married to Dorit. I had to remind myself again that I'm about to embark on this new life in the context of an old romantic relationship now rekindled at the fringe of the millennium. I had to remind myself again that the life I left behind in Missoula a little over a month ago is gone, and that I never want to hear from it again.

When I got back to the apartment I went online to check my e-mail before I resumed writing these entries. Dorit's e-posting was in My Yahoo mail in-box.

Date: Tue, 20 July 1999 22:14:25 +0100
From: "Dorit Levin" <doritlevin@onebox.com> **Add Block**
Subject: Hello again from Paris!
Message: Yo again from Paris! Thanks for depositing the check.Actually Emilie lent me some money when she finally got back home before we left to meet Eliane.

We had a great time! Eliane took us to CAFE BEAUBOURG for apéritifs, then we took a cab to THE COUPOLE at Montparnasse, where we ate and drank and danced with some male admirers. My mother said you guys had a great time as well at. I'm glad you called her.

Again: I can't wait to get back to you in New York. My flight leaves at 1:10 PM Paris time. I get into JFK at 3:30 PM New York time. I'll just take a cab home. No problem.I'm so wired! I love you and will see you tomorrow.

Bises.

––––––––––

Dorit Levin—Staff Writer
THE NEW YORKER
Condé Nast Publications
4 Times Square
New York, NY 10036
Voice/Fax: 1-212-421-8774
e-mail: doritlevin@onebox.com
Website: http://www.newyorker.com

*   *   *

Getting this posting from Dorit at this point of my writing was good timing in my opinion, aiding me in my endeavors to free myself completely from Missoula and Katya, to expunge Katya-Glen thoroughly from my system. I also know my next task after that: decoupling the tandem Katya-Missoula that I also realize I'm beginning to assume, because I never ever wish to arrive at the point when I will automatically equate Missoula with Katya in my future to come with Dorit.

Right now, today in New York, and even right this moment, Dorit and Katya both have equal claims on my psyche: the latter because I'm writing about her, and in doing this I'm remembering her in the past; the former because I'm anticipating her arrival in New York tomorrow and looking forward to my future with her, even if my history with her reaches further back than my nine-month history with Katya. So then I'm more determined than ever to terminate this literary rememoration as swiftly as possible. So then back to Hong Kong.

Hong Kong: Friday, November 27, 1998

Yesterday, Thursday, was Thanksgiving Day in the US. And so instead of roasting and eating turkey with countless relatives and friends while negotiating the cranberry sauce and the white or red wine, Michael and I spent the whole day "in the field"(while Eva again was out on assignment): in the Tai Po District of the Northern Territories of Hong Kong, specifically, on Fu Shin Street, the L-shaped mall-street (closed to traffic) that was straddled between two historical monuments: the Old Tai Po Market to the north, and the Man Mo Temple to the south—all near the Larn Tsuen River that wound its way horizontally through the Territories.

In fact, local residents considered these two monuments as one inseparable entity. Man Mo Temple, dating from the Ming Dynasty, which had public access but whose use was reserved for special events on traditional days and festivals, was a huge tourist attraction, and all kinds of people (except women, whose presence was greatly frowned upon) hung out in walled-in Man Mo Temple Park (behind the temple), amid its bamboos and plants, playing cards or chatting while sitting on its permanent concrete benches.

Fu Shin Street itself was built at the end of the nineteenth century as a marketplace, and its physical structure and shape haven't changed since then because shop and stallowners on the street resisted government plans to reconstruct it. On Fu Shin Street—accessed either through Shung Tak Street, considered the

beginning because the house numbers progreesed from there nu-
merically, or through Pak Shing Street, considered the end—the
road blends with the sidewalk to produce an uneven-level surface,
and aside from the fire hydrant in front of the temple, the street
was quite unique in all of Hong Kong: It had no benches, barners,
or garbage bins. The street was stuffed with restaurants, salons,
supermarkets on the ground floors of buildings, and with stalls
and makeshift "shops" on the street displaying groceries and fresh
vegetables.

Fu Shin Street was also packed with an admixture of shoppers,
illegal street vendors (selling everything from cell phones to laptops
to pagers to leather bags of all brands), street residents, stall and
shopowners, kids, nuns, monks, preachers (because of the temple),
and transients, beggars, tourists, and pickpockets (because of its
tourist attractions). The illegal vendors sold from makeshift
structures (what in the US is called "lean-tos) that they could
collapse within thirty seconds when they got wind that police
officers (called Hawker Control Teams) were on their way for
unpredictable and infrequent "raids." These teams were not really
confrontational or antagonistic with the locals, and some were said
to be "on the dole"—predictably enough.

On that Thanksgiving Day, thousands of miles from Missoula,
Montana, Fu Shin Street itself seemed to me a microcosm of all of
Hong Kong: an interesting and coloful farrago of objects, people,
chaos, noise, and smells—and a curious medley of first-world high-
tech items (cell phones, laptops, pagers, digital watches) and third-
world ones (fresh produce, monks, makeshift structures). And the
ambiguous boundaries, between street and sidewalk, and between
the shops and the street itself (shopowners sometimes "colonized"
street areas and in some cases "rented" these spaces out to "ten-
ants") underlined the fact that Hong Kong was a highly condensed
city-state and open port where most of the spaces were highly
contested.

I played ethnographer while Michael interviewed the locals
(in Cantonese and Mandarin), and out at lunch, as we were

sampling some delicious Hong Kong cuisine at a restaurant (frequented by the locals) in Park Cheung Court on Fu Shin Street just opposite the temple, I proposed another project (in addition to the documentary I was helping him with) to him that had occurred to me all morning as I was watching all the activities on Fu Shin Street: that we collaborate on a screenplay together on those aspects of Hong Kong that had been missing in *Chungking Express*—named for the notorious transient hotel, ChungKing Mansions, on Nathan Road in Tsim Sha Tsui—Kar-wai Wong's film that was released in the US in 1995: Hong Kong straddling first-world and third-world identities, underscored by the fact of having a stock-exchange, the only one in the "third-world"; and Hong Kong's curious and complex connections to China and the United Kingdom, signified by the ninety-nine-year lease from July 1898 to July 1997, with the end of the lease and the Handover ceremoniously and elaborately played out before the media-saturated world in July 1997—and most significantly, with the current international machine of capital on the brink of enslaving China, China's own ambiguous attitudes toward Hong Kong itself currently and into the future, since speculations abound about whether China will simply leave Hong Kong alone to continue its way of capital as an historical experimental window into its own future, or whether the communist regime in Beijing will simply annex the former island-colony.

One evening Michael and Eva rented the video of *Chungking Express* so we could refresh our memories of what the film did not accomplish, and consequently, what our own ambitious film project would strive to achieve.

Chungking Express engages two narratives: the first, a romantic relationship between May (Valerie Chow), a Cathay Pacific flight attendant, and Qiwu (Takeshi Kaneshiro), a policer officer also known as "Cop 223"; the second, another romantic tango between Faye (Faye Wong), who tends the counter at a take-out junk-food outlet (that calls itself Midnight Express), and a nameless "Cop 663" (Tony Leung). These two narratives unfold in all the classic

Hong Kong locations: convenience stores; mangled indecipher-
able streets; fast-food stalls; open marketplaces with make-shift
"restaurants"; airport check-in areas where world-cities click by on
departure-boards. All the scenes accompanied by a synthetic blast
of masala music, Canto pop, and "California Dreaming." Ever
upbeat at her food counter, Faye dreams of being a Cathay Pacific
flight attendant, and ends up being one at the end of the film.

Chungking Express focused on the middle-to high-end aspects
of life in Hong Kong and elided almost everything I witnessed on
Fu Shin Street: its underbelly of gritty and hybrid transactions
and identities, its delicate and rough balance of deeply traditional
practices and displays of high technology.

The current complex relationship between China and Hong
Kong was apparent to me during my visit. The fact that: mainland
Chinese needed "visas" to get into Hong Kong; Hong Kong was—
to all intents and purposes—still functioning as an "open" port,
providing its citizens with both the benefits of an "alternative"
capital system, signified by the "lean-to" stalls and structures selling high-tech items on Fu Shin Street and on the heavily traf-
ficked "PolyU" bridges—and also the benefits of the "legit" system of capital, signified by its stock-exchange tied to the daily
fluctuations of "near-by" Tokyo-Nikkei and the "distant" NYSE-
Dow Jones and NASDAQ.

My exposure to "life" on Fu Shin Street and on the "PolyU"
bridges also showed me the different inflection that the term
"homeless" had in Hong Kong. Unlike within the new machine of
capital and time that Dorit and I talked about in an earlier entry,
where the homeless had no skills that no employer wanted to buy,
even at a discount, and where the homeless had only their own
naked time to waste, in Hong Kong the "homeless" had skills (to
sell high-tech goods: high-end products of the new capital) and
no naked time: They "lived and worked" on the streets, in the
provisional structures that they could transform from "shops" during the day to "sleeping quarters" at night, and that they could

swiftly collapse and make portable when the "Hawker Teams" were in proximity.

Briefly, as Michael and I ate our noddles at Park Cheung Court, and later sipped herb tea at Jade Plaza in Tai Po, and a little later, watched the street vendors sell their high-tech items on the "PolyU" bridges connecting Hong Kong Polytechnic University and Hunghom Kowloon Railroad Station, and as we discussed our film-project collaboration (to which he was extremely receptive and enthusiastic), the whole Katya-Glen psychosexual charade that had unfolded in Missoula during the two months before my visit, and even Missoula itself, had vacated my psyche. The Hong Kong visit turned out to be a tonic (spiked with delicious noodles, abundant wine, and city noises and smells) for my blasted psyche, and it turned the angle in my one-year sojourn in Missoula, although I was only to realize this later. And the fact was that my full day on Fu Shin Street in the Tai Po District of the New Territories—"Tai Po" in Mandarin loosely translated means "big step to pass," in the new territories of my psyche and my life, as it were—signaled the beginning of this turn of (the worm of) the metaphoric angle. My junket to Jerusalem in March and April 2000 was to complete this 90-degree angle. But I'm getting ahead of myself. To repeat somewhat, my distance from Katya at this point was underscored by the fact that as of November 27, I still hadn't responded to the e-message she had sent ten days before, on November 18.

*   *   *

34

New York: Tuesday, July 20, 1999

I just came back from another walk outside: this time, I walked several blocks on 57th Street to Fifth Avenue, then all the way down to Bryant Park behind the public library—where a mid-afternoon concert was playing live to a packed audience—in order to mingle with tourists, corporate workers, freelancers, and the homeless, and maybe to: remind myself of the tumultuous scenes of Hong Kong that I had been writing about minutes before; contrast scenes between Hong Kong and New York; ground myself once again on the gritty sidewalks of the high-flying financial and media capital (in all senses of economics and geography) that New York is, and so therefore, be ready for Dorit and my future, for Dorit *in* my future. In any case, I felt compelled to close the Microsoft Word file, leave the apartment on the 28th floor, take the elevator downstairs, wave to a smiling and it seemed to me obsequeous Carlos in the lobby, walk out the door into the simmering heatwave on 57th Street, and turn right on Fifth Avenue.

I went online as soon as I got back in. I had the usual forty messages within two hours, some from friends wishing me "mazel tov" on my impending marriage to Dorit, some from new-media news network editors looking for freelance "content-providers," and nothing from Dorit, and of course I wasn't really expecting anything from her. E-postings from paramours should now take me back to Hong Kong.

Hong Kong: Tuesday, December 8, 1998

Two days after my experience on Fu Shin Street, I got another e-posting from Katya:

Date: Sun, 29 November 1998 07:45:15 -0800 (MST)

From: "Katya Brodsky" <kbrodsky@selway.umt.edu> **Block**

Subject: (no subject)

Message: Hello Sweetie. Why haven't you responded to my letter? Are you all right? Are you having a great time? Please give me the phone number of your friends, the ones you're staying with. I want to call you. Last night I went to Charlie B's with Sigi. We had a great time. Later on this morning, Sigi and I are going to hike up to the M. She's been keeping me company while you're away. Please write me today, as soon as you read this. And don't forget to give me the phone number! I love you. Bye bye.

Katya Brodsky—Assistant Professor
Department of Foreign Languages and Literatures
University of Montana
Liberal Arts Building
Missoula, MT 59801
E-Mail: kbrodsky@selway.umt.edu

*   *   *

I responded to Katya right after I read that e-posting, and gave her Michael and Eva's phone number. She called the day after, and for th7e first forty-five minutes, we had a very unremarkable conversation for about an hour. I kept wanting to get off the phone, telling her it must be costing her a fortune, but she insisted on talking some more. Then she mentioned that Glen had wanted to go to Missoula to spend Thanksgiving with her, and she had dissuaded him from visiting. And the agony that had been suspended all my time in Hong Kong resumed—but only briefly.

That last week in Hong Kong before I flew back to the US on Monday December 14, the day Hanukkah began that year, Michael and I did some more "field work" talking to more people and "observing" scenes in a few more areas: city parks sandwiched between Public Square and Market Streets in Yau Ma Tei District; Kowloon Walled City Park and Shatin Bicycle Park in Kowloon Tong; and Hoi Pong Square in Sai Kung. I also did a lot of running in scenic Kowloon Park, running there and back from Woosung Street.

Then, on December 14, 1998, Michael and Eva drove me to the airport on Lantau Island, where I got on my flight back to the US. The Northwest flight I got on originated from Tokyo, and I got on it in Hong Kong, then it went to Beijing, then over the North Pole to Detroit, then to Minneapolis (where again I had a two-hour layover and where again I saw Shoshana at the airport), then finally to Missoula and back to Katya-Glen, Jacques, Bryn, and Rob.

*   *   *

35

New York: Tuesday, July 20, 1999

My time is running really short for Missoula entries, which—to repeat ad nauseam—I *must* conclude before Dorit gets back here from Paris tomorrow afternoon. Therefore I want to confine these entries to three exchanges—spanning the period from December 21, 1998, the day Hanukkah ended, to Sunday June 20, 1999, the day Katya and I broke up, which I narrated in my first entry in these pages—that I had with three people in Missoula: Katya, the evening after Rob and Laura's holiday-season party at their house on Lolo Street (December 21, 1998); Bryn, one night at Charlie B's (February 14, 1999); and Rob, one afternoon at the Union Hall shortly after Laura left him (June 13, 1999).

This period was punctuated by my two-month junket to Jerusalem from Sunday, February 28, 1999 to Sunday, May 2, 1999, when I went there to do some freelance work for *The Jerusalem Post*, Israel's only English-language daily. When I began these entries, I had intended a full narration of my remarkable sojourn in Jerusalem, but I'm bound by the same temporal constraints that limit my Missoula entries. So therefore I will simply condense my experiences in Jerusalem to the few paragraphs that follow.

On Sunday, February 28, 1999, I took a Northwest Airlines flight from Missoula to Minneapolis, with the customary two-hour layover and visit with Shoshana at the Red Concourse of the Lindberg Terminal at the Minneapolis-St Paul International Airport, then to New York's La Guardia, where Dorit and I shared a nice dinner at one of the "two-star" restaurants at JFK while waiting for three hours for my El-Al flight to Ben-Gurion Airport in Tel Aviv-Jaffa, by way of Athens.

Nina Jacob, the *Post*' s editor-in-chief—Katya's friend, whom she mentioned in my Entry 3 "Missoula: Wednesday, June 23, 1999"—was generous enough to drive all the way for an hour from Jerusalem to pick me up at Ben-Gurion, and to drive us back for another hour on Highway 1, gradually climbing the hills of Judaea till we got to the city-entrance sign, then into Jerusalem, when Highway 1 became Yafo Street (Jaffa Street). We stayed on Yafo all the way to Jaffa Gate at the edge of the Old City, then drove past the Tower of David on David Street (which straddled and divided the Christian and Armenian Quarters), then straight ahead to Hal-Shalshelet (which straddled and divided the Muslim and Jewish Quarters), where I had arranged—before I left the US—to stay in a house with the owners Ben-Avi and Zev, a gay couple, for my entire tenure in Jerusalem.

Within a week in Jerusalem, I developed a routine—with a few variations—that lasted during my entire stay there. I also spent most of my time there with my little group of four new friends from the *Post* : Nina, a Sabra; Edith, who was born in Beirut, with a Lebanese father and Israeli mother; Meir, Brooklyn-born; and Ella, born in Baghdad, of Sephardic parents.

So then this was my skeletal weekday routine: After I got up in the morning—say around 10 AM—and did my ablutions, I would take the number 1 bus from the Old City into West Jerusalem to the editorial offices of the *Post*, where I had to be at 1 PM, and where I would get online and scout news web-sites for items from France that would be of interest to Israelis, then translate and transload them onto the Post's online edition (at http://www.jpost.com). Sometimes I would simply substantively edit news items written by the *Post* 's regular nonnative English-speaking reporters.

Around 3 PM, my new friends and I would take a break and walk to Ben Yehuda Way, the bustling pedestrian mall, and have coffee and chat at one of the cafés before heading back to the *Post*. For me and my friends, work at the *Post* ended for the weekday at

6 PM, then we would head over to Zion Square for drinks, then later to dinner at a restaurant at Hillel or Ben Shira before ending up at the Underground, a hip-hop nightclub near Independence Park, off Gershon Agron, where we were more or less regulars for the time I was in Jerusalem.

The hip-hop music at The Underground was always deafening, the air thick with sweat. At the bar, I might see a young Israeli woman wearing a black halter top, heavily tattooed and multiply pierced, writhing to the music with what seemed to me to be an African-American man. Or a brown-eyed Palestinian wearing a crisp Ralph Lauren T-shirt hanging out with glass of whisky in hand and with what seemed to me a Jewish-American woman who seemed to me to be from Brooklyn—or The Bronx: In another era she might even be a "Bronx Bagel Baby" who took the A-train all the way from Riverdale through Harlem to the West Village, to listen to jazz with the black Beat poets at the Blue Note or the Bottom Line. The scene at The Underground attracted all kinds: tourists, gay-lesbians, soldiers, Arab-Americans, and even Jews who wore skullcaps. Around midnight, my friends and I would disperse, and I would head back to the Old City to Ben-Avi and Zev's house on Ha-Shalshelet, where they would most certainly be asleep. I hardly ever saw those two all my time there, since they would also be gone when I got up in the morning. In any case, after I got "home," I'd use the desktop in their living room (which they were extremely generous to let me use) to get online to read and sometimes answer my e-messages, mostly from the US, and mostly pithy ones from Katya.

One of Katya's pithy e-messages told me Glen was coming to Missoula to visit her for a week, and my fresh agonies resurfaced with a vengeance, somewhat mollified by the time I was spending with my Jerusalem friends, especially with Nina, with whom a close friendship was beginning to slowly develop. Also during that first week, I saw my in-laws, Nigist's parents, Solomon and Miriam (Biblical names for sure!), at their place on Me'A She 'Arim, near the Ethiopian Church. Before I left the US, Dorit had given me the name and coordinates of one of her aunts whom she wanted

me to look up, and whom she said she would warn to expect my
visit. (I eventually hooked up with this aunt my last week in
Jerusalem.)

By the second to the third week, I had been to enough places
to begin to grasp Jerusalem as first of all a place of limestone and
concrete, glass and steel, built along the craggy hills on the desert's
edge. And that the city's residents were simply a diverse gathering
of people struggling to find jobs or to make sure that their kids got
a good education, as in every other big "world city." These included
bankers and computer engineers, students, and soldiers, who played
squash at the YMCA or caught a movie at the Gil Cineplex or
picked up the latest CDs at Tower Records, also as in any other
"world city." And as I walked the city streets, I saw people either
outfitted for the nineteenth century or others who favored nose-
rings and shaved heads and black high boots and clothes: icons for
a "hip" contemporary Western urban subculture. On those streets,
sometimes on those rare evenings when I was alone, I heard the
peals of church bells and the calls to prayer of Muslim muezzins
and the latest hip-hop throbbing from one of the nightclubs.

In Jerusalem, I found what I thought was the world's best
konafa—an exquisitely sweet Arabic treat made of syrupy pastry
and soft cheese—and also first-rate Hungarian goulash, acceptable
pasta, and a delightful couscous prepared by a chef who used to
work in the royal palace of Morocco.

But I knew from everything I'd read and seen that Jerusalem was
also imbued with the blood of the ages, and was deeply steeped in
symbol and myth. Jerusalem was also the theological battleground
where Jews, Muslims, and Christians argued most fervently over whose
God was the True God, and over whose history was legitimate.

On weekends, we sometimes drove all the way up to Haifa
and lounged on the beach, drinking beer or chilled white wine.
Or we went to Nazareth or Bethlehem (which in reality was more
or less a suburb of East Jerusalem) in Palestinian territory, where
my friends , all Jews, would tease me by saying they felt safe
because I was with them, or because they were with me, since

Palestinians wouldn't dare "set off a bomb at a bro." One day we went into the Negev Desert and spent the weekend at Beersheba.

One Saturday (Sabbath) morning I ventured out on my own in the Old City. I ambled through a maze of alleys, past pleasant-smelling falafel shops and a run-down Turkish palace, until I got to the Western Wall. The Wall was a small part of Herodian-era Jewish Temple that was destroyed by the Romans in AD 70—or 70 CE. When I got there that morning, a group of ultra-Orthodox Israelis were chanting and boisterously debating Talmudic interpretations of something. Then I walked on to the Little Wall, which was actually in an Arab neighborhood, and then on to the Temple Mount, which was under control of Israel. I wanted to see the mountaintop from where Mohammed was said to have ascended to heaven, and also the spectacular Dome of the Rock and its gilded roof that had cast an ethereal light over the Old City every night that I was in Jerusalem.

On Jerusalem's sun-drenched streets every day, I saw the most beautiful olive-skinned women on earth, it seemed to me. I exchanged furtive "magical" glances with a few of them while my heart throbbed, all the while comparing them to Katya, as my mind's theater contructed and repeatedly rewound scenarios of Glen making love to her again and again on her bed, the same bed that I had made love to her, and in the same mode that I had as well. Angrily but methodically seeking some form of revenge, I started spending more and more time with Nina Jacob toward the end of my sojourn in Jerusalem.

And yes, Nina did treat me to a delightfully long cozy dinner at a restaurant on Ben Yehuda Way the penultimate night before I jetted back to the US from Ben Gurion. And in fact that penultimate night, Nina did lure me back to her "postmodern" apartment on Derekh Ha 'Shalom, where we spent the night together. This weapon was about all that I had left, it seemed to me, to combat the psychosexual torment that I felt—rightly or wrongly—Katya was inflicting on me.

*   *   *

36

New York: Wednesday, July 21, 1999

I'm writing on Wednesday after I thought I would not be doing that. I had planned to type all evening last night. But then early last evening, May called me to invite me to dinner at their place in Park Slope. And so I took the number 1 train from Columbus Circle, changed to the 2 at 42nd, and took that all the way to Grand Army Plaza in Brooklyn, then walked on Prospect Park West to have dinner with Al, May, and a bunch of their usual friends: a mixture of traders, writers, and lawyers. May made a truly delicious dish from Indonesia that consisted of chicken, peanuts, and rice. We ate, drank, gossiped, and watched a video of something called *Chasing Amy*, an Indie film that my friend Derrick Tseng, a close high-school friend who went to NYU film school, worked on as a line producer. The dinner party broke up around 1 AM. I took the usual trains back to Columbus Circle and walked the two New York blocks here to West 57th, then went to bed immediately because I wanted to get up early and finish my task before-you-know-what. And of course I woke up with a hangover, as usual. I booted up Dorit's desktop, logged onto My Yahoo, and saw that I had sixty messages, none of them of any significant importance: a few more from friends, something from Jacques (about his colleagues in the department no doubt), something from Rob (titled "Love's Labor Lost," referring to his split-up from Laura, more on this below), and lots of spam: somehow my e-address had gotten on several mostly high-tech and media-related lists. For some of these, I used to deploy the "block address" option of Yahoo Mail but soon stopped bothering and imply deleted them en masse. In any case, I didn't bother to open any of these messages from Jacques or Rob because I wanted to get to work on these entries, and so onward—or backward—to Missoula to finish the task.

Missoula: Sunday, December 21, 1998

Rob and Laura had a huge holiday-season party at their sprawling house and yard (which was surrounded by a corral fence) on Lolo Street that last day of Hanukkah, in the Rattlesnake section of Missoula. The party, which included a munificent buffet dinner, "began" around 8 PM, and wound down about 2 AM. Almost everyone I knew in Missoula was there, and by midnight or so, everybody was drunk. Katya and I left at 2 AM with the stragglers, and we walked to her car about the same time that Jacques and Christine were walking to his car. I'd stopped and said a few words to him, and I saw that Katya was seething.

Katya had been bugging me since 10 PM that we should leave the party and get back to her house and make love, as she was wont to do. And also, as she was wont to do, she had said to me at some point:

—Let's go home, I'm tired.

To which I responded:
—I like to stay some more.
—Why?
—I want to talk to these people some more.
—You and your discourse. Let's just go home and make love.
—We'll do that later. As I said, I want to stay and talk.
—I don't give a fuck about your discourse.
—Well . . . Look, you can go home. Someone will drop me off later at your place. Or I can go to Jacques's house. I'm supposed to be living there after all.
—OK, we'll stay, but for only for another thirty minutes. OK?
—Only for another thirty minutes.
—Promise?
—Promise. Why don't you get yourself another glass of vodka.

Then I scurried off, eager to detach myself from her, looking for Bryn, who was also there somewhere with Mirta and Vanessa. Ever since I came back from Hong Kong, Katya and had argued almost every day about something or other. And I was getting more and more irritated with her, especially since the Glen phone-call charade was continuing. We had fallen right back into my pre-Hong Kong Katya-Glen practices, it seemed. It was as if my Hong Kong trip and my remarkably rich and almost "spiritual" experiences on Fu Shin Street never happened.

In any event at Rob and Laura's, thirty minutes soon became one hour, then two, then four, untilwe got to 2 AM. And by the time we got back Katya's, she was clearly on the warpath:

—I'm getting so sick of your discourses. And of you and your Jacques.
—You know something? I don't care anymore if you're sick. I like discoursing. And I like Jacques. He and I go way back. And I won't let you ruin the friendship.
—After everything he's said about you?
—That's your story. Why should I believe you?
—You know well he's a liar. And a sexist racist to boot.
—These are strong words, Katya.
—They're true.
—Well . . .
—Look, I don't feel like fighting tonight. I just want us to make love.
—When will you break up with Glen?
—I will soon.
—When? When?
—I told you to be patient with me.
—If you don't break up with him before Christmas I'm taking myself out of the relationship. Seriously.
—Oh, please. I told you the thing with Glen has no future.
—We will have no future if you don't break up with him.
—Let's go into the bedroom and make love, please.

—I don't feel like it tonight.

—You don't?

—No I don't.

—I want to tell you something.

—Tell me.

—You've been using sex to blackmail me about Glen. By doing this you're making it more difficult for me to break up with him.

—Is that right?

—Yes that's right. Pleasurable sex opens up other lines of communication between the two members of a couple. If we had good sex then maybe we won't be arguing so much.

—That's bullshit.

—Listen: I want you to win me from Glen .

—Oh yeah? Are you kidding? And how do I do that?

—By fucking me and fucking me again and again.

—You're a sex addict.

—Now you're insulting me.

—Good! I'm glad I'm doing that.

—That's mean. Why are you being mean to me?

—You know why.

—I take care of you. I cook for you. I buy your wine. I do your laundry. I even got you a new strap for your watch at South Mall. Why are you being mean to me? If you tell any of your New York friends that there's a woman in Missoula who is doing all these things for you, they'll say, this woman is in love with you. And they'd be telling the truth.

—As a point of fact, I have a dear close friend in New York who thinks I must be out of my mind to put up with what you've been putting me through with Glen.

—Did you tell your friend *everything* that's been going on between us? Did you tell him that I'm more or less supporting you financially here in Missoula?

—It's a she.

—A she?

—The friend I'm talking about is a woman.

—A woman? A girlfriend?

—In a manner of speaking.

I meant Dorit, and obviously at that point the exact nature of our relationship was ambiguous at best. She was simply my subletter. But I hadn't fully realized she was much more, and I couldn't have predicted that I would be getting ready to marry her about a year later.

—You have a girlfriend in New York? So you've been lying to me all this time we've known each other? And meanwhile, I've been up front with you about Glen.

—Look, I was just trying to make you jealous. She's my subletter.

—She's also your close friend?

—Yes she is. I've known her since 1989. And since you and I are being up front with each other: she and I had a romantic entanglement for a year or so in 1991.

—And it's all over?

—As far as I know. I've had two serious relationships since we split up: with a Karyn, and with Sarah, whom I married.

—But this woman is now subletting your place. I'm not very comfortable with that.

—I don't care if you are or not.

—Look, let's go into the bedroom and make love. I'm tired of fighting.

Then she forcefully dragged me into the bedroom, made a beeline for my zipper, unzipped my pants, took out my penis, and started fellating me.

Missoula: Sunday, February 14, 1998

Bryn, Mirta, and I were having drinks at The Old Post in the evening. We'd gotten together after Bryn got off work at Worden's, in the same building around the corner. Katya and I had had a big fight the night before, and we had decided to give each other some space for a few days, even on Valentine's Day. I was a little late getting to The Old Post. I had taken the last number 12 bus of the

day from Jacques's house in South Hills, and arrived at The Old
Post to find Mirta and Bryn waiting for me. As I approached their
table, they both looked up and stopped talking immediately when
they saw me: a clear sign that they had been talking about me
before I got there. Bryn and Mirta, both at once:

—Hi.
—Hi. You guys have been talking about me?

   Bryn:
—Yeah we have, as a matter of fact.
—What about?
—About how I should rescue you from Katya.
—*What*?
—You heard me right. You know me. I'm kinda direct.
—Mirta: You're in on this?
—I'm afraid so.
—Oh boy. How can you rescue me?
—I'll tell you about all that later. Mirta and I want to take you out
    to dinner, and then she's going home. She really can't stay up
    late. Her pregnancy won't let her.
—Where are we going for dinner?
—How about the Thai Restaurant on Main?
—The one right across from 201 Main—Rob's company's office
    building?
—Yeah.
—OK.
—Let's drink some more first. What do you want—merlot?
—How could you guess?
Bryn motioned the waitress over and ordered a merlot.

   I:
—So how do you know I've been having problems with Katya?
—Shh. I told you we'll talk about all this later.
—Mirta, how you been?

—OK. Can't complain. I'm directing a docu I'm really proud of.
—Yeah? On what?
—On preserving the national forests in Western Montana.
—Sounds exciting.
—Hey! Don't be too condescending. We can't all be working on
    politics and culture!
—I wasn't condescending. At least I didn't mean to. I'm sorry.
—You take things too seriously. Loosen up! I was just pulling your
    leg.

Bryn:
—Drink up you two, before you tumble into bed together. I'm
    starving.
—So am I. I've got to eat for two.
—So let's go.
—Let me finish my merlot.

So we piled into Bryn's car and she drove a few blocks to the
Thai Restaurant (which in fact was the name of the restaurant!).
After dinner, Bryn dropped Mirta off at her house. Then we went
to Charlie B's. Bryn got each of us a pint of Summit Pale Ale. She
lit a cigarette, then said:
—Jacques told me you and Katya have tons of problems. He said
    Katya has you under sexual bondage.
—He did, did he?
—He did. Totally. Listen: I've been thinking.
—About what?
—Us.
—Us?
—Us. Let's totally take off together on the road for about a year.
—On the road? Have you been reading Jack Kerouac?
—I've read a lot of Kerouac. But that's not what I'm proposing.
—What are you proposing?

—That you and I travel the US together for a year. Your experi-
    ences will make you a totally better writer. You'll be less stiff
    about all that theory bullshit.

—You sound like Katya.

—Listen: Don't you ever ever compare me with that bitch!
    I was startled. Bryn again:

—I'm sorry I said that.

—I forgive you. What you propose sounds like Kerouac.

—OK, no contest. What do you think about what I propose?

—You want us to be an item?

—Yes. Totally.

—Yes, but . . .

—I've been seeing a therapist about all that.

—Where did you get the money?

—My dad gave it to me.

—Did you tell . . . ?

—Yes I did. So he insisted on taking care of his little girl.

—Bryn . . .

—Come to the road with me. I like you a great deal. I'll try to
    totally take care of you. You can take care of me. We might
    even have great sex after my therapy.

—How will you continue your therapy on the road?

—My therapist and I have talked about having phone sessions.

—Oh boy.

—Think about it. Katya doesn't know what you're all about. She's
    totally abusing you. And I know what she thinks of me too.

—Yeah? Jacques told you that too?

—Yeah.

—I wish you would take everything he tells you with a grain of
    salt.

—I do. But I choose to believe what I believe.

—Oh Kay!

We stayed at Charlie B's until closing time at 2 AM. Bryn then drove us to her place just a block and a half away, where again, we slept on the same bed without making love.

Later on in June, the Sunday that Katya and I broke up, Bryn was one of the people I called. She told me she was heartbroken when I said I was quitting Missoula. She made me promise to keep in touch. And indeed I have. I plan to fly her to Dorit and my wedding on January 1, 2000.

Missoula: Sunday: June 13, 1999

Rob's wife Laura had left him for a famous writer a week previous. I got wind of this when I went into DragNet and was told Rob had taken the whole week off—and why. So that's how I got the news.

Rob himself got the news about his divorce when he and Laura were coming back from South Mall, where they had gone to get some clothes for their two kids. Laura was driving. As they turned onto Higgins Avenue, heading for the Clark-Fork Bridge, Laura told Rob she was leaving him for Chuck MacMahon, the famous writer who had made Montana famous in his novels about Montana. Rob immediately told Laura to stop the car, that he wanted to get off. He then got off after Laura stopped the car and ran to the Clark-Fork River, then walked along its banks for about two-hundred meters, then, a few minutes later, on impulse, in his words to me later, "ate a bunch of poisonous plants." (He was an amateur naturalist, so he knew quite a bit about plants.) Then, realizing what he had done, what he was doing, and remembering that he had two kids, he first made himelf sick, then after vomiting, he ran home and took some antidotes. Laura, suspecting what Rob might be up to, drove straight to the police station after Rob got out of the car, and accompanied by an officer, went looking for Rob by the river, then went home, where they found him.

Rob told me all this as we sat drinking some alcoholic beverages at the Missoula ("Mo") Club that June Sunday afternoon.

I had called him at home after his assistant gave me the news, and he had agreed to meet me.

—So you wanted to kill yourself.

—Yeah, that was stupid.

—Yeah it definitely was. I felt like killing myself also when Sarah left me, but I could never bring myself to act on it. I simply absolutely am not capable of committing suicide. My genes are not programmed for that.

—You're lucky. Twelve years of marriage down the drain! And two kids. I can't believe these past ten days. You know what I did with my week off?

—What did you do?

—I got drunk everyday. When I got up in the morning, I poured myself some vodka before I got online. I drank vodka all day. So now I feel really really shitty.

—Sometimes you have to go all the way, and then reemerge as a different person.

—You make sense. You always make sense.

—I'm simply speaking from experience, Rob.

—God! I can't believe she left me for Chuck MacMahon. That really hurts. You'll never know how much that hurts.

—I do, believe me.

—You don't. This one is a special kind of hurt. I'll explain.

—OK.

—Laura and I both admire Chuck's novels. We've both read everything he's written.

—Really?

—I'll tell you something about me you don't know.

—What?

—I'm a writer. Before I got very technical and worked for Microsoft I was a writer. I made my living as a writer.

—Really? A writer of what?

—Short stories.

—You made a living as a short-story writer?

—I certainly did. I sold my stories to *Redbook Magazine* every week. They paid me a thousand dollars for each story.

—Really? And you gave all that up?

—I did, for Laura. When I met Laura I was a writer. I think that's what attracted her to me. I gave up writing to make more money for us, for our kids, and this is how she's repaid me: By leaving me for a famous writer.

—So she was attracted to you because you were a writer?

—I'm convinced of that.

—Then she must be a writer-groupie. She's perhaps attracted romantically and possibly sexually only to writers.

—I guess. That's quite ironic, don't you think? Damn if you do and damn if you don't.

—I'd like to read some of your stories.

—Sure. I'll make copies of the *Redbook* stuff for you. And even stuff I've never published. I also have the finished manuscript of a novel.

—You do?

—Yeap.

—And are you going to publish it?

—No. I'll never publish it.

—You're a writer! You have to publish it.

—I'm a dot-com person. If I publish the novel, people will see me only as a writer.

—What's wrong with that?

—That will distract me from my DragNet work.

—Why can't you do both?

—I can't. I'm committed to the Internet. I'm focused on it. I don't want any distractions.

—You're really a piece of work, Rob.

—God, I'm hurting. Laura's fucking that guy. Probably right now. She's fucking him!

—How you feel right now will most surely get worse. Trust me.
   You'll go through hell. And then you'll recover. Trust me on
   that. You'll recover and find yourself another partner. You'll
   be a different person. You'll see the light at the end of the
   tunnel. You'll come out on the other side.

—I never figured you for clichés.

—Clichés are clichés for a reason.

—What reason?

—They're true.

—I'm glad we're having this talk. I'm feeling a little better already.

—Good. But trust me when I say it'll get worse. If you feel like
   crying, cry. If you feel like drinking, drink. If you feel over-
   whelmed, let it wash all over you. Don't fight it. You'll only
   get better. If you fight it, you might somatize it. Then you'll
   end up with some God-awful disease. Only, please promise
   me one thing.

—What thing?

—Don't ever try to kill yourself again. Ever.

—I'll never do that again. That was stupid.

—It was stupid. One day, one day, I swear, Rob, you'll fall back
   into your life again. One day, you'll look back at all this, you'll
   look back at this period you're now going through, and you'll
   think: What the fuck was that all about? Was that really me
   back there? That day is very difficult for you to imagine right
   this minute. But trust me . . .

— . . . you're speaking from experience.

—Absolutely.

—Let's have some more drinks. And then let's go to Marianne's
   and spend some cash!

—Sounds good to me. But don't you need a jacket and tie to get in
   there?

—Marianne's a friend of mine. No problem.

—I see.

—When is Katya coming back from Moscow?

—She's coming back next Saturday. June 13th.

—How's *that* going?

—I don't really know. I'm not sure what's going to happen. She won't like it when I tell her I'm going to Paris.

—She won't. Especially if you tell her you're going there with a woman. What's her name again?

—Francette.

—Nice. Let's have some more drinks and go to Marianne's and spend a pile of cash..

*   *   *

37

New York: Wednesday, July 21, 1999

Dorit is coming home in a few hours. I'm now done with my Missoula entries. After my last entry, I went online to check my e-messages. There was a posting from Francette, which I reproduce below.

––––––––––––

Date: Wed, 21 July 1999 15:38:27 -0100

From: Francette de Vallières <francette@arts.ucla.edu> **Reply to**: <francette@hotmail.com>

Subject: Félicitation!

Message: Hello there! I want to congratulate you and Dorit on your impending wedding. As I told you before at my apartment in Paris: I wish you both the best of luck! I want to apologize to you for the way I behaved in Paris. I was jealous, insanely jealous, but now I'm over it. Things wouldn't have worked out between us anyway. It was only my fantasy.

I'll get back to the US end of August, to Los Angeles. I'd love to go to your wedding in New York in January if you invite me. If you don't, I'll understand. Also, you and Dorit are welcome to visit me in LA. And if you both come back to Paris, you can always stay at my place. I'll warn Michel. I know you can stay at Emilie's, but my place has more space.

That's all. I hope this message meets you well. Say hello to your little friend for me.

Bye bye.

—————————

Francette de Vallières—Professor
Cultural Studies
University of California
Arts and Sciences
Los Angeles, CA 90021
E-Mail:francette@arts.ucla.edu

*   *   *

38

New York: Saturday, July 24, 1999

Dorit got back to New York Wednesday afternoon. Yesterday she left for Montréal for two months. She'll be back the end of September. Thursday night we had our first fight. All couples fight sooner or later, even if the two people think they have a mind meld. Here's how ours happened.

New York: Thursday, July 22, 1999

There's only one desktop in this apartment: Dorit's, the same one I'm using right this minute. Around 7 PM Thursday night, Dorit was writing on the desktop. I had told her before she started working that I needed to get online with Michael Pang for several hours before 2 AM Eastern Daylight Time, which translated to 3 PM Friday Hong Kong Time, Michael's and my self-imposed deadline for completing the final draft of the screenplay, so that Michael can give it to the producer to read for the weekend. The plan was that the producer would then take a meeting with Michael and other "executives" either on Monday or Tuesday, a crucial "power" meeting that would decide the fate of our fine movie about what *Chungking Express* elided about Hong Kong.

Around 10 PM, Dorit was still working on her desktop. I reminded her about my own project. She finally yielded the desktop to me at midnight. Then she sat on the couch and turned on the TV. She then watched *Star Trek: Voyager* and sipped some merlot while I worked online with Michael until about 3 AM, when I went offline. I then pour myself some merlot and sat on the couch with Dorit. At some point during a commercial, she said:

—Too bad you had to work all this time, so you couldn't join me
    earlier to watch *Star Trek* with me.

—Yeah, too bad.

I said nothing more. Then she said:

—What's wrong? Something's wrong. I know you.

—I'm pissed at you.

—Why? Did I do something?

—I told you I needed the desktop for several hours before 2 AM.
    You knew how crucial that was.

—I'm sorry. But what I was working on was also very important. I
    had my own deadline to meet.

—This is not going to work.

—What is not going to work?

—This arrangment.

—What arrangement? Can you be more specific?

—The space. The desktop.

—Listen, so we'll get another desktop. Big deal.

—Where will we put it? Also . . .   I can't afford a desktop.

—I'll get us another desktop.

—Still, where will we put it?

—In the bedroom.

—No way! Neither of us can sleep when the other one is using it.
    So therefore we have a big problem here You know that being
    online is my work.

—Mine too.

—We need more space. And I know that in New York that's easier
    said than done.

—The solution to that will come soon enough. Please be patient.

—What solution?

—Just be patient.

—Tell me what solution.

—OK, since you insist. I might as well tell you about our wed-
    ding present.

—What wedding present?

—The wedding present my mother is planning to give us.

—How will that resolve our problem of space?

—She's buying us a two-bedroom apartment.

—*She's what?*

—You heard me. She's buying us a two-bedroom apartment.

—Are you shitting me?

—No. Why would I shit you about something like that?

—You're not joking.

—No. I'm not.

—A two-bedroom apartment?

—Yeah.

—Where, in Park Slope?

—In Manhattan.

—Oh my God. I'm not sure how I feel about that.

—What do you mean? I thought you said we needed more space.

—We do. But I don't think I want to be beholden to your mother in that way.

—Oh come on! My mother wants to do it. She's happy to do it. You'll be part of our family when we get married.

—I don't want to be a kept husband.

—You won't be. You're in the media. You have an income. And who knows? You might even get a break with your novel and your screenplay.

—I don't know, Dorit.

—What don't you know?

—I don't know.

—You're repeating yourself.

—So I am.

—Listen, you don't feel right. And you're starting to piss me off a little bit. So let's just bag this argument right now.

—OK.

—I'm going to bed. We'll talk about it tomorrow.

—But I want to talk about it now. You're leaving for Montréal tomorrow.

—We'll talk about it before I leave.

—Let's talk about it now.

—OK, then.

—Look: I have a solution. Your mother can buy us the apartment, but I want her to put only your name on the contract when she signs it.

—What?

—You heard me. I want only your name on the apartment con-tract.

—Absolutely not. The apartment is for both of us. Both our names will be on the contract.

—No way.

—OK, suit yourself. I'm going to bed.

Then she got off the couch and stormed into the bedroom. I stayed in the living room for another hour, drinking more merlot and watching TV. At about 4 AM, I turned off the TV. Then I decided to sleep on the couch. About 5 AM, Dorit came out to wake me up, and pulling me into the bedroom, she whispered:

—Come to bed, you silly man.

*   *   *

39

New York: Wednesday, August 11, 1999

This will be my last entry. Dorit is still in Montréal. We voice-connect every night. We also exchange e-messages at least two sometimes three times everyday. I want to close out with two of her e-postings: one I got yesterday; and the other ten minutes ago. The one I got ten minutes ago threw my psyche off-balance for about a minute or so after I read it. The first e-message was about Dorit's typical weekday morning in Montréal that she wanted to give me a feel of. The second e-message: Dorit had forwarded me the typing she sent to Sarah, in response to the one Dorit got from her. Dorit did not include Sarah's posting in what she forwarded to me.

The first e-message:

Date: Tue, 10 August 1999 19:19:09 -0500 (EDT)
From: Dorit Levin <doritlevin@onebox.com> **Add Block**
Subject: My Typical Montreal Morning
Message: Yo. I want to give you a sense of how my mornings are.

I take a bus to the subway in the morning. The subway stop is called Mont-Royal. I take the orange line in the direction of Henri Bourassa, then change at Jean-Talon. From there I take the blue line in the direction of Snowdon. On the blue line, there is a subway stop called Acadie, which was beautifully conceived. The walls are black and gray marble, and the seats and light fixtures

344   BIODUN IGINLA

fire-engine red. The floors black and red tiles. The walls have one thick line of blue that takes over the center. Each morning, I am sitting (or unfortunately sometimes standing) engrossed in a magazine. I don't hear anything around me until the woman comes on and says in French Next station, Acadie. At which point I start waking up. The train pulls up at Acadie, and she says Station Acadie. I look out, craning my neck if necessary, smile, devour the colors, and you cannot imagine my childish good mood. Station Acadie makes everything worth having gotten out of bed for.

Speak with you tonight, my love.

Dorit Levin Staff Writer
THE NEW YORKER
Condé Nast Publications
4 Times Square
New York, NY 10036
Voice/Fax: 1-212-421-8774
e-mail: doritlevin@onebox.com
Website: http://www.newyorker.com

*   *   *

Now the second posting:

Date: Wed, 11 August 1999 09:18:34 -0500 (EDT)
From: Dorit Levin <doritlevin@onebox.com> **Add Block**
Subject: FW: My Future Husband
Message: Yo bro! I'm forwarding you a message I just posted to Sarah. She had sent me a weird message last night, saying all kinds of things about you that I don't feel like repeating here, although if you read my posting you'll get a general idea.

Have fun reading it. I'll call you tonight and we can talk about it if you want. I love you.

Dorit Levin—Staff Writer
THE NEW YORKER
Condé Nast Publications
4 Times Square
New York, NY 10036
Voice/Fax: 1-212-421-8774
e-mail: doritlevin@onebox.com
Website: http://www.newyorker.com

Forwarded Message
Date: Wed, 11 August 1999 08:32:06 -0500 (EDT)
From: Dorit Levin <doritlevin@onebox.com> **Add Block**
To: Sarah Guggenheim <sguggenheim@walkerart.org>
Subject: My Future Husband
Message: Dear Sarah:

Thanks ever so much for your message, and for telling me about my future husband. You were wondering what I was getting myself into. You said he has a lot of baggage. Well, we all have baggages.

I love Jamil deeply, in spite of what you say about him. And I know he loves Shoshana deeply, and that's all that matters to me. Whatever happened between the both of you in your marriage is none of my business. From what I understand, it was a bad marriage. But all that is in his past. I know he suffered a lot because you left the marriage. He lost you, his job, and his house. That's a lot to go through in one lifetime. But he's still standing, and Thank God for that! Again, all that is his past.

It's his future I'm focused on. I've known him since 1989. We had a romantic affair for about a year. And we were close friends since the affair ended, until we hooked up again romantically in Paris last July. He cried on my shoulders after you left him. And I saw him through all that.

Anyway, I know my future husband in a way that you don't, perhaps even didn't, and perhaps never will. He told me he never felt that you were his "buddy" when you were married.

As for Shoshana, I only wish to be her friend and *not* her stepmother. I want my own kids with Jamil (I'm only 30). And all that is in the future. Again: I'm looking forward to it all. I know he really loves Shoshana, and that she means a lot to him. I can live with that. I also know that he likes the way you've been raising Shoshana, and that you're a good mother. However, I also know that good mothers can make for bad ex-wives. Not a fair statement, since I don't know you at all.

I look forward to meeting you, however. I hope we learn to deal with each other in a civil manner. We're getting married at my mother's, on the Upper East Side, on January 1, 2000, the first day of the millennium. We will send you and Shoshana an invitation. Hope you both can come.

I wish you my very best.

Dorit Levin—Staff Writer
THE NEW YORKER
Condé Nast Publications
4 Times Square
New York, NY 10036
Voice/Fax: 1-212-421-8774
e-mail: doritlevin@onebox.com
Website: http://www.newyorker.com